Revolution's Fire
The Spirit Callers Saga #2

OJ Lowe

"Divines save us from the politicians. They say religion has been the cause of every war for the last two hundred years. I always personally think that's not entirely true. If there weren't our leaders and their followers around to exacerbate the situation, I think we might have had a lot less bloodshed. Nobody should ever have to die because someone with more power than sense wanted a war."

Corbyn Jeremies, Canterage revolutionary politician and self-proclaimed pacifist.

The eighteenth day of Summerpeak.

"This is disturbing on quite a few levels."

Terrence Arnholt did sound unnerved by what he had in front of him and neither Nick Roper nor David Wilsin could blame him if they were honest. It felt good, Nick had to admit, to be back in the fold, albeit how temporary it might be. Several days after he'd been put on leave, he was back here now. This ramshackle hamlet put together to form the Unisco command post hadn't changed, still had that sense of quaintness other parts of Carcaradis Island lacked. "Not just about Mazoud, about Leonard Nwakili as well…"

"Once a spy, always a spy," Brendan said dismissively. "I can't see why this unsettles you so, Director. We both know what Nwakili is capable of. Whatever he needs to suit him, he does. That's probably why he's survived so long. He's a sly animal."

"We should know. We train them that way." Arnholt still sounded tired. As Nick looked closer, he saw dark rings around bloodshot eyes and the way his shoulders threatened to sag. "We just never expect them to live as long as he did."

"Nice to know there's faith in us," Wilsin said.

"Hope for the best, expect the worst, Agent Wilsin," Brendan said. "That's always our plan when we send agents into the field. We know there's a chance that you'll never come back. You should know that as well. It's drummed into you enough."

Now that was true, Nick thought. Divines above knew it was true that they put it into you about how you were one mistake away from being a corpse. It was a make or break truth. Some couldn't handle that pressure. In a way, he'd always wondered if it depended on how much the trainee wanted to live or not. Did Unisco find itself made up of those who secretly had a death wish? Or really, was it only filled with those who wanted nothing more than to live? An interesting conundrum, something he'd considered more than once, if only to understand himself a lot better. Who is better suited to the job, someone who isn't afraid to die or someone who wants nothing more than to survive at all costs?

"Nwakili isn't the problem here," he said aloud suddenly. "With Mazoud behaving strange, I'd say the Vazaran Suns are probably more of a threat."

"If you believe Nwakili isn't a threat, then you're sadly misinformed about the state of the world," Brendan said.

"I didn't say that. I'd say right now that the Suns are more of an issue. That much firepower... Nwakili said he wouldn't have a chance if they suddenly snapped tomorrow. They have one of the largest standing armies in the five kingdoms. Easily since the Senate made everyone else trim their own down. And I don't know about you, that terrifies me, Field Chief. If they went rogue tomorrow, it'd be a very bad thing."

"Yes, well what you perhaps don't realise about Nwakili is that he's a master manipulator. He's capable of holding a dozen strings and make them all dance to his tune. More than that, what makes him exceptionally dangerous is that even when you know he's working you to do his bidding, you still can't help yourself."

"Make no mistake," Arnholt said. "I was Nwakili's friend once. I knew him well. But I don't trust him. Only an idiot would. You two..." He gestured to Nick and Wilsin. "What do you honestly think he's inferring here? Letting us know about this now? Pointing the finger at Mazoud, telling us how dangerous he is, coinciding with my own failed negotiations with the man." Neither of them replied and the director sighed. "Combined with his own inability to withstand an assault from the Suns and the repercussions if he made a move against them..."

"Are you saying he's wanting us to take him out? Mazoud?" Wilsin sounded surprised. "He has the gall to do that?"

"Of course, he does," Brendan said. "What do you think all this data is? It's his way of saying this man is a threat to me, but also you. Here's the damning evidence, bring your own blaster and shoot him in the head for me. I'm washing my hands of the entire affair but don't want the political backlash. What, you mean that also does me a massive favour? What a happy coincidence. Well, it was just my duty," he scoffed angrily. "Someone ought to tell that man duty and self-interest are two polarising ideas."

"He wouldn't listen anyway," Arnholt said. "My point, Agent Roper is that if you think Nwakili isn't a threat in all this, you're mistaken."

Nick said nothing.

"What are we going to do then?" Wilsin asked. "Because the Field Chief is right. Just because you know he's trying to play you for his own ends, doesn't mean he's not right in what he says."

Arnholt considered it for a moment and Nick knew from the look on his face Wilsin had made a good point. After all, he was right in what he'd said about Brendan's assessment.

"For the time being, we do nothing. We have only Nwakili's word that Mazoud is acting strange, or we would, had Mazoud not been complicit in the attack on Wolf Squadron. That alone should be enough to bring about an investigation on him under normal circumstances. That said, however..." He seemed to struggle with the word and just for a moment, Nick felt a little sorry for him. "Right now, any sort of direct action against Mazoud is not a recommended course of action. I do not feel it would be a good idea."

Both Nick and Wilsin opened their mouths to protest, only to be silenced as Arnholt sighed. "Sometimes, it's best to know when to do nothing. I don't feel happy about it. Mazoud is a legitimate business man. It's a questionable legitimacy but what are we if we ignore the laws laid down by the Allied Kingdoms Senate? Sometimes we can bend them but to break them is to bring down a shit storm none of us can survive. We need more evidence. It's a hard path we walk."

"So that's it then?" Nick asked. He couldn't help himself. "We just ignore him and hope he goes away?" That was frustrating but still, he couldn't blame Arnholt. He wasn't as autonomous as he liked people to believe, Unisco still had to answer to the Senate and Divine forbid something catastrophic should happen under Terrence Arnholt's watch. About the only thing to be said was he wouldn't be the first one kicked out of office following a disaster beyond his control.

"I didn't say that, Agent Roper. Watch your tone. If Mazoud is acting erratically, he's done well to keep it from showing so far. But he can't keep the façade of sanity up forever. Sooner or later it will slip. And the Suns are a ruthless organisation. The moment he shows himself unfit to lead, someone will slip a knife in his back. It has been their way for years. We have a happy retirement plan compared to the leaders of the Suns. None have ever lost control of the organisation and gone onto a new career after. The rest of their lives have often been numbered in hours rather than days."

"Right. I see." He couldn't help but feel the plan lacked for something. It might be okay to just sit back and hope it all sorted itself out. But Arnholt had made his point about sometimes nothing being the best thing to do and he couldn't help but hope it was the right call. "I back your judgement, Director."

"Good," Arnholt said, in a tone that said he'd expected nothing less. "Thanks for bringing this to my attention. And I hope you've both learned something here. Mainly, don't take politicians at face value."

"Oh, I already knew that," Wilsin said perkily. "Especially not Vazaran ones. Aren't most of them the most corruptible people you could ever meet?"

"On that regard, Premier Nwakili is not as bad as you might think," Brendan said. "He might be a snake, but he's not corrupt as far as we can tell. He seems to genuinely care about doing a good job for the people. He just has his ways. Schemers and spies and all that."

"What does that mean?" Wilsin asked.

"It means that if you're raised a schemer, you scheme. If you're a spy, you spy. How you got this far is usually how you continue. You stick to what you know." It was Nick who replied as he stretched out his arms behind his head. "Am I right?"

"Exactly."

"Am I the only one who hates this political thing?" Wilsin asked, the two of them making it to the range. Mel Harper was already there, X7 in hand and firing at makeshift targets, double tapping them with disinterest.

"You're not wrong. It's supposed to make things simpler, but it feels like it just makes the water dirtier. You can't see the riverbed for the slime," Nick mused. "But it's the way of the world. Can't change it. Can't change human nature."

They stopped, Harper ceased firing and lowered her weapon, ejecting the power pack and turning to face them. "I'm amazed to see you two walking around together. Thought you'd be fighting like alley cats to avoid each other before your bout."

"Professionalism, Melanie," Nick said. "Want to try it sometimes?" He grinned at her, before tilting a head towards the range. "Nice shooting."

"You're a comedian, Nicholas."

"Yep."

"Don't encourage him," Wilsin said, mock pleading. "Don't feed his ego, whatever you do. It's already spiralling out of control."

"Really, now I'm hurt," Nick said. Harper stepped aside, holstered her weapon and let the two of them onto the range. "Cheers, Mel. Got to keep the eye in."

"I think we've all shot more people than we thought we'd have to on this mission," Harper said. "It was supposed to be a quiet trip."

"Yeah but nobody's died," Wilsin said. "Nobody important anyway. Apart from Inquisitor Mallinson. And Jeremiah Blut."

That shut Nick up mid-sentence. For the moment anyway as he picked up the goggles and strapped them to his face, handing the pair just vacated by Harper to Wilsin. They were required for keeping track of scores on the range. Every Unisco base had a target range, all of them higher tech than this, but they'd done their best to ensure their agents could keep their skills up in the field. "Low blow, Dave."

"Oh, I just know your bout is going to get a bit tasty," Harper laughed. "If you're flinging comments around like that."

The range consisted of a large expanse of field covered with large rocks and a single big tree stump, the grass burnt where stray shots had landed over time, the acrid stink lingering over the area. Holographic projectors lay scattered about the field, throwing up targets in random sequences, not only hostiles but also civilian targets to avoid being fired on, one of Alvin Noorland's proud little inventions. Nick hadn't been here for a while, but he knew from experience knowing where the holo-projectors were hidden didn't make it easier.

"First to fifty kills?" He asked, raising an eyebrow at Wilsin. "Loser writes a letter of apology to the others other half?"

"Now who's throwing out low blows?" Wilsin asked dryly. "Struggling to get my dick wet out here."

Nick laughed, drew his X7 and ran a quick check over it. "Okay, okay. Loser buys drinks after the bout?"

Wilsin shrugged. "Okay. Acceptable. Ready when you are."

They started to fire simultaneously as the first target emerged behind the tree stump, the red colouring designating it an enemy. It dropped quickly as the flurry of shots hit it and the goggles awarded the kill to Wilsin. Nick swore angrily, swung around and shot the second target in the face. One-one. More started to emerge and they continued to fire, pausing only to replace energy packs in their weapons. Plenty of spares lay around the range, secreted away inside waterproof casings, as well as the recharge stations. It was a good way to whittle away the time, useful too. It might have been a while, but Nick felt the muscle memory returning to him after the brief period of inactivity. Granted it wasn't quite the same as being shot at in the field but he'd never met anyone who relished field training, given they tended to simulate it with stun balls and a tactical team. It wasn't fun in anyone's mind, the sort of experience that gave you just that, experience, as well as the incentive to avoid being shot with a stun ball again. They were painful, the blasts fucked up your nervous system, simulating getting shot to the exact detail.

Melanie Harper wandered into Noorland's laboratory, not entirely sure what to expect. It wasn't an unusual feeling. Plenty who entered Noorland's rooms found it that way. It was an ever-changing hole of chaos, his office and labs at the Unisco building in Premesoir were the same. Various tools from laser cutters to automated welders to sealant gel dispensers lay on tables, bits of half-finished equipment and bits of tech which might never see the light of day all being assembled. Some of them she recognised vaguely, others she couldn't even try to give a name to.

The man himself lay on the ground, a mug of something black and steaming by his head as he held a gadget about the size of a human palm to the light, the other running a scraping knife delicately across the grooves in it. She could hear the faint sounds of knife on metal, his face screwed up in concentration. Harper chose not to announce herself until he was done. Doubtless he knew she was there. She could smell his drink, it had an odour of chicory and rice, some sort of local delicacy whose name escaped her right now.

For five minutes or more, she stood there patiently, not entirely sure when he'd be done or if she'd be better off coming back later. He hadn't reacted to her presence, maybe he truly wasn't aware of her being there.

"Are you going to say something Agent Harper or stand there all day?" he suddenly said, his expression not moving towards her. "Nice perfume by the way. That's your giveaway."

She tried not to react. It was a nice trick but one any half decent Unisco operative would have observed. The fact Noorland worked in a place like this didn't mean he was incapable. Far from it. He'd been a highly competent field operative before it had been decided his future lay elsewhere. "You're needed for a briefing. They've gotten everyone up there. Arnholt sent me down to get you."

"I'm busy." Noorland didn't sound impressed. "Hold on..." Still his scraper ran across the metal disc, no sign of getting up coming from him. "This is delicate work. The key's in the grooves."

"I'm sure it is." She tried to sound polite, difficult when he was doing his best not to acknowledge her. "What are you building, anyway?"

"Projector plate for a particle barrier."

"I didn't know Unisco needed a particle barrier right now."

"No, you wouldn't. It's classified. Need to know. Eyes only." He sounded disinterested and she felt a flash of annoyance rush through her. That was the thing about Noorland. Everyone said how much of a genius he was, nobody ever mentioned what a dick he could be while doing it. Outside the office, he wasn't too bad. On duty, he was a nightmare.

"You going to come over when you're done?"

"I'll be a minute."

"Okay. I'll pass it on." She still wasn't entirely happy about being relegated to the role of messenger. "See you over there."

"Okay. Have fun."

She paused a moment. "Why are you building a projector plate from scratch?" She couldn't help but ask the question. "You can buy them, right?"

"Not to these specs. And well, the ones you buy are limited. They run on limited power and lifespan. Try to modify them, they'll stop working. It's like they build them to fail. Meh they probably do. Who wants something that works brilliantly for the rest of your life? It's a consumer business after all, right? Sell cheap and frequently. It's what's wrong with the kingdoms, I tell you. Meh, mine's better. Sorry, what was your question?"

She got the feeling she wasn't going to get anything useful out of him. "Sorry. I'll leave. Bye, Al."

"See you in a minute." Finally, he turned to look at her. "Seriously. Just let me finish this. It's delicate. Once you start, you got to finish. Otherwise it compromises the entire pattern. We don't want that, okay?!"

Okocha was bent down by a central projector in the middle of the floor of the briefing room, his fingers working overtime to set it all up. The call had come for all available agents to attend, Nick even told to come despite his leave. Brendan had informed him they wanted another set of eyes, another opinion and nothing had changed with his situation. A little frustrating but not unsatisfying. He'd given him a nod and gone to sit down near Lysa Montgomery, David Wilsin and Tod Brumley.

Arnholt was stood by the wall, tall and straight backed, no hint of a leaning and he watched Okocha like a hawk. Seconds later, a hologram flashed into life and a figure Nick didn't recognise appeared in the image, a tall woman with short cropped black hair and iron coloured eyes. Neither did Wilsin or Lysa but Brumley nodded.

"That's Agent Perrit," he said quietly. "She's a credit sniffer."

"A what?" Lysa asked, glancing around at the combat instructor with interest.

"She follows the credits," Wilsin said, adjusting himself in his seat for comfort. "You never heard that term before?"

"I've never heard it called that before," she admitted. It was true, she hadn't. "But why's she here."

"Guess we're about to find out," Nick said as Okocha stepped away from the projector and nodded at Arnholt. Roughly about the same time, Al Noorland sloped in, stretching his arms with a mug in his hand.

"Okay, attention," Arnholt said, his voice calm and quiet but drawing maximum attention. "We're here because Agent Okocha has a presentation to make in regards of our situation, a collation of the events here over not just the last several weeks but several years. We want operational theories and thoughts. Anything looks suspicious, you bring it up. Those of you who don't know, this is Agent Beverly Perrit, she's been following inquiries in conjunction with Agent Okocha at the other end of the line."

"Hi," Perrit said brightly. "How's the weather out there, guys?"

Okocha cleared his throat, a ball of holographic jumble appearing out the top of the projector and he reached down to it, pulling it out to scatter the one image into a variety.

"Right," he said. "Okay so it starts with this tournament. Always does. There's been some strange stuff ongoing here. Let's look at that first. Six years ago, Reims decided to bid to hold the Quin-C here and made all the arrangements. They managed to outbid Cerulia and Litnos in Serran and Tam Rivers in Premesoir to hold it here. But the big problem they faced was it was highly inadequate to hold a tournament. So, they needed huge amounts of revenue to turn it into what we've seen today."

"Speak for yourself," Perrit said dryly, bringing a laugh from some members of the team. "It's raining where I am, and I can see a hair salon for Vazarans out the window."

"As we all know, the cities bidding for the tournament usually end up paying for getting it all up to scratch," Okocha said. "It's different in this case. There's no real government out here, Reims offered to pay for it. Hence the fortune it no doubt cost. These hotels and stadiums don't come cheap." He paused to take a drink of water. "Agent Perrit, you've been checking into Reims' financial activities. You found anything untoward?"

"Only that they're absolutely haemorrhaging money. I'm not joking. Not just Reims but every company under their remit, every company Claudia Coppinger has a controlling interest is slowly being gutted so gradually it's hard to spot unless you're specifically looking for it. Profits are down massively, they're making just enough to keep afloat, to pay their employees and their taxes but that's it. Companies excelling before Reims got their hands on them are now struggling to keep their heads above the water."

"So, is it bad management?" Fagan asked. "Or..."

"I don't think so. They've not dropped the quality of their work. They're still making a stupid amount of credits in theory but they're spending them as fast as they make them and it's not entirely clear as to where they're going. Some of them were earmarked for the Quin-C development, some are marked for going down on research and development. Judging by some of the sums here, they're sinking more into R and D than any other company in the five kingdoms. In short, they could pay for the tournament and they have but they might have overreached themselves with it."

"Bad management and greed," Fank Aldiss mused. "Is there a worse combination?"

"Yep, anger issues and live ammunition," Wilsin said. It brought a smattering of laughter, Brendan cleared his throat to warn them back on the issue.

It was Okocha who spoke next, rubbing his hands together before moving a holographic file close to the centre.

"I went back and did this digging, I wondered why Claudia Coppinger wanted so badly for this tournament to be in Vazara. I mean, she isn't Vazaran, so she can't claim national pride. I did find this, and I just want to share it with you all, see what you think. Very rare footage, she doesn't like to be recorded apparently."

He pushed down on it and the video clip started to play, a picture of a middle-aged woman with brown hair stood on the steps of the Ubiqitor. Everyone recognised the structure, they'd all seen a picture of it at some point, the big temple in Tagos, the former capital of Vazara. She'd chosen a good spot, right in front of the bust of Gilgarus and Melarius. The sound abruptly came on, catching her halfway through a sentence.

"… Lovely country. Why do I want it here? I can't give you just one answer. And I don't think I should be able to either. What I should ask you, not just you the media but the ICCC and everyone who loves spirit calling, why shouldn't you want it here? I've spent a lot of time in the kingdom over the years and it's been good to me."

Nick pricked up his ears, considered the figure. She didn't look like much. Certainly not the richest woman in the five kingdoms. She looked like she should have been organising her grandchild's first birthday, something like that. There was something familiar in the way she held herself, he couldn't quite place it right now though he was sure he'd seen her before somewhere. That would irritate him now until he worked it out, he knew.

"Throughout my life, I've had two loves, one of them my family, the other being Vazara. I first came here a little girl, I saw the amazing indigenous wildlife wandering the plains and I was awed. I wept because I'd never seen anything so beautiful. This place has a lot of negative press but no worse than anywhere else. Somebody gets shot in Vazara, it's a big story. Same thing happens twice as often in Premesoir, nobody bats an eyelid. You know what, I want to give something back to a country that's given me a lot of good memories over the years. I want to give it an honour many would shy away from."

Her voice rose several octaves before she took a drink of water and licked her lips. "I want to be the one to see the first ever Competitive Centenary Calling Challenge Cup come here. I have a location in mind, I have a development plan and I intend to use local resources to create jobs and make this a reality. Together, we can make an idle impossibility a reality. This is very much in my plans, if it fails then I have failed…"

"Strong stuff," Okocha said as the video finished playing. "And of course, she succeeded. Nobody saw it coming. After discussions with Ritellia and Nwakili, Carcaradis Island was awarded the tournament."

"Why this island?" Leclerc wondered. "You have an answer to that? Because nobody else seems to."

"I did wonder myself," Okocha replied. "Best I can work out is some sort of compromise from the ICCC and the Senate about security. They were leery as hells about having it on the mainland. This was a happy medium. I'm not happy Coppinger and Nwakili bent to Ritellia on that but hey, still here so… Sorry, I digress." He moved another image to the centre, a shot of an untamed jungle from the air. "This was Carcaradis Island before it all started. Looks different now, huh? She was as good as her word; she saw that thousands of Vazaran workers were shipped out here to clear it all away…"

"This before or after the natives all got wiped out?" Nick asked, the question bringing silence to the room. He wasn't about to forget that, even if Okocha hadn't brought it up yet. He remembered that night in the sewers all too well. The key word there might have been 'Yet' but given the way Arnholt had danced around releasing the information to the media, he wouldn't have been surprised if it had been omitted deliberately from the brief.

"That came later. Apparently, nobody realised they were here until the workers started dying," Okocha said. "I found correspondence, some of it official and well, it looks like Reims might have brought the Vazaran Suns in to pacify the natives."

"Huh, Mazoud again," Wilsin said in Nick's ear. "What are the chances? It proves there's a connection between Coppinger and Mazoud."

"It took them a while, it took a lot of the Suns to do it and possibly the reason that Nwakili was able to bring them under control,"

Okocha said. "Because there were that many out here protecting the workers while they did their jobs, it left them underpowered on the mainland. Eventually they got rid of the natives and the island was built up from scratch."

"Remember those scare stories?" Derenko asked. "How they didn't think it'd be ready for the start of the tournament? I can see why when you look at it like this."

"Never underestimate the power of credits and an eager Vazaran workforce," Okocha said. "You'd be amazed what those two things can accomplish. Before long, all the materials were being shipped in to create the resort and the stadia from the ground up. Thousands became tens of thousands of workers…"

"Resources!" Pree yelled, before adjusting herself. "Sorry. When she said resources, where did all this material come from to build it? I mean, you're talking hundreds of tons of concrete and metal here? Maybe more. I mean, it's not a number than you can easily lay your hands on."

"Not a bad question, Agent Khan," Okocha said. "I'll check into that. I mean, I don't remember seeing too much mentioned, maybe I'll find answers. You see anything, Agent Perrit?"

Perrit shook her head. "No. Nothing. I did see credit payments to Local Vazara Haulage, Echedjile…" She cleared her throat. "Sorry, it's a tough word to pronounce that. Echedjile Excavations and Tom Harper Drills."

"Doesn't sound local, that last one," Derenko remarked. Nobody laughed. "Suggestive, I think. Are there any good drill places in Vazara?"

"Yeah but they're expensive," Okocha said. "I think. And good by Vazaran standards is still inferior to other kingdoms top standards. I'll try and talk to the companies, see if we can find out what they got. They should have it on record."

"Amount of credits that went into them, they should remember it off by heart," Perrit said dryly. "Unless they've been paid to forget."

"We all seem to be operating under the assumption Reims has done something wrong here," Noorland said suddenly, slurping down some of his ricefee. The smell of soy and rice filled the room as the film across the top of the liquid was broken. "Whatever happened to innocent until proven guilty? What happened to a little objectivity?"

"It doesn't look good, Al," Wilsin said. "There's something going on here. We're just missing a piece of the puzzle. Something we're not quite seeing."

"That's not assuming guilt. That's trying to work out what's going on," Lysa said, not entirely gently. "Remember? That's what we're supposed to do."

"When you're quite finished," Brendan said sourly. He nodded at Okocha who cleared his throat and folded his arms, not quite in a huff yet, but close.

"Right so, basically built the island up from scratch from the drainage to the buildings in six or so years…"

"Wait a second!" Nick said. "So that chamber we found in the drains, the one with the Kalqus statue. If they built around it, they should have known it was there. More to the point, why the hells would the workers build around it. Divine of water in a country that has a lot of desert. Seems like they'd be bowing to it right there and then while offering supplication."

"Maybe they'd built around it, so it'd be left alone," Aldiss said. "Possibly. They wouldn't want people to come and disturb the Divine."

"Which is just supposition," Fagan remarked. "From both of you."

"Shame there's nobody we can ask," Pree Khan said. "Reckon there's any workers still out there who'd tell us?"

"Might be hard to track them down," Okocha said. "But I'll dig into it, see what I can find. Or maybe there's some of the Suns who were there who'll talk to us. Probably harder to get rid of a group of comrades armed with powerful weaponry than it is a bunch of unarmed workers."

"Harder but not impossible," Arnholt mused. "There was a rumour of a V.S commandant who did break free of the organisation a few months ago. Maybe he's still out there. Think his name was…"

"Joseph Itandje," Brendan offered. "I remember it. If they did catch up with him, they probably wouldn't advertise it. Probably just one more corpse in the street nobody wants to identify."

"Will, you're better than anyone the Vazaran Suns have," Arnholt said. "See if you can track him down. Double priority."

"Gotcha. So, they absolutely work like the forges of Ferros to get it all together, taking the natives of the island hostage while they do apparently and slaughtering them daily over an altar. And then when the tournament starts, you have monsoons linked with the very chamber Agent Roper just mentioned, a vanished doctor who was paid by Reims, three genetically identical soldiers guarding said doctor. We have attempted kidnapping of the director's daughter, also by someone who worked for Reims in some capacity."

He wrinkled his nose at the odour from Noorland's drink. "We have dead Sun soldiers wiped out by Agents Roper and Wilsin, the

15

same group later took out a Unisco flight squadron to get back the same kidnapping lunatic associated with Reims and might have enough credits to pay them to do the same again. We have terrorism and murders, neither of which can be linked to Reims, but just because we haven't found a connection doesn't mean one doesn't exist," Okocha said, pausing to draw a grateful gasp of breath as he ceased speaking. "As you can see, Agent Noorland, this isn't supposition. This isn't just taking shots at Reims. There is something happening here."

"You know, that might be the understatement of the year," Noorland said, rubbing his chin, before putting his mug down. "We best get working on tracking down Itandje then. If it's important. See what he knows."

"I want a team ready to go retrieve him if he's confirmed alive," Arnholt said. "He was senior enough to know what was going on back then, even if he wasn't involved directly. Perrit, keep up the work and follow up on those companies, I want it found out what business they did with Reims, I want numbers and I want details. If one piece of information is out of place, sit on them until they tell us the truth. The rest of you…"

He looked around the room. "Fagan, I want you and Leclerc ready to get out there the second Okocha makes a location for Itandje. Aldiss, you and Derenko run backup for them. Anything you need, take. The rest of you, keep an eye out. Anything trivial, anything out of the ordinary, make a log of it. There's something going on here might slowly be appearing to be our motto for this mission, but it doesn't make things anything less true. If there is a bigger plan, then something else will happen and I want to be prepared. We've been too reactive here, I want more proactivity. The best way to foil an attack is to make sure it doesn't happen in the first place. Even if there isn't something going ahead, a little extra vigilance won't hurt. Remember, the safety of everyone here on this island is on you. On us. If we fail, then they will fall. It will be our fault and I for one do not want to live with that. Can you?"

The question was met with silence and contemplation, just the reaction he'd been expecting. Nobody made to move, nobody went to leave. He let them, allowing the words to sink in before nodding his head at them. "You're all fine agents. I'm honoured to have you working under me here. If anyone can figure out what's going on, if anyone can stop it, it's you. On other matters, good luck to Agents Roper and Wilsin. May the best man win."

The twenty second day of Summerpeak.

May the best man win…

Those words still echoed through Nick's head as he stared across the icy battlefield towards David Wilsin stood looking ultra-confident on the other side, arms folded, and summoner nestled on the crook of his elbow. The crowd were getting riled up and the announcer was doing his absolute best to whip them into a frenzy. He felt confident himself. He had a plan and he intended to stick to it.

The video referee buzzed to start, and he shot Wilsin a cool grin. "Shall we start then?"

"No rivalry is uglier than that between those who call themselves friends."
Former spirit caller, James Carter.

The twenty-second day of Summerpeak.

Three each. Pretty standard. Nick grinned, sent in his first choice of Bish, the garj for the first time since that ill-fated bout with Scott Taylor. His one black spot in the tournament so far. Redemption would come. It was the garj's time to renew the faith Nick felt he'd shown in him. His grin grew as Bish saluted with a bladed appendage, raising limb to forehead in a graceful sweep before turning to face Wilsin.

Neither of them showed any reaction as Wilsin brought his spirit into play, a golden-furred elephant with three tusks and a powerful trunk. Nick counted four cavernous nostrils at the tip, hot breath exploding from them periodically. The size difference immediately worried him, Bish was slender and graceful, the rapier while the elephant, Chydarm, was a tank, power and durability. This might be interesting, he thought, studying the enemy spirit with cool disinterest. He folded his arms, observed as it took one trundling step forward and peered at Bish through small dull eyes.

The starting sound rang out with shrill familiarity and he cracked his knuckles. Wilsin reacted first, the elephant lunging on the attack with deceptive quickness, four huge feet pounding into the ground. He was surprised the spirit didn't slip on the ice, but he couldn't let bemusement nullify him. He gave his commands and Bish vanished, a faint shimmering around his body before reappearing across the arena, suddenly between spirit and caller. Nick hadn't expected it to fool his opponent, not even for a moment, the elephant spinning surprisingly gracefully for one so large, twisting on the spot before unleashing a uniblast in the direction of Bish.

It was what he'd have done in the same situation. In graceful motion, Bish sprang out the way of the blast and retaliated with an attack of his own, sending a trio of rainbow coloured balls of energy towards Chydarm. All three landed, smashing into the broad face, flattening across the skin. In seconds, they'd moved to crawl across the eyes, seeking the dull watery pools.

The attack had been good, one he was proud to have developed. The energy had been telekinetic in nature, controlled by the power of Bish's mind and still moving despite impact. Ever since that failure against Scott Taylor, he'd decided to work with some of his lesser spirits and he'd trained plenty with Sharon, Wade and Lysa to make that happen. It wasn't the first time he'd faced an opponent like this with Bish. Strength didn't trump style every time, but it made things interesting.

With a crash, Chydarm's trunk thrust into the ice, breaking through with a deafening clang, Nick fought the urge to wince, suddenly curious as to Wilsin's plan Still the energy fought its way across rough fur, desperate to get into eyes, to scour and scrape, to blind the giant foe. He could see movement in the giant proboscis, tensing and quivering beneath the ice. Nick watched, curious, before the trunk erupted as rapidly as it had entered, water and ice slathered down Chydarm's face. Nick barely had chance to react before the last of it was shot towards Bish. The garj teleported again, vanishing before the makeshift quad of icicle spears could land fatal blows. He felt a second of relief, saw Bish reappear behind Chydarm, blades raised just as he'd commanded.

The elephant wasn't fooled, brutally kicked out with a back foot the same moment the blades came down and Nick winced as he heard something snap, the huge foot meeting Bish's body in less than gentle fashion. Simultaneously, Chydarm let out a great bellow of pain, blood suddenly staining both the ice and Bish's blades. Still the garj moved, staggering back as Chydarm rounded on him, suddenly on the offensive as the tusks rose to try and impale its opponent. Blades came to block them, batting them aside but he could see his spirit wasn't moving easily. The movements were laboured, sluggish. The determination was there, he could feel it feeding back to him and he urged Bish on. He'd taken a blow, but he wasn't down and out. To give up now would be to fail. The garj were a proud species, they didn't do well with failure. and he grinned as he felt a spark of defiance flood the spirit.

The next exchange saw blade meet tusk, both blades holding the giant spike at bay before retaliating with scissoring pressure. He doubted they'd be able to cut through the ivory, those blades were meant for rapid-fast slashes, leaving bloody gashes rather than sawing through tough bone, but they'd keep it off balance. Now he could see a look of frenzied determination on Chydarm's face as the elephant tried to bring its greater strength into play. He saw Bish's feet slide on the ice, traction slowly lost as Chydarm jerked its head.

Bit by bit, it was gaining an advantage, he knew that wouldn't suit Bish if they went toe to toe. The garj wouldn't survive a punching match Hitting and running wasn't an especially viable option either, not with that wound. He could feel the backlash of pain, fire from a broken rib or twenty. Not fatal but debilitating. The garj was fighting on though, determined not to falter. Nick wondered how long determination would conquer pain. It was a battle that couldn't be drawn out. On the other hand, Chydarm wasn't moving easily either. Blood stained golden fur where Bish had thrown a slash into the rear leg. The cut was deep, maybe severing a tendon or a hamstring. A couple more, it wouldn't be able to move at all.

The uniblast nearly caught him by surprise. As tactics went, it was a risky one at close range but usually an effective one if the wielder was strong enough to survive the backlash. Uniblasts generated a lot of light and heat, combined into an incredible destructive force, at close range they were as dangerous to the attacker as the target. He saw the mouth open, Wilsin throwing caution to the wind and he gave the teleportation order. Bish vanished, not quickly enough as the smell of scorched flesh permeated the arena, Nick wrinkled his nose as he caught it, didn't know whom it had originated from, but it couldn't be good.

Ahead of him, Bish reappeared in a flash. His worst fears were confirmed, the garj was wobbling on unsteady long legs, flesh blackened and burned, one blade corroded to half size. He grimaced as he saw his spirit totter for a moment, almost slipping. By the looks of it, Wilsin could smell blood. Chydarm bore blisters about the mouth and face but they were little more than superficial, and Nick had a horrible feeling the charge was coming. He wasn't wrong, the elephant dropped its head and broke into a lumbering run, ice shattering beneath it. Within seconds, it was sliding, building momentum while gliding across the frozen surface like the kingdoms biggest figure skater.

Bish couldn't move. Couldn't teleport again so soon. That was a weakness he'd yet been able to address, though given he'd been able to achieve it in the first place was remarkable. It was a tricky skill, handy but sometimes unreliable.

It was nearly over, about the best he could do was try to take the elephant down with him. He gave the command, Bish steadied himself, digging toe claws down into the ice and levelled the blade point first towards the oncoming elephant. Wilsin's reactions had to be good, it was better to overestimate an opponent than the reverse, but by this point Chydarm was moving too swiftly across the ice to manoeuvre, sliding wildly out of control...

A sickening sound filled the arena followed by a bellow of agony as blade went through bone and into brain, Chydarm's momentum carrying it straight through Bish who was press-rolled underneath, bones crushed, the arm bearing the blade shattered as it tore free amidst a shower of gore. Bish was down, defeated, dead but Chydarm was struggling, rampaging blindly in its death throes and Nick felt no satisfaction. He brought the garj back to the container crystal, pondered his next move as the struggles became less and less frenzied, fatigue and blood loss finally catching up with the injuries. Ice shattered beneath the great furred frame as the elephant keeled over and the crowd sounded their approval.

Empson came out at the same time as Wilsin unleashed his veek, Scales, if Nick remembered right. A twee name but surprisingly accurate. Normally he liked to save Empson for last. Right now, the penguin felt a good choice. Never make your tactics too predictable. If the opponent could make a reasonable guess as to what you would do, they could counter it. Tactics instigated beforehand were usually more effective than those concocted on the fly although it worked both ways. You couldn't plan for every contingency and a plan made up as you went along might be more effective given circumstances. Scales was starting to stalk around in listless circles, Empson puffed up the feathers on his chest and tried to look self-important. It was a look the penguin could pull off with aplomb, casual disdainful arrogance.

Then they were underway and the veek continued to prowl, Wilsin unwilling to make the first move so Nick made the decision to force it for him, Empson's beak clacking open, launching water bullets towards the creature. Five, six, seven, eight blasts of water, each packed with enough concussive force to deal serious damage should they land. Scales lunged sideways, evading the attack with smug ease, claws snicking into the ice to halt its movement. From motion to motionless in half a second. The furred tail swept about lazily, Scales bared pointed fangs in a low growl. Neither of them was intimidated. It looked like Wilsin was hesitant to attack, a mirror of Nick's stance in the previous match, a waiting game being played. Keeping a safe distance across the ice, Scales looked content enough, like the caller knew he'd be okay if he kept out of range. Either he was playing some game, or he really hadn't considered the full implications of the opponent he was facing.

There was a reason Nick had chosen Empson. Empson was a penguin. On an icy battlefield. About as close to home as you could get in a tropical clime. He grinned and Empson belly-flopped down, shot across the ice like a feathered blaster bolt. Taken by surprise, Scales sprang into the air, hoping to evade. On another day, in another bout, the veek might have succeeded. When their paths intersected, the beak opened again, water gushing out at point blank range. Suddenly the normally flightless penguin was propelled into the air, thrown skyward by the momentum. They were in close, Scales letting out a yowl of surprise as razor-sharp flippers rose to try and deal a deadly blow.

Surprise turned to pain, a fresh streak of crimson hit the ice, gore staining Scales' stomach. Both came down simultaneously and

Scales was suddenly atop Empson, leaping in to bite and scratch the enemy spirit. The flippers rose to block but while they might be tougher than normal penguin flippers, their main modifications had been enhancements to the edges and tips, not to the wings themselves. Nick heard squawks of shock and pain and tried to avoid wincing. Instead he chose to counterattack, the beak viciously jabbing at the scale ball in front of him. Scales flipped back, evaded the poke but swiped out with a fortuitous blow that sent Empson recoiling, blood billowing from his face. Nick caught the faintest blowback of pain, he winced but urged Empson on and the penguin obliged, dancing across the ice. Talons dug through the frozen water and shredded wings flailed, injured but still capable of dealing a potent blow. Scales went back on the defensive, weaving out of range, always threatening to slip yet always retaining its footing. The once flawless sheen of ice was starting to look uglier by the second, pockmarked and shattered, glancing at it gave Nick an idea.

The bloodied beak sprang open and another spray of brine erupted out, covering the frozen surface below Scales, some of it soaking the surprised veek. Wilsin looked surprised for a moment, not least because his spirit was apparently unharmed by the soaking it had received. All until it tried leaping back again and hit the ground gracelessly, any sort of momentum lost on the soaked ice. The crowd let out an ooh of derision and he saw Wilsin's façade of calm crack briefly.

"Cheap tricks?" he called across the field mildly.

"Always." At the same time, he urged Empson to press the advantage and the penguin leaped, flippers positioned to deal a penetrating blow should he land where Nick intended, right above Scales. If it was a penetrating one, it would also be fatal.

It wasn't. Just. The veek managed to roll aside, blade-like flippers cut deep into the ice and it took Empson a second to yank them free. But that was all Scales needed to leap onto the penguin's back, biting the exposed neck.

Nick smelled blood and suddenly the penguin went into a frenzy attempting to shake the veek off, only succeeding narrowly. Scales hit the ice, rolled a couple of times and then rose, fur caked in ice flakes. As Empson turned to the smaller opponent, Nick saw the mangled state of his spirit's back, deep bites and blood and knew immediately he might be getting into trouble. Wilsin's veek was a lot better trained than most seen in this competition and there'd been a few, it was his main battling spirit when on Unisco duty and had plenty of experience. That much blood loss couldn't be sustained. The problem when fighting spirits with claws or fangs. When they went deep, the wounds couldn't be staunched, and they'd continue to be a problem until their end.

He had to win fast then. At least Scales hadn't come out unscathed either. At least one cut had gone deep, the veek was moving more gingerly than at the start of the fight. One leg trembled when weight came down on it, an unseen injury Nick couldn't remember dealing.

Penguin and lizard-cat came at each other again, razor sharp claws and bladed flippers meeting mid-air, a deafening scrape ringing out as they clashed. Empson withdrew, a trio of deep grazes left across the metallic edge of his flipper before slashing backwards in an exaggerated bobbing motion. Had it landed, it might have cut Scales' head in two, but the veek ducked and the blow went high above its head. Suddenly open, it went for the stomach but Empson was already ducking his head to meet it with his beak. A sudden screech and Scales' face was covered in blood, a good chunk of skin missing. The veek shook its head, spraying claret everywhere. Empson rose proud and fired a series of water blasts from the beak, each hitting the target hard with deadly accuracy and just for a moment, Scales' eyes went blank, unfocused. The veek tottered, legs almost giving way beneath it.

Nick saw the opening and took it, once more Empson shot forward on his stomach across the ice, wings outstretched in front of him like spears and this time Scales couldn't do anything to evade. Both blade-like flippers tore into the veek who let out an agonised roar, suddenly impaled hard. Empson rose back onto his talons, the enemy spirit still skewered, Nick urged his spirit to go for the kill. He could see the muscles in the penguin's ruined back tensing as he slowly tried to pull his wings free. It took a lot of strength to pull a knife from a body, natural healing abilities of a living being meant wounds already tried to close around it. Still, the penguin was strong. Scales was in its death throes, he could see the veek struggling but to little avail, the flailing limbs losing their vigour little by little.

One final wrenching motion and Empson tore his wings free, twin halves of the veek's body falling apart with their release. There was a scream from the crowd, one solitary cry of shock amidst the stunned silence as the segments hit the ice and the blood-soaked penguin let out a squawk of triumph. Even the stadium announcer had gone silent, a void soon remedied although the shock remained in his voice at the brutality seen.

"Okay… On that note, Roper takes that round. He must defeat one more spirit to triumph. I don't know what it is with veek, you know, we've seen some defeated in absolutely brutal fashion in this tournament so far."

Wilsin's last choice was a dragon.

Nick was no stranger to dragons, this one lean and packed with muscle, the body covered with acid orange and soot black scales while its wings were the colour of musty green leather. Unlike most dragons he'd seen, it had six limbs, four for standing and two forearms, each leg culminating in six spike-like claws. The forearms did look more developed but still way short of human standards. The face was a blunt triangle, pointed jaws with beady little eyes. When the jaws opened, he saw an impressive array of fangs. Strangely enough, it lacked for a horn which some dragons bore.

On the battlefield, Empson was panting, bleeding from various cuts across his body. Although it was hard to tell which blood was his, it didn't take a genius to realise he was struggling from the efforts of the previous fight. Still, they would go until the end.

"What, you didn't know about this one?" Wilsin asked, hands in his pockets. He looked utterly relaxed, like a man who knew it was in the hands of the fates and had ceased to care about the pressure. "This is Aroon. He's a special dragon."

He chose not to reply, just flexed his fingers out in front of him, felt the muscles stretch and contract. "Prove it then," he eventually said.

The buzzer went, giving them the signal to start and Wilsin smiled. "Okay. Let's get this shit going then?"

"What, you mean you weren't already?"

Even as Nick said it, the dragon was already moving, taking to the sky with a flare of the wings. This complicated things. Fighting an airborne opponent wasn't easy with something left grounded, and for all Empson's qualities, the penguin was still flightless.

More water barrages tore out, cutting through the air where the dragon had been seconds ago, Aroon ducking beneath them. The dragon was agile, Nick had to give it that, but it was also a bloody big target to miss in the air. The water blasts stopped, Aroon didn't and he gave the order for Empson to jump. From a standing start, it wasn't a powerful jump but as the enemy flew overhead, it was enough for the tip of a razor-edged flipper to rake across the stomach. He heard the roar before Aroon reacted as Empson fell. The dragon seized the penguin, wrapped his forelegs around him to add his weight to Empson's fall and the two smashed into the ice. Dragon claws tore at the penguin's body, ripping through feathers and muscle with almost arrogant ease. As Empson struggled, suddenly on the verge of falling, the pointed jaws opened, and dragon fire erupted, engulfing the bird at point blank range.

Nick's face betrayed nothing as Empson fell, he only let out a sigh inwardly. That cut had been a costly one. It had been a calculated gambit that hadn't paid off. On the other hand, to deal any sort of blow with a spirit in worsening condition wasn't to be sniffed at. Could have been worse. And now, he could focus on the finish. Sudden death. Loser went out. He needed something special to beat Aroon. He brought back Empson, smirked thoughtfully and took up Carcer's container crystal. It might not quite be fighting fire with fire, but it would be an even contest. Carcer could match Aroon in the air and take those fire attacks.

He had a good feeling about this.

"And this is it, folks, the final clash in this enjoyable bout between David Wilsin and Nicholas Roper. Neither of them has held back, both have put in every inch of cunning and power they have, and it's come to this. Dragon versus draconic-looking lizard. Wilsin's Aroon has felled Roper's famous penguin and now it looks as if it's the turn of the shark-lizard. Let's get this on."

Carcer lunged, went for Aroon with claws outstretched, going into a dive under a stream of incoming flame. Nick felt the temperature rise around him from the blast, felt a wave of exhilaration flood him as Carcer hit Aroon in the sides, claws punching against dragon scale. The dragon let out a whoomphing sound, lashed out with fang-filled jaws to try and rip Carcer's throat out. Both had serpent-like necks, Carcer lunged back to evade and hit the dragon with a uniblast at Nick's mental command, the attack throwing sparks across scales as the black glowed orange under intense heat. Some of them melted, struggling to hold up under the force and the heat.

Aroon responded with another stream of white hot fire, Carcer weaved away from the blast, unable to keep his own attack up under the threat. In a flash, Aroon was homing in on Carcer, would have been on him had Nick not given the order to kick it up a notch. Aroon might be larger, Carcer was faster. If it was an open-air battlefield, it might have been more of an advantage. Here in the Ice Hall, as large as it might be, it was negated. The Ice Hall was still as large as most mainland stadiums, small by the standards of the others on this island. He'd once fought atop a volcano with Carcer and that had been something to behold as the shark-lizard had used the sky to full advantage.

As it was, it took a few moments to cross the battlefield, Carcer turned, flared his wings and let out a challenging shriek towards Aroon who bellowed back in response. He felt a simmering of dislike burning through him, surprising him. Spirits normally didn't feel emotions like that, maybe dislike was the wrong term. But there was clearly some sort of pride thing going on here. Maybe Carcer saw the bigger dragon, the more majestic one as some sort of insult to his presence and was determined to put it down. Something we both have in common then, he mused. Who am I to hold you back?

Carcer shot through the air, evaded the cumbersome snap from Aroon's jaws, the dragon looking a little sheepish at being so easily embarrassed, before raking his own claws across the broad back. Go for the wings, Nick urged him. Knock Aroon out of the sky and it'd be a lot less dangerous. The dragon twisted out the way, swiped out its powerful tail and caught Carcer a glancing blow across the chest. Nick winced as Carcer screeched, temporarily halted by the blow before resuming flight, the scales across his chest bent and scuffed. There didn't appear to be too much damage, certainly not debilitating.

Then let's carry on, Nick urged silently. Carcer hissed angrily, a sign of complicity and then shot into the air, almost to the roof and certainly to the extent of the protective field ensuring the audience weren't in any danger. He saw Aroon's eyes follow the lizard into the air, tracing the upward path before Carcer fell, only gaining acceleration as he tore through the air to smash into Aroon's right wing. Powerful claws shredded leathery flesh and Aroon howled, entire body twisting around to grab at Carcer like it had with Empson. Only Carcer wasn't there to be grabbed, claws clutched at empty air, suddenly the lizard was at Aroon's throat, clawing and biting, the surprise not just from the spirit but from caller and crowd as well. Wilsin looked surprised the scales were holding under the assault, even if Nick wasn't. It only made sense a beast as majestic as a dragon would have stronger protection in exposed areas.

It was all entirely natural as well. Dragons were mystical creatures and like most in that category, were resistant to any sort of genetic modification. Something about them prevented it. Maybe some higher power had decided they were as close to evolutionary perfection as could be gotten and so couldn't be changed. It wasn't important right now. All that happened was Aroon didn't even try to twist to attack, just pushed through the air on only half a wing-set and hit Carcer with a body check that looked like it hurt. The weight differences between the two suddenly became painfully obvious, it wasn't a fatal blow, but a stunning one. Carcer took a few seconds, head shaking as he sought to recover…

It would never come as Aroon's jaws snapped open and a stream of fire struck head on, the blast engulfing him completely. Suddenly Nick was worried. Carcer's scales could stand up to high temperatures. The problem was, that fire was beyond hot. It was a beautiful shade of blue white, probably would have been more impressive had it not currently been swallowing up his spirit. Life fire… He'd heard of it. Never quite seen it employed like this. Nick gulped, urged Carcer to break free. Hoped. Prayed. As the fires died away, Carcer fell to the ice, Nick heard it melting with a disgusted hiss as the smouldering body landed hard. Within moments, Carcer was laid in a pool of steaming water, Aroon landing on the ice ahead with an intensely proud look.

Ah…

Just briefly, Carcer managed to raise his head an inch or two out the water, struggled to hold it before sinking again with a dejected splash. If the burns didn't defeat him, drowning would. It was over. He saw the timer counting down on the video referee, allowing Carcer twenty seconds to get back up. Twenty seconds that lasted a lifetime. There wasn't even any hint of resistance from the pool, the steam had died down; frost was already starting to settle on the water.

Undoubtedly over. The buzz of the video referee only settled it and he let out a dejected sigh, fought the urge to kick at the ground in front of him. Instead he brought back Carcer, heard the applause from all four corners of the stadium and realised that it could have been worse. He'd done all right, not terrific, not as well as he'd hoped. But he'd competed. He'd made it this far. And with all that in mind, he couldn't help smiling with relief it was over as he walked into the middle of the field and embraced David Wilsin.

"Congratulations my friend," he said, surprised to find he meant it as well. He gritted his teeth together. "If it was going to anyone who beat me…"

"You glad it was me?"

Nick stared at him like he was simple. "Hells no. I didn't want to lose at all. But seriously. Good luck, man. Go on and take it all, yeah?"

One part of defeat he'd never enjoyed was having to face the media afterwards, sometimes it wasn't as necessary as it was here, but with the bigger prizes came the potential for a bigger fall. And with the biggest fall came the bitterest pills. They were all out in force, ten, twelve, fifteen journalists all jockeying for their quote. Anyone who thought they'd seen chaos before had yet to experience the press pen on Carcaradis Island. It had been bad in previous rounds, it felt like they'd reached a boiling point now.

Still Nick plastered the grin on his face and made decided to keep his answers brief. Sometimes callers came out shouting the odds after a bout, it didn't do them any favours. The articles that followed were usually mockingly cruel, sadistic even.

"You're out. Do you think you fought to the best of your abilities?"

First inane question of the day. He fought the urge to roll his eyes. "I think my opponent did very well."

"Does that mean you think you didn't fight as well as you could have?" This one came from a particularly loathsome looking character and Nick swallowed down a retort.

"Well, all things considered, I don't think it was that bad a performance. I can't blame my spirits. They fought to their maximum, sometimes you face someone who outperforms you on the day. Nothing to do with complacency. Nobody wins every time."

"You were one of the favourites. Does it feel like an underachievement to go out now?"

"Nope. I didn't name myself one of the favourites, everyone else did. I would have liked to have gone further but it wasn't to be. Stuff happens. No point getting upset about it."

"Where do you go from here? Do you continue to fight? What now for Nicholas Roper?"

Not that it's any of your business, he wanted to say. Instead he smiled. "Well, next order of business is getting married. Beyond that, it's hard to say. I don't want to walk away from the sport. Far from it. I'm not a fortune teller, I can't say what the future holds. I can't wait to find out, your guess is as good as mine."

That was six questions, if he'd had it right. ICCC rules said that the contestants were obliged to answer at least seven, one of the pointless rules and fines they'd brought in with to line their pockets with credits if the competitor stepped out of line. He had the feeling annoyed spirit callers had paid for local ICCC branch staff to come to this tournament in the first place with post-match fines.

"One more question," he said. "Make it a good one."

"How do you feel about defeat here?" Kate Kinsella. No failing to recognise her, not since that infamous article that could well have gotten her banned from the competition media circle in another time. He'd heard Ritellia had been furious with what she'd written about him and his running of the tournament to the point that he'd tried to have her expelled. She'd cited the freedom of the press and it being in the public interest. Good on her for beating it. Anyone who managed to fight off Ritellia's influence was okay by him.

"Upset. Tired. Been a long few days. Been a long few weeks really. I'm sad it's over but at the same time it means I'll finally be able to relax, step away from the edge. Appreciate this place for what it has become. Reims did a good job fixing it all up. I'd come here again, if I came into a spare couple of hundred thousand credits."

That brought some laughter. "But on a more serious note, about my opponent." He heard inhaling, breath being held in expectation that he might be about to insert his foot into his mouth. "David Wilsin... I didn't know him much before the tournament. I knew of him but never met him. Since it started, I've gotten quite good friends with him and if anyone left was going to beat me, well I hope he lifts the trophy. Best of luck to him."

That was it, all he would say on the matter as he inclined his head towards them, a respectful half-bow and he turned to walk away up out of the bowels of the stadium. Alone. But not for long. He already knew Sharon would be waiting for him. This defeat didn't hurt anywhere near as much as he'd thought it might. It was only the start. They'd both gone out, but things were looking up. After all, today was only the first day of the rest of their lives...

"You know you're in trouble when the spirits start calling the shots in battle. Personally, I believe the caller can't always be in control. But there must always be control, if you understand me."
Professor David Fleck on when bouts get tense.

The twenty-second day of Summerpeak.

"So, what exactly is life fire?"

The question came from Matt Arnholt as he leaned back in his seat, the very sign of relaxed as he drummed his fingers. Mia didn't have an answer, Scott made to open his mouth before realising he couldn't explain it well. Pete, on the other hand, did clear his throat to let loose with an explanation, wearing a smug look as he did. He gripped a glass of beer and took a swing before opening his mouth to speak.

"Life fire is one of those techniques," he said. "It's a similar to... Remember when I fought Sharon in the group stage?"

"Yeah." Matt was nonchalant. Around them, the bar was full, people watching the highlights of Roper versus Wilsin and despite the early hour, the alcohol was already starting to flow. Only Scott chose not to drink, given his bout later in the day. A glass of lemon sugarwater sat in front of him which he occasionally sipped, his expression as bitter as the drink. "I do. Vaguely."

"Well remember that breath attack she used on me, which drained her and made her susceptible to my knockout blow?"

"Yeah. Still, yeah, I remember."

"Okay so that's known technically as a Burnout Technique. They're advanced techniques, dangerous not just to the opponent but to the attacker if they're not used properly. All the user's strength is focused into one powerful attack, usually a fatal one under the right circumstances. But there's a downside, all that focused energy leaves the user exhausted and unable to defend itself. I managed to take out Sharon's spirit before mine collapsed. It was a gambit on her part that failed. Here, you saw it work."

"I'm surprised though," Scott said. "I mean Roper looked like he was on top. Guess you never can tell."

"Nope," Pete said thoughtfully. "You never can. If it's used right, Burnout Techniques can turn the tide of the battle. This might become the textbook example of how to use them."

"Think I've heard of them before," Mia mused. "Never used them. They're hard to teach, right?"

"Yeah," Pete said. "Hard but useful. There're a few notable ones. Death breath and life fire, I know of. Think there's an ice based one..."

Matt burst out laughing. "Death breath? They really called it death breath?"

"Oh yeah. You got a better name for it?"

Scott rolled his eyes, settled back in his seat as Pete and Matt continued to debate it back and forth. Mia leaned her head over to rest on his shoulders. "You ready for later?"

He nodded. "Always. Going to win, I'm feeling lucky."

"I know you can do it," she said. "You've beaten better than her."

"That's when you should worry though," Scott said. "When you get complacent. When people think you're better than you are, they put you on a pedestal and try to knock you off." He grinned at her, rested a hand on her knee. Her skin felt silky smooth beneath his fingers. "Good thing I got good balance. And you at my back. That's all I need." He almost said want, rather than need, stopped himself in time. That'd have been weird.

"How about gas blast?" Matt asked unexpectedly. Scott grinned, nothing like saying that to kill the mood. Mia furrowed her brow and glanced around at her brother, shaking her head.

"Really?" she asked. "You want me to tell you all the things that's wrong with that?"

"You have a list?" Matt's words were just as sarcastic. "Because if you do, I'd love to hear it."

Scott wasn't surprised to see she wasn't going to oblige him as she turned back to him, rolling her eyes. Her mouth curled into a little twist of frustration, he fought the urge to laugh.

"You're cute when you're annoyed," he said, not quite able to stop himself.

"Spend a lot of time with me when I'm around him and you'll think I'm cute a lot," she said dryly. Still, a grin broke across her face as she said it. "I joke. I love my brother. Even if sometimes I'm sure he's adopted."

"Low blow, sis." Even Matt laughed as he said it. Scott laughed along before stopping suddenly, a whip-like shudder piercing his spine like ice. He sat up bolt straight, immediately on edge, eyes whipping across the room for whatever had caused it. Nothing. Strangely enough, Pete's reaction was similar, he rubbed at his back and swore angrily. Gooseflesh rose over his skin, despite the warmth, he felt suddenly cold and clammy.

"S'up with you two?" Mia asked. "Someone walk over your graves?"

"Don't care if they did or not, I'm not dead yet," Scott said. "Just… Weird that. Weird feeling in me."

Pete said nothing, just nodded. "Must be all this talk of burnout. Guess I'm just tired."

"It's not even midday yet," Matt pointed out.

"And your point is?" Pete's voice remained deadpan, emotionless as he said it, but Scott could see it in his eyes. There was something troubling him.

"You sure neither of you felt that?" he quickly asked, looking at the siblings. Mia shook her head. Matt replied in the negative. "Huh. Weird."

Sharon wasn't there. Nick frowned as he studied the area, saw no sign of her, of anyone and then relaxed. Try not to read too much into it, he told himself. Maybe she's waiting outside the stadium. She wouldn't have forgotten. She'd been really into it that morning, running her hands over his body while they were in bed, playfully raking her nails over his hard muscles as she'd told him what she was going to do to him if he won. He loved it when she talked dirty. Nothing quite like hearing pure filth from the mouth of an extraordinarily beautiful woman. Even with the aching in his heart, the pain of defeat lingering, he smiled. Or maybe she had some other plan. He frowned. Sharon's ideas of planning often sometimes had an element of unpredictability about them, often exciting and potentially dangerous in equal measures.

The ache grew, every heartbeat suddenly hurt, and Nick couldn't help himself, doubling over in agony. Breathing suddenly became a chore, he gasped for air and his eyes watered. Bursting fire broke through him and just for a moment, he thought he was having a heart attack. That really would ruin his day, the faintest bitter thought passed through him. Yet, as soon as it had started, the pain faded, and he found himself not quite on the floor but his face close enough to kiss it. He soon remedied the position, slowly standing before straightening out. He adjusted the lapels of his coat. Breathing had never felt so good, he gratefully sucked in sweet air and allowed himself a moment to catch his composure.

What the hells was that?

The pain hadn't completely gone, still lingered in him. His heart felt heavy, like a part of him had been burnt away. He wiped his eyes clean, shook his head. Maybe he'd get something to kill the pain before he went back to the hotel room. He'd see if he could spot Sharon on the way to the apothecary. Maybe she was having trouble getting down here.

So many maybes and not enough answers.

The irony of ironies, it often felt that way in his duties with Unisco. Now with it seeping into his personal life too, he couldn't help feeling something bad was coming. He tried to ignore it, rubbed at his chest. The pain didn't feel physical now he thought about it. He'd been shot and stabbed before in the line of duty, it wasn't anything like those.

He tried to put it out of his mind as he went for the exit, leaving the squalid little corridor behind him. It'd be nothing but a memory after now. Wasn't ever going to be back here again any time soon. Nick decided he wouldn't miss it.

The silence between them was awkward, Anne had to admit as she looked at Theo and he stared back impassively. She could feel his emotions and although he no longer quite had that bubbling cauldron of seething rage and resentment lingering beneath the surface of his being, he still wasn't as emotionally adjusted as most. Still it was an improvement. She no longer had to fight the urge to hug herself when he was nearby. If he had been fiery before, he was threatening to turn to ice now, his emotions in check but still powerful. She'd studied him when battling and concluded his emotions weren't an impediment but rather the opposite. He battled with passion, never hesitating or quitting. He had himself convinced his own skill and power would drag him through. And he was powerful. Harry Devine had been the victim of that power the previous day. She had struggled with him in their practice bouts, even drawing on considerably more experience than he could.

"I have to admit," she eventually said. "I'm proud of how you've come on."

He gave her a grin, one that only looked partly forced, and she felt the ice in him thaw a little as pride shone through. "You had plenty to work with though, didn't you?"

"I did," she said. "I really did. Whoever taught you, they did well. And I was wrong about you. Maybe you didn't need my help."

"I'm not stubborn enough to turn down good help," Theo admitted. "Besides, it's not like you don't know what you're talking about. If it was some rookie, I'd have probably thrown him in a lake."

She narrowed her eyes. "You've actually done that, haven't you?"

He nodded. "Yes. Part of their education. In hindsight, probably not good, but at the time it felt the right thing to do."

She kept her face neutral. "I see." Her voice might have betrayed some of her disapproval for he shook his head at her.

"I was young. Stupid. Angry."

"You're not angry anymore," Anne said. "At least not permanently irritable. You never told me what made you so angry to start with. Not that I need to know," she quickly added, as she felt his emotions flare like a supernova. "It's just if you ever want to talk about it…"

"It won't be with you," Theo said, not aggressively but with the definite hint he was holding back. "No offence, but you're my teacher, not my therapist."

"Okay," Anne started to say. "I'm…" She narrowed her eyes in bemusement. Something had changed, something she couldn't explain. She dipped her head, trying to see what it was. Whatever it was, it wasn't here. Everything looked in order, she could tell without needing to dig deeper. No, it wasn't here. Anne focused her mind, tried to think back on the brief sensation. Brief was about the best word for it, didn't mean it lacked for impact. Like a moment of pain, betrayal, despair, all snuffed out from existence in the space of a second. It left her feeling more sorrowful than she wanted to admit, she felt a tear run to her eye and she didn't even know why. Then, she felt concern flash through Theo, felt his surprise at the sudden emotion. "You okay?"

How best to answer that? "Honestly?" she said. "Not even close."

"What, just because I said…"

It was her turn for her voice to come out cold. "Not because of you. Never because of you."

He'd never seen a spirit like the puttlebut before and it was starting to unnerve him. Just a little. Permear had it. The ghost hovered onto the field and gave an exaggerated little stretch, stubby arms tensing out to touch his giant ears. The spirit across the field, Martial's last was little more than a big pink blob with arms and legs just as stubby as Permear's if not more so, the limbs little more than oversized feet protruding from the bottom of the bulky bulbous body. The arms lacked anything more than claws Scott thought were almost cute in an ineffective kind of way. They reminded him of Palawi's claws, canine in nature rather than made for cutting. The eyes were huge and green, the size of saucers while the mouth was little more than a giant slash amidst the pink skin. It had four pointed ears, two out the top of its head and two more at the sides while lacking a nose. Its scalp was covered in bristly cream coloured fur sticking up in places. Privately he wondered where she'd found it. Such a creature, by rights, probably shouldn't exist in the wild. He'd investigated her beforehand, seen pictures of the puttlebut but had never expected it to be so…

Bouncy? That was the right term. When Palawi had faced it in the previous round, it had been unpredictable in its movements, the bulk might look solid and heavy, but it was considerably floaty and mobile. He'd thought of Permear immediately, and his newest spirit was eager to get out and fight. They were down to their last and he'd rolled his dice. He smiled, took a deep breath and nodded at Permear.

"Okay, we can do this," he muttered out the corner of his mouth. "Let's smash it up."

"You know it, bagmeat. You want it fast and painful or slow and excruciating? Because I got all the tools to do it both ways."

At least the ghost packed some enthusiasm about the task ahead, waving his fists in exaggerated motions, like a shadow fighter trying to out-psych an opponent. Scott knew it was all bluster. The moment the buzzer went, Permear spun and hit the puttlebut with a spin kick that sent it crashing across the arena, bouncing off the protective barrier and into the ground face first.

"Oh yeah! Number one! Eat that, fat fuck!"

He wondered who'd taught the ghost language like that. Because he was certain it wasn't him. Maybe he'd been listening to Pete. He smirked at that, gave Martial a grin. The cockiest he could manage. She returned his gaze with little more than barest acknowledgement. A little annoying but he shrugged it off. Across the way, the puttlebut floated back up, not needing to bend any part of its chubby body to rise.

"What hells? That was a good hit." Permear sounded outraged. "Come on chief, let me at that thing! I wipe that smirk off its face."

"You can't wipe the smirk off its face," Scott pointed out. "It's got a permanently curved mouth." Instead he gave the mental command and Permear charged, fists glimmering with a shining purple energy as he went for the eyes. They were big enough targets; the ghost could hardly miss. Apparently Martial had other plans, the giant cheeks swelled powerfully, the mouth opened, and the spirit exhaled. It had twin effects, one the blast threatening to topple Permear from his feet, the other sending it hovering just out of range. Permear swore as he struggled to keep his feet, had to drop to all fours to regain stability.

"Can I push its brains out through its skull?" he inquired, his voice harsh in Scott's ears. "Because this thing is really asking for it."

"I'm sure it's not. Come on Permear, stop dicking around and start landing some blows." Silently he added what he wanted the ghost to do and Permear nodded, begrudgingly pushing a hand inside his body. Scott heard the grunt of discomfort as the ghost tugged free a large handful of ectoplasm and brought his arm back, pitching it through the air towards the puttlebut.

It struck the big pink spirit straight between the eyes and immediately Scott caught the scent of burning, smoke rising from the wound. They'd come up with the attack together, the lump was about as toxic as you could without inserting a face into a puddle of nuclear waste. Truth be told, he'd enjoyed working out what Permear could do.

"Pinky!" Martial yelped, her face suddenly contorted with dismay. Any composure she might previously have had lost amidst panic. "Try to get it off!"

Good luck with that, Scott thought as Permear snickered in agreement. Pinky's arms weren't long enough for it to scratch its ass never mind wipe something off its face. The stuff on its face continued to smoulder, Scott caught another whiff of flesh charring in his nostrils. He tried to ignore it, the one thing you got used to as a spirit caller was the way flesh reacted under extreme abuse. The puttlebut dropped to the ground and tried scraping its face against the grass to little effect.

"Well that went better than I thought it would," Permear mused, taking one bobbing step towards the downed opponent before turning it into a run-up. He sprang, landed down on the giant fat back and Scott heard a great jeer erupt from the crowd, about the same time the sound of breath being expelled from Pinky's body exploded around the arena, an almost vulgar sound which made him smirk. The puttlebut tried to rise, turn to face Permear and Scott saw smoking footmarks across the back.

Okay, that's just improvising, he thought. He could have sworn Permear turned back and winked at him. But good job. Sometimes it was hard to remember that the ghost could hear his thoughts. Granted that was how he gave him most of his orders in battle, but when Permear started talking back, it was a little distracting.

"You a little distracting," the ghost said bitterly. "I don't want you tipping around in my head."

"Can't imagine it's crowded in there."

"Oh, you bitch!"

Anything else Permear might have said was cut off by the stricken puttlebut hitting it with a body check which almost knocked him off his feet. It was replaced by rampant swearing, Scott blinked several times, not quite sure he'd just seen what had just passed before his eyes.

"How…"

Pinky came around again and this time he ordered Permear to dodge, the ghost leaping into the air above the lumbering spirit. Scott peered close, still trying to work out why the attack had landed.

Permear was a ghost, the blow shouldn't have landed. Physical blows against ghosts usually had the same effect as trying to punch smoke. Or fire. It was a stupid idea and probably shouldn't be attempted. But elemental attacks could hurt, so presumably it had been something along that line. Now Pinky was in the air as well as Permear and the ghost was on the defensive, weaving to evade a flurry of blows. Scott was galvanising him on, he didn't want to take a chance if the ghost could be harmed.

"Nice you care so much," Permear grunted. "This exhausting. Can't I just hit it until it falls down?!"

Await an opening, you'll get one, Scott urged silently. Just try and keep it up. It might be tiring but it's better than being dead.

"Who for, me or you?" The words came out in exaggerated huffs as the ghost gasped for breath, Scott now sure the spirit was being entirely unnecessary in his actions. Now you're just being unhelpful, Perm.

Once again Permear winked at him, wove his face away in to avoid being hit. Pinky's fist flashed through the space where he'd been a moment earlier and Scott reacted.

Now!

He almost yelled the word out in his head and Permear grabbed the outstretched arm and made to spin around, hurling the puttlebut into the ground face first. It would have been a painful hit against any opponent, except apparently this one, Pinky hit hard and bounced straight back up, the great bulk checking Permear head on and the ghost went sailing higher into the air.

"Okay, this is just getting humiliating. I hope nobody's watching this," Scott heard the ghost grumble. He didn't sound hurt anyway, at least that was one positive out this whole fiasco.

"Just my pride," Permear added, hovering near the peak of the protective shield. "Think I might just hover here for a few. Catch my breath. While you think of a new strategy because this is bogus."

"Diplomatic."

"Screw diplomacy, bagmeat, I… What the hell's diplomacy?"

I'll answer that for you later, Permear, Scott thought with an inward groan. For now, just get some pain laid out on that damn thing.

"Thought you'd never ask." The ghost sounded almost cheery as he lunged into the fray, ducked beneath a stubby pink arm as it flailed for him and landed a trio of punches into the bulbous body. Thick sludgy stains stuck to its skin as the blows landed, slowly bubbling as the poison started to take effect. "It's better than hitting a bag this. Reckon they make punch bags out of dead versions of these things?"

To that, Scott had no answer. He didn't even want to consider it.

"You can't keep ignoring me, you know that. I never go away. You can't silence the Permear."

"You're the stupid," Scott muttered. "Nobody refers to themselves like that."

"I going to start a trend."

"Might be hard when I'm the only one who… Keep your bloody mind on the fight!" Out on the field, Permear had to sidestep a body check and made a point of kicking the puttlebut viciously in the back. There was a faint slurping sound as he tugged his foot free of the hefty skin.

"Stop bloody distracting me then!" Permear almost howled, sarcastically mimicking the words Scott had thrown at him moments earlier. "You want to do this, or you want me to do it my way?"

What's your way? Scott wondered silently. Pulling brains out through skulls? From the other side?

"Nah, that's an easy trick. All you have to do is manipulate a void inside the skull and…"

"Yeah that!" Scott almost screamed. "That! Do that."

Martial looked at him like he was losing his mind. Some of the front row sections of the crowd had surprised looks on their faces, he tried to ignore them. Using Permear here might have been a mistake, he was willing to admit that. There was still a lot he didn't know about the ghost and it might cost him.

"You know I can hear you, right?"

Yeah, you've reminded me several times. Just do it! He studied the puttlebut, shook his head. Wait, wait!

"What now?! You want me to do this or not?"

Just, think about this. That worked before because… MOVE!

Permear was already hurtling out the way as Pinky came charging in like an out-of-control mag-rail train. The ghost whistled as Scott silently cursed the annoying opponent.

"Ooh you got a really dirty mouth, bagmeat."

The veek he'd unleashed Permear against had been a completely different shape, entirely unlike this thing. Given the puttlebut didn't appear to have a head, it'd be hard to pinpoint exactly where its brain was. Given it was all body, it'd be almost impossible to guess where the vital spots were. Having Permear randomly throw voids into it would be a bit of a fool's errand without a specific idea where to start. A waste of time and effort on their part.

Okay, can you form up a series of voids, one after another?

"Probably. You want me try that now?"

"Well yeah, that's why I asked you." He fought the urge to kick something. Probably not a healthy urge. Aim for the arm. See if you can do some damage.

"You know what I do when I want to kick something? I kick something." Permear broke into a stream of manic laughter before staring at Pinky with an evil grin. The onrushing puttlebut suddenly stopped mid-rush, a bemused look on the giant features. Scott saw saucer-sized eyes move to the left arm, he saw the skin bubbling like it had been exposed to acid.

"My pretty?" Martial asked, her words puzzled. They almost mirrored the surprise on her spirits face. "Is something concerning…"

She was cut off, almost screamed as Pinky's arm exploded in a shredded mix of blood and flesh and bone. Only a useless stump remained, Scott turned his face to avoid taking a chunk in the eye, felt it hit his cheek and slid onto his shoulder. Calmer than he truly felt, he flicked it away and deliberately rolled his eyes. He imagined it looked exceptionally cool for the cameras, typical really there'd be something recording his reaction right now. Martial looked like she'd avoided it, uneasily slipping to the side as a big lump of fatty flesh hit her technical area.

"Want me to just keep doing that?" Permear asked. Casually he reached to grab a piece of already baking meat and took a bite from it with a crunch. "Because…"

"Eyes!" Scott yelled. "Now!"

This time he made sure to cover his face, watching only through the cracks of his fingers as Pinky's eyes started to bubble, one stubby arm and one stump struggling to get to them, seeking out any sort of reprieve from the pain. A dull moaning sound emerged from its cavernous mouth, he almost felt sorry for it. Almost. Not quite. He couldn't afford sympathy at a time like this. The moan turned into a scream as twin brutal pops broke the suddenly stunned silence of the stadium. Scott allowed himself a momentary look, satisfied he wasn't going to be struck with eye gunk, saw twin gaping caverns staring back at him.

"Eye see you!" Permear chortled, dancing around just out of reach as the puttlebut flailed ineffectually at him. "Want me to lend a hand? Or an eye?!"

"That's terrible," Scott muttered. "Just let it go. No more eye jokes. Put it out of its misery."

He could hear the ghost sigh. "Just once, I want to be allowed to express myself. Just once. None of this 'do this Permear, do that Permear, kill this for me Permear.' I feel like a slave sometimes…

When I could be having a ball! An eyeball! Hahahaha! Come on bagmeat, tell me that wasn't hilarious."

Scott ignored him as the ghost hopped into the air, floating listlessly above Pinky's head before dropping a punch onto the puttlebut. The enemy spirit never saw it coming, flattened under the force of the blow only to contort back into shape almost instantly like it was made of elastic. Had he not dug in, Permear might have been thrown clear, instead ethereal hands dug in, tearing away at mangled flesh. It probably wouldn't be the cleanest win he'd ever be awarded. But as the damn puttlebut finally went down, he couldn't help but be relieved. A tricky opponent and he'd conquered her. He'd bloody done it. Quarter finals, here he came.

"What do you mean, you did it?" Permear sounded irritable as he strode over, shaking himself off. "You did nothing but flap around like an idiot. I was the one who had all the good ideas. I should get the trophy."

"What trophy?" Lost in the heat of the moment above the applause of the crowd, Scott stared at the ghost in confusion.

"You know, for winning." He threw a hand out at the fallen puttlebut. Martial looked upset. Scott wasn't surprised.

"You don't get anything for winning at this point," he said. "Got to win four more bouts yet. This was the third round."

Permear's eyes widened bulbously. "You joke with me, right?"

"Nah, there's a long hard path ahead. This was probably the easy bit."

"You call that easy?" Permear sounded outraged, like he wanted to give the puttlebut one final kick to emphasise his displeasure. Scott paid him no attention, walked past the ghost and over to Martial. Behind him, Permear continued to explode with disgust, words fading to sound as he tried to hide his enthusiasm.

"Hey," he said to Martial. She looked despondent, he could almost feel the sorrow radiating from her. "Well done."

"Suppose you expect the same from me?" she asked, her accent heavy with grief. Her eyes remained dry though, her expression steadfast. She folded her arms and fixed a beady stare on him. "I will give you one. Congratulations, good luck with the rest of the tournament? Satisfied no?"

It lacked for sincerity, he had to admit that but there wasn't anything that he could do, nothing in the rules that said you had to lose with grace. Sometimes when he'd been on the wrong end of a defeat, it had been all he could do to get to the locker room without kicking something.

Still, it sure was something. Him, Scott Taylor, into the quarter final of the Quin-C. The last six… Of all the spirit callers in the five kingdoms, he could say he was in the top six… Well he could say it anyway. Part of him felt like there'd be plenty who'd dispute it.

The twenty-third day of Summerpeak.

Okocha had had enough and judging by the look of frustration on his face, Noorland had too. They'd both spent way too much time in these makeshift offices on this trip and right now, Okocha felt if he never saw another cabin again in his entire life, he'd be deliriously happy.

"Hey, Will."

He tried to ignore the voice, didn't need the distractions, just wanted to keep working until stuff made sense. Just keep turning the facts over and over in his head until something clicked. There had to be some sort of connection, all of this, Reims and Blut and the Quin-C and everything that had happened since.

"Will." Something hit him on the back of the head and he snapped back to attention, just about managing to suppress the urge to flail his hands about wildly.

"Wha-what?" He shook his head violently. "Sorry, miles away there. This whole thing is starting to get to me."

"Yeah you look stressed," Noorland said. "Want me to take over a bit?"

Okocha shook his head. "Nah, I'm fine. Got to keep working. Got to keep going. Need to find a connection. If one exists…"

"I already brought this up," Noorland cut in. "I don't think we should solely focus our investigation on Reims. There's a chance they have nothing to do with this."

"And there's an even bigger chance that they don't," Okocha shot back. "There's an even bigger chance that they're a snake in the grass and they're just waiting to strike. Without warning!"

"Will, piss off and get some sleep," Noorland said as gently as he could manage. "You're not doing anyone any favours working yourself into the ground like this. We're all tired, we're undermanned and someone's going to have a breakdown if things stay like this. Don't let it be you."

"I'm fine. Just…" He let his sentence hang to yawn. "Just…"

"Yeah, I got that," Noorland said. "Seriously. Clear your head, clear your mind. I'll stay here, hold the fort. You know I got this."

"Not as well as me." Okocha's voice was stubborn, angry, the tone of voice that said, 'aha but you aren't me so stop trying to be.'

"I can match you right now," Noorland replied. "Because you're that out of it. When was the last time you got a full night's sleep?"

"When was Arventino's fight with that freaky he-she?"

"Wow…" Noorland sounded like he was straddling the lines between impressed and disgusted. "That long?"

"Aye… Next tournament, we should bring more people…" Okocha cut off with another yawn.

"I agree with Agent Noorland."

Both looked up, saw Brendan stood staring into the room, patience etched across his craggy features.

"Will, go get some sleep. Think we got some sleep tablets in storage. Take a couple. You'll feel better in the morning. I'm ordering you to do it. Agent Noorland, I need you to do something for me. My biometrics are fritzing again. See if you can fix it for me."

"And therefore, you need me," Okocha piped up. "If he's fixing that, who's going to be watching this." He gestured at his screen. "Who's going to…"

"Get out!" Brendan jerked his thumb towards the door. "Don't make me…" He was cut off as his summoner buzzed. As did Okocha's. Then Noorland's.

The same screen next to Okocha was suddenly alight with activity and the three men looked at each other, a sudden collective of heavy hearts present in the room. Eyes went to display screens and all messages read the same. It was a picture of someone they knew of very well, a perky blond figure and the heart-breaking message beneath it. All three of them felt it and they suddenly found themselves worried for what would come next.

Sharon Arventino found dead in hotel room at Quin-C.

"Everyone dies. Some deaths are just more pointless than others. I can't think of anything I'd want more than for my death to matter."

Alison Teserine, former highest of the Vedo.

The twenty-second day of Summerpeak.

He waited patiently while the two of them spoke, the traitorous Silas and the self-styled Mistress. Wim Carson didn't like the moniker she'd bestowed upon herself. If he chose to address her with it, it was with great reluctance. He could have overheard them if he chose, yet he didn't. The less he knew of this scheme, the more comfortable he felt he'd be, if only for his conscience. What he knew, he didn't like. Besides, he had something he needed to do. He knew he'd need her leave to succeed, therefore no point in antagonising her unnecessarily. If she chose to engage in discussion with a man like Silas, then that was up to her. He could feel the duplicity radiating from him. From her, Wim just got the same feelings he usually did. Deep calm, smug authority, an unshaking sense of belief in her own justification. There was nothing more dangerous than someone who truly believed what they were saying to be the truth. Therein lay the musings of a dangerous lunatic.

Still he'd rather be here than prowling the Eye for the missing Cavanda. That girl had to be here somewhere, but she'd proven evasive. That the ship was large, and therefore an easy place to find somewhere to hide, lay in her favour and she'd taken advantage. It felt like a fool's errand to seek her out, if she was still here then she'd show herself eventually. The only question remained how many she'd kill when she revealed herself. They'd discovered the hole she'd cut through the hull; they'd been at work patching it up ever since. No sign of her, no trace of her in the Kjarn. She was chameleoning herself, he'd guess, making herself impossible to find through mystical means. Not a hard technique but infinitely useful for one in her circumstances.

He felt a tinge of disgust, saw Silas rise and make for the door. Though his face was neutral, there was no hiding his feelings and they sickened him. Silas was the sort of man for whom being drowned at birth would have made everyone's lives easier.

"I loathe that man," the Mistress said as the door closed behind him. "I truly do."

"And yet, you're willing to work with him." There was no amusement in Wim's voice, just a statement of fact, cold and unyielding.

"Well yes." She sounded by surprised by what he'd said. "If I only worked with people I liked, I wouldn't have much of an army."

"And the fact he's proving himself to be a traitor doesn't worry you?"

"Everyone's a potential traitor. The known ones aren't a problem. It's the unknown ones I worry about the most. You know what they say about keeping your friends close?"

"Enemies closer?"

"Absolutely. I need the assistance of everyone here for now. I know some of them are already plotting to stab me in the back. If others want to stab others in the back, then at least the knives aren't pointed at me. It buys me time."

"It's a dangerous scheme you've embarked upon. I see at least you are prepared for the realities of the path you've chosen to walk."

She gave him a smug look. More than that he could feel it radiating from her. Like poison. "I've spent years planning this. I have foreseen every detail. I have my confidants, they've thought of things I haven't, and we've accounted for as many variables as possible. When all the pieces come into play, we will be victorious." She didn't mention his own part in proceedings, but he could tell she was fighting the urge. People like her always did, they had a tamborlute and they wanted to play their own tune.

"I have a request," he said. There was a viewing screen in his quarters, he'd spent a lot of time watching the Quin-C tournament, not normally something he'd done throughout his life but now he had the opportunity. Thus, the purpose of his visit had come into existence.

"Really?"

"I need to go to Carcaradis Island. I need help in regards of the problem, some brains that need to be picked for extra information. There is someone there who can help me with that. I require transportation. Are you willing to provide me with it?"

He left no room for interpretation in his voice, resisted enhancing it with the Kjarn to power his suggestion. He had the impression she'd be resistant to it, would have the willpower to see through it. If she was feeble minded, she wouldn't have gone ahead with this entire scheme. It wasn't a theory he was curious to test.

"Who?"

"Excuse me?"

"Who do you need to see? I'll have them brought here."

He shook his head. "They are like me. Or they were. You would struggle to restrain them. And it is one thing doing it in a remote area like you did with the girl. In the middle of a public place, someone would spot it. Secrecy would be lost. I imagine you don't want a scene. It undermines everything you've done so far."

He trailed a finger across the table top. "No, I must see her in private. It is the best way to engage cooperation. I hope we have enough remaining history to ensure that it can be done amicably."

"You speak wisely," she admitted. She didn't look happy about it, didn't feel happy in the slightest. "I want you to take someone with you. A witness. I don't entirely trust you. You might run."

He almost laughed out loud at her words. "Where am I going to run to? It's an island and I have no credits to get off it. As much as you might have faith in my abilities, I'm not in the habit of abusing them just to get out a deal I made willingly. If I were, we wouldn't be having this conversation. When are you going to work out my word is my bond? This trip is in your interest. There is no need for a witness."

"I think there is. It's not that I don't trust you..." He could tell immediately those words were a lie and he fought the urge to give her a sarcastic smile. "It's not. I don't trust those you might talk to. You've shown your own opposition to my undertaking and I do not wish to have it undermined by anyone you might contact. Some people have stronger consciences than you."

"No." Wim sounded strangely defiant as he said it. "They really don't."

"Regardless," she said, insistent in her words. "A witness is what you need, and a witness is what you shall have. Of my choosing and of my command."

"I do not think..."

"That it is a good idea? But I do, my dear Wim. It's with a witness or without."

He felt a stab of annoyance. "You'd really sabotage your own efforts?"

"What I need from you is a part of my plan. It is not the be all and end all. If needs must, I would do without it. But should I not need it, then I wouldn't need you. And do you really think you'd be able to make it off this ship alive?"

Anger rushed through him as he stood up straight, his hand twitching to go for his weapon. He took several deep breaths and tried to push them down inside him, not look threatening. That wasn't right. He shouldn't have risen like that. "Do you?" he asked quietly.

"You have so much you want to live for," she said. "I'm prepared to die in the pursuit of my undertaking. I've made my peace with that." He could feel the steel in her words, they rung with true conviction. "Can you say the same?"

He glared at her. "Talk to me of witnesses. I want someone reliable."

As it happened, she had just the person in mind, someone she wanted out of her hair for the time being. Someone useless here for the time being but had experience of Carcaradis Island. Someone who Wim would be able to intimidate into good behaviour. She smiled at him coolly. He undoubtedly wouldn't like it. What he did or didn't like wasn't her concern.

They'd arrived on Carcaradis Island shortly after mid-morning and Wim was already regretting that she'd made him bring Rocastle along. The man had proven himself to be a truly disgusting individual and already he was looking for an excuse to either cut him loose or cut him down. Either would suit nicely. Until then though, he'd play nice.

A pair of pilots sat up front, guiding the craft down to the aeroport, him and the fat man stuck in the back. Rocastle dug under his nails with a flint of metal as they sat in silence, neither of them willing to speak to the other. He'd grown a beard to help disguise his identity, wispy and dyed black, contacts in his eyes to give them a watery brown tint, his long hair cut short. Wim couldn't keep his eyes from his prosthetics, the new fingers he'd been granted following his aborted attempt to keep the girl prisoner.

He had no sympathy for him in that regard, nor for his bloody Mistress. They should have informed him they had a prisoner with such abilities, he would have been able to assist in keeping her contained, rather than have her screw things up the way she had. The fingers hadn't been covered with synthetic skin yet, they were a dull blue colour, every joint exposed. Every time he moved them, Wim saw the flinch on Rocastle's face from where the clasps dug into his knuckles. Due to the cauterising nature of the kjarnblade, they'd been unable to reattach the original digits. He might learn a lesson from this about going up against an opponent with a kjarnblade with a blaster. That wasn't a fair contest, not even for a skilled combatant against a novice bladesman. Nothing about Rocastle spoke to him of skill. He was a bully and a coward, those were his impressions and he'd seen nothing to say otherwise.

Granted he did have a weapon in the interests of protection, be it from Wim himself or from the target but somehow Wim didn't find that too worrying. How accurate he was with it would be open to debate. He could sense unease in the man, buried beneath pain and resentment, maybe a little worry. He wasn't happy to be back on the island. There'd been some sort of trouble weeks earlier, Wim wasn't clear on the details. He'd asked as much and Rocastle had refused to answer, giving him a sarcastic sneer that told him it was none of his business. Wim had probed deeper across the surface of his temporary partner's being, an act he found disgusting, but he sensed no regret to balance out that fear. All Rocastle had said was he didn't want to be recognised or there'd be trouble afoot.

With that in mind, it had made Wim wonder why she'd picked the fat man to go with him. Surely there'd be someone less likely to bring trouble down on them. Or maybe she'd just decided to cut them both loose and to hells with the consequences if they didn't come back. Either way, it meant he'd need to ensure Rocastle wasn't recognised. Some sort of abject lesson in teamwork he really didn't need? If that was the case, he could do with teaching that bloody woman a lesson. Who the hells did she think she was, interfering with him like this. He clenched his fists, ground his teeth and felt himself shaking under the righteous indignity of it all.

Something wasn't right with him, he realised, and it worried him. He'd always been tightly restrained with his emotions before this. He'd needed to be. Vedo didn't react like this to adversity. They faced it steadfast, ready to do the right thing. They didn't fall into their anger. That was a Cavanda trait. Wim knew he needed to be more careful, especially when the entire future of the Vedo was at stake. He needed to restore them, but not at any cost and not by building on such a tenuous base.

It was an old trick but one he relished being able to employ again as he strode through the hallway like he owned it, secure in the knowledge neither he nor his blaster rifle toting companion would be picked up by security footage. Maybe he could own it all. One day, he might be wealthy, have financial influence to back up his power. Having gone from having it all to having nothing, Wim didn't intend to reach the point where it was scooped from him again. He couldn't. He wouldn't. Vedo of the past would never have aligned themselves with someone like her. That was why they were gone and despite everything, he was still here. He would be triumphant. The last of the old Vedo, the first of the new.

Of course, that wouldn't quite be true. It was an idle thought but another disturbing one. Until he'd known true poverty and despair, he'd never thought of greed or desire in these ways before. They were something beyond him before, he'd never wanted for anything but neither had his life been awash with affluence. He'd been comfortable in it. That was the best way to see it. But to want it all was a new one. He couldn't think like that. Of course, saying it was easier than doing.

Then again, the path of a Vedo was never an easy one. He hadn't been one for a long time, understandable he'd have trouble readjusting. Understandable but unacceptable. He wouldn't allow himself to fall even further than he had. There was no path back from that. Wim had a task to do here and he couldn't fail. There were still a few pieces yet to slip into place.

One of them more pressing than anything else. He knew she was here. All that remained was getting her to talk to him. What sort of condition might she be in, he couldn't say with any degree of confidence. Once the Kjarn had been corrupted, it had happened, and it had sent the unprepared Vedo who touched it mad slowly but completely. Many of them needed to be put down. He was lucky that he'd been saved, everything happens for a reason and he was to be the architect of a rebirth for losing it had undoubtedly been what had kept him sane. There'd been many times in the past, he'd rather have died than live in the squalor, but some spark inside had kept him going. And now he knew why. It was better now. Once it had been filthy and malignant. Some of it still was. He could feel the remnants of it as he sent a lens flare across the recording image of the camera. It was better but still not perfect. Time was apparently a natural healer. Now he was better and rising again. He would do what he needed, including, apparently, making deals with someone he would have avoided in the past.

It appeared you couldn't escape the rot. Sometimes it was in your head, sometimes it was in the world outside. Here they stood, room three twenty-eight and he could sense the remnants of her presence. She'd spent time here. Enough to imprint a sense of feeling on the room. Expanding his mind into the area around him, that sense found everyone, the presences of those in their rooms minding their own business. It no longer exhausted him to do so. He didn't want to encounter them. If they interfered, Rocastle would put them down, he didn't want to be responsible for their deaths.

With a wave of the hand, the lock on the door clicked open and he grinned at Rocastle, pushing it open. "Easy."

"You're quite the little cat burglar, huh?" Rocastle said. "You fancy giving me a hand with something while you're here? I've got some unfinished business with someone…"

Wim shook his head. "I've been warned about you," he said sternly. "Any of that business and you'll lose a hand. The other one." He nodded his head towards the prosthetic fingers his companion wore, his own hand tapping the hilt of his kjarnblade.

"The Mistress warned you about little old me? She tends to overreact."

Without bothering to correct him as to the impressions the Kjarn was giving him, Wim trailed into the room and took it in. He could smell the perfume, azelberry and jasmine. Some things never changed. Back in the day, she'd tried to keep a single azelberry flower in a jar in her quarters in the temple. It hadn't survived. She'd gotten over it a lot faster than he thought she would, had taken the lesson to heart. Despite your best effort, things always die. "Sit down," he said, glancing back to Rocastle following him in. "We don't know how long she'll be, but I don't want to spook anyone before we're ready. And I have work to do."

"Fine by me," Rocastle said, dropping into one of the plush chairs, the kinetic disperser resting across his knees. Wim had chosen the weapon himself, had explained it as the best choice for the task. He didn't know what sort of reaction he'd be greeted with; it was harder to defend against the wide spread hammer-like blasts than against a single narrow laser blast. When you didn't quite know what to expect, it was better to be prepared. Even the few scant meditations he'd employed to scan out his path ahead had been clouded, too many variables to read what the future might hold to the outcome of this meeting. One could only plan so far ahead.

As Rocastle sighed aggressively, Wim started to move across the room, running his fingers across the walls in deep sweeping motions, careful to not overextend himself. His connection with the Kjarn was still new, still fresh and while it was growing stronger every day, it still would have been all too easy to exhaust himself.

"I had a room like this," Rocastle continued wistfully. "Bet they gave it to someone else. I miss that room, even after it flooded. Best gig I ever had doing the scouting here. What the hells are you doing, anyway?"

"Soundproofing," Wim grunted. "It's a big job, I need to concentrate."

"Why the hells you soundproofing? That really the best use of your time?" Rocastle sounded petulant like a spoilt child and Wim wanted so very much to ignore him. Instead he sighed and turned to face him, eyes narrowed. The fat man wilted under the glance and privately he was pleased with the reaction. The fear amused him.

"Are you really as ignorant as you appear? If this turns out badly, do you want every person on the island to know? With your record, they'll probably shoot you on sight."

He clapped a hand on Rocastle's shoulder and squeezed, letting just a little bit of Kjarn slip into his fingers to prove a point, saw the fat man's eyes widen as his grip bit down on the muscles. "Me, I'll be fine.

Might have to make a swift getaway but I will survive. No, this requires a delicate touch and that is something I do not think you possess."

"I'll show you delicate," Rocastle muttered. Wim increased the pressure; a yelp escaped his lips. Idly he thought about breaking his shoulder or at least dislocating it, a tempting thought but he chose to refrain. He might still need this noxious little weed yet. Still…

"Can you repeat that?" he asked mildly, applying more pressure and the yelp turned into a low howl, a moan of desperation. Rocastle tried to shake him off to no avail. "I thought I heard you say something."

"I didn't!" Rocastle almost screamed it out. "I didn't say anything."

Finally, Wim let him go and settled on the floor across the room from him. "I thought so," he said as he closed his eyes. "She'll be here. Soon. Stay patient. Don't alert her or your life won't be worth living."

Threats? From him? That was interesting. And worrying. What was he becoming? And more to the point, why did a tiny part of him enjoy it?

Slipping into meditation was easier than ever, a nice drift into another state of mind, one of hyperawareness and sensitivity. Yet at the same time, he felt so much more alive than he ever had before. He could feel them all, connected to everyone on the island, a collective mass too densely packed together to make out as individuals. Searching for one specific person however would prove to be more challenging, he found himself grasping several times to no avail before finally locking down her position. This used to be so easy… He tried to quash the resentment down inside him. It wouldn't help.

Through his meditations, he heard her approach through the Kjarn long before the sound of the key in the lock and slowly he opened his eyes. This might need to be a swift job. With the door open, the soundproofing he'd thrown up around the room wouldn't be as effective and she could still run. Could, but she wouldn't. She surely knew he was here, and still she'd approached, unless she'd completely lost touch with her heritage. She was curious, and that curiosity would be rewarded tenfold. Yet as the door swept open, he found his hand dropping to his newly constructed kjarnblade for reassurance. He wasn't expecting to need it. If he had to ignite it, then he had already failed his mission.

In truth, Wim Carson had already arrived at the conclusion he was more likely to use it on Rocastle than on his prey. He smelled her before she entered the room, she saw them almost immediately, tensed up, only to enter regardless. Good, he hadn't fancied chasing her through the hotel. Him, she recognised. To Rocastle, he registered a flicker of fear and surprise, of the unknown emanating from her.

"I thought you were dead," she said to him, her voice calm. Apparently, she hadn't forgotten how to keep that level of poise. "I thought he killed you."

"Ascendant Arventino," Wim said, his voice respectful. "I think you'll find I am very much alive. And harder to kill than you might have been led to believe."

"Apparently so, Master Carson."

There it was. Not deference in her voice, that was too much to hope for, but an acknowledgement of the authority he'd once held. She kept his eyes as she bent down to remove her ridiculous heeled shoes, he nodded slowly and relaxed.

"I see this is what you've been doing since the Fall," he said. "You became a spirit caller."

"I was always a spirit caller at heart," she said. "Training to use the Kjarn didn't change that. So was my master."

"Your master was a lot of things," Wim said coldly. He watched her remove her other shoe, shaking his head. "Not many of them good."

"He was a good teacher."

"As a Vedo, he was lacking. Dangerously unfocused on what he could have been. It was a mistake to give you to him. And now look at him. He abandoned you. The two of you could have done so much more. You lead the life of someone else not befitting to us, he hides away who knows where."

She said nothing, he felt a stab of anger filter through her. That had touched a nerve. Several maybe. "Neither of you are fit to bear the name."

"Master Baxter was a great man. He did…" She struggled with the words before getting them out. Idly he wondered if she believed them or if she was just paying lip service to someone she'd idolised. "He did what he thought was right. And that's something not many of you ever did."

"Interesting you don't count yourself among us," Wim said.

"He didn't run," Sharon Arventino insisted. "He had a plan, he was going to make it all better. If anyone could have…"

"Do you even hear yourself?" Wim asked incredulously. "If he had this master plan to fix everything, where is he? How come he never came back for you? Why are you limiting yourself to being ordinary when you could be exceptional?"

"Maybe some of us don't want to be your kind of exceptional," Sharon said. "My father, Alison Teserine… They pushed me into this. I never wanted it. But in a way, it made me, so I can't complain. No changing the past, but my future is something I can do something about."

"Yes, I hear," Wim said smoothly. "I hear congratulations are in order of your upcoming nuptials."

Rocastle let out a whistle of demented glee. Sharon ignored him. "Why are you here?" she asked instead. "Because the Vedo are gone, barring my master…"

"And I!" Wim snarled, surprising himself with the venom in his voice. "If there are Vedo to hear the voice of the Kjarn, then their hope will never leave the world. I'm here to take you back."

She rolled her eyes, an expression of audacity that would have infuriated him then and infuriated him now. He wanted to strike out at her for her disrespect, held his temper.

"I recently encountered a Cavanda apprentice," he said. "That means there are more still out there. And only the Vedo can stand against them. I've seen it!" The words weren't entirely true, but he believed them. He knew what those unchecked Kjarn wielders could do. "Without us, they will overrun the world."

"Then go to Master Baxter, find him and tell him."

"He's not my master!" The venom returned to his voice. "He's not fit for that mantle. Just because he survived doesn't make him the head of the order. That right should be mine! He's a pretender. He should be coming to me. As should you. I forgive your transgressions if you accept yourself as my apprentice and come back to the path you never should have been allowed to leave."

Sharon blinked. "Master Carson. As much as I hear what you're saying…" She hesitated for a moment, he thought she might go for it. He'd given her an order after all. She'd stand with those that she belonged with. "I'm going to have to decline. That part of my life is long over. I'm not interested."

"You assume you have a choice!" White hot anger flared through him and he didn't even try to restrain it. He revealed the hilt of his weapon, almost drew it. She did react to that, her eyes widening, and she threw out an arm, Wim grinning inside as he felt the Kjarn surge through her in a way denied to it for so long. It looked an effort, but the cylinder flew to her outstretched hand and he sighed as she thumbed the activation switch and the blade burst into life, a silver blade with flecks of gold and black running through it emerging. He could smell the acrid scent of white hot energy, the odour of disuse. How long since she'd last activated it? A while, if that smell was anything to go by.

"Still works then?" he said dismissively. His own kjarnblade crept into his hand but he didn't move towards igniting it. "Ascendant Arventino, I'm asking you to stand down. I do not want to fight you."

"And I don't want to listen to you," she said. She shot a sideways glance to Rocastle who made a hurt face and gripped his weapon tighter. She brought her blade up, shielding her body pointedly. "Or him. Both of you, leave! Now!"

"I can't do that," Wim said sadly. "I need your help and…"

"No!" She sounded furious as the words left her mouth. "I'll never help you! I remember you, Wim Carson and I know what you're capable of."

"You remember what? That I was friends with your teacher…"

"You tried to murder him! And me."

That much was true, he had to admit. It wasn't the entire story, but that fact was always going to condemn him in her eyes unless he could make her see sense. A lot of bad stuff had happened back then during the Fall and he couldn't defend himself against the accusations. "I wasn't myself. Nobody was that day. The madness had taken us all, bar you and your master. I don't know why you two were spared…"

"No, I wouldn't expect you to," she cut in with a sneer.

"If I had been able to stop myself, I would have done so. But I'm better now. It took us all by surprise. But now my eyes are open, and I will conquer this. I will bring the Vedo back. You and I will be the first of the new…"

"You can't control this. I don't know how you got your connection back but…" He took a step towards her and she raised her weapon. "Get back! I don't care. You might be able to touch it again but you're making the same mistakes as the old order did."

"The old order was perfect," he said, trying to keep the control in his voice. "Cut off before its prime."

"You're in denial," Sharon said scornfully. "The old order deserved to die."

"You!" Something in him snapped and his words came out harsh and angry. His blade snapped on and he didn't lower it, pointing it level at her throat. She didn't move to knock it away, but he could tell in her eyes she wanted to. "You don't know what you're talking about, stupid little girl! Just because you survived doesn't give you a Divine-given right to comment on our ways. You or your deviant master."

"And why was he deviant? Because he chose not to follow blindly down paths trodden thousands of times before by you and yours? Because he was different? That made him the greatest of them all. Have you ever wondered why he and I were the only one unaffected by the Fall?"

Wim had, but now wasn't the time to debate it. She couldn't know why. She wouldn't. Didn't. She was lying, trying to psych him out. "It won't work!" he yelled. "You don't know what you're talking about! How could you? What we did was magnificence, the work of the Divines and if Baxter survived it, then…"

It felt like the pieces were falling into place. "Did Baxter get involved? Was he complicit in our destruction?!" Suddenly a great weight felt as if lifted from his shoulders, realisation dawning within him. "Were you?"

"I wasn't, Wim. Neither was he. It hurt him badly to have to dismantle it…"

"But not enough to crush him! You're both a disgrace!" Fury coursed through him now, as he'd never felt before and part of him knew it was wrong to feel like this, but he couldn't stop it. All his reservations were pitiful against the anger bellowing in his being. "I came here to ask for your help but…"

"I will not help you on your mad quest. Let things be. You can't resuscitate the order. Not as it was."

"Ascendant Arventino," Wim said through gritted teeth. "I do not, I repeat, do not…" He let the Kjarn burst go he'd been building up inside him, emphasising his words, the sheer power forcing her to take three steps back. She nearly lost her footing. Rocastle nearly fell back off his seat. "WANT YOUR OPINION!"

As she righted herself, she glared at him. "I was so hoping you would do that." And then she was on him, swinging her blade at him and that was that as his own blade came to block, the clash of light hurting his eyes as they met.

"So much for never striking first," she said. "You've forgotten that code you claimed to live by. Now who's disgracing the order's memory?"

He didn't reply, just blocked her next three strikes as she continued to shoot her dirty little mouth off. "No hate, no anger, just duty and the greater good. Sound familiar? It's the opposite of…" She swung out again, a two-handed swipe at neck height that would have broken his head from his neck if it had connected. He didn't recoil at the flare as blade met blade. It wasn't anything he hadn't seen before. Next, she went low, and he slashed to block her from taking his legs away.

Even amidst the anger, he found he truly didn't want to hurt her. He wanted her to see sense, which had been the true purpose behind the harshness of his words. But if she wouldn't see it, that only together would they be stronger, and she didn't seem to understand. Or want to. He moved his blade in unison with hers, never pressing an advantage, just halting her attacks before they reached him. He was rusty. But so was she. They'd been suffering from the same malady in a way. The ability to touch the Kjarn in them had threatened to atrophy through underuse. Her movements were stiff, unfamiliar, but it looked like there was some sort of muscle memory remaining with her.

Of course, her bastard master had ensured she was well drilled in that. Ruud Baxter, the disgrace of the Vedo, always chose a fight over another solution. Still their blades met, neither given as much room to move as they might have liked given the layout of the room. He swung at her, missed and cut a great scar down the middle of her, only barely blocking her counter attack as he pulled free. In retaliation, she sent a weak burst of Kjarn lightning towards him, the smell of static sulphur thick in the room. He caught it in his hand, felt his skin fizzle under the charge and he tossed it aside, blackening the wall with the blast. Once more she came at him and he brought his blade up to defend...

Rocastle's kinetic disperser boomed and suddenly her eyes widened as she was flung forward, he couldn't have twisted to evade her even if he'd wanted to, reactions just too slow, he heard the gasp as his blade went through her body and out the other side. Nothing held up against the power of the Kjarn, it was what made the blades so formidable as weapons. As soon as he saw the look on her face, he felt the regret, deactivated his blade and she fell to the carpet, the back of her head a mess, her neck at an awkward angle. Wasn't dead yet but...

The wave of power hit him like a tsunami, almost hurling him from his feet and rendered him insensible, everything she was, everything she had been and what she could have become forcibly being expelled from the slowly dying shell that had once been her body.

He'd felt it. Anyone with a single iota of Kjarn sensibility, within a hundred miles would have felt it. Anyone even who had a strong connection to her might even have felt it, such was the power he'd felt behind it. For several long moments he sat there slumped against the wall where he'd fallen, staring at the body. It wasn't supposed to go like this. She was supposed to have listened to him. If she would have...

"That was intense," Rocastle said breezily. "Shame she had to twist. I could have..."

What he could have done was lost in the moment as Wim rose to his feet angrily and flung out with the Kjarn, grabbing him by the throat and holding him upright in the air. He wanted so badly to kill the fat fuck, make him suffer like Sharon had. Nobody should die like this!

"Why the hells did you do that?"

With pressure on his windpipe, Rocastle couldn't answer but still he managed to smirk as the force on his throat only grew. Killing him wouldn't be the right solution. But right now, if there was a correct solution to the whole mess, Wim Carson didn't know what it was.

He felt like he didn't know anything anymore.

"Once more, like an overindulged child, the more attention spins away from him, the more he clamours to pull it back to him. Ronald Ritellia will speak today about the latest tragedy to hit his grossly ill-thought out attempt at running a successful Quin-C in Vazara…"

Kate Kinsella article ahead of Ritellia's press conference.

The twenty-fifth day of Summerpeak.

In front of the media of the five kingdoms, Ronald Ritellia gripped the sides of his podium for reassurance, gnarled knuckles going white from the exertion. He didn't look well, the colouring in his face faded and despite the best efforts of his makeup team, the fatigue made him look each of his seventy plus years of age. Thomas Jerome stood by his side, the Falcon with him but with the look of one ready to plunge the knife. In the crowd, he saw dearest Alana, the sole bright light in a dimming sea of sharks. Still he straightened himself up and adjusted his tie.

"Ladies and gentlemen," he said, his voice dull and almost lifeless. The stories of how he had reacted upon hearing of another setback was already legend, rumours let slip by an onlooker seeking quick credits. Cynics had said he had wept for the increasing untenability of his own position rather than the lives lost. His most vociferous supporters had said his tears were ones of sorrow that such a tragic loss of life should have occurred under his watch. "Over the last few days, there have been plenty of debates not just about the future of this tournament but also my future as the head of the International Competitive Calling Committee. And today I have come before you to make an announcement that will greatly affect the way we view our sport."

He felt the collective assortment of press draw a breath of surprise as one. They thought they knew what was coming, could sense sudden hope he'd finally be out the door. That made him want to scoff. It made him want to curse each of them. How little they truly knew about real life.

"What happened with Ms Arventino was a tragedy among tragedies. There have been fewer callers of her generation more loved and respected and a beautiful life was cut short. We can't change that. Nothing will bring her back." His voice took on a note of derision, losing its humility just for a moment. "My resignation will not bring her back, nor will it change anything that has happened. Therefore, I do

57

not offer it. It would be pandering symbolism of the lowest possible order and I will not give you the disrespect of doing it. Instead, what I will do is continue to embody the qualities that has made both this organisation and this sport the finest example of competition that the five kingdoms have ever known…"

He tailed off, suddenly aware the mood had turned ugly. Some had started to mutter amongst themselves, the cameramen recording him looking like they were about to go into a frenzy. They might not have heard anything after his refusal to leave. He spoke louder, not quite shouting but determined to make his point.

"We do not forget those we've lost. As of the culmination of this tournament's final, the trophy will be renamed the Sharon Arventino trophy as a reminder of what it took to lift it. It will not be cancelled. To do so would be to allow these cowards who would slaughter an innocent woman to win and I refuse to do that. My administration in this office will not bow to glorified terrorism. I can assure you I have been in contact with Unisco and they've put their best people on the investigation. Somebody will be found. We will have justice."

Behind him, the Falcon crossed his arms with an exasperated look. "If we cannot have justice, then we have nothing. Our hearts and minds go out to those who she left behind." He regretted asking it the moment the question left his lips. "Any questions?" He tried to ignore Kate Kinsella. He wasn't about to dignify any poisonous bile that woman might spew with an answer. Instead he gestured to a clean cut Burykian gesturing impatiently for his attention.

"Yes, you."

"President Ritellia, do you personally accept any of the blame directed at you by some sections of both the Senate and the media?"

He shook his head. "No. None of this is my responsibility. There was nothing I could have done to prevent it; I don't lose sleep over it. Granted I feel sorrow for the loved ones of not just Sharon Arventino but also Darren Maddley and anyone else caught in the events transpiring here, but some people want to blame me for everything and that I find unacceptable." He tried to avoid looking at Kinsella as he said it. He gestured for another. "Go on?"

"Have you spoken to any of Ms Arventino's close family since the death?"

"Mr Roper does not desire to speak to me, I've been told. Nor does her brother or her mother nor her step-father. I have made efforts but been shot down. What more can a man do?"

"Why would Mr Roper not wish to speak to you?"

A tricky question, one he was prepared for with a quick deflection. "You'd have to ask him. I imagine that he's going through some tough times and the shock of losing someone can be quite overwhelming. Doubtless he wishes to assign blame and instead of putting it where it is due, he apportions it to me. It's a tactic slowly becoming more common in damaged societies as our lives go by. Sad but the only thing we can do is give him time and let him heal." He could have gone on about the injustices of it all but chose not to. Better to keep it succinct, more quotable rather than airing his true grievances. Whine too much to these people and they'd go for the kill.

"When do you see the tournament resuming?"

"As you all know, the service for Ms Arventino is this afternoon, we hope to resume in two days' time. A period of respect has been given, we can do no more. She'd want the show to go on and therefore that is what it will do." If it was questions about the tournament, he'd field them all day. He preferred it to talking about the emotional stuff. Ritellia felt uncomfortable with the whole thing, still a little irked Arventino had had the temerity to be killed while the tournament was ongoing. It brought up all sorts of questions about the whole damned mess he'd rather not answer. Given another choice, he'd tell Reims and their bloody Coppinger woman to take a hike. They'd been nothing but trouble since it the start.

Of course, if he'd done that, he wouldn't have met the charming Ms Fuller. She smiled at him, her eyes neutral but her mouth warm and welcoming. She ran her tongue over the outline of her lips, he smiled back. Still Kate Kinsella tried to get his attention and just as pointedly he ignored her.

"Yes?" He gestured for another question, saw Kinsella leaning forward to talk to the journalist in front of her, a younger redhead with nervous eyes. A protégé perhaps? Both irrelevant. The question came from a tall Vazaran, his hair in those ridiculous dreadlocks. No wonder people didn't take his kingdom seriously with hairstyles like that. It was either those or big bloody beards that spoke of a serious lack of personal hygiene.

"Mr President, is there going to be any extra security put on with the continuation of the tournament to ensure the safety of the competitors and the spectators? And the press?"

Ritellia wasn't alone in laughing at that last comment, it brought many cackling brays from the press pack as well. Privately he wouldn't have been bothered if some lunatic chose to open fire in this room right now, provided he had the chance to get down behind his podium first. Still, he had an answer for this, a solution he was particularly proud of. "Yes. Yes, I have arranged for an extra security presence on the streets for the remaining weeks of the tournament. Thanks to a productive discussion with Mr Mazoud of the Vazaran Suns, there will be twenty of his best units keeping an eye out on safety concerns for the…"

"You're joking!" Kinsella said loudly. More laughter from the crowd, Ritellia frowned in her direction.

"If that's your question, Ms Kinsella, I'll be happy to answer it when it's your turn to ask one." You know, first stop after never, he wanted to add but chose not to. He hoped she was suitably chastened by his reply. "But no, I'm not joking. As shown a week ago during the hostage event, our island police force is greatly inadequate for situations of that measure. With the support of the Vazaran Suns, plus the vaguely defined help from our friends at Unisco, I feel certain that we can get through the rest of it without any more trouble."

In the cabin, Okocha and Noorland looked at each other, hearing the smug condescension in Ritellia's voice at the mention of their organisation, both rolling their eyes while across the room, Fagan let out a snort of derision. "Typical. I hate that fucking guy so much. Vague help… There'd have been way more people killed if it wasn't for us." Both he and Leclerc were getting ready to travel, Aldiss and Derenko doing the same in the other room. It had taken a few days longer than Okocha would have liked it to, but he'd gotten a hit on the location of Joseph Itandje and they were getting ready to move on it.

"Can't do much about the politicians," Leclerc said. "I've seen things under stones preferable to Ritellia. But he'll do anything to avoid taking the blame. Technically, none of this is his fault…"

"Well it is," Noorland said. "He saw the tournament was staged here. Sure, they say it's an impartial vote, but you really think he doesn't tell them where he would prefer it to be. And I'd imagine there's a few lives made an unmitigated disaster because they didn't comply with him."

"Any of you spoken to Nick since it happened?" Fagan asked, fastening a muffler to his belt.

Okocha nodded sorrowfully. "I did."

"How's he taking it?"

"About as well as you'd expect him to be. Suffice to say not at all. Think he's in denial."

"Got to feel sorry for the guy, no?" Leclerc mused. "He'd thought he'd got it all worked out and now this. One of those bad days I think. Out the tournament and out of love… No, that's not right."

"He'll still love her," Noorland said. "It just… It's never good when your loved ones die. You feel it, you know."

His voice took on a dull tone as he said it, as if remembering. "You'll carry on living but it feels like your heart got ripped out your chest, like there's a great hole where all the love and joy you once had should be. And everything you see, everything you do just makes it hurt more. Because there's reminders everywhere."

"And it's a bad way to die," Okocha said. "I saw the autopsy reports. Massive trauma to the upper back, neck and head, they reckon it was a kinetic disperser. Those things are meant to be used against shields so have a guess what they did to her head, and then impaled on something that burned straight through her. They don't know what did it. They're genuinely stumped. Seen nothing like it. Wound instantly cauterized but there was no saving her."

"Poor bitch," Fagan said. A sentiment most of them echoed with Ritellia's press conference slowly reaching its conclusion on the screen in front of them

"Funny though," Okocha said. "I took Arnholt the report, was there when he had a read. There's something going on there. There was a look on his face."

"Like what?" Noorland asked.

Okocha shook his head. "Not sure. Like he recognised something. Anyway, not that it matters. No idea who did it, there's no evidence of anyone going in or out of that room bar Arventino herself. The footage is too badly messed up to tell us anything."

"Messed up?" Leclerc asked. "How?"

"Keeps going into static," Okocha said. "It's actually pretty incredible, each recording camera along the path from the elevator to her room goes down one after the other and starts to work again a few seconds later after the next one fails. And then does it again in reverse after we guess when the murder took place."

"Well that just sounds deliberate," Noorland said. "Nothing you can do to repair it?"

Okocha shook his head. "Nope. I already tried, I already failed." He let out a sigh. Admitting you'd failed what should have been a simple task was never easy. He'd found the whole thing to be completely frustrating if he was honest. "Seriously! This was supposed to be a relaxing trip." He hit his desk with his fist and bit back a yelp as pain shot through his hand.

"Okay Will," Noorland said. "Chill out. Told you before, it's not your fault. If it's beyond you, it's beyond anyone." He clapped Okocha on the shoulder. "And just for the record, ain't no such thing as a relaxing trip. Not in this job. But I got to say, I didn't think it'd be this bad."

"At least you're missing out on this trip," Fagan said. "The armpit of Vazara. Cubla Cezri. Worst hive of snakes you'll ever find."

"I thought Tatmanbi was the armpit of Vazara?" Noorland asked. "Remember that place where all those kids got shot?"

"Nobody ever remembers the good stuff about Tatmanbi," Okocha said. "I spent some summers there as a kid, it's not that bad a place. It just has a bad rep."

"Yeah child murder will do that for you," Leclerc said serenely. "Is Cubla Cezri really as bad as my belligerent friend makes out?"

"Probably worse," Okocha deadpanned. "It's not the sort of place you go unless you're either hiding or hunting. Place is a mess, a warren of streets and alleys, it's easy to get lost in there. And once you do, it's hard to get out alive."

"Well, pack the Featherstones then?" Fagan grinned. "And a map."

"And don't turn it into a war zone. Even the Sun's don't like going in unless they've got to," Okocha added. "There's more illegal ordnance lingering unchecked per head in there than the rest of the kingdom combined."

"Maybe just grenades then," Fagan said. "Sounds like we don't want to get made here too early."

Noorland shrugged. "Ah, maybe I'll come along. Sounds like my sort of place. Besides, if it's that dangerous, you need someone to stick with the ship. Make a quick getaway. It's not like we're brimming with pilots out here, eh?"

"I don't have a problem," Leclerc said. "If you really want to come, more the merrier. Just approve it with someone first, yeah?"

Noorland snorted. "Yeah, obviously."

Theo had mixed feelings about the whole thing as he stood in the afternoon sun, watching the procession move down the street. On the one hand, he genuinely didn't have a bad word to say about Sharon Arventino. On the very few occasions he'd had any interaction with her, she'd always been nice to him, courteous and never condescending. He'd found that rare from someone in her position. Pretty and powerful. In short, an absolute prize of a woman. On the other hand, she'd been a powerful caller in her own right and there was a part of him left a little smug knowing he'd be the last person ever to have battled her competitively. And the last person to have beaten her. That sent a warm feeling through his stomach, would do no end of wonders for his own legend.

He felt uncomfortable in the formal wear, the stiff black tunic and pants but showing respect meant doing things you didn't like apparently. Beside him, Anne wore a simple black dress as they stood, a pair of faces amongst thousands as the coffin made its way down the streets of the resort, suspended on a quad of repulsorlifts. Black banners adorned the streets, hung from the awnings of shops and stalls and from the street lights. Just plain black with the occasional picture of Sharon's face transposed onto them in liquid silver, some bearing the message for her to rest in peace and how she'd never be forgotten.

Six walked with the coffin, guiding it on its way, Nick Roper and Peter Jacobs at the head, the other four Theo didn't know but given one looked like an older version of Jacobs, he'd have hazarded a guess at him being his father. The silence was everywhere, occasionally broken by the squawking of gulls and ocean birds as they made their way towards what was to be her final resting place. Next to him, Anne's eyes were red and blotchy as she hugged herself, her skin a little cool despite the afternoon sun.

"It's not fair," she muttered. "So many assholes in the world and only the good die young."

"Life's a bastard sometimes," Theo agreed. Feeling monumentally awkward, he reached to put an arm around her. She was shaking slightly, he felt a faint twinge in his gut for her, an emotion he wasn't entirely familiar with. It felt weird. Sorrow? Pity? Either of them could have felt like the right term "You just have to keep going despite it, I think."

She rested her head against his shoulder, he could smell lilac from her shampoo, a clean, fresh scent he found soothing. For a moment, he found it difficult to form the words. "Because... I don't know. Something about taking a beating and getting back up. Never going to stay down. She wouldn't have wanted that. You get what I'm saying."

"Yeah." Anne sounded better as the words left her mouth. More than that, they sounded amused, just about avoiding any hint of disrespect considering where they were. "You really suck at the consolation; you know that?"

Theo said nothing. Privately he agreed. Outwardly, he kept his face stoic, ran the tip of his finger through the locks of her hair. She let out a little sound of contentment, it almost startled him into ceasing. "Don't," she said. "It's nice."

"Okay," he replied, a little bemused. "I'm sorry. I try to avoid funerals. First one I ever been to."

"Really?"

"Yep. Don't like to think too much about the past. Or I didn't used to. Too painful. I grieve in my own way."

"And what's that?"

"Trying desperately not to," he said, meaning every word. It was true. He'd never gone to his mother's funeral, despite his father begging him. In a way, he regretted it the more he tried to avoid thinking back to it. He'd loved his mother just as much as he hated his bastard of a father. He'd missed out on the chance to say goodbye because he wanted to stick it to the old bastard. What the hells was wrong with him?

Sure, it wouldn't have been a turnout like this. Not for some woman whose name wasn't anywhere near as well-known as her husband or, Divines willing, her son. But still, that was irrelevant. She was his mother and suddenly he found himself filled with regret. He'd been to the grave since but never stayed long, it made him feel things he was uncomfortable experiencing. "Some pain I just don't need."

"You're a complex individual," Anne mused. "Stubborn too. Have you ever thought that the pain serves a necessary function? You can't heal without it. Bottle it all up and you'll suffer and burn far more over the course of time."

"I've done okay so far," Theo said defiantly. She looked at him, gave him the fish-eyed look of disbelief. "And I'm not in pain over Arventino's death. I didn't know her that well."

"And you're in denial."

"No, I am..." He almost fell into the trap, gave her a sarcastic grin. "So, if I deny that I'm in denial, doesn't that make it true? Sort of?"

"I think you're thinking too hard about it," Anne said. "All I'm saying is you can't cut yourself off completely. We all have demons, we can't always exorcise them completely. But you shouldn't let them control you. That way lies ruin and the point of no return."

"The point of no return," Theo said softly. "Used to think that sounded like a pretty good destination, if I'm honest."

"What do you mean?" Anne looked surprised at his words. "Are you mad when you say that?"

"No." He paused, not quite sure how to explain what he meant. "What I'm trying to say is it's all about progress, right? You start on a journey, you mean to get somewhere and eventually you'll either get there or you'll fall short, right? But there's always a point where there's no going back. As you go on the journey, you change, you mature. You're not the same person come the end as you were when you started and sometimes I just wonder when the point is you can't come back. I wanted so badly to get away from who I was that I couldn't wait to leave."

"But you'll still be the same person. You'll still have the same problems in your past, you'll still be running from them..."

"I've never run from anything," Theo said suddenly, his voice cold. He didn't like the way it sounded, he tried to temper it without success. "What I mean is... Ah, I don't know what I mean. We've all got things we'd rather forget."

"Yes," Anne said simply. "And sometimes we have to face them rather than flee. You can't outrun your past, it has a horrible way of catching up with you. You think she'd know that more than anything."

She gestured to the coffin, now almost out of sight. Some of the crowd were following it, others were already milling away. The funeral was being broadcast across the five kingdoms, it had dominated the media despite Ronald Ritellia's earlier attempts to steal back some of the limelight for himself. The actual service had been victim to only a limited number of places despite heaving masses desperate to attend. Theo thought that was a little disturbing if he was honest, so many people so desperate to do something morbid. Granted, it was part of the unofficial caller's code. If someone dies, even if you don't like them, it's just good to honour their memory even if just briefly. He'd done his bit here, both him and Anne.

"Did you know her?" he asked. "Arventino?"

Anne shook her head. "Not well. But we have some mutual friends. I knew her vaguely, spoke to her a couple of times. Fought her once or twice..."

"You win?"

Anne scoffed. "Draw and defeat. She was one tough cookie."

The faintest embers of a fire started to burn in Theo's stomach, a blister of pride mixed with guilt. "Yeah, she was," he said. "She sure was something."

The zent conducting the ceremony had been flown in from mainland Vazara especially for the event, Stoatley, Pete thought he'd said his name was. Apparently amidst all the desperation to construct the resort, one thing the builders had conveniently forgotten to add was a church. Pete didn't know if that was significant or not. There were all sorts of resort towns that had churches, like that place in Premesoir notorious for drunken couples getting married without thinking it through.

He shot a glance over at Nick, he was pale in his face but keeping stoic. There'd been a few awkward moments between them. At least he hadn't been the one to find her dead like Nick, bones shattered, and her body impaled. When he'd heard... Well he'd not taken it well. He wasn't proud to admit he'd shed tears but at the same time he was glad Scott hadn't used it as an opportunity to take the piss. Neither had Mia. He felt like the odd one out between them, a little like he had when Scott had been with Jess, but here they'd been good to him. He was grateful for that.

The zent's white robes shone in the afternoon sun, contrasting violently against his dark skin as his deep voice spoke powerfully. He didn't know many of the faces here, but there were some he recognised. Many of the great and good names of the spirit calling world had managed to make their way here, some he didn't even know Sharon had been on speaking terms with. "The Divines above have a way of operating," the zent said slowly. Although his voice was languid, it was deep and had a way of drawing attention to his presence. "A way many of us cannot claim to understand or even approve of. Their way can seem cruel, it can seem unjust and harsh, but it is necessary for without death, there cannot be life and it is often in the most painful of times we find the strength to carry on."

Pete didn't know if he found this comforting or not.

"When Gilgarus took on human appearance and was subject to brutality and death to safeguard those who couldn't defend themselves, future generations were reminded that although it may hurt now, there can be no pain without joy, just as there can be no good without evil to counterbalance it. No good deed can be performed without opposing acts of depravity to weigh the levity of it. That is why we were given choice. Because the decision of what to do with choice always will be what gives humanity its place in this world. Sharon Arventino was well loved, well known but at the same time humble. Nobody ever had a bad word to say about her and she was taken all too soon."

Long pause. Pete thought he heard someone sobbing in the background, he wasn't entirely sure who. "But take solace in your memories of her, remember both the good and the bad for she is with the Divines now, away from the stresses of a world that ultimately she was too good to remain a part of. It's a worse place without her, she might have gone on to reach even higher plateaus of greatness, she might have gone on to fall so, so far. Ultimately, we will never know, for she leaves this world as we would, given a choice. At the top. At the peak. Greatness personified. Kind. Gentle. Unselfish. To honour her, take a moment to join me in prayer, to remember her as she was and to try and touch the Sharon Arventino in all of us. There is no greater privilege than to be remembered and to try living life the way she conducted hers." He cleared his throat and began to chant. This one Pete knew, he kept trying to blink back the wetness in his eyes.

"Oh Gilgarus, high and mighty above, take her into your embrace. Let her not miss those left behind, nor mourn what might have been.

Griselle, guard her shade from the blackest eternity, let her never forget that which has been.

Dainal, take the time that passes and let the pain lessen as the sun rises and falls, let her eternal spark never burn out, let her name never fall from history.

Pellysria, as memories fade, let them remain strong and undiminished, let her inspire and keep her mark on a world, let future people hold her as an example.

Garvais, let her body nourish the soil so even in death, she will continue to do some good, that one final act might ensure the survival of others.

Kalqus, let the tears of those left behind nourish the kingdoms as final tribute to a beautiful soul, let us see a remnant of her face in every beautiful raindrop.

Rochentus, skyrider, let her forever watch over those she loved and loved her, allow her the knowledge she made a difference to sooth her passing.

Melarius, mother of all, take your newest daughter under your wing, love her as we loved her, and may she be the best of them all.

Temperus, Stzorn, Incenderus, take our despair and keep the snows falling, Stzorn, take our screams of pain and make thunder with them, Incenderus, take our pain and use it to fuel the fires ever burning.

Leria, grant us knowledge that we might spare this pain ever again, Farenix, let her greatness be reborn anew. Ferros, spare her your fiery punishment forever. Divines take this lost beautiful soul and see that what she left behind might never fade, that what she might have done yet still may come to pass. Divines above be praised."

The echo of the last four words rang around the funeral. Pete felt a little queasy. He'd never liked overtly religious ceremony, he was sure Sharon hadn't either. So, all of this felt a little tasteless, he wanted to say. Sure, it was nice and twee and all that stuff but given the choice he felt she'd have picked otherwise. Then again, given a choice he was pretty sure she'd have kept on living. Bile threatened to rise in his throat as the zent continued to drone on and he found himself trying to pick out the bits relevant to her. He wanted to say a few words, they still hadn't quite formed yet in his conscious mind. He wasn't sure he could plan something long and concise ahead of time, just go up and say it off the top of his head. Not like that zent. He had no emotional attachment to the whole thing. It was just a job, do it, go home, go to bed.

That time came before he was even close to being ready, he found himself making the walk to the podium amidst the smatterings of applause, displacing the zent there with a heavy heart. He adjusted the microphone, straightened his tie and cleared his throat all while trying to avoid the dull ache in his heart.

"Good afternoon," he said. "My name's Peter Jacobs and Sharon was my sister. Well half-sister. Or so we used to say. We used to joke about it, but the truth is she wasn't my half-sister. She was my sister. We might have had different fathers, but we shared a family. We were blood. I loved her, and I like to think she loved me. For my whole life, she was there, something to live up to. I always thought that was an impossible task. Maybe part of me resented that, just a bit but you know what? Overall, I didn't care. It's in the past now, seems stupid when I think about it. Whatever stuff someone may do when they're alive, you'll miss it when they go. Knowing you'll never see them again makes it that much harder."

He tried to keep the quaver out of his voice, couldn't quite manage it. He took a few breaths, managed to hold his composure. Breaking down here would be exceptionally embarrassing. And no matter how justified it might be, he'd probably not live it down. Best keep it short. "I'll really miss her. A sister is like... Well you can say the same about family really. You appreciate them more the older you get. You never realise just how much having them being there for you if needed means to you." He turned to look at the coffin, grateful they'd closed it up. He'd been to see her before the ceremony, she'd looked so peaceful, though he was truly grateful the wounds had been hidden from sight, that they'd fixed the back of her head up. "Life is short, I guess. Sometimes we don't realise quite how short." He bowed his head. "Thank you."

More applause followed him from the podium as he made his way back to his seat, slightly more enthusiastic than it had been for the zent. Next, he announced Nick Roper to the podium, a sombre looking figure making his way up there. It was a very different Roper from the one he'd first met, he looked drained, older and tired, clenching and unclenching his fists as he strode past.

"Thank you," Nick said quietly. There was no emotion in his voice beyond pure control, keeping it together with supreme calm. In his position, Pete was sure he'd have been doing much worse. "Well I don't want to have to follow what Peter just said for long, so I'll keep this short. Sharon Arventino was a wonderful woman, possibly the best I ever met and as much as this might cause some hurt around the five kingdoms, maybe the only one I ever truly loved. People like to dwell on her achievements, how she was this master caller, how she took on all challenges and conquered them, but I'm not going to remember that. I'm going to remember who she was as a person. I have genuinely never met a kinder soul in my life. I remember there was a time when we were in Premesoir, she'd just won this tournament and I think the first prize was something like eighty thousand credits."

He managed a weak grin, looked like he was struggling to speak. "She gave it all away to a local charity, a little girl who needed replacement lungs. Crazenbergs syndrome. The parents had been in touch, asking for some signed stuff to auction off. And I remember what Sharon said to me as she handed the credits over. She said, "It's only credits but for them it's a life," It's a true story she asked to be kept out of the media because, as we all know there's those who try to find a negative in any positive situation. She was happiest with knowing what she'd done and that the parents were grateful. That was the sort of woman she was. That's the sort of memory I want to keep of her. Thank you for hearing me out."

As he made to walk down back to his seat, he hesitated as the zent announced Ronald Ritellia was to say a few words. Pete stiffened, he hadn't heard about this. As far as he'd known, their mother was to speak next. What Ritellia had to say about Sharon, he didn't know. The applause for Nick died down as Ritellia made his way towards the podium, waddling his way there in a too tight suit.

"Speaking of people who like to spin the facts," Nick suddenly said loudly, startling everyone into silence. "Or ignore them completely." He moved from the podium, past his seat and towards Ritellia. "Who gave you the right to speak here?"

For once, Ritellia seemed at lost for words. "As president of the International Competitive Calling..."

"You've clearly misinterpreted what we're trying to do here. It's not about you, it's about the woman whose death you're indirectly responsible for!" Nick said viciously. Any hint of control he might have had earlier was dangerously failing. "You chose to have the tournament placed here, you ignored the earlier warnings and you carried on regardless."

"Is this the time and place for it?" Ritellia asked.

Nick looked to be considering it for a moment, before visibly relaxing his body, his mouth twisting into something resembling a weary smile. "Probably not."

And that would be that, Pete thought with relief. A dangerous situation defused. At least until Nick stuck a punch straight on Ritellia's mouth and things descended into chaos...

"Once again, Cubla Cezri comes up for discussion. Once again, we need to decide what to do about it. And once again, it seems we don't have a reasonable answer."

Premier Leonard Nwakili, to his advisers and ministers.

The twenty-fifth day of Summerpeak.

An aura of silence pervaded the cockpit of the Unisco hoverjet as they made their way first across the seas and then into Vazaran airspace, Leclerc and Noorland seated behind the controls. Neither of them felt like talking, only communicating with the kingdom below or occasionally to the people in the back. Derenko, Aldiss and Fagan had nothing to say for the time being, just sat content to their own devices. The holding area of the ship was roomy enough for the three of them to be comfortable. Fagan worked nonstop, cleaning the individual parts of his disassembled X7. Derenko lay back on a bench, eyes closed and oblivious to the world. None of them had been sleeping well recently, hard to find a peaceful night's rest when the call to action might go out at any moment. Privately they envied him for being able to get away with it right now. And ever since Sharon had been killed, the level of tension around the island had only grown. People had started to leave, potential newcomers had stayed away, worried they might be next.

Max Brudel, the first high profile victim had been ruled a suicide for the time being, given they'd never had a chance to fully interrogate Harvey Rocastle over any possible involvement. Darren Maddley's cause of death had been deemed down to snake venom administered by a species not uncommon to Vazara. More than that, some nests had been seen on Carcaradis Island, he'd even had bite marks on his body. It wasn't impossible someone could have commanded a spirit to do it, but the case was slowly spinning into inactivity. Privately Fagan was convinced Ritellia had done some begging to play them down for the time being, anything to avoid a hint of controversy on his precious tournament. The incredible nerve of that man...

But when someone was brutally murdered in their hotel room without anyone in surrounding rooms being aware, it really put things into perspective that maybe you'd be better not being here. Aldiss was reading something, Fagan saw him out the corner of his eye and wondered what he found so interesting. He and Leclerc were taking point on this mission, Aldiss and Derenko backing them up if it went wrong. Given where they were going, that was always a possibility.

They'd been flying above Vazara for a good hour, past most of the major cities as they left the coastland and were above the deserts when Leclerc suddenly jerked the ship to a sharp left, the action bringing Derenko straight up into a sitting position. Beneath them, he saw nothing but useless desert wasteland for miles, nothing but sand and faded scrub. Looking at a map, the settlements were usually classed as the Vazara Ring of Cities, for they formed a large ring around the biggest expanse of desert. And of course, Cubla Cezri was over the other side. Fagan had been trying not to think about what would happen if they went down in the middle of nowhere.

"What's going on?" he asked, his voice not fogged with sleep. "What happened?"

"Apologies," Leclerc said. "Should have warned you. Will asked me to check something out while we're here. Something he was curious about. Taking a quarter hour detour. Just look out the windows, tell me what you see."

A strange request but one Fagan was willing to comply with. Quickly he put his X7 back together, stopping short of reloading the power pack. He took aim, dry fired it twice to check all was in working condition before slotting the load back in and holstering it. He was the last to the window, curiosity biting at him now

"Will transmitted these records to Agent Aldiss and I before we left," Leclerc said. "According to what he had to say, this is where Reims acquired most of the building material from for the Carcaradis Island project."

"The desert?" Derenko said. "Interesting. Suggestive I think."

Below them, nothing but sand. If there were any people down there, they were too high to make out. The people weren't the issue here. Sure, there were nomads in the desert, but they weren't important. If Okocha wanted them to scout something out, hopefully it'd be noticeable.

"Aye," Fagan said quickly. "I think it'd be something like that."

He blinked several times, not quite sure what he was seeing. Noorland got up and left the co-pilot seat to get a better view of the ground far below, seeing immediately the huge black serpent winding its way across the sands. He had to blink several times to register what he was seeing. "Oh shit!" he said animatedly. "They scar mined the whole thing."

"Scar mined it?" Aldiss asked. "I thought that was illegal."

"Yeah, it is," Derenko said. He folded his arms grimly. As far as Fagan could see, deep ugly scars had been carved into the ground, the area around them blackened and burnt beyond anything recognisable.

They extended out for miles and miles, spread in every direction. "If you get caught. And I don't see many environmental cops out here."

"Scar mining?" Fagan asked. "Divines weep!"

Scar mining had been an illegal process in the five kingdoms for years now, it had started back when someone had come up with the idea of fixing a wide-range high-intensity low-power laser to the bottom of a hover jet and running it over an area rich in minerals.

Here it would be ideal, the sand would have been superheated to the point of shattering, whatever was in the ground below exposed and melted in the same way to the point suction machines could suck it out and it could be transported in liquid form to be reconstituted and then shaped into whatever was needed, an easier process than it before, due to a new type of nanite designed to help shape it while still in liquid form. The scientist who'd created it had made an absolute fortune out of the process. Judging by the extent of the scarring, they must have taken easily a couple of thousand tonnes of metal out of the ground. Even that, Fagan realised, might be a conservative estimate.

"I can't believe they did this," Noorland said. He sounded annoyed. "What the hells is wrong with people?"

"I imagine we could throw this at Reims," Leclerc said. "This is evidence of clear wrongdoing. Breaking the laws of not just Vazara but the five kingdoms. I don't think they'd get away with it unscathed."

"At the very worst, they'd be fined," Derenko said wearily. "Maybe some minor custodial sentences. It's easy for the people at the top to shout innocence, be that true or not. It always looks like a worse crime than it actually is." He sighed, lay his head back down on the bench. "No, I think this is only part of a bigger picture. We'll report this back to command, see what they want to do with it. For now, gentlemen, we have an appointment with Joseph Itandje."

"Maybe he'll have some answers about this whole thing," Aldiss said. "Somebody has to. Resume course for Cubla Cezri."

"Speaking of unsightly scars on the landscape," Noorland offered. He sounded like he meant it to be a joke. At the same time, his voice carried very little trace of amusement in it.

He was sort of right, Fagan considered as he glanced out the window as they came in for descent. Comparing Cubla Cezri to a scar on the ground wasn't as unfair a comparison as it might have once sounded. The stories went it had once been quite a decent place to live, until undesirable criminal elements had moved into one of the neighbourhoods and slowly started to drag the quality of living down until once affluent areas had been submerged beneath the squalor. Mansions had been broken down into shanties, boutiques into brothels, still regular people trying to make enough credits to get out toiling down there. By the looks of it from the sky, the town was split into three distinct sections, each an ugly overflow of building spilling out into the desert around it.

"Man, this looks rough as a bear's arse," Noorland said, shaking his head. "If this place was hit with an airstrike, it'd cause millions of credits worth of improvement."

"Don't let Okocha hear you say that," Derenko remarked. "He'd agree with you, but he'd still be annoyed. You know how people get. They can insult their homes and their family but if you get involved, they take offence. Especially round here."

"I don't think that's a solely Vazaran thing, you get that everywhere," Leclerc said, moving to activate the comm system. "Ah, Cezri Air Traffic Control, this is Unisco Aitch-Jay-One-One-Eight-Nine, requesting permission to land immediately, over."

"Never said it was," Derenko muttered in the background.

The voice that came back through was heavily accented with thick Vazaran overtones, the language broken but understandable. "Permission granted, keep in mind you not be too welcome here if you want reception, over."

"No reception is necessary, over," Leclerc said. "Just a place to refuel and restock supplies, as well as check some minor errors in our system. We'll be gone ASAP, over."

"Understood, Unisco Aitch-Jay-One-One-Eight-Nine, enjoy your brief stay, over."

"Well that was more civilised than I thought it'd be," Fagan commented.

"They don't all scream about the pale infidel," Aldiss said wryly. "Not while there's credits to be had. Be glad we do carry official ID, they'd be asking us for bribes otherwise."

The larger a settlement tended to be, the more docking stations it usually had. Regulations said any place over a certain number of people had to have at least one, by order of the Five Kingdoms Senate, not just individual kingdom law. Apparently Cubla Cezri met that standard. It rose high into the air, almost touching the sky, easily the tallest building in the town, Leclerc deftly guided it into one of the allocated landing slots, bringing the hoverjet to a gentle halt. They were the only one there, not another airship in sight. That, Fagan thought, truly was a depressing insight into the town if nothing else.

"Easy," he said. "Okay, shall we get this show on the road, I think."

They took the speeder in the back of the ship, Derenko behind the controls with Aldiss riding shotgun, Fagan and Leclerc in the back.

All had outfitted themselves with body armour under their shirts, as well as carrying both their mufflers and personal shields for protection. Fagan and Leclerc had their X7's hidden about their person, Derenko and Aldiss had a Featherstone each, a contingency plan.

They left Noorland in the docking station to oversee the supposed maintenance on the hoverjet, soon speeding out of sight and over the sandy road. The roads were narrow and unmaintained, filled with carts and old speeders that couldn't have matched their own in speed or durability. Still, Noorland and Pree Khan had taken some special measures to ensure it didn't stand out in the crowd, scuffing the paintwork and spreading liberal measures of dirt and grime and spray-on rust across sections to ensure it didn't look like a Unisco speeder.

They aimed to get in and out as quickly as possible, no lingering to fight. They needed to talk to Itandje, get him into custody for his own protection if need be and survive the trip. The air was hot and stifling, the people looked beaten and sorrowful. Fagan lost track of the number he saw begging at the side of the road. More than once he saw men armed with assault weapons trying to move them on. One woman refused to go, she took the butt of a Vazaran Hornet to the side of her face and went down bleeding, her shattered teeth exposed as she screamed.

More than once, Derenko had to nudge it around debris threatening to block their path. Halfway into their journey, they saw someone being speeder-jacked, the driver yanked out at blaster point and tossed into the overflowing gutter, getting up, covered in filth and yelling as his speeder vanished into the distance under new ownership. At that point, Fagan slipped his X7 from his holster and let it rest on his knees. Another contingency plan. Hope for the best. Prepare for the worst.

"Okay, Control," Derenko said into his earpiece. "Where are we going here? Do you have us?"

"Yeah, I see you," Okocha's voice came out over the connection, Fagan heard it loud and clear. "Man, I'm glad I'm not with you. That place makes my hometown growing up look like a reward."

"Should come on one of these missions sometime," Aldiss said. "Remind you what you missed out on when you came to work for us."

"Yeah, I'll pass," Okocha replied. "Okay, you need to take the next left, look out for a café named R'achelle."

"Strange name for a café," Fagan offered.

"Yeah, don't eat or drink anything from there. Not the smartest thing you could possibly ever do. It's not the best."

"You ever eaten there?"

"Yeah I've eaten somewhere a couple hundred miles away from the only place I ever lived while growing up and at the same time have no desire ever to visit." The sarcasm was palpable. "Nah, I've got the reviews of it here. Even in a scumhole like that, someone still took the time to give it a one-star rating. Anywhere other than Cubla Cezri, it'd probably have been shut down years ago. Since their health system is on a par with the status quo seventy years ago, I'd say take care."

"Really?" It was Fagan's turn to be sarcastic. "Looking at this place, I'd never have guessed to do that." Leclerc laughed at the comment.

"Think I've been here before," Derenko said wistfully as he glanced around. "Long time ago. Back before it was this... does it sound harsh to compare it to a shit hole?"

"Seems about apt for me," Aldiss said. "Not one of the better places I've ever been."

"Yeah, I'm sure there's some lovely places to bring the family," Fagan remarked. "Just beyond that burnt out speeder and past the next heap of trash." His voice tailed off as his gaze landed on the building in question, a shabby looking café with the name R'achelle painted above the door. Some of the letters were peeling away from the board, one of the windows boarded up, the other with chicken wire threaded through the glass. Underneath the sign, something had been scrawled in the local dialect that Fagan didn't understand.

He saw Leclerc glance at it and smirk. He'd forgotten he could speak a little Vazaran, enough to get by. That infamous Unisco policy. Have all agents fluent in at least two local kingdom languages as well as the united tongue.

"Something funny?"

"Says it all," Leclerc said, jerking his head towards the sign. "Someone does have a sense of humour. Nice place for nice people. Come in and be proved wrong on both counts."

"Meaning it's a dive for scum," Aldiss said as Derenko brought the speeder to a halt. The two of them looked back, gave their comrades their full attention. "Right, you know the drill. We'll be in touch all the time. You need any help, give the signal and we'll be in there with you, weapons blazing."

"Keep it in mind there's a large civilian population in there," Okocha offered. "Some of them won't be armed. A lot of them might be."

"Just to make it that little bit more bearable," Derenko said. "You know the drill, you've done it before. We need to find out what Itandje knows. Might be nothing. Might be everything."

"You read the briefing on him," Okocha added. "Remember, nobody leaves the Vazaran Suns unless dead. You're in for life. Might want to remind him that if he's being uncooperative."

"Will, we got this," Fagan said as he rose to leave the speeder, sliding his weapon back into his holster. Both he and Leclerc wore loose fitting button up shirts beneath local tu-yak cloaks buttoned around the neck and covered their upper bodies. It did the job of hiding what they had on underneath. "See you on the flip, guys. We'll be back."

"Until the end," Leclerc added as the two of them sauntered towards the entrance of R'achelle, trying to look casual. It was late evening, not quite night yet and although it was still warm, the heat had died down enough to avoid discomfort. Regardless, he felt a rivulet of sweat streaming down his forehead and Fagan hoped they weren't here longer than they needed to. It probably wouldn't be any hotter here come the peak temperatures than it would be on Carcaradis Island but at the same time, the island bore a much more hospitable surrounding. It was hard to feel at ease here.

They entered the café to a raucous roar, most of the patrons stood circled around a table, a series of ferocious hisses and squawks erupting out from the midst of them all. Fagan and Leclerc looked at each other, shrugged and made to move past the crowd towards the counter. It wasn't easy, the spectators had packed themselves tight, often the best way around them was to weave closer to the action and soon they were close enough for Fagan to spot the source of the amusement. Lizard fighting.

A tame sidebar, not really a comparison to spirit calling but given the place lacked a viewing screen they had to do what they could with the entertainment. Vazaran fighting iguanas, if he had it right. Long bodied, squat-built multi-coloured lizards scrapping with each other ferociously, each trying to overcome the other. Plenty of credits were being thrown around, punters determined to bet which would kill the other first. Maybe somebody would spirit claim the loser, Fagan thought. They didn't look like spirits. They were too uncoordinated. It wasn't uncommon in places like this, let wild animals go at each other for the sport of it.

When they were through, he could hear himself think again, as well as the tinny voice of Okocha in his ear. "Target is situated towards the back of the room, one of the booths." Fagan looked up instinctively, the back of the room only sparsely filled and running through the faces there didn't take as long as it might have done if the target was amidst the action. Maybe ten people sat down, showing a morose lack of interest in the entertainment on show. They looked like they'd had enough of life. Living here, he couldn't blame them. He spotted Itandje sat nursing a glass of something amber, the local brew most likely, a heavyset man with a scarred face. He carried himself awkwardly as he sat, favouring his left side. A cold pack rested against his shoulder, one large hand holding it there. If he was in pain, he was taking tremendous efforts not to show it.

Leclerc took the lead; a situation he was only too happy to acquiesce to as they approached the table. "Mind if we sit here?" Leclerc said. The great dark face looked up at them, eyes narrowed with suspicion.

"Fuck off," he said simply. "Plenty of other tables."

"Regardless," Leclerc said, pulling out a chair and dropping down. "Those lack something. Mainly you."

Suspicion turned to dislike in the brown coloured eyes that stared them down. Fagan had to admit, Leclerc's sense of cool fearlessness did come in handy sometimes.

"You got some place you want your remains posted?" Itandje demanded. "Because…"

"Mr Itandje, my associate and I just wish to take up…"

"How the fuck you know that name?" Itandje almost rose to his feet, would have done if Fagan hadn't held out a placating hand.

"We just want a quick chat," he said, Unisco ID badge in the hand he'd offered out. Itandje's eyes met it, he hesitated just for a moment before sitting back down. He clearly was bearing an injury on his left side, Fagan noticed. Something wasn't right there. "Officially. Talk to us and we'll let you get back to your drink."

Itandje laughed out loud, a sarcastically cruel bray that sounded like a buzz saw making an unfortunate union with something that was still alive. "And why the fuck would I talk to you? Piss off or you get hurt."

"Don't worry, you've not done anything wrong," Leclerc said. "We just want some information about some of your former employers…"

That laugh again, this time even more derisory than it had been before. "Oh, now I know you joking. I'm not informing on the Suns. There's not enough credits in the five kingdoms for that."

"Good thing we're not trying to pay you to do it then," Fagan said. "It's not about the Suns. We already know they're an inglorious bunch of bastards. It's about a contract you might have been involved in."

"Nope, rings no bells," Itandje said stubbornly. He drained the rest of his drink in one gulp and then stood. "Now if you'll excuse me…"

"What did you die of?" Leclerc asked.

"What?!" There was more than a faint hint of outrage in his voice at being asked such an impertinent question.

"What killed you?" Leclerc repeated, folding his hands over each other on the table in front of him. "I mean, I heard the Suns only let out those who died. The fact you're here…" He let it hang airily, the corners of his mouth threatening to twitch.

"It's true," Fagan added. "I mean, I heard the Suns don't have much of an official presence here. They don't like it. It's a bit rough for them." He managed to keep a mocking tone out of his voice. Technically it was true.

"Neither of you know what you speak of." Itandje's voice was little more than a growl. "How about you stop talking about what you know fuck all about."

"So, there's no reason to be here," Leclerc added as if he hadn't said anything. "Right?"

"Right," Fagan agreed. "I mean unless you'd done something stupid like deserting? They shoot their deserters, right?"

"If they're lucky," Leclerc said. "I heard they skin the real high-ranking ones who try it. An object lesson to the rank and file, I think is the phrase, am I right Commandant?"

"How high were you?" Fagan asked. "Or maybe they just want you dead. You must have pissed someone badly off to get that reaction."

Somewhere amidst it all, Itandje had hesitated and now he slid back towards his seat. "Either of you have a point?"

"Just that we're not on bad enough terms with your former employers not to mention that we've seen you. I mean, it'd take a quick call and then they'd be here in force," Fagan mused. "If they really wanted you, that is."

"Or we can offer you some protection," Leclerc added. "We don't have a gripe with you, Mister Itandje, we just want to know a few things and if you prove helpful, we'll put you out of reach of Mazoud and the rest for the rest of your natural life."

"However long that is," Itandje growled. "I won't sell out Mazoud. Mainly because he's done nothing wrong…"

"I doubt that but go on," Fagan said. Itandje did, carrying on as if he hadn't been interrupted.

"But also, if I said a bad word about him to you, my life really wouldn't be worth living. He'd find some way of finishing me off. And there'd be someone to sell me out. There's always someone who needs credits."

"We're not interested in Mazoud," Leclerc insisted. "Rather some work your organisation might have been involved in. On Carcaradis Island."

Itandje sighed, let his head loll back and finally swallowed the rest of his drink. "That fucking place. Should have known."

"Should have known what?" That he remembered it was a promising sign. Maybe they'd get some answers, Fagan thought. This whole trip might have been worth it after all. They were due a break, it would appear.

"That island. Never going back there. Not for any credits, not for any offer… It's not natural." Itandje's eyes widened as he spoke, almost theatrically but there was something behind them that spoke volumes. Fear. "Whole mission was a mess from the start. They tried building there, clearing it all out… They blasphemed. It wasn't meant to be tamed."

"It's turned out nice," Fagan said. "They did a good job. I'd go there on a holiday, given the chance. And a decent wage."

Itandje gave him a dirty look. "You know nothing. Only those outside the kingdom call it by the name Carcaradis. Vazarans… Those who haven't had their minds ruined and corrupted by excess… all know it by its true name. Ai-Yal'Sanhim. Those that lived there were blessed to survive it. To protect it. And we fucked up royally by being brought in to pacify them. Some we wiped out. Some we captured. I don't know what they did with the poor bastards, but we heard them screaming. They died noisily."

Fagan held his breath as he spoke, letting it out in one soft exhalation. He recalled the bodies of those natives too well to ignore it. Any sort of flippant comment was lost as he tried to forget those rooms just a few dozen feet under the affluence of the island above.

"I blame that woman. And that mad doctor. They were obsessed. They thought something was there and well, they turned out right. I lost my faith about the time they found it. Fucking proof right there and I didn't want to accept it."

"Proof of what?" Leclerc asked.

For a moment, Itandje didn't answer and then he laughed bitterly. "Eternity. The answers to it all. The proof of the power is in the wielding of it. Just because she hasn't set it all off yet, doesn't mean she won't. Mazoud is in thrall to her." He stiffened. "Speaking of…"

Across the room, the door to the bar had opened, Fagan glanced back, saw it out the corner of his eye. He relaxed only for a second, saw the glint of metal and the hint of black uniform and suddenly he was in motion, overturning the table and yanking Itandje down behind it. The sound of blaster fire tore through the bar as Leclerc joined him on the ground, X7 already out. Screams and shouts of terror broke through the bar as bodies hit the floor, people made runs for it and Fagan felt sick as he realised they'd run out of time.

"Friends of yours?" he asked, drawing his own weapon out. Itandje had a Rellman in his hand, a stubby blaster pistol with an elongated barrel. Nothing fancy about it, a good weapon for circumstances like this, close-range combat. It did what it was intended to do.

"Guess they found me," Itandje said with resignation in his voice. "Don't let them take me!" Resignation quickly became overcome by terror. "Don't let them take me!"

"We made you a promise," Leclerc said. "We get you out, you talk, we make you safe."

"Wish we could skip straight to step three," Fagan muttered, pointing his weapon over the table and firing blind. He doubted he'd hit anything, but it made a point they were armed and anyone approaching would be shot. The table was thick and heavy, he'd nearly wrenched his arm out of his socket overturning it but at least they were protected. Maybe they were only trying to stun them. The force behind a stun shot might be greater but the actual penetration was virtually non-existent. "There a back door to this place?"

"The fuck you think?" Itandje said. He pointed his Rellman over the top of the table and squeezed off a few blasts, before jerking his head over towards the counter. Fagan could see a door behind it, he hadn't noticed it earlier amidst all the chaos. "There. Through the kitchen. This is all your fault, y'know."

Neither Leclerc nor Fagan deigned to respond. They looked at each other, heard the shots crashing against the table. So far, they'd been unscathed, but they'd been lucky. If Fagan hadn't seen them when he had... "Okay, on three," Fagan said. "Two of us lay down covering fire, the other moves. Joe, work with us here. Jacques, move! One, two... Three!"

Fair to Itandje, he did join in as they fired over the makeshift barricade, the flurry of shots silencing the ones coming their way for a moment. Leclerc moved, out of cover and towards the counter, his X7 reporting twice as he caught beads on foes who had ventured into his view. Fagan could see them properly now, they looked like Vazaran Suns operatives, right down to the uniform and the weapons. Thankfully none of them were packing shields. He said as much to Itandje who laughed derisively.

"You think they give their ops teams shields? The whole fucking point is they get encouraged not to be shot." He broke into a bray of laughter. "Numbers and firepower. Their two main tactics in pacification."

"Sometimes that's what you need," Fagan said grimly. If there were a lot of them right now, he'd fancy their chances against the three of them. Leclerc fired his X7 again, emptying the power pack in the direction of the door, the wild shots sending the enemy scattering. "Go!"

Itandje didn't hesitate, jumped up and sprinted the short distance across the floor as Fagan gave him the cover he needed, adding his few remaining shots to those Leclerc had spray fired into the crowd. At least three had gone down, still too many more for the odds to be good. He ejected his spent pack and fixed a new one in.

"Will," he said into his ear comm. "What's happening outside."

"Derenko and Aldiss are pinned down. You need to get out there, maybe find another way out. Withdraw to the air station on your own."

He almost swore. "You're kidding?"

"They're having to pull out, they're taking heavy fire. You're on your own for the moment." This time, he did swear. Twin pistols continued to fire over by the bar, he added a few of his own to the flurry, just enough to keep the Suns at bay before making his move. It wasn't a comfortable crouching run, but he kept his head down, hissed as one of their shots grazed his shoulder and soon flopped next to them. His shoulder was on fire, even with the shield and the armour.

"You hear that?" he gasped to Leclerc who nodded.

"Ah yes," he replied. "Only too well. Shall we?"

Through the kitchen door they went and just for a moment, Fagan thought they might make it as he spotted the back door. It was a dangerous light of hope, he tried to push it out of his mind. They couldn't afford to be distracted now. Leclerc went first, crashing through the door and pulled up short outside, Fagan and Itandje coming up behind him. Itandje cursed violently as the five men took aim at them. Same uniforms, same weapons, they'd walked out of the lion's den into the bear pit. Their faces were uncovered, all Vazarans of differently intensifying darkness to their skin.

"Shit!" Fagan said. It was no use trying to fight back, they had them outnumbered, outgunned and dead to rights. They'd made to flush them out and they'd succeeded. Split the team up, make them weaker, cut them off from backup.

"Could really use a miracle right now," Leclerc muttered. He sounded like he agreed with his teammate's sentiment. Between them, Itandje began to speak rapidly in Vazaran to the men, Fagan couldn't work out if he was begging for mercy or trying to feign innocence. He saw Leclerc roll his eyes. By the looks of that, he might be trying both.

"Miracles don't come cheap," Fagan muttered. Why hadn't they killed them yet? They honestly couldn't be that interested in what Itandje had to say, could they? He glanced around, they'd found themselves in a back alley. The street was only a dozen or so metres away, so close to freedom. But that aside, there was nowhere else to go. Overflowing dumpsters hemmed them in either side, thick and heavy and good cover but the moment they made for it, they'd be blasted.

Itandje finished speaking, a pleading expression on his face as he tilted his head to the side. The lead guy shook his head, squeezed the trigger and Fagan yelled in frustration as the trio of blasts hit Itandje in the chest, hurling him back towards the exit of the café. Both he and Leclerc dived towards the dumpsters, taking advantage of the confusion. Blaster fire followed them, some came close to landing, concrete chips tore into his hands and face as he hit the ground. All until he heard the most beautiful sound he'd ever know, the familiar roar of the Unisco speeder's engines, followed by the even more familiar sound of Featherstone fire roaring through the alley. He peeked out, saw Aldiss spraying them with his weapon, Derenko quickly joining in. Within seconds, they'd taken all five out and Fagan felt a sudden sense of elation. They were getting out of here.

Itandje wasn't. He could see that; the wounds were fatal and there was no changing that. They were under fire in a hostile environment, they wouldn't be able to get him to a hospital. He slid over to him, saw the last breath had already left his body. Angrily he hit the ground with the flat of his hand before making to get out. The speeder had seen better days, nicks and burns covered the sides and half the windshield had been melted by blaster fire. But the engines still worked, and they soon quickly picked up speed, covering the distance between them and the crime scene in little time. The sooner they were in the air, Fagan thought, the better. This whole mission had been a bust from start to finish.

They'd failed, and badly.

"You must be joking if you think I enjoyed any part of that."
Nick Roper in his statement to the Carcaradis Island authorities following his arrest.

The twenty-seventh day of Summerpeak.

Obsolete?

Special Correspondent Kate Kinsella writes from the Competitive Centenary Calling Challenge Cup.

To say the enthusiasm for the tournament has been kicked out of a shell-shocked crowd is an understatement. Although the quarter finals did culminate last night, few of the victorious callers did celebrate as they might under less stressful circumstances. To make the semi-final of this tournament is a grandiose occasion but looking at the faces of Theobald Jameson, Katherine Sommer and Scott Taylor, you wouldn't have guessed it. To describe celebrations as muted is an understatement. Even Taylor, perhaps shown as the most passionate of the three over the course of the tournament didn't seem as overjoyed as he might have.

The feeling of uncertainty hovering over the competitors following the vicious murder of one of their own has failed to disperse and even Ronald Ritellia having his nose broken hasn't cheered most of them up although it has spared us from listening to his delusions of everything being okay over the last few days. In this case, the evidence to the contrary sits right in front of his eyes, even if his nose no longer does the same. With this sort of apathy settling over the tournament, after all there are only four bouts left before a winner is declared, and at the point when the excitement should be reaching a fever pitch, this correspondent asks if it is perhaps time to abandon the whole format in favour of something new. Something fresh and inspiring, untainted by the scandals plaguing it for years, mostly brought in part by ICCC members and their desire for recognition most of them do not deserve.

Five years ago, there was the Pro-Spirit-Plus scandal which was very quickly outlawed when discovered, younger readers might not remember ICCC member at the time Werner Jackson was also a part owner of a company that produced the spirit enhancing drugs, providing an effect not unlike banned steroids. The lengthy court case that followed did nobody any favours. With everyone and anyone at the ICCC being implicated and only Jackson being convicted and later

banned from involvement with the sport, the results were
underwhelming to say the least.

Then there was the bout fixing scandal of the previous
tournament, allegations dredged back up during this very tournament
in the Arventino versus Jacobs bout, allegations that bore very little
fruit and were the purview of people either bad losers or who knew
very little about spirit calling at this level in the first place, sneery
armchair fans who contribute very little to the great game other than to
indirectly swell the coffers of the people who take and take and give so
very little back. No tournament has been free of scandal since Ronald
Ritellia took over, but it is only in this one that the scandal has turned
into death and murder rather than corruption and dishonesty. Not the
sort of legacy anyone sane would wish to leave behind.

It might be the time for these swollen egos to put aside thoughts
of their own personal gain and for once in their careers, do something
to benefit the sport in a positive way. This format has become unwieldy
for years, a series of increasingly predictable rounds which threaten to
dull the excitement the longer it progresses. Granted there have been
some shocks this year perhaps more than the past three tournaments
combined when this new format began, yet it becomes a predictable
pandering towards those watching at home. More bouts equal more
credits in the eyes of the powers sitting on their behinds. More bouts
equal more chance for sponsorship, more money from the companies
that want to screen it all. The ICCC boasted proudly before the
tournament that every bout would be broadcast live, you could hear the
back slapping and the self-congratulating braying from a mile away.

But perhaps, for once, they should think of us. Granted, when
you put it into perspective, Ritellia has done some good things but the
negatives far outweigh the positives. For every free spirit summoner
device given out in Vazara, there is the question of where the rest of the
money to be spent on them went. For every free tutoring class in
Burykia taught by retired spirit callers, there is a deep sense of
foreboding that he's about to release some bombshell brought about by
the incompetence of his management.

"Am I the only one wondering why Kinsella hates Ritellia so
much?" Lysa Montgomery asked as she lifted her eyes from the article.
"I mean every chance she gets; she goes to town on him. It's sad and
predictable but kinda funny. Every chance, boom, she hits him hard."

"I don't think Ritellia cares," Anne said. She, Lysa, Okocha and
Tod Brumley had taken the chance to get out of headquarters and into
one of the cafés on the island, indulging in a spot of lunch. "He's got a
thick skin. Like a rhino. It's why he gets away with so many public

appearances. If someone wanted to shoot him, knowing our luck he'd survive it unscathed."

Brumley laughed at that. "Yeah, he's one of a kind. Unfortunately, not in a good way. I'm surprised at you, Anne. I thought you tried to see the best in everyone."

"Yeah, I tried," she said. "You ever met Ritellia. He's a strange one."

"Not like Nick met him," Okocha said, that single comment bringing laughter from both Lysa and Brumley. Anne frowned at them in dismay.

"You shouldn't laugh at it you know. He's in serious trouble."

"Yeah, Ritellia's trying to press charges and sue him and get him banned from ICCC competition for life," Okocha said. "All at the same time. He's throwing enough shit at him hoping some of it sticks. All of which is going to be a pretty nice distraction until Arnholt gets hold of him."

"Was he annoyed?" Lysa asked. Okocha nodded and laughed.

"Oh yeah. Absolutely furious. Never seen him so angry."

"It's true," Brumley offered. "I was there. Even I was scared. Thought he was going to start shooting."

"Any of you seen him?" Anne asked. "Because I heard Dave Wilsin tried to get in to do it…"

"Yeah, I heard that," Lysa said. "He's not having any visitors. By choice."

"Maybe he's ashamed." That came from Okocha. "It's possibly not something he'll be proud of in the cold light of day." He said it lightly but with a real sense of seriousness behind it. Anne narrowed her eyes at him, a look of bemusement across her pixie-like features. Lysa couldn't work out what she was thinking. "I mean if I was him, I'd feel pretty stupid."

"It was funny though," Brumley said. "Really funny. Just didn't see it coming."

"And neither did Ritellia," Lysa grinned. "Not even in the slightest. Bet he couldn't believe it. Think the whole five kingdoms was surprised. Could hear the sound of high fives from all around them."

"Shame he managed to spoil such a beautiful occasion," Anne mused. "I bet he regrets that?"

"Who, Ritellia?"

"No, Nick. I mean he loved Sharon, he was really hurting when I saw him. His brave face is just that. A face. He's put on such a façade we're missing how badly he's suffering."

"And hitting Ritellia was supposed to be a soothing balm for that hurt?" Brumley couldn't keep the sarcasm out of his voice. "As much as any of us might have enjoyed it under other circumstance."

"Just saying. And hey, I don't think Ritellia should have shoehorned his way into there like he did. It was asking for trouble. We went from brother to fiancé to someone who wanted to use the moment to grandstand." Anne shook her head bitterly. "Well he got his moment in the sun and it bloody well burned him. That's irony for you. If he didn't try and stick his fat nose in where it didn't belong, then it wouldn't have been broken."

Lysa laughed suddenly aloud, not entirely solely just at Anne's comment. "Anyone else think we were going to expect a tournament where the focus was just going to be what happened on the battlefield? Because this has been... different. Memorable. And not really in a good way."

Okocha said nothing. But everyone was thinking it, how the first tournament staged in Vazara had threatened to descend into farce. Beyond the murder, attempted kidnapping and the terrorism, there'd also been the first monsoon the kingdom had seen in years and it had nearly ended in tragedy. It didn't do a kingdom with an already bad reputation any favours. He was as prideful as the next Vazaran, Lysa thought. Nobody wants to admit where they come from is a dive. Maybe a bit harsh on the kingdom overall. Plenty of the other four had bad parts in spades but they didn't get anywhere near as much bad press as Vazara did.

"You see the team since they got back from Cubla Cezri?" Brumley asked suddenly. She hid a roll of the eyes. Somehow it always had to boil back down to the job at hand no matter where they were. They all shared that bond between them, the five of them. Unisco. You couldn't escape that bond it fostered.

"They were down," Anne said. "A failed mission can do that for you."

"I wouldn't have said it was a complete failure," Okocha mused. "Arnholt didn't hold it against them. They couldn't have accounted for a V.S strike team hitting them at the same time. They're lucky to have gotten out of there alive."

"Still..." Brumley said thoughtfully. They were all thinking the same thing, Lysa would have wagered. Nobody liked to be tarred with the taint of failure, no matter the circumstances. Nothing less than coming back with the objectives completed and everyone healthy would have been enough.

"They're still in debriefing," Okocha said. "Having reports compiled together on the whole thing. They did get some information out of Joseph Itandje before he, ah, expired." He said the word with a little twist in the corner of his mouth as if it made him physically uncomfortable. "Just not enough."

"It's never enough," Lysa said. "We'd all like to have all the facts in hand before we do anything. I guess sometimes it's not happening."

"Try any time," Anne muttered waspishly. She then perked up and gave them all a big grin. "So, who do we fancy to win the Quin-C then?"

"Sommer," Lysa and Brumley both said, with Okocha half a heartbeat behind.

She smiled at them all, a smile hiding a hint of superiority behind it. She revelled in the mystique, bearing the impression she knew something they didn't. "I don't think so."

Granted, it had been a pretty sad time and he'd tried not to appear too overjoyed in front of Pete, but Scott was privately having an absolute blast. His best buddy was still grieving; he'd done his best for him but really, he was uncomfortable with it. Being consoling wasn't really his thing, no matter how much he tried, the words always felt hollow and lacking. Pete hadn't complained, he hadn't done much of anything other than retreat into himself to the point Scott had troubled recognising him for who he was. It was not a nice feeling. Probably on a par to how he feels himself, he reminded himself.

But Scott himself… Semi-finalist of the Quin-C tournament on his debut. He still couldn't believe it. He really couldn't. How'd he ended up here? He'd been asked the same thing in an interview after his last bout and he'd not been able to answer then either. He'd just grinned inanely and shrugged, the words about how he genuinely didn't know spilling from him. He'd found some composure too little too late to stop cruel words in one of the less reputable media outlets. Describing him as slack jawed was a little harsh. He was even too overjoyed by his performance to fantasize about revenge, something he might have done in the past. Permear had wanted revenge, especially when the ghost had also been criticised for being 'in high spirits' and 'disobedient'. Those were the polite ways it had been written.

It felt like he'd earned a reward, time away from the grind, as much as doing something he loved well could be described as a grind, and so he and Mia had made their way across the island to find a secluded spot away from everyone else for a picnic, maybe other sort of fun times if he was lucky. Just the two of them, nobody else. He was hoping for a private beach. Granted there were some sands back at the resort but with the island holding as many people as it did now, privacy wasn't quite a guarantee. And there was always some idiot with a picture box who thought they'd make quick credits by capturing a few images of callers engaged in personal time. As that idiot in the after-bout interview had proved, there'd always be someone to put them out there given the chance and the means.

Mia just looked stunning today, wearing nothing but a pair of shorts and a bikini top beneath a light flowing beach robe fashioned of cotton but resembling something more appropriate for the bedroom. It was see-through enough to leave little to the imagination, he could see the butterfly wings tattooed on her upper back, the yerley fairy she'd had inked on her side, to the Burykian woven rings inscribed on her ankles. He kinda liked that, it was cute without being over the top. More than once he'd linked his arm through hers and kissed her, still giddy with the good times. Right now, he felt like he'd fallen on his feet. So why did he have that niggling feeling that something wasn't quite right with the world? He couldn't say. Maybe he was feeling guilty about being here while Pete moped around the resort. He'd been spending a bit too much time in the bars since the funeral and it wasn't like he was a fun drunk to start with. It wasn't like he could even hang out with Nick Roper, going through the same thing, given he'd wound up locked up after Sharon's funeral.

To say Pete had gone berserk been an understatement. If Scott was honest, he'd found it hilarious, he thought he'd done an admirable job to not laugh when Ritellia had hit the ground like a sack of shit. But it hadn't been his sister whose death they were there to mourn, was it? Pete had spent the rest of that day stalking around like a tiger with a headache muttering about how they better never let Roper out on the grounds he'd kill him if they did.

Privately, Scott thought that was wishful thinking. He wouldn't have picked a fight with Nick Roper. There was something about him Scott didn't quite trust. Every time he saw him, he got the impression he was... Well, he might not be hiding something, but there was something going on there, even if nobody else saw it. He'd seen people hit out in anger and nearly break their own fists. None of that with Nick. There'd been something not right about it. He might have looked angry on the surface but... He didn't know. Something was missing, something he couldn't place.

Why was he thinking about this? He chided himself for it, rolling his eyes in bemusement. Here, alone with a beautiful girl, having the time of his life and he wanted to think about other stuff. Stuff that, grieving best friend aside, didn't really matter to him in the long run. He pushed it aside, let out a laugh. Mia looked at him, a little bemused, one of her eyebrows raised in surprise.

"What?" he asked.

"You," she said. "Something funny, flyboy?"

He shook his head. "Nah, just thinking about stuff. Just that it's been a weird few weeks since I got here. I mean I spent most of my life thinking about getting here and now that I did, I got to say it's not like I expected it."

Mia said nothing, instead let him continue. "I mean I guess I just pictured it as chill out stress-free stuff between bouts. I figured it'd be the bouts that'd be full of drama, not the stuff in between. Not people getting killed and buildings getting blown up."

He toyed whether to mention kidnapping effeminate lunatics but chose not to. He wasn't entirely sure what sort of reaction it might get, he didn't want to bring it up and upset her. She'd not spoken much about that night, at least not to him and if she was having trouble he didn't want to dredge up bad memories.

"It's never like you expect it," she said eventually. "That's why they call it expectation. You spend so much time building up to it, thinking about how it will be yet when it does come around, so much is different. Some find it underwhelming."

"I wouldn't say I found it underwhelming," Scott said. "Just different. Different in a good way. Don't get me wrong, it's shaping up to be the best month of my entire life so far if things keep going as they are."

"Glad it's going well for you," she said. "Hope you haven't jinxed your tournament by saying that. You'll look a fool if you crash and burn in the semis now."

He managed a weak grin. "Hey, I made the semis at least on my first try. Not many say that. And hey, I got you, didn't I? That's better than any trophy and huge amount of credits. Y'know if you want to make comparisons."

She went red at that, he didn't think it was the sun bearing down on her skin either. She'd built up a bit of a tan since being here compared to how pale she'd been beforehand. Several times in the space of a few short seconds she made to open her mouth as if to say something and then words failed her. Privately he was pleased with that effect.

"That's a really nice thing to say," she eventually managed, her voice quiet and surprised. "Might be the nicest thing anyone's ever said to me. You know, who wasn't family."

"I mean it," Scott said. "I really do."

It was her turn to surprise him as she stopped and almost leaped on him, crushing her mouth against his, pushing him into a sitting position on an overturned rock with her legs almost wrapped around his waist. The sudden intensity of the surprise was almost as potent as the glee that rushed through him.

"Sorry," she said as she broke away. "That was…"

"No need to apologise," he replied. He could taste her lip gloss. Cinnamon. "You're not going to hear me complain. Not about that, anyway. Might complain that you stopped." He managed a weak grin.

"I've known a few spirit callers like you," she said. "Not one of them ever said anything like that to me. Probably thought the reverse to be exact."

Heh… His grin grew, her skin was warm and smooth, and she was close enough for him to feel her heartbeat. His own was thudding wildly in his chest. Good move, Scott, he congratulated himself silently. "Still, I meant it, you know. Always." His stomach was twitching, like he'd swallowed a storm of millibugs and he suddenly felt the grin growing idiotically against burning cheeks. Oh Divines, he thought to himself, suppressing a wince. He very much got the impression he was falling for her completely. And right now, that suited him.

Terrence Arnholt and Brendan King looked at each other, neither feeling particularly cheerful at present. Neither felt like this whole mission to police the Quin-C was doing them many favours in front of their own people, nor in front of the people they answered to. It was slowly turning into the biggest farce either of them had ever known under tournament circumstances. They'd never experienced anything like it for the constant exacerbation of problems. Now Ritellia had announced he was bringing a Vazaran Sun presence in to see that things went smoothly for the last few days. Arnholt hadn't been pleased to hear that, had retreated to his office and viciously described Ritellia in a number of anatomically improbable ways.

"Did you know this island was supposed to be some sort of sacred site?" he eventually asked, looking across at Brendan with quiet resignation in his eyes. "For the Vazarans anyway?"

"Ai-Yal'Sanhim," Brendan said, deliberating on each section of the word thoughtfully, moving it over in his mouth. Both had read the reports from the failed mission into Vazara. They'd read about what little Itandje had had to say on the matter. "Ai-Yal'Sanhim. I didn't know this was supposed to be it. I've heard of it, of course."

"What's the significance?"

Brendan considered the question for several moments, flexing his callused fingers in front of him absentmindedly. "Ai-Yal'Sanhim is first mentioned in tales of the Belleric Empire some couple of thousand years ago. The Bellericians, they inhabited what we now call Vazara, they believed originally the Divines were men and women. But at the same time, they knew how to manipulate the fervour of those around them into holding them above the crowd. They used all that strong feeling about them, the adulation of their supporters, the fear of their enemies to rise. To ascend from man to something more. Something eternal, if their names were remembered, their power would be absolute. Of course, when they did ascend to paradise, the first of the few, the first thing they did was wipe out what was there before so what we know now could come into existence. Their pantheon would become the forefront of their new world, they wiped out any other competitor for divine affection by killing their followers."

"As fascinating as this might be," Arnholt said icily. "What does this have to do with Ai-Yal'Sanhim and this island."

"Giving background, sir. To understand the story, you need the context," Brendan sounded pissed at being interrupted. "Anyway, the story of this island is that before they departed their newly formed kingdoms, never to return, Gilgarus left this island as a gift for a worthy one. Something would be hidden here that only the worthy may find and use."

"The worthy what?"

"The worthy heir," Brendan said. "An heir to the mantle left behind by the Divines long ago. An heir to the kingdoms. Someone who would do what they did long ago and rise to join the Divines, sparking a new world order along the way. Whatever was hidden here would bring about change. That's how the story goes anyway. How much you actually believe in it is…"

"Is it a weapon?" Arnholt interrupted.

Brendan frowned at him. "Not everything has to be a weapon to initiate change. Of course, in theory it could be used as one. There are those out there who always find a way."

"Brendan," Arnholt said, his voice soft and tired. He sounded exhausted, nobody knew when he'd last slept, least of all him. "Tell me you don't believe in this."

"Personally, I want to," Brendan replied. "But whether you do or not, I think the main thing here might well be that our enemy believes in it and seeks to take action which could be catastrophic for the five kingdoms. I believe not believing could be a foolish mistake we'd do well to avoid."

"You might be right there," Arnholt said. "Do all the research you would for any other case, inform Okocha to do the same. I want you to try and narrow down an exact objective, a plan of action, a way to stop them. Maybe use this insane idea against them." He sighed, managed a very weak grin to spread across his face. "Never thought I'd deal with something like this."

"Sir, there's also the question of Roper…"

Arnholt smashed his fist down onto the desk, his reaction sudden and unexpectedly violent. Breath exploded out of him in a sharp rupture, he took several long seconds to regain composure. "There's no question about Roper," he said simply. "He did what he did. He's got to live with that. We can't interfere."

"Can't or won't?" Brendan asked.

"Both," Arnholt said. "I'm aware of his circumstances, I'm aware of what he's feeling, and I don't care. I expect professionalism from my agents always and he's violated that. We're not lifting a finger to save him and if he's got any gumption left about him, then he's not going to expect us to."

"I see," Brendan said. "Very well sir, just making the inquiry." He bowed his head slightly. "If there's anything else, Director, then I'll see myself out."

"Yes, yes," Arnholt said. "Thank you, Brendan. Take care of yourself."

As the field chief left the room, he rose from his seat and made his way to the window, staring out the glass at the island beyond. All the regret and the pain caused by what was out there was starting to wear him down. So much that could have gone wrong with this tournament had. There was no winning in this situation, just making the defeats less severe. And there was still one more task ahead of him, one he'd known was coming when he'd seen the footage of the so-called Vazaran Sun attack on his agents.

"Damn you, Roper," he said, looking at the sun going down. "I really hope you know what you're doing here."

He turned back to the holo-projector on his desk and cleared his throat. This would be an interesting conversation as he reached over to it and made the call, punching the numbers into it and waiting.

It took minutes rather than seconds and throughout, he could imagine the wheels within wheels turning, the conversations over whether to accept, whether to put him through and who'd get the blame if it didn't go as well as the recipient hoped. Vazaran political households were notoriously treacherous. At least he didn't have to talk to Mazoud, rather, it was the holographic image of Leonard Nwakili that emerged in front of him, the eyes tired but alert. He looked as bad as Arnholt himself felt. Probably worse.

"Good evening, Premier," he said pleasantly. "I trust I didn't disturb you from something important."

"Well actually..." Nwakili started to say before Arnholt cut him off and took great pleasure in doing so. It was perverse, he couldn't help it. He rested his elbows on the desk in front of him and gave him a big grin.

"Good, good," he said. "I got in touch because there's ever such a sensitive matter I need to talk to you about. Dae'sutaka." Wrapping his tongue around the Vazaran language had never come easily to him, the best thing he could do was try not to sound inept when he spoke it. He'd like Crumley or Okocha here for that, both spoke it better than him, Crumley with her gift for languages, Okocha being native to the kingdom.

Nwakili blinked. For him, it was the equivalent of being an admission of guilt and Arnholt felt a flood of satisfaction rush him. "Dae'sutaka?" He couldn't pull off the sound of innocence as well as he thought.

"Yes," Arnholt said. "You know them, I assume. We both know what that translates as." Death squad, basically, he thought to himself. Not a lot of people knew about that, he'd chosen to keep it that way. He knew Nwakili better than he wanted to and him not knowing you knew what cards he had was preferable to him knowing you didn't know what he had.

"Director Arnholt, I'm not sure..."

"Don't play dumb with me, Leonard, it doesn't suit you. Besides, I've played Ruin with you, I know when you're lying. You know exactly what I'm talking about. Yohan Isiah. Fabrice Townsend. Didier Kondogbia. Solomon Bennet... You want me to keep naming your operatives in there? I have them all. How many of them are still alive by the way?"

He gave Nwakili a cold smile, not giving anything away. All those names had been members of Dae'sutaka confirmed dead at the scene of the Cubla Cezri mission, a little gift from Okocha's marvellous hacking skills.

"Of course, not many people know about them. And what they don't know is that your own private death squad wears a uniform very similar to the Vazaran Sun basic one. Easy mistake to make, I imagine. I mean there can only be so many uniforms in the world, some are bound to have similarities. Vazaran Sun grunt uniforms are black with a red stripe across the shoulders. Dae'sutaka have a red stripe across the shoulder, dark and grey under the arms. An easy mistake to make but I imagine a costly one if it came to light."

"What's your point, Terrence?" Apparently, they'd abandoned formalities now, another sign he might have Nwakili on the ropes. The man never broke protocol unless he was seriously struggling.

"Someone wearing those very uniforms just tried to kill four of my agents and I take that sort of thing very personally. More than that, they were responsible for the death a man in custody of those agents, someone with vital information regarding blowing open this whole case. That sort of thing I take even more personally."

"Well my condolences. Was anyone hurt? Beyond the guy who died?"

"They'll live," Arnholt said coldly. "I also had one of my guys examine some things and he discovered that an unidentified hoverjet departed for Cubla Cezri the moment my guys announced to air traffic control their destination. Vazaran Sun craft are still required to identify themselves, are they not?"

"I believe so," Nwakili said, still a great deal of even control in his voice.

"And given what you tried to talk two of my agents into relaying back to me not so long ago," Arnholt continued. "I have reason to believe you manipulated this whole thing to make it look like the Suns attacked my agents and executed our suspect. All so we'd retaliate and wipe out Mazoud for you in revenge." He clucked his tongue. "That's a rather desperate gambit for you, Leonard. It truly is."

"Prove it!" Nwakili suddenly snarled, true venom in his voice. "Go on! If you can…"

"Oh, I can't," Arnholt said. "Not beyond reasonable doubt right now. Even if I could, I'd probably let it go. For old times' sake, this once. But I will give you fair warning. If you try anything like this again, I won't be so restrained. If you do it again, I will speak to Mazoud anonymously and inform him what you're doing. Because I think he'd be interested, even if nobody else would. Having your people put on V.S uniforms to execute undesirables… That sort of thing tends to piss off people in high places. I dread to think what would follow such an act."

Nwakili had a sneer in his voice as he spoke again. "And you the great champion of law and order."

"I get the job done," Arnholt said. "Sometimes a compromise is needed. You're the politician, you should know that." He smiled politely at the seething Premier. "Very nice talking to you again, Leonard. We must have a catch up at some point. Old friends and all that." He paused a moment, toyed with the idea of hurling something else in front of him. Just in case it got a reaction. Arnholt's grin grew even wider. He shouldn't be enjoying this as much as he was. "By the way, you ever hear of Ai-Yal'Sanhim?"

"Stop wasting my time, Director Arnholt," Nwakili said. "If you don't desist, I'll see that the Senate hears of your false allegations towards a duly elected head of state. Without validation, I'm afraid they're just that. False."

He had, Arnholt mused as the connection died away, truly enjoyed that. Rattling Nwakili wasn't easily done, he felt he'd handled it in the right way. At the very least, it might have convinced him to change his ways in regards of using an incognito death squad. He wasn't worried about that final threat. Nobody made threats from a position of strength.

Now he just needed several more pieces to fall into place.

The twenty-eighth day of Summerpeak.

At least it wasn't one of the worse cells in the jail. Not that he couldn't have dealt but given a choice, he shouldn't have to. He'd seen some of the cells in this place and honestly wouldn't have minded. It would have been nice to suffer in a squalid little windowless hole that matched the way he felt inside right now. There hadn't been much need for policing this island by the local force, meaning the cells were empty.

He'd slipped one of the guards a hundred credits to ensure he didn't get visitors unless they were a magistrate. He didn't want to see anyone right now, just be alone for the time being. Not his friends, not his enemies, not Ritellia come to gloat. That sort of petty small-mindedness was just the sort of thing he'd do. They'd kept a stoic face on, but the two officers who'd arrested him had both been laughing about it. Maybe they'd read his statement.

He perched on the bunk, rested back on it and closed his eyes. It didn't help. Every time he did, he saw her blank eyes staring at him. He saw it all, the scenes when he'd entered the room, the chaos and the destruction and at the centre of it all, the death of the woman he'd loved. Nothing would ever scrub that sight from his mind. Nor, he reflected, should it be able to. He didn't want to forget. Nick wanted to remember that pain, use it to forge himself and grow strong off it. He couldn't let it conquer him for if he curled up into a ball and reflected on his misery, he'd never get back up. He couldn't do that. He wouldn't.

He remembered how Ritellia had tried to barge his way to speak at the funeral, aware he wasn't welcome there and he remembered how the anger had rushed through him, the desire to do exactly what he'd wanted for a very long time. Of course, it had been live. Thousands, if not millions of people had seen it by now. They'd seen what he'd wanted them to see. A high-profile spirit caller disgruntled enough with the establishment to strike the public face of it.

He heard the door at the end of the corridor scraping open and he opened one of his eyes a fraction wide enough to see what was going on. One of the uniformed guards was already moving away, a short Serranian stood across from him, dark hair greased back and his suit likely expensive. He was chewing on an edible tooth cleaner, Nick could smell the bitter mint on his breath from across the room.

"Mister Nicholas Roper?" the man asked. "I'm your magistrate."

"I was expecting a Vazaran," Nick said dryly. He hadn't but that was neither here nor there right now.

"I'm a better one," the man said. "Here to get you out."

Got you, you bastards!

"Okay, I'm listening."

"Those two won't tell me anything. Carson chooses not to; I think Rocastle is too scared of Carson to tell the truth. That unnerves me. Because it means Carson is getting stronger. And what happens when he grows too strong to control?"
Private musings of Claudia Coppinger.

The twenty-eighth day of Summerpeak.

Jake Costa, he'd said his name was, and he'd proved to be as good as his word. Nick had been out of the holding cell within fifteen minutes, he'd been out of the building inside half an hour, he'd even gotten an apology from the guards holding him. Nothing personal, they'd said. He believed them, they were only doing their duty. Ritellia had probably been kicking up an unholy shit storm to try and keep him here for the time being. Hence the reason it had likely taken days to get out. He'd lost track of the time; he'd had to admit. Locked in that room, he'd been pretty funked out, alone with his thoughts which hadn't been pleasant. A couple of times he'd thought he'd heard her voice and it had slowly been driving him crazy. Getting out was good, he hadn't realised how good fresh air on his lungs would be. He didn't want to think too hard about what had happened, instead preferring to focus on what was to come. That was the important part.

Costa led him over to a speeder, an easy swagger to his walk, which Nick could hardly blame him for. The man was good, he radiated confidence and so far, he had every reason to believe things were going well for them both. They both thought they had their man. Nick had a strange feeling he wasn't the first one to be approached like this.

"Talk to me of the price," he said thoughtfully. "What is this going to cost me?"

"There is no cost," Costa replied. "I was amused by the way you struck down that buffoon. Someone should have done it a long time ago. Anyway, there is no price, but just a simple request."

"Okay." Nick nodded in agreement. "I see. What's the request? I have to hide something for someone?"

"No, you just need listen for a few moments of your time," Costa replied. "You might do very well out of this, it's a once in the lifetime opportunity. You know how rarely they come along, right?"

"Well that sounds interesting. It from you? You want me to invest in something? Because I got credits to spare." He shrugged. "Hey, you got me out of a spot. Right now, I'd probably consider doing

anything to return the favour. Short of breaking the law again, I guess."
He shrugged again, spread his hands out in front of him. "Don't want to
end up back there, right? Not something I want to go through with."

"You seemed to cope okay," Costa said, his accented voice faint
with sarcasm.

"All a brave face I'm afraid," Nick replied, hesitating a little
between the words to build on his point. "Okay, what's this offer?"

"My boss will tell you. In person." Costa grinned, hands in his
pockets. That grin sent a chill through Nick's flesh, something about it
he didn't like. They approached the speeder, he saw two guys with it
and narrowed his eyes at them as he took them in. Wait... He continued
to study them, tried to work out what it was. They looked familiar,
more than familiar. They had the same nose, but their eyes were
different, the mouth smaller on the guy on the right, even the skin was a
different colour. One Vazaran, one probably Premesoiran. But an
identical nose?! His instincts were telling him something was wrong
here. He stiffened up, the bad feelings pushing over him. Maybe this
hadn't been the best idea, but it was too late to back out now. He
gulped, swallowed and managed a weak grin.

In the hesitation, he took his eyes off Costa and suddenly he felt
the prick in his arm, turned and fought the urge to react as he saw the
fake magistrate pulling a needle out of him. Costa grinned lazily.
"Apologies but necessary." His voice took on an echoey tone, Nick's
vision swam, Costa's face little more than a blur, Nick reached out to
steady himself and suddenly his legs couldn't hold him anymore.
Strong arms caught him as he fell, the last sensation he remembered.

The twenty-ninth day of Summerpeak.

She looked across the desk, first at Wim Carson and then to a
bemused Harvey Rocastle, something about the fat man unnerving her.
Not that he was usually the most pleasant of company but today there
was something not quite right. It was the eyes, she'd gazed into them
and they were like cut glass. Very little feeling. Perhaps no emotion.
None of it was there. He was humming just below his breath, perhaps
the most irritating thing close at hand.

This wasn't the first meeting she'd had with them since they'd
returned to the Eye following their disastrous trip. Every day she'd met
with them, got them in front of her in attempt to convince them to
reveal what exactly had happened. Seven meetings. Seven wasted
hours. Carson politely pushed aside any attempt to probe into what he
knew, intimidation didn't work on him. He was only growing stronger
and it worried her, those powers of his. She'd seen what he could do,

and it was necessary to ensure he didn't turn against her. He said he wouldn't, he'd made his promises, but she didn't trust what came out of his mouth. Who knew how far the depths of his powers went. Plus, she was leery as the hells about him arming himself with one of those laser swords. But she couldn't call him on it, not while she still needed him. When it came down to it, when his usefulness ended, she'd put him in front of a firing squad. Perhaps better to be safe than to be sorry where her own life was concerned.

And as for Rocastle, he'd been different since he'd returned. Maybe sending him had been a mistake. She was sure he had something to do with the death of Sharon Arventino. Nothing she could prove, but maybe, just maybe the time was coming to cut him loose. The man was a liability, but he had enough credit in his bank to think himself safe. It irked her, but she did try to reward loyalty. If you couldn't inspire that or even move to show you valued it, then there was little point in expecting them to give it freely. Doubly so if she couldn't inspire two men like this, then the whole undertaking was futile.

"Are either of you ready to talk today?" she asked. She wasn't expecting anything but still when she was obliged, she harshly exhaled her breath out between her teeth.

"Talk about what?" Rocastle was being perhaps more vocal than normal with those three words, a tone that defined innocence. She didn't buy it.

"You know," she answered quietly. "I still want answers about what happened with that trip to Carcaradis Island."

"Madam," Carson replied. "I believe I am almost able to help you. Maybe a day or two and I will have everything I need."

Okay, that changed things. She sat bolt upright in her seat, allowed a smile to play across her lips. That changed things a lot. "I see," she said. "Do you care to explain further?"

He shook his head. "Not right now. I'll tell you on the way. We need to travel; I trust this won't be a problem."

"No. Not at all." She smiled again, more elation spreading through her than she'd allowed herself to feel for a long time. Nearly. Oh, so very nearly. It was within her sight. She could already feel her fingers itching to reach out and touch it. "Very good, Master Carson. Very good indeed. Carry on."

"Oh, are we done for today?" There was just an inflection of sarcasm in his voice and it didn't suit him. She chose not to dignify him with a response as he left the room, Rocastle trotting after him. Maybe she should have Domis kill him. There wasn't too much more Rocastle could offer the project. Nothing she could see right now anyway. Down the line, maybe. Maybe she'd need someone killing or to make a scapegoat. He had some limited talent at murder and the five kingdoms already thought he was a psychopath who'd tried to kidnap a beloved spirit dancer. The latter appealed at some point. She could use that. If it was the last task he ever performed for her, she could live with that.

He didn't know how long he'd been out as he stirred awake, his head threatening to split as he rolled onto his back and tried to sit up. He ignored it as best he could and took in his surroundings. Not much to go on. Four walls. Grey. Metal. Bare floor. Sparse decoration. Just a cot in one corner and a closet. An empty closet. Not much indeed. The toilet and tiny sink made it even more depressing. He glanced down at himself. Still wearing the same clothes, albeit a little dishevelled. Nick patted himself down, found his pockets still contained everything they had before. Credit chips, spare crystals, old water tablets and gum. He still had his calling crystals, yet they'd taken the summoner. Probably didn't want him making an outbound contact.

Whatever else happened in the immediate future, he was suddenly glad he'd left his badge, muffler and X7 with Okocha. They would have given the game away. He'd been taken, he didn't know where. Unless they had definitive proof, unlikely at best, his identity remained a mystery. For now, he was just Nick Roper, Spirit Caller. Nothing more. That was the way it needed to be. He'd put his neck out and now he was on the block, there couldn't be any regrets. He had enough without adding to them. Fair enough most concerned what had happened to Sharon and the means he'd employed to get into this position. Sharon… Oh Gods, Sharon. He let his head fall back onto the bed, exhaling harshly as he stared at the ceiling. He didn't want to think about her now. He needed to keep his head together, not let it all fall loose. This had been the very first thing he'd ever learned in the Unisco academy. Cool head under pressure, no matter the circumstances. Those who lost the plot invariably went on to lose their lives and he couldn't afford that. Still he couldn't deny the empty space inside him ripped into existence ever since he'd pushed that door open and woven his way into the chaos. She'd been there right at the epicentre of it, sprawled out and bloody… Her eyes… He gulped and tried to blank it out. He could do that. He didn't have to dwell on it. Shouldn't. But there it was.

That was about the time he heard the door grinding open. He turned his head, watched as it swung slowly open. He'd already taken note of the weight of the door. Heavy enough to be automatic. Pushing it from either side would be a futile exercise. Probably operated with a card reader. It opened all the way and he saw he was right; one of the guards had a key card. The other held a big bag, plain black with no hint of a logo or anything fancy. He tossed it in. Both were Vazarans, he'd guess at them being the slow and simple type. Big but he'd seen bigger. The one holding the bag looked like he'd had his nose broken a bunch of times. That told Nick he was an inept fighter.

"The Mistress requests you join her for dinner," the first guard said. "Fresh clothes. We'll collect you in twenty minutes."

"No shower?" Nick asked. "Could do with one." He kicked the bag with the toe end of his shoe. It didn't feel like there was much in there, the sound felt horribly hollow in the echoing room of the cell. Outside, the corridor didn't look much better. Both had weapons but neither had them pointed, only holstered. UP40's by the look of what little he could see. Interesting...

Take them... Take them now before they can draw.

He ignored the voice in his head begging him to act. It wasn't an imperative at this moment. For the time being, it would appear he was being treated as an indentured guest rather than an outright prisoner. Go along with it for the moment. And if the Mistress... Several images rather a little more graphic than he wanted to think about bounced through his head... wanted to meet with him, then why not see what she wanted. The only answer to his question about the shower was the door swinging shut with a click.

So... Twenty minutes then.

He might not have been able to get a shower, but he'd gotten the next best thing. The bag contained fresh clothes, shoes, towel, toiletries and right at the bottom, clealine tablets. He'd not seen some of these since his early days on the road. But very handy indeed. He stripped off, broke two of the tablets against each other in his hands and felt the soapy lather start to form almost immediately. They weren't a particularly good option, but it was better than nothing. And if nothing else, it took his mind off the other problems at hand as he scrubbed himself down, rinsing himself off at the sink, before towelling himself clean. He felt human again at least, refreshed. It would appear for the time being they were interested in his well-being. A chance to ensure things stayed that way would surely follow. If he was going to be trapped here, better to do it in comfort. His allegiance would always be to Unisco. Nothing they could do would change that. But what lay ahead, he couldn't say, and it worried him as he started to dress.

Okay, these were nice. The shirt was a cream coloured silk, the trousers and jacket an almost leather texture of black. He ran a hand over it, found himself wondering if it cost more credits than he'd ever seen at any one time. It was expensive, any fool could tell that. And he looked good in it. The shoes fit okay, a little tight on the left foot but he'd live with it. He'd just finished shaving when the two guards returned, the door giving that same creak as it swung open. He turned, gave them a grin. "Almost done, guys. I'd hate to keep your boss waiting, so..." Nick finished rubbing in the cologne and tossed the empty bottle back into the bag. "Shall we?"

"Step outside, please," one of them said. "And don't try to run."

"Why would I run?" he asked, letting a note of puzzlement slip into his voice. "You've got me interested now. Besides I assume I'm meant to be here, right?"

No reply. As he stepped out, he saw only the quickest glimpse of them, but he immediately blessed his decision not to try fleeing earlier. Both guards were missing their ring fingers on each hand. Some might have dismissed that as unlikely coincidence. Nick knew what it meant. He'd seen it before.

Taxeens!

He hated fighting guys with knives. Even with a clear shot, there was a chance an enemy could still miss with a blaster. It wasn't in human nature to kill. Those who did had to overcome that block. Knives would still cut you though. And Taxeens were excellent knife fighters, especially when one considered the poisons coating their blades. That was why they'd kept their blasters holstered. They didn't need them. Not against an unarmed man distracted by grief. Not with two of them. One, he might be able to take by surprise. To face two at the same time was an act of suicide. They cut away their ring fingers to let the weapons spring into their hands from special spring-loaded gauntlets strapped to their wrists. There'd been one or two in Unisco over the years he knew of, and he'd seen how impressive they could be. Not just with knives but in unarmed combat as well.

He followed them through the maze of sterile corridors, trying to memorise the torturous route until finally giving up. The laws of physics didn't seem to make any sense here, unless they'd purposely been disorientating him. It felt like they'd been past the same fire extinguisher three times, before finally they'd arrived at a room and the door opened to allow him access. Dressed in the unfamiliar black suit, he adjusted his tie and stepped into the room, stopping short from entering as he took it all in.

Oh my...

To say it was a far-flung shot from his cell was an understatement. A very drastic understatement. This was... This was gorgeous. He'd been in classy hotels which paled in comparison to this place. The carpet was a lush crimson that felt like walking across spongy moss, the support beams of the walls lined with gold trim. Diamonds hung from the chandelier, a dozen twinkling lights reflected a hundredfold. And the table could have seated fifty easily. Who had a place like this? He thought he knew the answer. Something had been going on around the Quin-C. They'd been following the patterns and that was indisputable. Someone was pulling strings, there'd been too many seemingly isolated incidents to not be worried. Someone had arranged the natives to be wiped out. Someone had sent that mercenary team the night of the storm. Someone had attacked Wade. Someone had arranged for the hospital to be attacked. Someone had killed...

Sharon...

For a moment he'd thought it was her. He'd been wrong. The woman across the other side of the room looked nothing like her. Wrong age, wrong build, wrong colouring. Maybe she was about fifty, tall but fighting a losing battle with age, brunette and pale. Too pale. Maybe she was sick. She looked tired. If she had enough money to afford a dining room like this, a terminal illness would be ironic. A tasteless thought, he knew that. Somehow, he couldn't bring himself to care. And then she spoke and despite her outward appearance, he found himself surprised by the strength in her voice. The resolution strong.

"Mr Roper," she said. "My apologies and my condolences." She didn't look particularly apologetic; he had to admit as she approached. Her mouth thinned as if trying to look sorrowful, but it wasn't a particularly effective effort.

How to play it? The question rushed through his mind in that moment and he found himself momentarily perplexed. There was something about this whole thing that stank, and he wasn't sure he liked it. Grieving. Grieving and hurting. If he could pull those off, he could take it from there.

"Who are you?" he asked quietly. Privately he was quite pleased with the note of self-pity in his voice. He'd buy it. "What is this place and why have you kidnapped me?"

"Again, I apologise," she said, coming to a halt. "But you've seen this place, I think it's better you don't know where we are. That way it can't be taken from you by force and there are those out there who would. Besides, I think you're being rather ungrateful considering the efforts we went to in securing your release."

She let it hang and Nick shrugged. "Just nervous I guess. Been a rough few days. But grateful, I am. Thank you." He looked her up and down. The hurt in his eyes wasn't false at all. Thoughts of what he'd lost kept battering away at the back of his mind, demanding his attention. He tried to ignore them. It was a losing battle. "Why collect me in the first place."

She sighed. "I wanted to offer you my condolences in person. It's partly my fault that your fiancé died, you see."

It took considerable restraint honed over years of working for Unisco that stopped him from grabbing her by the neck and demanding answers. Restraint he'd made a big show of shattering when he'd smacked Ritellia in the nose. He took a deep breath. Another. And another. Anything to remain calm and composed. "Your fault?"

A nod answered his question. "Partly. You see, I'm the one who arranged for this tournament to be here on Carcaradis Island. In a way, that makes it as much my responsibility as anyone else's. Mr Roper, my name is Claudia Coppinger."

Ah... He owed Will Okocha credits, it would appear. "I've heard of you," he said. "I feel like I've seen you somewhere before." He closed his eyes and focused on her face. "Just there. You weren't at the opening ceremony or something were you. Sorry, if you weren't, I guess I got you confused for someone else."

She raised an eyebrow, a sudden flash in her eyes a little too quick for him to be sure he'd seen it. "There's just one of me, I think you'll find," she said, suddenly haughty. "I am unique."

"Just like everyone else?" Nick quipped. That brought a small smile from her. It probably warranted the reaction. It was an old joke.

"Exactly."

"You're wrong though," he said softly. "I can't blame you for Sharon's... I can't blame you for what happened. It wasn't your fault." He gulped. Felt sick suddenly. Talking about it hurt like the hells and especially to a stranger. Double for one whose motives weren't quite clear yet.

They'd sat down and made small talk over dinner. The main had been a roasted leg of lamb seasoned in mint and nuts, served with honey glazed parsnips, fluffy potatoes cooked in rich goose fat and drenched in meaty gravy so brown it was almost black. It had been outstanding; he'd openly admitted he'd never eaten such fine food before. Claudia Coppinger had smiled and winked at him.

"My own personal chef, Alphonse, came aboard," she said, almost conspiratorially. "The best. I'll be sure to see that he hears your compliments."

"He's not for hire, is he?" Nick asked. "I mean... He doesn't own a restaurant, does he?"

She laughed. "I doubt you could afford him. And no, not yet. One day I mean to set him up with an exclusive establishment in one of the biggest cities in the kingdoms. For the time being, I enjoy him too much. Wine?"

"Maybe one," he said. He didn't want to refuse. If the wine was as good as the food, he probably wouldn't stop at one. He needed to keep a clear head. Something was up here, he couldn't place what, but to say he didn't trust her was an understatement. She'd given nothing away in her small talk, refusing absolutely to talk about business amidst the food. It would sully the food, she'd said, and he agreed politely. What sort of business she wanted with him, he couldn't guess at. The plates had been cleared away and the wine had been served. He swirled it about in his glass before taking a sip.

Wow... To say it was good wine was doing it a disservice. It was fantastic. Normally he wasn't a big wine drinker, but this was something he could enjoy. He didn't know much about the stuff, but he knew what he liked. This, he could cheerfully drink every day for the rest of his life. "Life has clearly been good to you, Ms Coppinger," he said politely. One sip turned into another. She waved a hand dismissively. "You've been an excellent host here. Other than the whole kidnapping thing. And I can't help but wonder why."

"Why?" she asked coyly. "Well, why wouldn't I want an interesting dinner guest up? That whole thing with Ritellia, just marvellous. I truly despise that man, even if he does have his uses sometimes. Everyone does, you know? You'll probably be remembered longer for taking that swing at him than if you'd won the tournament."

"It's not really the sort of thing I'd like to be remembered for," Nick said. "It was a dumb thing to do and well, I suppose I'm going to have to live with the consequences."

"Not necessarily," Claudia said. "You see I happen to know President Ritellia quite well and after a quiet word, he's dropped all the charges."

Interesting, very interesting. Nick let a relieved look flit across his face, even if inside he was maintaining a sense of icy calm. "You see he's come to accept that everyone makes mistakes and you were grief-stricken..."

"I'd prefer not to use that as an excuse. A lot of people were. Her brother was. He didn't act like that." Here, Nick had to admit that he wasn't entirely acting. He'd genuinely considered all of this before putting his little charade into play.

"Could you not say that was down to your passion? Would you say you're a passionate man? I've seen it in the way you fight."

"Passion unrestrained is like fire. Tough to control, harder to contain, difficult to stop," Nick said. "I'm not proud of it. It's going to be hard, but I'd like to move past this."

"Exactly. Life is tough, wouldn't you say? There are no prizes, but living is its own reward," she said.

"All this is just a check-up on my well-being? You're not worried I'm going to sue you, are you?" he chuckled. Apparently, she didn't find it funny, her face didn't change even for a second as she leaned on the table and made a pyramid out of her fingers. He genuinely couldn't tell what she was thinking. Somehow, he felt he didn't want to either.

"Talk to me of faith," she then said suddenly. "Are you devout? Do you feel that the Divines benefit from your supplication?"

"Honestly, I think my supple has been vacated long since," Nick replied. "I'm all out of it. If I wasn't before, then I'm hardly likely to suddenly start believing because they took the one thing I loved beyond all other away from me."

"Or maybe they did that to punish you," she said.

He shrugged. "Perhaps. But I doubt it."

"Why?"

"It seems kinda petty to be honest."

"Pettiness is a human emotion; wouldn't you say? You'd expect something so divine to be above it."

"If you're wanting a debate on the nature of theology, I'm afraid you've probably picked the wrong dinner guest for it," Nick said apologetically. "I don't think I'm being punished."

"Just for the record," Claudia said. "I don't either. I think it'd be a cruel being who would punish someone for not seeing things their way by taking a life not theirs to take. All life is precious is what they teach us. Not to be taken in anger or revenge, not even in justification."

That's me fucked then, Nick thought dryly to himself.

She paused, truly thoughtful for a moment. He could see it in her eyes. There was something there, maybe not madness but not sanity either. "You know," she said softly. "Once I met a holy man when I was a little girl and I spoke with him about faith. The nature of it and the reality. How we take so much of it on little more than a whim. I believe in Divines. I truly do. Yet at the time I found myself wondering why the secrecy. Why not reveal themselves, why not rule? All that power and yet they limit themselves to little more than the imagination. What was the point?"

Nick said nothing.

"He wasn't your usual holy man. Had a decent church, nice office. And in the corner of the room, there was this old chair. He got up and pointed to it, asked me with a smile on his face what sort of proof would suffice. If he prayed to Gilgarus or Melarius and asked them to lift the chair up and down as a sign of their existence, some would regard it as a miracle. Some would see it as a trick. And some would be scared. Because power scares people. Especially when it's used so brazenly. But with some subtlety, you can never know. Do just the right thing and people won't be sure if you've done anything at all.

So, what if everyone loved each other like family, if there were no more wars or sickness? Wouldn't that be greater proof of a higher plan than this chair rising up and down?"

"You seem to forget one thing with that argument," Nick said. "Families fight all the time. That's when it gets personal when the family is involved. I've seen some of the worst arguments ever spring from people who should know better."

"You're missing the point, I see."

He felt the ire rise in him, a hot hard feeling in the base of his stomach. "You know, you're not persuading me with this story. That's just the story religion likes to perpetuate. You're right. We'll never know. We shouldn't. Otherwise it'd be worship for the sake of it. We wouldn't do it because we believe, we'd do it out of fear."

"I've always found fear to be an excellent motivator," she said. "But only a fool uses it as their sole weapon."

"I wouldn't disagree. There are forces stronger than fear."

"Greed for instance. That's served me just as well," Claudia said. "I'm a very wealthy woman. One of the five wealthiest in the five kingdoms. Well I was before all of this. You see to accumulate, you need to speculate. I've been hunting a dream for a very long time because I believe it to be attainable. I have thrown a great deal of credits towards this venture and my rewards are almost near. To acquire the priceless, you really have to pay through the nose for it."

"Oh yeah?" Nick wondered if he was supposed to sound impressed. Given she'd spilt very little information; he was probably entitled not to be overwhelmed with emotion.

"You know the story of Ai-Yal'Sanhim?"

He shook his head. "Sounds Vazaran though."

"Close but not quite. The gist of the story was how those who were exceptional found themselves elevated above the ordinary. The ordinary started to believe in them and thus they became extraordinary. They became more than mortal, they shaped the world in their image and did what we could not. In short, they became divine." She smiled faintly. "I want that."

"And you want me to help you attain it?" Nick couldn't believe his ears. As farfetched ideas went, this one took the cake. "I think you might be overestimating what I'm capable of there. Because…"

"No, no, no," she said. "You can't help me there. But once it is attained, I must take steps to ensure it is kept. I will need those who are loyal to me to build a power base. Those who know how to use the weapons in my arsenal. Those who will ascend with me." She smiled coldly. "I've been recruiting from the Quin-C, you know. I wanted those who had nothing to lose and everything to gain to come to my side. Those who wanted change, those with grievances against what had come before. I offer them what nobody else would. A chance for change."

"A noble goal," Nick said. "But seriously, you don't really believe that story, do you?"

She narrowed her eyes at him. "And why would I not? There might be some fanciful elements to it, but I've always found there are some elements of truth behind the frippery of every tale. You have suffered, you've struck against the establishment, you are strong and capable. You are exactly the sort of person I want at my back when I ascend and bring my new world into being. It won't be easy but nothing good ever is, I think you'll agree."

Claudia Coppinger smiled at him. "So, what do you say?"

Nick exhaled sharply, dabbed at the corners of his mouth with a napkin and put on an expression of deep thoughtfulness. He leaned forward to look her in the eyes, trying to keep down the feeling of disgust he felt deep within him.

"I believe you believe what you're saying is true," he said. "You seem so damn confident about it, I think you might actually have the stuff to back it up. That equal parts thrills and terrifies me. But it's a big decision." He paused to finish his glass of wine, made a big show of swirling the dregs down in the bottom of the glass before swallowing it. "Life changing even. Can't just say yes or no like that. Allow me some time to think it over and I'll get back to you."

She raised a hand. "But of course. I'd be more than a little worried if you just blindly accepted it. Return to your accommodation and perhaps we can arrange a tour of the facilities for the morrow. If you can see what we've already got, then it may change your mind." It wasn't so much what she said that caught his attention as what she didn't say. He got the feeling she was omitting the part where if he didn't sign up, he wouldn't be leaving alive.

He'd known the risks. He'd just have to try and get some sort of signal out before things went sour.

Silas was already waiting for her as she entered the room. Amidst all the excitement she'd almost forgotten their little arrangement and he looked impatient to be kept waiting, a situation she could care less about. "Mister Lassiter," she said. "Sorry to delay, there were circumstances beyond my control. This entire project is poised in a very delicate position as we speak."

"Hey," Silas said angrily. "Don't talk to me of delicate positions. I'm in a precarious one myself. I think Cyris suspects I'm trying to stab him in the back."

"Really?" She sounded amused, she couldn't help that. "And pray, why would he think that? Have you been careless?"

Silas shook his head. "No, I've been quiet as a mouse in my movements. Not a hint. So, how's he...?"

The curtain at the back of the room opened and John Cyris stepped out, no anger on his face but rather disappointment, a look of hurt disbelief. "Oh, I told him," Claudia said nonchalantly. The look on Silas' face was priceless, outrage, disgust and hurt betrayal all rolled into one.

"You did what?"

"See I have no wish to ally myself to promises from the bottom when I can get the same with a vow from the top."

"You're making a mistake!" Any hint of cool in Silas' voice had gone and he was starting to sound desperate. High and shrill, she could see his eyes darting back and forth as if looking for a way out. "He'll betray you."

"I'll have to watch out for that then," she said sounding amused. "He has no sense of irony, does he John?"

"Not at all, Madam Coppinger," Cyris smirked. "Simon, I gave you everything when you had nothing." His smirk faded and there was disappointment in his voice. "I treated you like a son and you do this?"

Silas snorted. "Yeah, I know all about your relationship with your son."

He said no more as Cyris swung a fist and Silas went down with a yell, blood spurting from his lip. He tried to fight back, all to no avail as Cyris swept in, hitting him again and again, fists meeting flesh over and over until he stopped moving. There was nothing to say to that, she studied him curiously as he got to his feet and straightened his clothes. "You have a strong reaction to betrayal."

"He knew what'd happen," Cyris replied, still staring at the man on the floor. His face had been pounded into something unrecognisable, he still lived but barely, his breathing shallow and laboured. "You think I acted irrationally? Maybe I should have spared him?"

She twitched her lips in amusement. "No. I wholeheartedly approve. Sometimes a strong hand is needed."

"Your mind will always be your greatest weapon. Everything else is superfluous."
First thing said to Nicholas Roper on first day of Unisco training.

The twenty-third day of Summerpeak.

He'd watched them take her out of the room on a hover-gurney, her face covered by a sheet. For that, he was grateful. He didn't want to see her face again, had witnessed it as he'd entered the room, fallen to his haunches and just been unable to move, just wanted to purge the last thing he'd eaten, just sit there unmoving. Arnholt, bless him, had come to see what was happening and they'd exchanged words. Nick could see that his boss was just as rocked by the whole thing as him, the shock plastered across his face. If Arnholt hadn't seen this coming, with all the resources at his fingertips, then it might be worse than they'd all thought.

He'd ignored the calls and there'd been plenty of them, had taken all he had to vacate the room. He'd still be there now if management and the forensic service hadn't made him leave, they'd moved him to another room with their condolences. Which was nice, he supposed. They'd have to be just as worried as he was, just as scared. Though theirs came from a professional point of view, they didn't know how this would impact on their reputation, he didn't care. Personally, he couldn't care less about that right now. Nick was too busy grieving. Somewhere across not just this island but the kingdoms, the news would slowly be seeping out a beautiful, kind, talented woman had died and those who had known her would never get the chance to see her again. They'd never get the chance to say goodbye.

They'd never get the chance to say goodbye. He found that thought perhaps the most distressing of all. He'd ordered a bottle of Serranian firebrandy from the hotel bar, had it delivered to his room but hadn't drunk any yet. The bottle remained unopened, though he'd been tempted. He should. It'd calm his nerves. But at the same time, he didn't want to be calm, he wanted to be with her. He should be with her, but he was here, and she was out there. Silent forever, never to make another sound or cast another smile. Already she'd be laid out on a cold slab in the mortuary alone. Alone. He was sure he must have wept, for his eyes were sore and wet, his nose clogged but more than anything he just felt numb. Like a part of him hadn't just died but had been surgically removed.

He didn't know how long he'd sat there, it might have been hours, might have been minutes. He finally broke the top from the bottle and took a long drain, the liquid harshly burning the back of his throat. It felt good, he felt the fires twitching through his limbs. Feeling slowly returned to him although he realised now he was shaking, his hands trembling as he held the bottle. Gently he put it down and sighed.

Now, he wasn't entirely sure where he went. Now he was alone. Sorrow coursed through him, the thought echoing through his mind before slowly he stood. Gradually the ice turned to fire, hot anger burning through him as he turned and smashed the bottle against the wall, silvers of glass cutting into his hand, alcohol stinging the cuts. It felt good, the pain brought things back into focus. He drew a deep breath and closed his hand into a fist, felt fresh agony assault his system, but he didn't make a sound, too busy thinking.

He hadn't slept as he made his way into Will's makeshift office in the Unisco headquarters, he didn't feel tired. Or hungry. He didn't feel much, just numb in everything but his desire for answers. And if anyone had them, he'd guess Will was the top of the list. And if he didn't, then he could get them. He wasn't about to take no for an answer. Nick entered, saw the Vazaran slumped at his desk, head on his arms and sleeping. The last few weeks had been rough on all of them, he supposed. Especially Will. He'd been here late every night doing the job of three people and right now, he looked so peaceful. The sleep would do him good. Then again, Nick realised he didn't care as he closed the door. Loudly. Okocha jerked awake with a start, mumbling out confused words.

"Morning," Nick said before acting apologetic. "Sorry, didn't realise you were asleep."

"Knock next time yeah," Okocha groaned. "Yipes." He yawned loudly. "Bloody hells I needed that." He felt a twinge of guilt. Not much but some. Okocha could sleep on his own damn time. Nick folded his arms and looked at him.

"You look almost as bad as I feel," he said, allowing some sympathy into his words. Okocha did look exhausted. "Almost."

"I know, right? Nick, I'm sorry for your loss."

It wasn't the first time he'd heard such sentiments and he nodded gratefully. "Thanks, Will. That means a lot. Now are you going to help me find her killer?"

An audible groan slipped from Okocha as he let his head fall onto the desk again. "Nick, I'm not sure you should be doing this. Shouldn't you be grieving?"

"I'll grieve when I've got an answer and someone's dead."

"You know Arnholt won't put you on this. It's way too personal." He didn't look convinced as he said it. "And if you go off without orders, you'll be in the shit?"

"And do you know I don't care?" Nick asked softly. "I'm not... Look just let me look at the evidence in the case. I know you can get hold of it. Let's look over it, I'll not abscond with it. I'll be under your supervision all times." He tried to grin at him, failed miserably, decided it wasn't important. "Maybe we can find something that's been missed."

"Well..." Okocha looked uneasy about the whole thing. That, Nick noted, was a problem. A rather big one. He couldn't do this without him. Okocha might sympathise with him but if he was unwilling to anything then he couldn't force him.

"Go on. What harm can it do?"

A sigh escaped Okocha's mouth. "Okay, okay, we'll have a look over it. But if you find anything, we take it straight to the director. No running off on revenge missions."

"Now would I do a thing like that?"

"Well you look desperate enough to do anything right now," Okocha said dryly. "I'm actually a bit worried about what might've happened if I'd refused to help you."

"Now who's being melodramatic?"

Okocha gave him a sarcastic smirk and folded his arms. "I'm going to ignore that. So where do you want to start?"

The crime scene hadn't revealed much, there'd been fingerprints all over the room but most of them belonged to either him or the victim. Thinking of her like that worked for the moment, made it easier. Looking at all this imagery reminded him of how he'd found her and the last thing he wanted was those memories troubling him now. He didn't want to break down, wouldn't do anyone any good. About the best thing he could do was stay focused on the professional aspect of the case. Some existed from the cleaning staff in the hotel, they'd been ruled out as suspects. There'd had been some sets of unidentified fingerprints, Okocha had run them against all known databases but come up empty. That troubled Nick more than he was willing to admit. Something about this whole mess troubled him. This didn't feel like an opportunist murder, they'd had to have done some planning, to get in the hotel room without a trace spoke of professionalism. But the way it had gone down felt sloppy. No sign of forced entry. Had to have been two people. Deep fibre analysis of the carpet spoke of three sets of footprints in the room in the time frame of death, one of them belonging to Sharon, one of them leaving the impressions that implied a tall heavy man, the other being rather vaguer. Average height and slender-to-medium build were about the best they'd come up with.

"Not much here, I'm afraid," Okocha said. "Believe me I already looked over it. And there's no camera footage showing who went in there. It's all been flashed out. But not in a way I've ever seen before. All very weird."

"Talk to me of the murder weapons," Nick said. "Maybe there's something there."

"Two injuries on her body," Okocha said, bringing up a holographic rendition of the body. Nick was grateful to see the face had been blanked out, leaving it featureless. That was appreciated. What hadn't been concealed was the damage to the back of the head, he found it painful just to look at it. Minus the blood and the gore and the smell of death, it looked like an egg that had been smashed half in at one side. "First injury which would have killed her was a kinetic blast to the back of the head, smashed her skull straight through and blew fragments of bone into the back of her brain which was already scrambled from the blow." He cracked his fist against the desk suddenly. "Dead on impact. We all know what a blast like that does to a shielded person, into flesh at that range, well that'd be all she wrote."

"How does someone get a kinetic disperser across an island and into a hotel room without anyone noticing?" Nick asked. "I mean they're not easy to hide?"

"We've been asking around," Okocha said. "But so far nobody remembers seeing anything. They're drawing a blank."

"Yeah that's helpful," Nick said. "Really is." He saw the look on Okocha's face and felt a bit guilty. "Sorry, I know you're doing your best. But... Come on, I need to find them."

There, he'd said it. He'd let it slip. He meant to find them and that was that, he didn't need Okocha knowing it. He tried to put his mind to it. Seeing the hologram was a little distracting. Kinetic disperser wounds all followed a similar pattern, narrowing them down to a single weapon would take more time than they had. "What about the other wound?"

Okocha hit a few buttons and the holographic image of the woman rotated, showing the entry wound across the chest. If he bent down and screwed his eyes up, Nick could see the exit wound on the other side.

"It sped death up, would have been fatal on its own, but appears to have been a superfluous injury added post-head trauma," Okocha said. "Weapon is unknown, appears to have been hot enough to cauterise on impact. Very little bleeding."

"What the hells does that?" Nick asked. "That doesn't seem possible. What did they use, an oxytorch?"

"Wouldn't have produced a neat wound like this," Okocha said, reaching his hand into the hologram. Nick fought the urge to wince as he waggled his fingers in the wound. "This was a straight in and out job, very little resistance to the entry wound. If it had been an oxytorch, there'd be a whole lot more damage to the surrounding area, it wouldn't have been as neat, it'd have had to have melted its way inside through flesh and muscle. You know how easily flesh burns? The room would have stank like a bacon factory."

"Nice," Nick said. "Well I didn't notice that. So, what sort of weapon does it?"

"Coroner couldn't identify it," Okocha said. "I think that's worrying personally. When the weapon can't be identified, we all need to sit up and take note."

Nick nodded, folded his arms and stroked his chin thoughtfully. "Okay, okay. So maybe look at it from a different angle."

"How do you mean?"

"You run a trace for similar sorts of wounds in murder victims recently? If it's that uncommon, then maybe we can narrow down a link."

"I did," Okocha said. "This is where it gets interesting." He pushed another button, more images materialised in front of them, two badly dismembered bodies. "This happened a few weeks ago in Latalya."

"Serran, right?"

"Yeah, just at the base of the Trabazon mountain," Okocha said. "It has a nice waterfront; they trade with Vazara a lot. Anyway, these two guys were found cut up in a cellar. Wounds were cauterised instantly, looked a lot like what we see on Ms Arventino here. Same weapon or similar."

"That does warrant a huh," Nick said thoughtfully. "So, what's the connection here? The two guys who died have a record? Anything to warrant violence?"

"Just drunken disorderly. And get this, they caught the guy who did it according to this." Okocha pointed to his screen. "Weird huh? They were found in the home of the guy who did it, Burak Hassan. They were friends. His first words as they came through the door were, 'I did it, it was me, I killed them.'"

"He in jail?"

"He's in an asylum," Okocha said, reading aloud from the screen. "Deemed mentally unfit to stand trial. Those nine words are all he says now. Hasn't said what sort of weapon was used, how he did it or even why. Just that he did. Doesn't even eat unless he's fed. He's pretty much a vegetable."

"So probably not our killer then," Nick said sarcastically. "Will, we've not seen a weapon like this before. You think it's really possible two of them exist?"

"Well you never know," Okocha said. "I mean this is just the most recent example. If we go back further…"

"I'm not interested in the past," Nick said, regretted immediately the way he'd said it. "I meant to say, I want to know about the present. So, if we take it that they're connected…"

"Perhaps a false conclusion but go on."

He ignored Okocha's comment and the sarcasm in his tone. "If we assume they're connected, then they had to have gotten here somehow. They can't have been on the island all the time. We need to have a look at arrivals on the island about the time Sharon was killed. Within a period of two days."

"I'm not sure," Okocha said. "I mean, okay, they were found on the ninth, assumed the kills were at max forty-eight hours old and Sharon was killed on the twenty-second… Who knows what happened in that period…"

"So, go back further then. It's a, what half day flight minimum from that part of Serran to here, assume that they got on a flight immediately after killing the men and framing Hassan, it'd still be late on the tenth, early eleventh by the time they got here. Earliest. We need to check it all out. Has to be something."

"Wow, you want anything else while we're at it?" Okocha asked dryly. "That still has to be hundreds of people. Conservative estimate. Probably closer to thousands maybe."

Nick leaned forward in his seat, his face screwed up in concentration as he thought things through. He rested his elbows on his knees and mused it over as Okocha sat watching him. He wasn't just thinking about Sharon now but about everything else that had happened since this tournament had started, the terrorism at the hospital, the attempted kidnapping, the murders, the attacks. So many isolated events to sort through. Isolated events across the same background. Something started to stir in the deep recesses of his mind, the gestation of an idea that sounded better the more it started to take shape.

"Ion emissions," he said eventually.

"Really?" Okocha asked, just as dryly as his previous comment. "You spend all that time thinking and you come up with ion emissions? Identifying the ion emissions of a ships engine drive is not going to…"

"Compare any ships that departed the Latalya area with any that arrived in this area," Nick said. "See if we can get a connection."

The reason most commercial companies used the slower, blimp-like methods of air travel was simply a matter of cost, their engines were smaller, more efficient, they worked with the air currents instead of against it, supporting rather than straining. When it came to fuelled aircraft, mainly used by industrial and private companies as well as the military for transport and travel, the engines were large, they used a great deal more fuel and produced a lot more energy, the resulting emissions producing an ion efflux residue exclusive to the craft based on the specifics of their engine and their output. A residue quantifiable and trackable, given the right equipment "And while we're on it, correlate any sort of data for ships departing or arriving this island since the tournament started. Both commercial and private."

"You don't ask for much, do you?" Okocha asked. That dry tone in his voice was starting to grate. He clenched his fist together, ground his teeth and tried to suck it up. It was quite an effort, he had to admit. Why couldn't he understand how desperate things were here? He didn't need this constant questioning. Unfortunately for Nick, what he did need was Okocha's help and kicking off about the way he did things wasn't going to help.

"Just a little peace of mind. Some closure. Justice. That all sound okay to you?"

He just about managed to keep the sarcasm out of his voice. If Okocha could do dry, Nick could do sarcasm. Anything to keep his mind off the chasm in his stomach.

"Okay, anything else?"

It had taken a good several hours to work across the data, considering most of the people who had arrived at the tournament for the start had come by boat, there'd been more air traffic coming and going than expected. It had all been a logistical thing. More people could be transported by boat than by air and it was cheaper for the ICCC who'd laid the boats on to the island. The same number of people coming by air as by boat would have been vastly more expensive. That said, it felt like the number of people who could afford air travel was rising. Several hours of gazing at incoming and outgoing aircraft via the spectrometer, cataloguing each into its own ion grouping, and he was ready to scream. This was the part of Unisco work that nobody ever spoke about. It wasn't all fights and shootouts. Sometimes you needed to think as well.

"Maybe they came by boat," Okocha eventually said. "You ever think that?"

"Thought they stopped laying on cheap boat travel after the knockout stage started," Nick replied, not taking his eyes off the screen.

His eyes felt like they'd start bleeding if he stared at it any longer, but he couldn't pull away. "It wouldn't be any cheaper to get here that way, it'd be a lot slower for sure."

"Security would be tighter in the air though," Okocha said. "How would you get a weapon through the aeroport checks?"

"We don't even know what this weapon looks like," Nick shot back. "It might be one of those that you know when you see but I wouldn't bet on it. Don't forget there are very few instances of weapons like these on record. Who's to say it'd even be picked up by a scanner?" Okocha's search on a different terminal had come up with more instances a similar weapon had been used on a victim, none of them recently. Most of them were more than five years old. Quite a few were older than ten. There was one which went back fifty years to Nick's home city of Belderhampton. Interesting but hardly relevant. "You know, compared to a blaster or a knife. And anyway, those scans aren't fool proof. They're only considered good until some idiot manages to fool them. And I know it hasn't happened yet, but there's always a way. Probably has happened before, we just haven't heard about it."

Okocha shrugged. "You know, there sure are a lot of Reims flights incoming to this place," he said. "Go figure that one out."

"Well they did pay for it..." Nick said, pausing midway through his sentence, his mind catching up with his mouth. "Hey, let's have a look at the times. Was there one in on the day Sharon was killed?" Her name brought a stab of grief to his gut, he allowed himself a moment to find his composure.

"Hold on..." Okocha hummed to himself as his fingers danced across the keyboard. "Oh yeah, there was actually. Landed in the morning, took off early afternoon. Two figures arrived and departed, in-kingdom flight so they didn't have to show any documents. Departure location not registered, destination unknown. Trying to get images of them now..."

Now visibly interested, Nick looked at Okocha's screen, footage from the Carcaradis Island aeroport hangar cycling swiftly, until it lit up like a firework display for a good several seconds before returning to normal to show the Reims ship in a hanger on its own. Only a few aeroport staffed lurked, none of them really paying attention to anything other than their job. "Well that can't be coincidence," Okocha said. "Just like the hotel."

Nick leaned back in his chair, thinking about what it might mean. Okocha was right, of course. There was not a way in the hells this could be coincidence. Two men got off a Reims airship, nobody seemed to have caught an electronic glimpse of them, someone died and not long after, they departed. It screamed guilty. Okocha's words echoed in his mind about plenty of Reims flights coming in and out. Surely if people were coming to watch from the company, it'd be easier for them to hire rooms and keep them there, rather than trafficking them in and out. Unless it was a rotation of people. Suddenly, he found himself thinking about all the other strange occurrences on the island since the tournament had started.

"Let's have a look at all the dates that Reims aircraft landed and took off," he said. "See what we can find." This had started by being about Sharon. Somehow now, he had the feeling it was going to turn into so much more, something that simultaneously terrified and excited him. Maybe, just maybe they'd stumbled on something. Maybe they'd caught a break. And if it did crack the whole mystery wide open, then he hoped wherever Sharon was, she'd consider it something they wouldn't have done without her death. It might console her. It wouldn't him though. The price would always be too steep from a personal point of view.

It was still a few long moments before Okocha returned with the relevant information, putting it up on the screen in front of them in double quick time. "Okay, so here are the dates," Okocha said. "Let's have a look through them, see if we can attach anything meaningful to when they were." He ran a finger across his screen. "Ouch! I remember that all too well. That was when the hospital was attacked. Came in with... Fifteen?! Bloody hell! An in-kingdom flight left with one man shortly before the siege was broken by Agent Derenko and Wilsin's teams."

"Two occurrences don't make a pattern," Nick said. "What else we got?" He ran his eyes down the list, drummed the desk with his fingers. He was starting to tire, his body ached with weariness and his hand throbbed from unhealed cuts. "Just let me see... Oh crap!"

He pointed to a date, grimaced and as Okocha saw it, he joined in. "Oh dear."

"Yeah. Starting to think this is a worrying pattern," Nick said. He jabbed it with a finger, bringing the details up in front of him. "Arrived on the morning, one arriving passenger... The boss herself. Claudia fucking Coppinger. Ship left several hours later, minus Ms Coppinger. Where the hells did she go?"

"Maybe she left by other means," Okocha said. "Let me see..." He tapped at the screen and several long moments later, a video of Claudia Coppinger appeared, showing her stepping off the ship, the footage temporarily replacing the flight details from Reims marked arrivals and departures. Nick studied it, blinked several times and swore loudly as realisation dawned. It was like a light had been flicked on and he cursed himself for not realising sooner.

"Son of a bitch, that's her!"

"Who?!"

"The woman who attacked Maddley the first time. The one who had an offer for him. I'm almost certain. The one who injured Wade." He was almost jumping up and down on the spot.

"Seriously, you're realising this now?" Okocha said. "How have you not seen a picture of her before now? We passed them around not long back." He tailed off. "Her face was covered. So how do you...?"

"It's the way she holds herself," he said. "You know how to tell the difference between a rich man and a poor man? A poor man lives on the streets. A rich man walks the streets like he owns them. And with women it's even worse." He pointed at the screen. "See that way she holds her shoulders back and stares at the world like it's her own personal playground. Same body language. Don't forget I saw a long-distance glimpse as well. I knew I'd seen her before somewhere!" He shook his head. "Plus, she's wearing the same bloody clothes!" He pointed to the scarf around her neck, the same one he'd seen covering her face. "Fuck sake!"

He strode back and forth, pacing frantically all while still squinting his eyes at the video. "Will, it's her. I'm telling you. They make us study body language at the academy. Because sometimes you can't see faces. I'm certain it's her. But why? She wanted to make Maddley an offer. Why Maddley?" He'd wondered this before. Why Darren Maddley out of all the callers on the island?

Except... Maddley had said no. It had backfired on him. That was the only reason they knew about it. Because he'd said no, she'd tried to kill him, and it had caused a disturbance. That had brought him and Wade to the scene. If he hadn't said no, she wouldn't have tried to kill him, nobody would have been any the wiser.

"Says she attended Maddley's bout versus Sharon," Okocha said. "Hold on..." He dragged up Maddley's statement about the whole thing, they both quickly read through and looked at each other. If it had answers, they weren't going to be immediately clear. Nick had always heard that a tired mind was a focused mind and right now he was focused solely on the problem, his grief momentarily forgotten, even a little excitement within him, the thought that answers were just out of reach. He read the statement again, not sure what he was looking for. "Let's see..." He started to read aloud in hopes of jogging his mind a little more. "Condolences. Offers. New world. Rage against the current one..."

"Irony," Okocha said. "Given she's one of the wealthiest in this one."

"Think she might want even more in the new one," Nick said. "Why Maddley?"

"He has that tragic family history," Okocha said. "There is that."

"Doubt it but maybe. He did have that run in with Sharon extending, but they made it up. I was there. It was touching." Remembering that was more painful than he wanted to admit.

"Yeah but Claudia Coppinger wouldn't have known they made up. She at least implied it once or twice..."

"Maddley went into meltdown too," Nick said. "Remember after the bout?"

"Oh yeah, classic. There's been a few of them here this time huh?"

Nick laughed along, nodding in agreement until suddenly he wasn't, the bobbing of his head stopping as another thought struck him. "Harvey Rocastle was working for Reims, wasn't he?"

"Yeah? What he claimed to Mia Arnholt."

"Looking for them to sponsor talent on the spirit calling stage."

"Yeah?" Okocha was starting to sound bored, like he'd lost interest in this track of the conversation. Either that or he couldn't work out where Nick was going with it. "What of it?"

"I always thought that sounded a flimsy excuse. I suspected, given what came afterwards, he was hunting Mia Arnholt. Her brother was here; she might show up to support him. What he tried with her might have been an opportunist attack. Suspected but didn't pay much creed to, anyway," Nick added. "What if, just humour me here. What if Rocastle was running the same deal to spirit callers as Coppinger offered Maddley?"

"I think that's a pretty big assumption," Okocha said. "And do you have proof?"

Nick shook his head. "Not right this moment. But it can be corroborated easily enough, I imagine. Consider she wanted to kill Maddley to stop him from talking. If someone did agree, she probably wouldn't want them to be in touch with the people they know on a frequent basis. It might lead to awkward questions." He pointed at the list again. "And they had to get off the island somehow. If you examine the passenger manifestos, I imagine..."

"Holy crap," Okocha said. "That's impressive." He paused for a moment, considering things in silence. "It also explains why they might have wanted Rocastle back. I wouldn't want him telling us all this if he was working for me. It explains why he couldn't pitch to Maddley either. He was on the run."

"Hello, is that Madame Ulikku?" Okocha asked into the caller. Between them, they'd gotten a decent list together of all the callers they'd either confirmed to have left on a Reims ship or who had taken some sort of swipe at the establishment, a competitor or the system following a negative result. There'd been a few over the tournament so far, though none recently. Privately Nick blamed the media, forcing the loser in front of the cameras when blood was still burning hot. Just because a lot of people took part in spirit calling didn't mean they had the temperament for it. Nick was running down video footage, Okocha had made the call to the family of the most prominent name on the list.

"Good, good. Yeah, this is Agent Okocha with the United International Spiritual Control Organisation, I just need to ask you a few quick questions... Yeah, it is a Vazaran name. Yeah, I do come from there. Nice place, I know. Madame Ulikku, it's about your..." Nick glanced sideways at this bit. He wondered how Okocha was going to deal with it tastefully. Reda Ulikku, that crazed Varykian had had that androgyny thing going on and although his bio officially listed him as male, it was hard to tell what sort of reaction it would get. Word of mouth told you all sorts of things.

"It's about Reda Ulikku, a relative of yours I believe. The name came up in the context of one of our investigations and I just wondered if you'd heard from him recently?" Nick nodded his approval and settled back to watch his reactions. "No, no, he's not in any trouble but we're just taking precautions. Yeah, I'm sure he's a lovely boy. Okay. Oh, that sounds nice. Yep. Yep. I see. Alright. Nice. Okay."

As he disconnected the call, Okocha let out a big sigh of frustration. "Bloody typical woman. Talk all day when it's not her footing the bill. Anyway, she heard from him about three weeks ago after he was knocked out, he said he'd gotten an offer from some big company and he was going to be out of touch thinking about it."

"Well that sounds promising," Nick said. "A few more?" He said it lightly, but he knew they had to. If they established a pattern, a series of connections, then they could take it to Arnholt. And then things would get interesting.

"We have a comprehensive list of all these individuals who have gone off the grid following contact with Reims," Nick said, looking his boss in the eye. "This isn't including Darren Maddley, but we've got Reda Ulikku, Weronika Saarth, Sophie Black, Paul Foster, Emma Johnson, Stewart Platt, Buck Brady... None of them are available. Most of them were good enough to make it here but they were roundly spanked when they did. They must have had a tempting offer."

"We have passenger records from Reims issued ships," Okocha said. "All of them left on them, all bar Ulikku and Saarth, in the company of Harvey Rocastle. All of them displayed a sense of agitation in the media a sense of dissatisfaction. Saarth complained her opponent beat her with a spirit he hadn't even claimed and was clamouring for the rules to be changed. Ulikku claimed Arventino threw her bout against her brother. Sophie Black said the ICCC had given her a tough pot because her father had annoyed Ritellia in the past..."

"Doesn't bode well for any kids Kate Kinsella might have," Arnholt said thoughtfully, before looking back across the files. "Anyway, I can't..."

"Reims ships were also on the island at the same time as the two major terrorist incidents, as well as one on the day Sharon was murdered," Nick continued. "And there's the little matter of Claudia Coppinger being the crazy bitch who tried to murder Maddley and Wade."

"You're absolutely sure about this?" Arnholt said. "Because if you're wrong..." He let it hang for several moments.

"It's her," Nick said. "Can't fake body language easily. It's something you need to work at and she wasn't even trying. Plus, what chance of two people wandering around in the same clothes. A dozen little things adding up to one picture."

"Huh," Arnholt mused. "So, with all this in mind, what do we intend to do about it? I can have an arrest warrant issued but most of this is circumstantial at best and I'm not sure whether it would hold up. We don't know her motives, other than some vagueness involving a mythical island and delusions of grandeur, neither of which are a crime. We'll have tipped our hand for nothing."

"It's a tricky one," Okocha said. "We need a plan."

"Sir," Nick said. "I didn't want to spread this wide. Just in case. I think the fewer people who know about this the better. I trust Okocha. He was the only one who could help me here. If he goes bad, we're all screwed." He shot a sideways glance at him. "No offence."

"None taken."

"And I believe in you to do the right thing," Nick said. "If I can't put you above suspicion..."

"I appreciate your loyalty, Agent Roper," Arnholt said. "Still, I agree with you. The less people that know about this the better. Things can't be accidentally leaked that way. I asked what we should do, I'll tell you what we're going to do. We'll flush her out."

"I'll do it," Nick said. "I'll find some way of getting my displeasure at the current system across, do it in front of the media and see what happens. Based on current form, I should get an offer. It might get me through the door, I could get something we need to blow this whole thing open."

"What do you have in mind?" Arnholt asked.

"Honestly?" Nick replied. "No idea." He meant it too. "But I'll think of something. It's got to be natural and spontaneous. It can't look staged or they might suspect something. If we're right." They'd trained him in improvisation as well. Time to put it to good use.

"A big if," Okocha said. "I think we might be on track, but I also think that we might be reading too much into stuff here we probably shouldn't."

"Yes, it's going to be one or the other," Arnholt said. "Every gamble can be split down into that fifty-fifty chance. Keep all the odds you want, always remember it'll either happen or it won't. We've suffered too much here to brush it all off as coincidence. Agent Roper, I am giving you an order to do what you can to crack this whole thing open. Do whatever you need to."

He paused, his expression softened, and he leaned forward in his seat. He almost looked father-like in his demeanour. "And one more thing, Agent Roper... Nick. I'm truly sorry for your loss. My condolences."

Nick bowed his head, grateful for the words. "Thank you, sir."

The twenty-ninth day of Summerpeak.

Nick genuinely hadn't known what he would do at the time. He'd mulled it over for at least a day after, had been the first thing he'd thought about on waking and the last conscious thought he'd held before trying to enter that troubled state. And it still hadn't come until the day of Sharon's funeral and the inspiration had hit him almost as hard as he'd hit Ritellia.

Pulling a punch wasn't an easy thing, not while making it look genuine. There was a way to hit someone without breaking a hand, elbows and forearms were better. The human hand contained some of the softest bones in the body, the fingers were quite delicate in comparison to the thick bone making up a human skull. But a simple spirit caller wouldn't have known that and so he'd thrown a punch, trying to make it look as ungainly as possible. He'd seen the look on Arnholt's face, he'd winked at him as they'd taken him away. It had been a gamble.

And when Jake Costa had come for him, he'd known it had paid off.

"I always find the semi-finals to be the last chance for shocks. Once it's out the way, you've got a fifty-fifty chance between two callers who deserve to be there. You've got half a chance of calling the winner. Out here in the semis though, anything can happen. It's all about who deals with the occasion the best."

Choksy Mulhern speaking from the pundit couch before the first semi-final bout between Theobald Jameson and Katherine Sommer.

The thirtieth day of Summerpeak.

The whistle blew, and Scott watched as Theobald Jameson and Katherine Sommer went for each other in the first of the semi-final bouts of the Competitive Centenary Calling Challenge Cup, their spirits tearing across the grassy battlefield, ready to lay into each other.

Scott had made it a personal task to be present. This stage of the competition was a little unusual in that the last three contestants competed in a round robin for the chance to fight in the final, they each fought each other across three matches for points and the top two advanced. He was here to watch Jameson and Sommer, before he fought Jameson himself and then Sommer last. Privately he was pleased with that. Common consensus was those who fought consecutively had a slightly better chance than those who to wait between their bouts. Theo had been given the so-called favoured draw because he would complete his bouts first. Scott wasn't sure. If Theo lost his two bouts, he wouldn't have to do much against Sommer at the last. He could pretty much relax, learn her strategies and take it to the final where he'd put all the effort in. He wouldn't be the first person to do that. These bouts were one spirit each, winner took the points. Not that he'd want to throw it but sometimes you need to employ strategy a little more judiciously than normal.

Both callers had chosen wolves to fight for them, strangely. Not the same breed though, Theo's wolf was thickly coated, its fur the colour of iron and one eye left white by a ferocious scar. Scott had seen images of wolves like it, he got the impression they lived in a forest environment. Meanwhile Sommer's wolf was easily bigger, despite the coat not being as shaggy. What the thinness of its fur emphasised was the contour of the muscles beneath its pelt. Crucially, Sommer's wolf had both eyes, both glowing like embers against the coal-coloured fur. Both wolves hit each other, the one eyed one going for the throat. With a nimbleness that belied its big bulk, the svartwolf... Scott had heard the commentator in the stadium call it that... had darted away and spat a great gob of fire towards its one-eyed opponent. It had been Theo's turn to call a dodge and the grass still smouldered as the fires licked at it. The one-eyed wolf bared its fangs, muzzle twitching under the growls. It was meant to look intimidating, Scott guessed.

He couldn't help noticing with some bemusement it looked to be a mirror of Theo's style. He'd had run-ins with the cocky arrogant son of a bitch once or twice before the tournament, and in his opinion, he was the absolute worst example of what a spirit caller should be, brusque and standoffish as well as downright unpleasant in battle. Of course, the flip side was he'd won a lot more bouts than Scott. So maybe he had a point. In another life, Scott could have been like him.

Everyone knew he'd been training with Anne Sullivan and it showed. Scott had fought Anne Sullivan before and she'd not just beaten him, she'd absolutely destroyed him in efficient fashion. Admittedly some of them had been a while ago but still, they rankled. He'd look forward to knocking out her pupil. And maybe something else, if the rumours in those blogs Mia read were anything to go by. Note to self, he thought, never let Pete know you've just thought that. Across the last few days, Pete had slowly started to come out of his shell a bit, he'd promised to come to Scott's two fights here and for that he was grateful. Having his buddy back would be a blast, he knew it'd happen sooner or later if he gave it time. There was nothing else he could do. Pete wouldn't get over it overnight; Scott knew for a fact given the same situation he'd be struggling as well so that Pete was slowly improving was impressive. He was glad that he was improving, he hated seeing his best bud like this.

More gobs of fire came the one-eyed wolf's way and yet none came close to landing, the smaller wolf was just as agile on its feet, easily darting out the way. If Kitti Sommer looked bothered by it, she wasn't showing it. She just stood there, chewing her gum, manicured fingers tucked into the waistband of her jeans, one leg crossed over the other. If there had been something to lean on, doubtless she would have been. This might have been a training exercise for all the stress and worry her demeanour showed.

Privately Scott envied her, as another fireball went wide. He'd been chewing down his nails to the quick the last few days, trying to fight off the nerves. Nerves were good, he'd heard somewhere. If he was stressed out with worry, it'd only urge him on to battle twice as hard. That was the hope anyway. He'd need everything to get past these two, knew he was already being talked about as the underdog and it was starting to aggravate him. He might not have the trophies to show it, but he was just as good as them. He'd need to prove it though.

The svartwolf did something very strange following the next missed attack, it let the fireball go and then followed up, launching a sudden beam of pure blue-white ice across the field, miniature snowflakes floating to the grass. The one-eyed wolf sprang to evade it, the svartwolf followed it with the rake of the beam, focusing it on the opponent, determined there'd be no chance of escape.

Theo's wolf rolled to the side, a tight controlled motion and then shot back an attack of its own. The ice beam died away, the uniblast tore into the svartwolf's flesh, burning away fur and filling the stadium with the stink of broiled meat and the eerie sole howl of a wounded wolf. It made Scott's skin go bumpy even in the heat of the Vazaran tropics. A weird sensation, it lasted only briefly but that made it no less unsettling.

Apparently ignorant of its wounds, the svartwolf lunged from a standing position, great paws tearing the earth beneath its claws as it sprang on its one-eyed opponent, the difference in their size even more palpable as they closed in on each other. The one-eyed wolf hadn't stayed stationary, it too had charged, and hit the larger opponent square in the stomach like a furry missile, jaws ripping at the exposed underbelly. The svartwolf let out a woofing bellow, Scott thought he heard a crack, he suspected broken ribs, before the svartwolf got off a blast of fire, singing the smaller wolf's tail. Another yelp of pain rang out, the svartwolf taking the chance to bring its jaws down on the scrawny neck of its opponent. Theo had other ideas, his one-eyed wolf rolled aside, dropped to its stomach and spun out the way, one powerful back leg kicking out, hitting it in the muzzle. Scott raised an eyebrow, a nice move he had to admit. It wasn't something a beast would expect in the wild, Sommer hadn't seen it coming either judging by the way her spirit was now spitting out its own teeth. Around him somewhere, the stadium announcer was commenting how this was the first time he'd seen someone really give Sommer the run-around. Normally she was already imposing her will onto the opponent, taking control of the bout.

He'd be fighting her second, Scott knew it might be decisive and he studied her, not entirely sure what he was looking for. It was hard to avoid focusing on her looks, she might have been Mia's older sister. He could see some clear similarities between them in their choices of clothing, jewellery and body art. They even didn't look a million miles different, both slender, both attractive, both dark haired. Kitti Sommer looked like she liked it dirty in the bedroom and she would be just as eager to return the favour in kind.

He'd been lost in his thoughts, he'd almost missed the way the one-eyed wolf had sprang up and landed on the much larger canine's back, digging claws and teeth viciously into flesh, tearing away. Blood shot out in crimson spray, staining the one-eyed wolf's face. The svartwolf went berserk, bucking and jinking to try and tear it off, suddenly panicked and the crowd went silent as if anticipating something special happening. It was not a pleasant silence, Scott noted, if you were in the section cheering out their hearts for a Kitti Sommer victory. Most of them appeared to be guys of a certain age and style choice, most had tattoos that, this made him smirk, weren't even good tattoos. They looked like they'd done them themselves with a poor-quality ink gun and gritted their teeth through the pain, even as their hands shook with the agony. Most had beards. Most looked like the idea of exercise was an alien notion. Premesoir burntnecks in the extreme. Scott smirked and settled back in his seat.

Summoning strength from somewhere, the svartwolf found a moment and twisted the one-eyed lupine down from its back, a dull crash as it hit the ground. Some sections of the crowd broke into applause, a little too enthusiastic for Scott's liking considering it wasn't even close to approaching a knockout. Still the one-eyed wolf looked like it was struggling to move following the rough landing, Theo's right eye was twitching badly like he was ready to lose the plot. He can't have been happy, Scott noted. He should have had this wrapped up by now, with how it's gone. He's been on top and now it looks like he might have blown it.

Personally, he'd rather be the other way. Defend for most of it and then come strong at the end. It's not how you start but how you finish. Those words had defined most of his career, been the bedrock of his strategy, the cornerstone of his planning. The first bit of advice he'd ever been given in regards of spirit calling.

The svartwolf went for the one-eyed wolf's throat, big crushing jaws clamping down around them. Scott winced, the crowd went wild, once again sensing something violent coming. Twisting ferociously the svartwolf looked all on to win, the one-eyed wolf was fading out, blood gushing from its wounds. He saw the first glowing hints and realised something was going to happen, Scott instinctively threw a hand up in front of his eyes to block out the blinding flash, winced at the thunderous crack echoing around the arena. He blinked away sunspots, shook his head to clear his vision.

Huh...

Both spirits were down in defeat. The svartwolf had something red and glistening caught between its jaws as it lay in a crumpled heap, fur and muscle burned away by the uniblast. Bone could be seen in places, protruding ugly through shattered flesh. The one-eyed wolf on the other hand was missing most of its head. Scott nodded to himself. He wasn't sure if a draw would do him any good, because both would be out to beat him now. If they both did, he'd be out. He couldn't let that happen. Still it was interesting to know Theo's strategy hadn't changed that much. He'd seen his spirit was doomed so he'd gone for the suicide attack. The one-eyed wolf's throat had been about to be torn out, not much could survive that, so he'd chosen the devastating power of an imperfect uniblast. With it being fired from the mouth and therefore up through the throat, said throat being blocked by the svartwolf's teeth, the power had intensified, reaching critical levels until the throat had been ripped away and the blockage removed. Kaboom. No wonder the one-eyed wolf was missing a head. Theo had obviously decided gambling for a point was better than losing all three.

In a way, Scott appreciated that sense of ruthlessness his opponent had in spades. In another entirely different one, he worried about what that might mean when he faced him.

The time had come quickly, only an hour since he'd stood in the stands watching but it only felt like minutes, the seconds rushing by and Scott was starting to feel queasy about as he strode onto the battlefield, ready to begin his first semi bout. Theo across the field, still the same grassy backdrop but with hasty work carried out to repair mangled sections, gave him a tight-lipped smirk. Scott got the impression he was looking way too forward to this. Hands in his pockets, his gaze followed the last of the grounds staff off the field.

He already had his summoner in his hand and Scott's nerves were intensifying by the second. It was the first time he'd experienced a bout of this magnitude, though he would have been amazed if he was the only one to feel nerves like this. As far as he was aware, Theo was a rookie at this level too, yet still he exuded calm impatience and it worried him perhaps more than it should have. Somewhere in the background, he was aware the stadium announcer was going through the rules for the benefit of anyone who'd been living under a rock for the past several weeks. He could hear the dull thud of Theo tapping his foot impatiently on the soft ground of his caller area, he could hear the throbbing anticipatory hum of the crowd all around him. Mia was somewhere out there, Mia and Pete and Matt and probably even Samandou N'Kong and although he didn't know where, he could feel reassurance from their presence. If he focused, he might be able to place them but that wasn't important. The where didn't matter as much as the actuality, he knew that they were there and that was all that mattered.

Across from him, the video referee was whirring into life, Scott took a few moments of comfort in that one familiar crumb of comfort and then he mentally berated himself. Pull yourself together, you dick!

This is the single biggest opportunity of your life and you'll never forgive yourself if you throw it away! You might never do this again, so you best have no regrets!

He felt a little better at the tirade Not by much but some. He had a strategy he'd have to stick to. He could even feel Permear tugging at his attention, the ghost perched in his shadow, but he ignored him. This wouldn't be the ghost's fight.

Theo sent out a huge grizzly bear and Scott grimaced. Huge didn't even start to cover it, the giant bear towered over them both, its claws the size of Scott's fingers and looked sharp enough to punch through steel. Still he'd done his research on his opponent and he'd made provisions over what he'd used to counter every possible combination.

His own spirit materialised from his summoner and Snooze entered the fray, the two ursine combatants easily matched in height though Snooze had a huge advantage in bulk. Snooze's fur was thick, damaging it wasn't easy. If he was hoping for some sort of roar and a show of bear pride, he was to be disappointed. The grizzly let out an angry bellow and rose to its hind legs, Snooze only grunted and scratched his ample gut.

"So, we have slow and sleepy versus angry and even angrier," the stadium announcer remarked dryly. "Let the second semi-final begin on the referee's mark. Three! Two! One! And… We're off!"

Already Scott had to react as a uniblast erupted from the grizzly's mouth and he ordered Snooze to fall backwards to evade it. The bright orange beam seared through the air, catching the top of his bear's head but other than the smell of singed fur, it looked superficial. Snooze had never been capable of nippy evasive tactics but had enough weight to fall quickly and evade that way if needed. The bad news was he was now on his back, temporarily vulnerable until he rolled back into a standing position. Mia had helped him develop the technique, the roll being one of the spirit dancer's tricks. Granted it had worked a lot better when smaller spirits like Seasel and Palawi were doing it, Snooze and Sangare had shown trouble with it. Permear had just stared at him like he was nuts and walked off. Still if he ever needed something to work…

It did. Just. Snooze twisted his neck, flexing the powerful muscles beneath the fur. Just because Snooze sometimes resembled the average house in width, it didn't mean he wasn't strong. Underneath that fat was enough muscle to crush the average house into tinder. In an instant, the grizzly was upon him, swiping out with giant paws like a great shaggy shadow fighter, a flurry of blows bouncing off Snooze's copious belly. The sloth-bear gave his smaller opponent a puzzled look, and then on Scott's command, backhanded it viciously and Scott felt a momentary thrill as the grizzly hurtled backwards across the arena, bouncing off the shield and into an undignified heap on the grass below. That had to have hurt. Anything else would have broken bones from an attack like that. If there was, it showed no sign of them, Theo's lip curled into a sneer and he folded his arms as the grizzly rose to its feet and shook itself off. "Griz," he barked. "You're not really taking that, are you?"

Griz bellowed out in disagreement and sent another uniblast screaming towards Snooze, Scott already utilising the same evasive tactics he had before. It might have worked, had the aim been directed at Snooze. Instead it tore through the ground at the sloth-bear's paws, punching a groove through soil and grass. Snooze tried to roll again, suddenly struggling in hot mud threatening to boil under his bulk. Burns covered his fur and then Griz was upon him, not in any way debilitated by injuries. Those big claws raked into Snooze's exposed rump and it was the sloth-bear's turn to let out sounds of pain as blood was drawn.

Just as the wolf had earlier, that memory flashed through Scott's head and he had Snooze kick out blindly, but it was slow and cumbersome, Griz was nimble enough to evade, shuffling onto all fours and darting out the way before powerful jaws bit down on Snooze's other leg, tearing into the muscles across the calf. Still Snooze struggled to get up in the slippery mud, more and more burns and filth covering his hide by the second as he flailed in the sludge, all while Griz chewed at the exposed leg.

It took an almighty effort but finally Scott managed to coax some retaliation from his spirit and he felt the flash of pain surge through him as Snooze managed to kick Griz off. It had very quickly gone sour, he noted as he studied his spirit. Snooze was bleeding and burnt, could barely hold his weight on one side where fangs had torn into muscle and one giant hamstring. Griz wasn't unscathed but, and he could have sworn he could almost feel it, the anger rushing through it was keeping it strong. Rather than succumbing to its injuries, it was ignoring them in blind rage, fighting through broken bones and wounds. It charged again, Snooze threw out a fist to try and push it back, but fell well short and in moments, the grizzly was on Snooze's arm, ripping chunks of flesh and fur out by the mouthful.

He could hear Snooze's wails of pain, couldn't do anything to avail them right now. The sloth-bear hurled out his other arm, crashed it into Griz's side with blunt claws out, the grizzly bellowed half in pain, half in shock as it was knocked away, the breath forced from its lungs. Snooze lowered his head at Scott's command, half lumbered, half fell forward with the intent of delivering a brutal head butt. With all that weight behind it, Scott had seen it flatten spirits bigger than this grizzly.

It landed, he fought the urge to wince as he heard the crunch of skull against skeleton, saw the flash of light all too late as the grizzly leaped back with the momentum of the blow, simultaneously unleashing a uniblast towards Snooze. This time he did screw up his face in dismay as the huge blast almost completely engulfed Snooze's face. Griz landed hard but the sloth-bear landed worse, piled in an untidy broken heap, with no chance of getting back up. Worse, Griz did rise again, slowly standing proudly and bellowing a roar of triumph.

Just for a few seconds, the stadium fell into silence as the crowd tried to work out what had happened. And then the applause started slowly, breaking out into the rapturous as the announcer went along with it, screaming out how Theobald Jameson had become the first spirit caller to make the final of this year's Competitive Centenary Calling Challenge Cup and Theo was there looking a little sheepish with the attention.

Somehow Anne Sullivan had found her way onto the field and there she was embracing him amidst all the attention. Scott pulled his gaze away, looked at Snooze. He'd seen more devastating injuries but there was something about the great furless face with melted shut eyelids that filled him with sorrow. Despite himself, he walked out and gave the sloth-bear a pat on his mangled head. The skin was hot beneath his touch, singed his fingertips

"Sorry dude," he said. "Better luck next time."

"Told ya bagmeat," Permear said from his shadow. "Should have used me."

He really didn't like a told you so. Especially not from Permear, not right now.

It was perhaps the most uncomfortable moment of the entire tournament for him so far, Theo reflected as he found himself facing the cameras, all the journalists determined to get him for the first quotes following his triumph. It should have been the most satisfying but… Natch. He grimaced, adjusted his jacket and tried his best to plaster a smile across his face. He was aware it made him look a disturbed but to hells with them. He was doing them a favour by talking to them. Anne had already slipped away, nice of her not to stick around for this, but it had been nice of her to show up. Really nice. She'd been warm as she'd hugged him, and he'd noticed she smelled nice. Like some sort of flower, he guessed. Don't ask him what sort. They'd hugged close and he'd enjoyed it, enjoyed the closeness and he'd looked down at her to see her smiling.

"I like it too," she'd said the way she sometimes did, that all too creepy manner before fading into the background, leaving him to face the vultures.

"Before you all start," he said to the media. There had been something preying on his mind for a while now and he wanted to get it away from his chest. Something he needed to say. "I just want to make a statement." He cleared his throat, waited for their chatter to die down and then he spoke. "I'm glad I get the chance to say this as finalist and at this point, the favourite."

It might have sounded arrogant, he meant it to in its truth. He was the favourite as the only qualifier so far. He hoped that Taylor kid made it through to the final, he'd be a lot easier to beat than Sommer. "Everything I've gone through in my life so far has got me here, I wouldn't have done anything differently. I just want to thank some people. Anne Sullivan for one, just for…"

He almost tripped over the words, such was their unfamiliarity in his mouth. "Just for being one of the most wonderful women I've ever had the fortune to meet. I'd like to thank my opponents for granting me some semblance of a challenge on the way here. And I'd like to acknowledge my father for it. Because we might not always have agreed on things, well anything really. But in a way, he shaped who I became more than anyone else, I suppose the message I want to pass to him, wherever he might be, look at me now you bastard!" Gloating felt good. Especially at that fucker's expense. To say their family reunions, when they happened, would be terse affairs would be putting it mildly. "I don't care what you think or what you care because I did it! Suck on that!"

He grinned at the cameras. This time it felt more natural, genuine. He was enjoying the moment, even despite knowing the ICCC would be sending a fine his way. "Sorry about that. But it needed to be said. I've looked forward to that for the whole tournament. Any further questions?"

Now Scott was pissed as he paced his changing room. Just a few more minutes and he'd be making his way out there to decide his future, whether he went home or not. Then again, even if he lost, he'd probably stick around for the final. It had to be done, he supposed. How many other chances would he get to attend a Quin-C final, even if it was one he could have competed for rather than watching?

Still he had to concede Theo's words were funny, even if he'd heard the venom in them. Some people really had issues. It made him think of his own dad. Scott had never met him; his mom had never told him anything about him other than his name had been Ronald and he'd been from Vazara. That second part he'd probably have been able to guess at, given the colour of his skin. He wondered if he was still out there and watching. If he'd know it was his son. If he'd care. Whether he did or didn't, it wouldn't matter. He still intended to win, no matter what.

It was with that mantra echoing through him he strode back out onto the battlefield, swapping ends for this round, moving to the same one Theo had stood in for the previous bout. Callers could be a superstitious lot given the chance, Theo had picked that end undoubtedly because he'd not lost in there in the first bout. The way Scott looked at it, putting Sommer into the other caller area meant she was in one neither semi-finalist had won in so far. It might play some part in her mind, it might just give him an edge. He hoped, anyway. He'd take any slim advantage.

Let's play, Kitti. All the picture boxes around the stadium, one of them must have caught his grin. He wouldn't have been surprised if it came across as a bit idiotic, he didn't care. This was his chance and he needed to take it.

Sommer was even more imposing in the flesh, arms folded in a position mirrored by the garj in front of her. Scott had studied her choice for a moment, seen those blades and considered going with Becko to fight it like for like, blades versus blades but he decided against it.

Although the grassy backdrop in the stadium would benefit his leaf lizard, he didn't want to turn it into a fight on her terms. Doubtless that thought was somewhere in her mind, she undoubtedly knew about Becko and maybe, that was what she was trying to do, subconsciously influence his choice. If you could make your opponent fight on your terms, you were halfway there. The stories about Sommer told how she was a meticulous study; she could guess at what you'd do before you'd even planned it. That unnerved him, hence he'd already made the choice to be as unpredictable as possible. He didn't go with Palawi or Sangare or even Permear, despite the ghost's angry mutterings.

He went with Sludge, already bracing himself as the spirit materialised on the grassy battlefield and the stadium was filled with the stench of rotting filth. The garj, blessed with enhanced senses immediately recoiled, its caller wrinkling her nose. Some sections of the crowd started to mutter in the front row. He was sure he could hear someone upchucking their dinner. Already going for shock and awe tactics then, he smirked to himself. The video referee continued to rattle on the rules for the bout.

Scott tried not to think about how he'd acquired Sludge, a beast that lurked in swamps and sewers, exceptionally predatorial and carnivorous. He resembled nothing so much as a pile of mud and dirty water, two great luminous eyes hovering above a cavernous mouth. Like a sand hound, a mud-stalker's body was exceptionally hard to damage, its skin loose like liquid rubber, a semi-permeable membrane difficult to gain a purchase on. That they were poisonous as well made touching them difficult with anything less than a hazard suit. Browns and purples and ugly reds swirled across the grass as he hoisted himself up and turned to look at the caller. Scott had always had a theory there was hidden intelligence inside something that didn't look like it had much of a mind.

There had been occasions throughout this tournament he'd toyed with using Sludge but something in the deep recesses of his mind had told him that the moment would come. That time had come, it appeared. He grinned at Kitti Sommer who had at least looked to have regained some composure. She rolled her eyes in his direction. If she was bothered by the smell, she didn't show it now.

"Cheap trick?" she asked. There was amusement in her voice.

"The cheapest," Scott replied. "We'll see. Good luck."

"Oh, I don't need luck darling," she said as the signal to start the bout sounded. "I just need to be me."

She winked at him and suddenly her garj's eyes began to glow with an eerie effervescent blue light. Parts of Sludge's body started to ripple and shake as if a dozen invisible hands were crashing repeatedly into him. If he was bothered, he didn't show it. Sludge made a bemused sound. Grass died as he moved across it, what was left behind rotted and wilting under his trail.

At Scott's command, the mud-stalker's mouth ripped open and he let loose a huge belch in the direction of the garj. He could smell the gas from here, fought the urge to breathe. You didn't want that in your system. Not even close. It hit the garj full on, didn't appear to have any effect. Not until the beast doubled over and purged the contents of its stomach loud and violent. The calm smirk on Sommer's face faded in an instant, replaced by concern as her spirit dropped, knees, paws and blades all hitting the dirt in the same instant. The garj's bright red plumage started to droop, dripping with sweat and sickness. He'd seen spirits in terminal decline looking better than this one did.

That had gone better than he'd expected as the garj slowly rose, still looking queasy. Then it sprang across the field, a lot more mobile than he'd expected after inhaling a lungful of toxic gases and swept its blades into an attacking stance. Within moments, it was dancing around

Sludge, blades whipping through the soggy body, a squelching sound erupting every time a blade landed.

Scott didn't even try to counterattack, just ordered Sludge to defend for his life. He had his strategy and he needed to stick with it. The poison was slowly killing the garj, all he and Sludge needed to do was outlast it. The downside of poisoning it so early in the bout was the garj could now hit Sludge at will without the danger of being poisoned given that ship had sailed. He'd turned it into a timed bout essentially, thrown all cards off the table. Who'd fall first? Because despite being hard to damage, Sludge wasn't even close to being invulnerable. Sooner or later those blades would catch something vital. Scott made his choice in a heartbeat, Sludge's arms shot out in the direction of the garj, didn't come close to landing but it made the opponent retreat.

It was starting to look sick, any idiot could tell that. The garj's eyes were starting to bleed even as they glowed once more, and this time Sludge was yanked from the ground before being forcibly slammed into it. Those, Scott reflected, might be a problem. A mud-stalker in the air was infinitely less dangerous than one on the ground. They weren't intended to fly for that very reason. Nothing enjoyed being smacked into the ground with that sort of force. Righting himself, Sludge yanked a handful of mud away from his body and threw it in the garj's direction. It managed to dance away, a lot less gracefully than moments earlier. One of its legs buckled beneath it, still it just about managed to remain upright, supporting its weight with a blade into the dirt.

Scott hadn't expected the attack to hit home, he just needed to keep it on the defensive a little longer, not give it chance to regroup. How long did that poison take? It was different for different species, the mud-stalker's natural prey was birds, rodents and small amphibians, on those it took effect in seconds. On something larger, it'd take a lot longer. On the plus side, it was in its blood now, the more it exerted itself, the faster the poison would pump around its body. The garj coughed and blood dribbled down its chin, Sommer was starting to look worried and Scott took that as a good sign. It came again and this time he rolled the dice, ordering Sludge to move.

The mud-stalker twisted away clumsily from the first blow, the garj overshooting itself and tripping, its legs no longer completely able to hold it up. One knee came down into Sludge's body and came away bloody and raw, Scott caught the odour of something rotten and fought the urge to gag, the acidic poison already corroding through the fine fur covering the garj's body. Sludge swung out, caught it a blow in the side and Scott could testify from experience those blows hurt when you didn't expect them. It left a black handprint on the garj's side and with a scream it went down flat on its face, Sludge immediately crawling all over it. If it were lucky, it'd suffocate quickly. If it wasn't…

It wouldn't be a particularly pleasant way to die. First there were struggles, Scott could see the ripples through Sludge's body but gradually they slowed until it moved no more

As Sludge slithered away to reveal the defeated opponent, Scott didn't know which came first, the sound of the referee confirming the bout was over, the roar of the crowd or his own sudden enthusiastic celebrations as he dropped to his knees and raised both arms to the sky, elation suddenly filling him.

He'd done it. He'd only bloody done it!

"Even the shallowest puddles can have hidden depths."
Old Canterage proverb.

The second day of Summerfall.

How long had he been in this room now? He didn't know, time had gradually been slipping by, devoid of a timepiece he had no way of counting the minutes. Of course, they didn't want him wandering this place unescorted. If he were in her position, he would want to keep track of visitors until he knew where they stood. He had no right to be here until he committed to the cause one way or another and so he'd stay locked up. The only times he'd been allowed to leave were under the supervision of the two Taxeen guards for meals and they'd not been particularly chatty. Any attempt to make conversation with them had met stony faces and stern expressions. Maybe he wasn't speaking their language. After all, she wouldn't want guards who could be persuaded to deviate. It made things difficult as he pondered his options. This had started as a mission to go undercover, he'd volunteered for it and between himself, Arnholt and Okocha, they'd put it into place. The less people knew about it the better. It was always better that way. Protocol demanded that they keep it secret.

Part of him wished he could have told Wade though. He'd been in touch since Sharon had… Nick swallowed hard. He didn't want to think along those lines right now. Too many bad memories, painful to the touch, and he needed to keep a clear head. He could lock them down. He needed to. Couldn't dwell on the past now, not with something this important. If he faltered, then he'd fall.

On the other hand, he was entitled to grieve a little. And it might be what his captors were expecting. Seeing someone sat there stony faced for a long time when they'd just gone through a traumatic event. He could try and second guess all he wanted but the likelihood was sooner or later he'd have to face it. Ignoring it now was only going to make the pain worse. That much was undeniable. He couldn't put it off for long. That he was doing as well as he was, he found nothing short of remarkable, if he did say so himself. The pain he was trying so hard to ignore was like a blazing ragged hole in his stomach, constantly screeching in agony and injustice. Why, Sharon? Why? Of all the beautiful radiant souls in the world, why did you have to be the one taken? What did you do to deserve it? His eyes felt wet, just for a second and he viciously clamped down on them, rubbing them more vigorously than necessary.

His hand still ached where he'd landed the punch on Ritellia, something he might have enjoyed in more satisfying circumstances. Some people probably would never forgive him for wrecking a funeral like that. It was okay, he probably wouldn't be able to forgive himself. On the one hand, it felt like he'd sullied Sharon's memory because he'd had a part in making it memorable for all the wrong reasons. On the other, it felt like he'd done something necessary to ensure somebody got punished. He might be trying to delude himself, in fact he knew he was, but if it got someone caught then, it was worth it. There would be no greater tribute to her memory.

He'd heard it said in the past that that would be what the dead wanted, to make sure their end was ultimately something that mattered. Everyone liked the idea of a last stand to save others, going out in a blaze of glory, but in the end, dead was dead. They were beyond caring. They were the lucky ones in a way. He knew how cheap life was, how easily it could be snuffed out and the dead had it easy. Their troubles were over. It was the ones left alive who had to keep on going. He didn't want to think about how many lives he had prematurely snuffed out and while you could go on about the greater good, it didn't change that they'd had families as well. Families who would feel like he did now. The irony was not lost on him.

He needed to report in at some point, a task appearing to become harder with every passing hour. No way was he going to be able to slip his Taxeen escorts, no way Claudia Coppinger would even let him go if he said no to her. He'd be getting shot in the head, one flash of light and that'd be it. But what if he did say yes? All in the purposes of getting more information, of course. He genuinely got the impression she believed what she was saying and that was perhaps the scariest thing of them all. Nothing more dangerous than someone who genuinely believes in the words from their mouth. Belief was good, but he'd also seen first-hand it was one of the most dangerous things in existence, it created mania, desire, the urge to cause change no matter the cost.

There was something untoward going on here, she'd kept most of the details secret, but he'd guess it'd be nothing good for anyone involved.

Cyris looked shifty as he walked into the room, she could tell that much. Privately she despised the man as she despised all those whom she had entered alliance but there was something in Cyris' swagger, that arrogant sense of self satisfaction that made her teeth itch.

"Madam Coppinger," he said, effecting a neat little bow he managed to pull off with hitherto unseen grace. "Thank you for granting me my audience. And for the aid in regards of Mister Lassiter."

"How is he?" She cared not for his health but rather the loose end he constituted. If he remained alive and breathing, then there was always a chance he could talk, and she didn't want that.

"He lives." That sent a stab of annoyance through her. "But for how long I hesitate to say. There was some bad damage done to him." A little note of pride crept through his voice, the bruises remained on his knuckles, ugly and purple against his pale skin. "Anyway, it might have been easier for you to ally with him. I appreciate you chose not to."

"I was tempted," she said. "He was a skilled orator."

"I taught him well," Cyris said. "Perhaps better than I did my own son." He hesitated, scratched the back of his hand. "Had I not been aware of the knife, it might have met my back and I'd have been gone."

"I made the deal with you," she said. "I know what to expect from you. At this point, I don't wish to deal with unknown quantities. Silas was undoubtedly that. If he rebelled against you, what would stop someone else rebelling against him down the line? I think you'll keep your people in line from now on."

"And it doesn't worry you he denounced me as untrustworthy?" A little grin crept across Cyris' mouth, cruel and twisted. "The desperate gambit of a man so in love with the idea of being leader he didn't think through all the angles."

"Let's not bullshit each other," she said coldly. "You ARE untrustworthy, John Cyris. That's about the only thing I trust about you. You've sold a lot of your people out down the line to keep yourself safe. I'll work with you; I might even enjoy the experience but don't mistake it as trust. It's not in your nature to follow. One day you'll start to think you can do a better job than me. And you'll make a play."

His grin grew, almost to the point of being ghoulish. He could give Rocastle a fight for his credits in those stakes. "If you feel that is true, then perhaps I should do so quickly. Before your scheme comes to fruition, for it may be difficult after."

"Or you could go against your nature," she said. "For once in your life. Either way I don't care. I won't be the one to break our peace. It's good to trust. Better not to." It was her turn to give him a cool tight-lipped smile. "No offence, of course."

"None taken. We all have our demons." Cyris made a show of deference, swinging both hands out by his sides, palms raised upwards and outstretched. If he was insulted by her words, he didn't show it. "Mine just so happen to be grander than anyone else's. We're all capable of greatness, Madam Coppinger. Do we wait for greatness to find us or do we just simply take it? Personally, I've always liked that last option. Find someone who's nearly there and usurp it for yourself."

"Of course, Silas doubtless felt the same way," she said. "And look what happened to him."

"Those who move close to the sun risk getting burned."

"No, those who move close to the sun are going to get burned, it's a matter of when, not if," she said.

Cyris let out a nervous bray of laughter, one that was entirely betrayed by his all-too calm range of body language. "And on that note, I require to ask you for a favour."

She balled her hands into fists, her nails digging rents into the palms of her hands. What the hells did he want now? She didn't know and honestly, she worried. She'd given him a lot, ensured he kept a hold of his power base, as well as his life as well and now he wanted more.

"Is that right?" she asked.

"I want off for a day or so," he said, gesturing around the room. "Off this ship. I'm getting restless being stuck here."

"It's for your own good," she said. And for mine, she added. I don't want you going off and talking to the wrong people about the wrong thing. That would end oh so very badly for you, Mr Cyris.

"It's not like that," Cyris quickly said. "It's… Okay, it's about my son. I want to go see him before we get this whole undertaking undertook. You've got a daughter, right?"

He knew damn well she did, the innocence in the question didn't come close to fooling her. "That is correct."

"I'm going to speak candidly to you on this, Madam Coppinger. I have not been a good father; I'll admit the ungrateful shite hasn't been a good son but there's been failings on both sides. I want to go make amends, see if I can reconcile with him before we start reshaping the world. There are going to be casualties, he might be among them. I might be. I might never see him again, I know he hates me, but whatever happens, I don't want it all to end without knowing I at least made the effort. If nothing comes of it, then it is what it is. I'll have failed, and I'll have to live with that, but I'll not say I didn't try."

He sighed sadly, it all looked a touch too theatrical for her. Like he really didn't mean it, his sorrow feigned for effect. The man was a master manipulator after all. Let your guard down with him and he'd sense it, he'd be all over you before you knew it. She'd known plenty like him and yet they always seemed to come up short. There was a reason she'd found herself where she was, on the brink of greatness and men like Cyris had failed time and time again doing it their way. Cyria, she'd snorted when she'd first heard the name. The true sense of a man's ego to name the organisation after himself. "Because," Cyris continued, oblivious to her musings. "They are our blood. We might not like them, but we love them unconditionally. It is the burden of parenthood."

"Admirable sentiments, John," she said. "But…" She paused to reconsider her refusal. If she let Cyris out of her sight, it could be catastrophic. Letting Rocastle and Carson go to the island had been different, a gamble but a calculated one. They could both be trusted, Carson with his strange notions of honour and his wild promises that some part of her doubted he could fulfil and Rocastle who despite everything about him hinting otherwise, did remain as loyal as a man like that could. He was too much of a coward to betray her, too afraid of what she could arrange to be done to him. Privately she detected a hint of masochism in his demeanour. After all, that he hated women was no secret. She knew about all his dirty little adventures, those he thought so secret. Walls had ears and he liked to brag in private. For him to let her lead him around by the nose, order him around like a dog, there was something not altogether right in him.

Still he had come in useful in acquiring the future controllers for the Ista Neroux, the spirits that would shape the kingdoms. That Rocastle still persisted in calling them his Angels didn't bother her. If he was thinking up pathetic little nicknames for them, he wasn't conspiring against her. As if he could! Not right now, not ever. Not with what she had behind her. Her clones. Her fleet. Her mini-Divines, bred to be faster, stronger, more durable and a thousand times deadlier than anything else in the kingdoms. Nicholas Roper would be the ideal leader for that group, the feather in her cap if he agreed to join her. He had the sort of presence to pull it off.

Did she think he would do it? Claudia didn't know. It was a problem for the future, for now she studied Cyris. He waited patiently, arms by his side and his face calm, expressionless. What if it were Meredith? She'd not seen her daughter since this had all started, not since she'd boarded the Eye of Claudia. Not much had changed in that respect truly, given the only times she had really seen her daughter was when she wanted something. Usually that damned wedding. Having a break from hearing about that had been such a relief. She didn't much care for most of the decisions her daughter had ever made, didn't care for the woman she was marrying either. That her daughter wasn't normal in that respect didn't bother her. That the whole thing was going to end in tears did, for Lydia was blatantly unsuitable, and she'd not been ashamed in voicing that opinion. But she only did it because she cared. Meredith would have no part of this, she wouldn't be the heir to everything done here, that honour would go to someone else unless things changed. But it didn't mean she didn't love her. Meredith was her blood. And that was all that mattered sometimes. She would have done a lot for her daughter once upon a time.

If Cyris was the same, she didn't know. Nothing about him spoke of a family man identity despite what he liked people to believe. It was common knowledge he made his son out to be the bad guy in their relationship despite the son claiming the absolute opposite. The two of them pathologically hated each other, the way she believed it. More than once in her research, she'd seen interviews where the son had dedicated victories and triumphs to the memory of his mother while shunning his father, sometimes mentioning him in derisory terms but never praising or thanking. That whole family was messed up. That the son had changed his name was suggestive, albeit it wasn't an uncommon practice. Hadn't her own brother done that just to get away from the weight of the Coppinger name? Alana had done well, in fact she had no complaints the way she'd performed over the last few weeks. Fucking Ritellia had been the one thing she'd thought Alana would quibble over, but she'd gone at it with gusto. Some of the footage was so vigorous that several times Claudia had thought Ritellia on the verge of a heart attack. That would deal with quite a few problems.

"Do you love your son?" she asked suddenly, her voice quiet and low. Up here, the engines couldn't be heard. It had been a requirement for her office.

"Of course," Cyris said. He looked offended she should ask. "He's family. All I want is the chance to talk to him face to face. Would you deny me that? If you might never see your daughter again…"

"The circumstances are different," she said quickly. They weren't that different, but she didn't want to hear more of his rhetoric. Too much of it would give her a headache. And reunions did happen. After all, Collison hadn't wanted anything to do with the family until she'd extended the olive branch. They'd reconciled, and he was prepped to join her in the upcoming war. "John, we are on the verge of something spectacular here. If we can keep the element of surprise, and strike at the right moment, we might be able to win before anyone knows they've got a fight on their hands. Because that's key. Getting it done before the counterstrike. I want the five kingdoms; I don't want a series of smoking craters following a long engagement. We have the firepower, but I don't want to use it unless needed. But I ask myself why I do this? These kingdoms are broken, and I want to fix them. They can't be allowed to evolve naturally for that will only allow more of the same selfish interests of the people running them time to flourish and that will not do."

He was nodding in agreement, an interested look plastered across his face, but she got the impression he was bored with her arguments. He wanted an answer. "It won't satisfy those who have power, but it will benefit everyone else eventually. The people nobody cares about. Those who have nothing but their families and sometimes not even that. These kingdoms could be a utopia but for now they're being dragged. But those who fight to claim it, you have families too."

She bit down a sigh, she knew this was a bad idea, but she couldn't help it. If Meredith had known her father, things might have been different. And she didn't want to deny Cyris a chance of a reconciliation with a son savagely indifferent to him. It might make him more amenable, buy her more time until he eventually attempted to stab her in the back. She wouldn't bet on it but at the same time, people were capable of surprising you.

"You can go," she said. She'd even surprised herself with that. "I'll see that a transport and a pilot is arranged for you."

"I can fly myself," Cyris said smoothly. That sent alarm bells jangling in her skull and she gave him a thin smile that made him recoil. Good. Nice to know she still held the capacity to intimidate.

"I'm sure you can," she said. "But you're not." You can get that idea right out of your nasty little mind. She didn't say the last part aloud. She wanted to. Antagonising him unnecessarily was dangerous, a risk not worth taking. "Our transports are unpredictable, and the weather is treacherous on approach to Carcaradis Island. I can't afford to lose you right now." Especially now your second-in-command is in a coma, inflicted by you, and there's no notable heir to commanding your men. "It is what it is." Her face gave nothing away. Neither did Cyris' but she got the impression from his body language he wasn't happy.

All one of a dozen little personal duels she needed to win every day with him and his ilk, those who each thought they'd best her when making demands. The trick was to give them something, not everything, just enough to feel like they'd come out of the deal if not winning but not losing either. It told them she had claws, she would use them and if she did, they would go empty-handed. Already Boka Arturs, one of the Vazaran Sun lieutenants had asked to bring his family aboard, his three wives and his dozen children. She'd flatly refused the request and he'd not been happy. She needed to talk to Mazoud about him. There'd been an ugly air about him and she didn't like it. Last thing she needed was him causing trouble.

"I suppose gratitude is in order then," Cyris said eventually. He bowed his head. "Thank you Madam Coppinger. My eternal loyalty to you and your cause."

More like to the rewards it offers. And by eternal loyalty, you mean until you to turn on me. I wasn't born yesterday, Cyris. Words she'd love to say. Instead she smiled graciously. "Of course, I reward those who serve me well. You should know that by now." Just a little jab but one that reminded him of his place. It could have gone worse. He looked contented enough as he walked away from her.

Seeing Collison again after all these years had been a thrill, one that still hadn't quite worn off whenever he came into her presence. The years had been better to her than to him, it would appear, it didn't look like it bothered him. Her brother had grown, not just older but physically, he was a girthsome man whose appearance hinted at a love for the finer things in life. He was running fingers through his ginger hair as he walked in, something he'd inherited from their mother. People had always said she looked like their father, he took after their mother. Weird how things worked out like that, she'd always thought.

"Claudia!" he said jovially. With all the bowing and the posturing from men like Cyris, it was refreshing to hear his enthusiasm. None of that Madam Coppinger stuff from him, they'd grown up together and he wasn't going to go on ceremony. And sometimes it was nice to be just Claudia. Something that probably wouldn't happen again if she succeeded. When, she corrected herself. When it succeeded.

"Col," she said. She couldn't help but smile. He'd always been the same, that sense of easy-going approachability that had infuriated their father. He couldn't give an order to save his life, he always managed to make it sound like a suggestion. And hadn't that just annoyed dear old dad? 'A Coppinger is there to issue orders, to be obeyed!' he'd said on more than one occasion. 'We do not suggest; we do not bargain with those beneath us. We see it is done.' He'd been the only one immune to Collison's charms, strangely enough. When Collison had left, she'd been the one to inherit everything. She'd had no problems giving orders. "What can I do for you?"

"Ah just checking in on my favourite sister," he said, dropping into a seat, spreading his legs with a content sigh. "Because you never know when the next reunion might be? Hey, when am I going to get to see my niece? Got about twenty years of birthday presents to catch up on, right?"

"Don't tell her that," Claudia said smoothly. "She'll take you up on it. Grasping little wretch. And it's closer to twenty-five."

"Ack, well I'm sure she's not done without," Collison said, spreading his hands out in front of him in a surrendering gesture.

"You have no idea how right you are," she replied, fiddling with the holocom. "Just stay quiet, I have a call to make. Something important."

"Always the same, always so serious," Collison laughed, yet he did oblige as the holographic image of Ronald Ritellia's porcine visage appeared between them.

"President Ritellia," she said airily. "How nice to see you again."

"Oh, it's you." Ritellia's voice sounded thick and slurred, like he'd been drinking. Or maybe it was the damage to his nose, there was still evidence of the medical work done to it there. When he breathed, the air could be heard whistling through it. Roper really had done a job on him. She hid her amusement, it wouldn't do to insult him. The man's pride only matched his stubbornness. To alter him from a pre-determined course often took a concerted effort and even more often, was just as costly.

The president of the ICCC disgusted her if she was honest. The corruption, the hypocrisy and the selfishness, all of them were flaws she could appreciate if not admire. But the way he'd sell out his own opinions for a few credits more was something that truly evoked her contempt. Before she'd met him, she'd always believed everyone had their one true point of strength, something they would cling to in attempt to salvage some of their conscience, a justification. As far as both she and dear Alana had been able to work out, Ritellia lacked it. Nothing was sacred to him other than the potency of the power he believed he wielded.

"It is," she said, keeping the loathing free from her voice. "I believe my condolences are in order, Ronald. How is your nose?"

"Sufferable," he replied. "But sore. Worse, the bastard seems to have vanished from custody of my island."

Your island? It was on the tip of her tongue, she swallowed it down. Apparently Ritellia also found himself in habit of claiming people's work across as his own. One more stone to be placed in the path leading ultimately to his deposition. By the time she was finished with him, he would have nothing, and she would have everything. She would have won, and he would be ashes in the winds of memory. She'd like dearly to be the one to set fire to him herself.

"Perhaps this is a warning," she said, unable to quite keep the amusement from her voice. "Only the righteous should seek justice."

"That man...!" Ritellia almost sputtered. "He broke my nose!"

"You sort of had it coming, Ronald," she said, electing to ignore his elected title. "There are those who fail to appreciate constantly reaching for the sun is the best way to get burned." She enjoyed that analogy, she had to admit. Maybe she was still thinking about watching him burn. "You intruded on a sensitive time, you poked the bear when he was hurting." The look of outrage on his face at her words was priceless. How could a man with so much supposed power be so clueless as to the way he affected the world? "Do you see my point? What the hells did you actually think you were doing?"

All the blood shot to his nose and suddenly she got the feeling she might have overstepped the mark. Of course, she found herself paralysed with not caring as to his reaction. They'd done all they needed to together, if he blew the whistle on what he knew about her now, he'd be going down himself. That would be anathema to him, would never give up willingly what he'd attained. It would be taken from him eventually.

"You... You can't speak to me like that!" He sounded insulted in his wheezing outrage and she hid her smirk. "I'm the president..."

"Of the ICCC, I know. I'm aware of that. Stop acting like a spoiled bloody child then. Your need to be the centre of attention at every given moment has long threatened to ruin what little shred of dignity you have in the real world." She smiled sweetly at him. Sweet but poisonous. "You really want me to tell you how it is, Ronald? I don't think you do. You won't want to hear it. Your precious ego might never recover." Still she smiled through every word. And she'd thought this might be a boring conversation. "They despise you. They think you're a joke of a president, someone who shouldn't run a street cleaning business never mind one of the biggest organisations in the kingdoms. Most of them wouldn't spit on you if you were on fire. Now, you might be able to deal with being hated, but not being taken seriously?" She laughed animatedly. "Oh, I imagine that's the real kicker."

His lips had almost vanished into the slit of his mouth as he stared at her through heavily narrowed eyes and she folded her arms, leaned forward to stare him out. He blinked almost immediately. "You want to be taken a bit more seriously, start acting like you deserve it. The first thing you could do is not press charges against Nick Roper, admit you were in the wrong and apologise for ruining the funeral of that poor woman! If you want to keep your job, I'd do that."

Some of the bluster that had previously been lost returned to him in a flash. "Woman," Ritellia said flatly. His choice of wording amused her. "If you feel that decision is in your own realm of personal power, you are flatly mistaken."

"For now, perhaps." She put as much menace in her voice as possible, even Collison sat bolt upright in surprised. "If you wish to gamble on that in the long term, then do so. A fool's gambit is named so for a reason. Think on what I've said. Is it really going to cost you anything to let something go and make a public apology?"

She disconnected the call before he could say anything else, the disconnection tone being drawn out in the same mocking sound as her brother's applause. "Damn, Claudia, way to put that guy in his place. That's something I ain't never going to forget." Collison sounded impressed, a big grin on his face.

"Ritellia is a parasite and he'll be squashed like one someday soon," she said furiously, finally letting her anger touch her. "Everything is falling into place, slowly but surely. My ascension is coming, soon I'll break beyond the failures of the flesh and into the pages of history." She noticed he was looking at her with something half-bordering on worry, half amusement.

"Sounds good," Collison said affably. "It's important to have goals."

If he had any other thoughts on the matter, he didn't voice them. Privately she was pleased. His lack of enthusiasm while unexpected wasn't to be discouraged. He couldn't depose her, plan to stab her in the back if he was apathetic about everything.

She didn't know how long Wim Carson had stood there before she eventually chose to acknowledge him. The man was like a spectre in the room, only the gentle rise of his chest and the flare of his nostrils showing any signs of life in him. His eyes remained closed, she turned her chair and cleared her throat. Still he didn't respond until his eyelids slid open to meet her gaze.

"Madam," he said. "I believe it is nearly time for our journey to start. I will help you with what you require, I have the power and the knowledge." He bowed his head low, glanced around the room. She'd almost felt like she lived in this office for the last several weeks, the one aboard the Eye of Claudia being an almost exact replica of her offices in the many Reims buildings around the five kingdoms, each built to the same design, awaiting her arrival. A bit of an affectation, an extravagant one she had to admit but she liked to know where things were.

Of course, some things couldn't be replicated. Not her most treasured possessions. She'd seen Carson eyeing them before but never with so much insouciance as he did now.

"There are some puzzles yet to have their pieces fall into place," Carson continued, moving towards her collection of artefacts. She couldn't afford to leave them away from her for any length of time, the smaller ones anyway. It wouldn't be practical to move the larger items around. The idea that some of them might get misplaced or damaged was just too painful to contemplate. "Have you ever heard of synchronicity, madam?"

It was a random question; one she hadn't been prepared to answer. Regardless she cleared her throat and gave him an answer. "The theory that everything in this life and any other is linked, that everything and everyone has a connection however trite?"

"You are a learned woman," Carson said, his voice lacking any sense of patronisation, which would have been easy for him. "One of many qualities, it would seem. But in some areas of knowledge, you are decidedly lacking. That link is the Kjarn." He smiled gently and moved to her collection. "Without it, life cannot function as it does. It is the force which lets us command beasts to our will, it is the fuel for existence itself. Some believe that is what made the Divines what they became. What we cannot deny for sure, is that we all have a path before us. Everyone has a purpose; they just don't know it."

"I see." She wasn't quite sure what else to say. The man unnerved her a little with his proto-philosophical musings and non-sequiturs

"But, sometimes they do know. Some have the self-belief that what they do is the right course for their life, they move their ship off the vector their life should have taken. They forge something different. Will the new future affect the world around them? Invariably, yes. Such individuals are rare, most lack the force of will to do so. But those that do are famous." He reached down, a sound of outraged died in her throat as she saw him touch her divine artefacts. "World changers. I see a lot of some of them in you, Madam Claudia."

Do you have a point with this? She found herself wondering, not quite daring to ask the question.

"I sense your impatience," he said. "And your surprise. My thoughts in this are that in the circumstances of these individuals, there are turning points in their lives, points that never they thought might be relevant and yet turned so important." He picked one of the items up, the one that Domis had recovered months ago unless she was mistaken. The bronze tigress, the bust of Melarius.

"Be careful with that," she said.

"Invariably," he continued as if she hadn't spoken. "The Kjarn makes its will clear to those who listen. If it is to happen, it will facilitate it. If not, well you haven't heard of anyone otherwise." He exhaled sharply. "I don't know how you acquired this piece, but it isn't coincidence. Where I will take you is a door and like most doors there are two ways through it. I intended to force my way, but that is the ill-advised action. No telling what could go through or come back or even if it could be closed again. You don't want uncertainty, I imagine."

With a sudden violent motion, he hurled the bronze tigress to the ground and before she could even make a sound, lightning erupted out from the tips of his fingers just as he had employed against the interloper.

A strangled cry died in her throat as she saw it strike the statue, saw the sparks dance across brown metal. All those credits and the time tracking it down had been wasted, she smelled burning metal harsh and acrid in her nostrils. She tried to move towards him, sudden irrational anger coursing through her at the casual destruction of her property but he held out his other arm and an invisible force gripped her tightly in place, too secure to move. She could only watch as the statue dissolved into a puddle of brown goop on her carpet...

Except...

Suddenly she could move again, watched as the small item hidden in the confines of the statue floated into the air between them, a jewel-like shape covered in melted remnants, molten slag dripping to the carpet below.

"Or you could use the key," Wim said simply. "Unnecessarily complicating things has never appealed to me."

"And when Gilgarus and Melarius first copulated, they gave love to the world. Although they felt nothing for each other before, the product of their union brought it into existence. The first rays of love touched their hearts when their first child, Griselle, was birthed."
The first book of Gilgarus on the creation of love.

The first day of Summerfall.

His head ached and as he slid his eyes open, he knew immediately he'd gone too far the night before. A soft moan escaped Scott's mouth as he rolled over to check the time, finding it a little past afternoon to be a touch distressing. His mouth tasted like sandpaper, he swallowed, found he had no saliva and let out another moan. Okay, the celebrations had been justified but at the same time, massively over the top. Some of the memories were already coming back to him, the drinking and the dancing among them. He shifted in bed and felt a stab of pain rush up his arm... Yeah, he'd fallen over at some point. Slipped! He didn't fall. He was sure there'd been some Vazaran food at some point as well, if the gurgling in his stomach was anything to go by.

He sat up, glanced around to see if Mia was okay. The bed by his side was empty, her clothes were gone... Had she come back? He couldn't remember. Sudden rushes of fright passed through him, he racked his memories, hoped he hadn't done something to upset her. Or insult her. Or both. Groaning, Scott let his head fall into the pillow. It'd been going so well too. His stomach churned, clamoured for his attention. Whatever the hells he'd ingested last night was disagreeing with him now. He supposed this was why they called it a comedown. The previous day, just wow... So good. Just so awesome, potentially up there with the chance to be the best day of his life and it may yet be topped. If he won, a big if. But more chance of it than four weeks ago.

His life had changed since then, Scott reflected, where he'd been upon arrival and where he was now felt like the lives of two different people. It had been, he supposed, a massively successful tournament for him. He'd won plenty of bouts, just as many admirers, shipped off the potentially biggest most destructive distraction in his life (Jess would have loved to hear him describe her so), acquired a potent new spirit and then there was Mia. Scott looked in the mirror, found himself grinning like an idiot and quickly stopped. Life felt pretty good right now, he wasn't sure if it was a good thing or not. Nothing lasted forever after all.

Be good if it could. Even if he won in a few days' time, what did it mean for his future? He harboured no illusions he really was one of the best in the five kingdoms. Part of him knew he'd had an exceptionally fortunate draw to get this far. He could already see the media calling him the most undeserving champion of all time, even if the upside would be that he was still a champion, deserving it or not. The champion of probably the biggest tournament ever seen, how he'd remain until someone took it off him at the next one. Nothing would ever tarnish the memories. He let out a bitter laugh, threw back the covers and rose, rubbing his belly to satisfy a troublesome itch and headed for the shower.

Hot water scalded his skin, he gritted his teeth together and bore the thousands of tiny hot needles bouncing against him, raking his skin, his hair, burning all the ill feeling away. It wouldn't be a perfect job but as he closed the water off and stepped out, he felt a little better. By the sink, he reached into the bag and popped an oral mint into his mouth, determined to wipe the taste of the purge from his mouth. That hadn't been pleasant, the sickly bitter taste still permeating his taste buds. Several times he sucked vigorously and slowly the minty odour replaced the aftertaste of bile. That was when he heard the door open. He wasn't worried. What was there to be worried about? Who else was it likely to be but Mia? And if she'd come back, he obviously hadn't pissed her off.

"Scott?!" She didn't sound pissed off at least. "Where are you?"

"Shower!" he yelled back. "Out in a minute." He finished towelling himself, kicked the towel around the floor to mop up excess water puddled around his feet and then stepped out of the bathroom. She wasn't alone. Of course, she wasn't. Pete was with her and suddenly Scott found himself wishing he'd wrapped the towel around his waist. Two pairs of eyes glanced over at him, he caught the roll of Pete's eyes, caught Mia's smirk and suddenly he wanted the floor to open and swallow him.

"I'm dreaming, aren't I?" he asked, more out of hope than expectation.

Pete laughed, just for a moment, he sounded like the old Pete once again. "It's not one of those dreams where we have a threesome, Scott."

Mia reached over and punched him on the arm. Still he laughed as he rubbed the sore area. "Oww, seriously? You got one hells of a right hook on you there, love."

"Don't love me," she said. "Not funny Pete."

Scott took that opportunity to nip back into the bathroom, wrap a towel around himself and slip back out, an uneasy grin plastered across his face. He could smell food, saw the bag from Willie's next to Mia on the bed. And fruit coffee. "My patent hangover cure," Mia said, holding a cup out. It smelled like roast strawberries. "Since someone got a bit too OTT last night."

"Was a good night though, right?" Scott asked hopefully. The fruit coffee did smell good, he had to admit. "Right?"

"I'm not going to forget you climbing onto that bar and dancing to Queen RaRa," Pete said, his smirk growing. "That was hands down one of the funniest things I've ever seen." He paused for a few seconds, his face wrapped up in concentration as if he were trying to remember something. "By the way, you can't ever go back to the King Ichehano ever again. Management asked me to relay that message to you."

Scott frowned his brow trying to remember the club in question. He vaguely remembered the bar dancing, felt the colour flood into his face at the memory. And now he thought harder, he could sort of remember a pair of doormen trying to throw him out. They'd been successful as well, unless he was mistaken. Maybe that was why his arm hurt. "Yeah that wasn't my finest moment," Scott said, glancing sideways at Mia. Still his fruit coffee remained untouched. Gingerly he broke the lid and took a small sip. It was bitterer than he'd expected but filled him with a scouring warmth he found unexpected. "Sorry if I embarrassed you." Pete opened his mouth as if there were something else he wanted to say but thought better about it and clammed up. Instead he shot Scott a grin.

"You seem in a better mood," Scott remarked. He took another draw from the coffee cup, sucked air through his teeth as he swallowed. "Less mopey."

"Want a Willie's sandwich?" Mia asked. "I brought some." She held the bag up. It didn't take too long to consider it, Scott took it and shot her a grin. He caught the smell of fried bacon down from the still-warm package and upgraded his grin to a hug.

"Someone's affectionate this morning," she said. "Or this afternoon, whatever."

"Ouch," Scott said struggling with the packet. He glanced out through the cracks in the curtains, saw the blaze of the sun peeking through and winced. "I really sleep through to the afternoon?"

"Yeah, you looked so adorable asleep," Mia laughed. "Thought I'd let you. Don't expect breakfast in bed every morning."

"I'll probably have to get you it at some point now, huh?" Scott grinned. Pete jammed his hands into his pockets and let out a long uncomfortable whistle.

"Well I wouldn't say no," Mia smiled, Scott finally wrestling the sandwich out of the pack and he took a few great bites out of it, feeling grease run down his chin and warmth rush through his body. It had been smothered in Willie's Warm Sauce, a condiment a lot better than the name made it sound. "Just enjoy it, yeah?"

"I wanted to run a joke on you," Pete said sourly. "Tell you that the final started in fifteen minutes, see how long it took you to realise…"

"But I told him it wouldn't be funny," Mia finished. "You're welcome."

"Wouldn't have believed you anyway," Scott said, glancing at Pete. "I'm not that slow and I'd have known you were lying."

"You can do that? I don't think so." Pete smirked at him. "And besides, I think you might have if you were half asleep and hungover."

"Well, you're back to normal then I see. Crap practical jokes and sarcastic smirks."

"Remember that time I swapped your shampoo for hair removal cream?" Pete asked with a grin. "That wasn't so crap, was it?"

"Yeah, it was terrible. You didn't have to wear a hat for three months while it grew back." Scott furrowed his brow, breaking into a smile. "And that did backfire on you, remember? Because Je… Someone else also used that shampoo and they weren't impressed." It was his turn to break out laughing at the look on Pete's face.

"Oh yeah…"

"Wait, what happened?" Mia asked, a bemused look on her face.

"Well," Scott said. "You're a spirit dancer, right? You remember about a year ago when Jess… Yeah, my ex-girlfriend, don't make a big thing about it… Remember when she was spirit dancing in a headscarf for several months?"

"I'm not going to make a big thing about it," Mia said, shaking her head. "But yeah I think I vaguely do… Oh… She lost her hair?" She suddenly burst out laughing. "Oh my… That's fantastic, bet it killed her that."

"Nearly killed Pete, that's for damn sure," Scott said.

"For starters," Pete said, his voice annoyed as Scott bit into his sandwich again. "She didn't nearly kill me, I had it under control the whole time. I was in no real danger. It'd take more than her to kill me. I regularly face down rampaging rhinos for fun."

"You've done that once," Scott said, licking his fingers where the remnants of sandwich, sauce and grease lingered. "And it caught you by surprise as much as it did everyone else. Plus, if I remember right, you didn't face them. You ran like a scared little bitch!"

"You did as well!"

"Yeah but I'm not professing to incredible bravery over it. Also, now we bring it up, that's not brave. More like suicidally stupid."

"You two have had some adventures then," Mia said. "Sounds like good times."

"Ah not always, you see," Pete said. "Might have been better if Jess wasn't there."

"You'd say that about anyone though," Scott said. "Unless it was just you and me."

"Well we did have some great times though. Not just the rhino thing. Which was also your fault anyway."

"How was it my fault?" Scott protested. He wiped his fingers on a napkin in the bag and went back to his cooling coffee. At the same time, he moved over to Mia, slipped his arm around her waist and kissed her on the side of the head. He felt her acquiesce, her body still warm from the sun outside. "Thanks, snicks."

"No problem, flyboy."

Pete raised an eyebrow. "Really? You already gave each other nicknames? When the hells did that happen?" Without waiting for an answer, he carried on as if he hadn't spoken. "Anyway, it was your fault because some idiot decided he was going to train a big fucking fire-breathing dragon and the local wildlife got a bit freaked out by the presence of such a big bastard on their turf."

"Oh yeah," Scott said, blanching at the memory. "I remember that. Good times. And well, Sangare was a whole lot of help that day too. About as much as Permear is now. You know, doing that thing where they refuse to completely acknowledge your authority? That sucks! Majorly."

"Where is Permear anyway?" Mia wondered. "Haven't seen him for a while. Not that I'm complaining," she added quickly.

"He's still sulking after I didn't use him in the semi," Scott said. "I'll occasionally hear him come out with some sarcastic comment about the way I live my life or the choices I make. I just try to ignore him."

"That should go well," Pete said. "You know ignoring the problem usually doesn't help, right?"

"It does for me," Scott said. "It's worked for me really well to this point and I'm not stopping."

"Wow," Pete said to Mia. "And you want to be in a relationship with this guy? Incredible. Can you spell denial much?"

"Hey, shut up," Mia said lightly. "Just because you got a bromance going on doesn't mean anyone else isn't allowed near him." She stuck her tongue out at him.

"Bromance?" Pete asked. "We're just good buds."

"Yeah," Scott agreed. "Nothing weird about that." He glanced down at himself. "I should probably put some clothes on."

For what felt like weeks now, Kyra Sinclair had hidden. It couldn't have been weeks, but it felt like it. At most, it had to have been one week, she guessed, though the truth was, she didn't know, and it annoyed her. She'd lost a week of her life hiding out on this bloody ship, not quite sure if the hammer would fall on her.

Not that she worried too much about some of the rank-and-file discovering her. It was unlikely they'd be able to cause her too many problems, yet if corpses showed up with kjarnblade burns, the Vedo would know she was still alive and be bound to hunt her down. She held no illusions as to whether she could best him, he'd matched her once despite being unarmed. In hindsight, she hadn't been attempting to kill him, so everything considered, the result had been fair. Only the outcome wasn't satisfactory, leaving her hidden and hunted like an animal. It was the way it needed to be for now, but it didn't mean it didn't piss her off.

She needed to escape, she wanted out of here, but it wasn't as simple as finding a back door and slipping ou. She'd tried that already once and had nearly died. She needed another plan, preferably one that worked. Kyra had all but healed her wounds, moving from area to area between meditations to avoid a concentration of energy in one place. That could be tracked to lethal effect. She was playing a dangerous game as it was, but it was a necessity. As the injuries had healed, she'd carefully set out to explore her surroundings, mindful always of what could happen if discovered. Over time she'd found a ship-issue jumpsuit and had put it on to avoid attracting suspicion. At least she could walk around inconspicuously.

Nobody had given her a second glance... Well almost nobody. Nobody important. The crew around here were an odd bunch, a mix between those with the strange overlapping Kjarn presence and those normal. If there was an explanation, it was beyond her now. Not without further information. She'd tucked her blade into one of the deep pockets of the clothing and tried to get comfortable wearing the blue-green jumpsuit that was just a little too big around the shoulders. She'd rolled them up four times at her wrists and ankles, just to be able to walk comfortably. So far, she was amazed nobody had commented.

There'd been a guy, easily twice her age, he'd noticed her and tried to strike up a conversation. She supposed he'd been cute, if that sort of thing interested her. It didn't. She'd tried to brush him off politely, last thing she wanted was to attract attention by causing an argument. Or by brutal decapitation which had been a thought lingering in the back of her mind. His eyes had been the same colour as her jumpsuit, the green bits anyway and he'd had elements of roguery about him. He hadn't taken kindly to her attempts to avoid his attentions in the eatery mess.

Down below, she might have made some subtle tweaks to his mind with the Kjarn, up here she was less inclined to do so. Never know who might feel it. Plus, it wasn't her strong skill. She'd never been overly talented with dealing with minds. Not with subtle tweaks. She could break it easily enough. Bending it... That was beyond her skillset. She wasn't a Cognivite, not like her master. Sure, she'd tried it down at the mountain but that had been different. Any result at that time would have been a good one. If his mind suddenly snapped in this confined space, last thing she wanted was a big investigation as to why. Expect the worst and that way you won't be disappointed. She couldn't take the chance.

Her clothing might have been oversized but at least it got her into the eatery with minimum fuss. If she kept acting like she belonged, as long as she kept exuding an aura of confidence then nobody would question what she was doing. The food wasn't bad; she'd had worse on the road on her travels. Cooking had never been her strong point, anything that kept her going would do.

She'd started to judge the days going by in conjunction with the meals after a while. Two meals she considered as one day, one in the morning, one in the evening. That sounded about right. What was being served, the way the time went by, made it a reasonable assumption to make.

Two days and four meals later, she made the decision that it was time to start looking for a way out. Her first realisation was different coloured jumpsuits meant different areas. And lacking an access card, she'd been unable to get out of the maintenance corridors running around the ship like a tir rabbit warren. It was immensely frustrating really, being able to see the other people in public areas of the ship moving around, cream coloured jumpsuits and invariably smug expressions. She'd needed a plan and so she'd turned to Thomas Quinn, her not-so-subtle admirer. She'd sat across the table from him in the eatery and gave him her sweetest smile. The unfamiliar sensations made the muscles in her mouth ache, but she did her best to bear it.

"Morning beautiful," he said. "You look cheery today."

Kyra fought the urge to punch him in the mouth. He'd find out just how cheery she really was then. "Well it's a good morning, I think," she said. "Time runs together down here. Forget how long it is since I saw sunlight."

"You never go up to the observation decks on your downtime?" Quinn asked.

She shook her head. "Never seem to get the time." There were observation decks? Of course, there was, by the sounds of it. And downtime… She'd never seen anyone have any. They all just seemed to wake, eat, work, eat, sleep, repeat. Then again, something had to break up the monotony, she supposed. Not everyone trained like the Cavanda. That whole experience of learning made what went on here look like a pleasant experience.

"Don't remember seeing you at orientation," Quinn said nonchalantly. "Think I would have. Why was that?"

"Must have missed me," she shrugged. An idea struck her. "I was a replacement. Last minute. Remember that guy who got killed?"

"What?!"

"Yeah, something about burn wounds. And some psycho. I didn't get the full story. Just wanted a last-minute replacement and, well I needed the credits." Describing herself in that abstract way, she found that particularly amusing if she was honest.

"Probably easier ways for someone like you to get credits than come all the way up here." He leered at her as he said it and the urge to strike him grew stronger by the second. Thomas Quinn was not an unpleasant looking man and as much pleasure as ruining that face might give her, there was still the need for secrecy and escape. In that order. Short term relief wasn't going to benefit her, she knew that. Employing patience was the only way she'd leave here.

"That's flattering," she said calmly. "But I like working with my hands. And it seemed like a good place to put my skills to good use."

"What do you do up here?"

"Maintain the rear power shield stabilisers and their control core," she said immediately. It was a lie, hopefully one he'd believe. She added just a little hint of Kjarn influence to her words, pushed the impression on him it was believable. "You wouldn't believe the rate they degrade under less than ideal circumstances. And this whole thing seems thrown together so rapidly in places I don't know how it ever got off the ground. You know what I'm saying?"

"Don't let the dupes hear you say that," Quinn said. "They report everything back." He jerked his head over towards one of the guys with the weird presence. "No scruples that lot. Soulless bastards."

Huh… So, there was something off about them, it wasn't just her having a weird feeling. "Ah, dupes? Didn't hear about those." She managed to sound offhand about it, shrugging her shoulders.

"It's a secret but not a secret sort of secret. We all have an idea. Just look at them." Quinn jerked his thumb towards the closest group of them. "It's like, really weird, you get me? You look at them and it's unsettling. You'll see one, you'll see another and another and another and then you'll start to look closer."

Puzzled by his words, she did just that, scraping her chair around to glance at them. For once, she tried to ignore what she could feel and focus on what she could see. Quinn did have a point; they did have a certain type of eeriness about them. There was something cold and mechanical about the way they all ate as one, uniform in their movements. Their faces were blank as if they lacked emotion and from what she'd been able to sense, that might well be the case. It took a good few seconds of watching but she thought she saw it. Two of them had the same nose. Not just similar but exactly alike.

Dupes... Duplicates.

Huh. Interesting. Just more of the reasons she needed to get out of here as quick as possible. One of them raised a head, a movement strangely out of kilter with the others as they continued to eat and sniffed the air. The emotionless eyes turned towards her, the head tilted, and they focused in on her curiously. She nodded her head at him, smiled and then went back to her food.

"Are you out of your mind?" Quinn asked. Perhaps there was a hint of jealousy in his voice, there clearly was in his aura. Lust made men do strange things. He was just about old enough to be her father and here he was wanting to fuck her. It was amusing.

"What?!" she asked, letting mock-confusion slip into her voice. "He's cute." Behaving innocent like that did have its advantages. If nobody took you seriously, it made it easier to stab them in the back when they didn't expect it. Quinn wasn't expecting it. She'd seen the ID card he had, and she'd made the decision immediately she might have to take it from him.

Of course, there were varying degrees of force she could employ in removing it from his possession. One would be to kill him and simply take it. But she couldn't take the chance that his remains would be discovered before she got out. Or she could steal it. Again, not without problems. When he discovered it lost, he'd doubtless report it, they'd cancel the access if they had any sense. A useless card would be no good to her, she'd be back to the start once more. No, she needed to play this cool. And by playing it cool, she needed to inflame Thomas Quinn's passions. He was attracted to her, she could sense it and she'd done very little to dissuade him from then on as distasteful as it might be. She'd given him enthusiastic greetings when she'd seen him in the corridor, letting parts of her out she'd long since thought had been quashed by her master and his training. More than once she'd purposefully rubbed her body against his while squeezing past him in the crowded corridors, she'd felt excitement boiling deep in him like a heating kettle.

Their chats had continued in the eatery; she'd created a whole persona for herself. She'd graduated from the university in Blasington, Premesoir with a diploma in specialised systems engine maintenance and had joined this mission to gain some experience. Because after all, the pay wasn't particularly good according to Quinn, but she'd trumpeted the value of experience. She enjoyed playing the harp, holo-dramadies set in hospitals and long walks on beaches in moonlight (She'd tipped him a wink as she'd said that) and seen him lapping it all up.

It was a strange feeling really, something in her she couldn't describe as she spoke to him. An emotion tickling deep within her, both disturbing and troubling. She didn't think it was love though. She didn't have a problem with love. Emotions were powerful things but sometimes she thought they could be a distraction, which could be fatal. Maybe she was investing too much in the part she was playing. She needed him to believe it after all. If Quinn doubted she was sincere for just a moment, then the whole jig would be up, and she'd need to resort to more extreme circumstances for getting out. Credit to her, as arrogant as it might sound, he never once doubted her.

The first kiss they shared was just as confusing, he'd surprised her with it but in a nice way, it had left the confusion more palpable inside her. Throughout her life, men had done nothing for her. She'd hated her father and as much as her master and Gideon Cobb had done for her, they hadn't exactly gone out of their way to ingratiate themselves to her on a personal level, affection something sorely lacking from their interactions with her. Of course, that was perhaps the way it should be. When you had a bond with someone, you couldn't teach them properly. She wouldn't have taken Master Amalfus seriously if he'd have been patting her on the head and showering her with praise every few moments. It'd have given her a false sense of accomplishment.

Most of her affections, when they'd manifested themselves, they'd steeped towards the so-called fairer sex. Those of her own. She'd never gotten that. The fairer sex. In her experience, women were just as bad as men when it came to matters of the heart. More than once she'd found that out, she'd seen the truth in that statement. It hadn't been pleasant but there'd been many a woman who she'd had to leave behind without saying a word when something had been on the verge of development. Attachment was wrong. Only destiny was something she should seek out, look to be forever partners with. A few stolen kisses, several long moments of pleasure in a clumsy fumble wasn't going to change that.

And neither was Quinn. As nice as he had turned out to be, she had no doubt it'd end with her breaking his heart in devastating circumstances. It was the way it would have to be. Would she feel sorrow? Some part of her knew she would, just as she'd come to accept it would pass. Some part of her had already moved on, determined to do it with as little pain as possible. But that was against what she'd been taught. Pain was power. Pain was striking back with relish against those who hurt you. Closing yourself off was never the answer, the master had always said, only weak-minded fools afraid of their own potential do that. The Vedo had cut themselves off from the word, looking inward rather than out. They'd do anything they could to avoid feeling. They'd had this power and they'd wasted it, let it stagnate in their caves like bloody savages. Who the hells lived in caves these days? She'd laughed when she'd heard it, dialling it down when the master had told her they'd all died. What was the point in an eternal enemy if there were none left to challenge you?

Clearly, she'd miscalculated on that part. There was one here on this ship and he'd managed to best her, unarmed, there'd been something about him she'd long considered since their fight. He hadn't been at full strength. His efforts had been cumbersome and laboured, like a man going out strong because he lacks the stomach to draw it out. Somehow, she felt that if it had turned into a longer fight, she would have dealt with him in the end. Escape had been her priority. Still was. Hence her dalliances with Quinn. She'd been trained to be ruthlessly single minded in her chosen path. That she wanted to do it without bloodshed was just a matter of practicality. Gid Cobb would have done it differently, but he wasn't her and she wasn't him. She was better than Cobb and one day she'd prove it when the master returned.

She'd made up her bunk hole carefully, avoiding the barracks they had down here. Staying there would offer up more questions than she'd be able to answer. She'd seen regulators moving around down here, checking cards and asking questions. She wanted to avoid answering them, just in case. It'd be easier this way. She'd managed to steal a blanket and had cut a hole in the wall behind one of the boilers where it was warm. Squeezing between the pipes, she'd made herself comfortable for sleeping purposes before replacing the section of wall. Probably not the best place to bring Quinn back to. If it came to carnal experiments, they'd go to his bunk not hers. She wasn't going to let it go that far though. Last thing she wanted was him writhing on top of her unless there was no other choice.

Still Kyra felt like she'd made good progress today and tomorrow might be the day she got out of here. Settling in her section of cut out wall, she took out her kjarnblade and twisted the casing open to remove the k-crystal. The small lump of rock held all the energies of the Kjarn and worked as a conduit to power the fearsome blade capable of cutting through metal and flesh alike with ease. She held it in the palm of her hand, closed her eyes and opened her mind. Like any power source, it could be depleted over time and she'd neglected it for too long, largely due to other circumstances. Still it flickered hard with power in her presence and she felt relief, letting some of her own latent Kjarn presence flow into it. Just a touch. She didn't want to attract the wrong sort of attention.

The third day of Summerfall.

She didn't entirely know how much time had passed when she saw Quinn again, hands in the pockets of his jumpsuit and a nervous look on his face. She could sense he was really struggling with something as he approached.

"Morning," he said. He didn't move to kiss her, she sensed he wanted to, but something held him back. He jerked his head towards a side room. "Can I have a word? In private?"

Her senses were warning her now, but she kept her face calm. Forewarned was forearmed after all. With people all around them, it wasn't the best place to cause a scene. Not her, not him. Kyra cocked her head towards the room, extending out her senses. There were people in there already.

What the hells? She could decline but that'd look suspicious. Really suspicious. She still needed Quinn to get out of here. Or she could accept and go in forearmed. A hand dropped to her pocket and her fingers rested around the hilt of her blade.

"Ooh someone looks serious this morning," she said in a teasing voice. She put her other hand on his and smiled at him. "Not about to tell me about your wife, are you?"

"Just... Just come on inside, will you?"

He looked like he was going to be sick as they stepped into the room, she paused and took in the uniforms of the regulators. Neither of them was a dupe, she realised immediately. They both gave her the sort of look a hungry cat gives a canary and now the Kjarn was screaming for her attention, doing its best to warn her to their intentions.

"Hey what gives?" she asked, doing her best to sound surprised. "What's going on here?"

"Ma'am, we're going to need to see your ID card," the regulator on the left said. He was tall and sandy haired, the other smaller and balder. Both were armed but not with anything heavier than hand blasters. In other words, about as much threat as toothpicks to her.

"I..." She almost said don't have one. "I... haven't been issued one yet." They scoffed at that. She tried to keep her face neutral, but she knew the ruse was up.

"I wanted to find you, surprise you," Quinn said monotonously. "Went and looked to see what barracks you were in. No record of you on the manifestos anywhere. No last-minute replacements or anything. So, I asked the regulators. Had to be some sort of error, right?"

Her heart fell. Oh Thomas, you soft fucking idiot.

"No card, no right to be here," the bald regulator said, his voice high but menacing. She almost laughed at hearing it. "You're going to have to come with us, right now Miss!"

"I said!" she snapped, putting the persuasive force of the Kjarn into her voice. A tricky gambit but a desperate one. "I haven't! Been! Issued! One yet!"

The reaction was immediate and noticeable, both recoiled like she'd slapped them. Doing two at once was tricky, the effect was diluted. As far as she knew, she'd done it perfectly. But would perfection be enough? "I'm sorry..." One of them started to say before hands dropped to blasters. Shit! Something had gone wrong! The confusion was clear on their faces, they didn't know who or where they were, she could sense their fear. Behind fear, she could sense violence wasn't far. Kyra couldn't hesitate, her blade came out and suddenly the shorter one was even shorter, minus a head. The taller one lost a hand first, then stared down in shock at the blade protruding from his chest. Quinn screamed, and she span, gesturing with her fist to grasp him about the throat with the telekinetic force of the Kjarn.

Before she could crush his windpipe, the alarms went off all around her, a sudden harsh burst of klaxon horns and wailing sirens and inwardly Kyra swore. Oh fuck!

"Some people are natural born liars. It comes to them as easy as breathing. If you believe even a single word they say, then you've already lost. Of course, what happens when you don't have a choice?"

Brendan King summing up Unisco's policy on making deals with known criminals.

The second day of Summerfall.

"Incoming!"

Okocha's shout rang through the offices, Arnholt on his feet in an instant and out to see him. He never belayed that much emergency in his voice unless things were serious. He left a surprised Brendan King and Allison Crumley in his wake, moving straight to Okocha's workstation.

"What is it?!" he demanded, urgency overriding his patience. He'd been on edge for days now, not since the reports of Nick Roper being bailed out of the Carcaradis Island jail and vanishing. That was good, it meant there'd been something to the plan, Roper had guessed right. That there had been no sign of contact since then was more concerning. It meant he could be anywhere. His instructions had been clear, find out what was going on, report back and get out. Don't be a damn hero! Contrary to popular belief, he'd always found the role of the hero was to get others killed. Arnholt didn't hold much stock by the one-man hero belief. He'd seen too many dead men to go along with it. Heroics and the job often went hand in hand, or so the new recruits seemed to believe. Too much time with the organisation and you started to think otherwise.

"We have an incoming Reims ship," Okocha said. "Same energy output, same contact codes as before. After our discovery, I set up an algorithm to alert us when they came back and they're here! They're here!" He was excitable now, Arnholt could see, it was almost infectious. "It's coming into land and we know they're here." He was chattering excitedly now, almost jumping with glee. "We've got them!"

"It could be nothing," Arnholt said in a tone of voice that suggested he truly didn't believe the words that had left his mouth. "Get me footage of who gets off that aeroship. I want to see who it is. And if we have another camera skip, I want everyone tooling up and we go wait for them in that hangar. Give them a nasty surprise when they return."

Of course, this job took incredible balls. The mortality rate amongst agents and operatives had dropped since he'd taken the top job and he was personally proud of that. Men and women weren't dying as often because of the way he'd done things as director. There'd been those who weren't as impressed by the statistic, of course. One of his bosses... He grimaced like a foul taste had entered his mouth... had asked if his agents were doing their jobs as thoroughly now they looked as if they were afraid of getting shot. Fair enough, he'd stunk like he'd been imbibing all day and he was a lunatic at the best of times, but it had been unfair criticism. Their mission success rate hadn't dropped or risen, rather it had stayed about the same level of consistency. Analysts reckoned somewhere about the seventy to eighty percent success rate. Given the number of potential interferences in some of their missions, Arnholt didn't think that was too bad. If someone failed, they inserted another agent as rapidly as possible. Or a team of them. You couldn't win every time.

"Just coming in for landing now," Okocha said, watching every moment of the landing on the screen with almost wistful envy. "That's a beautiful craft. I guess the wealthy can afford whatever they like, huh?"

"It would seem to be one of the perks," Arnholt said absentmindedly. In his head, he was already putting together a team to hit the hangar. Derenko would lead it, taking Montgomery, Aldiss, Wilsin and maybe Sullivan. Her talents would come in handy. He'd seen aeroships like it before, looking through the press releases of the Reims corporation. They had plenty of them but what nobody had ever looked to have brought up was the way they looked curiously like oversized Premesoiran Tu Lar bombers. Uncannily so, really.

Given what they were starting to suspect about Reims, he found himself wondering if there was something intentional there. The craft had a noticeable curve at the nose of the ship, almost like a hawk's beak, the wings broad and impressive, protruding at acute angles, all with intent of cutting through anything before them. They weren't the fastest or the most manoeuvrable, but they packed heavy firepower and armour, were the match of a HAX in the air one on one, in theory yet their cumbersomeness left them unsuitable for protracted dogfights.

All this information passed through Arnholt's head as he studied the video images. They even moved like the Tu Lar, descending in a fashion best described as like a flailing duck. Still the pilot had some skill about him, no small measure by the looks as he guided it gently to the ground until bringing it to a gradual halt.

"Here we go," Okocha said. "Moment of truth." He was shivering with excitement. Maybe, Arnholt thought, he was expecting Nick Roper to leave the ship, anticipating the all clear, that they'd been right, and it was time to go to war.

If he was expecting Nick Roper, he was to be disappointed. But neither of them could contain their surprise as they saw the tall figure with the aristocratic face. Okocha very nearly almost spat out the sip of water he'd been taking. "Now that just adds more questions!" he complained. Neither of them was going to fail to recognise the man walking towards the exit. Arnholt had to admit, he'd been taken aback himself by his presence. Unlike Okocha, he'd fought to retain his professional demeanour. Even if he very much would like to know what John Cyris was doing stepping off a Reims aeroship. And there was only one way to find out.

Theo had looked in a decent mood since his victory in the semi-finals, Anne thought. A lot more cheerful these days. Out of his shell might be the better term. He still didn't like people, still found them annoying overall. And sometimes she thought he had a point. Some people could be jerks, she knew that better than anyone. She'd known someone once who'd told her that in battle, all illusions were cut away and you saw someone for who they truly were. Either they lived or died by it, you saw them rise to the challenge, you saw some part of them you hadn't before and sometimes you might not like it.

She'd engaged in so many practice bouts with him by now, she could read him. Of course, practice bouts weren't quite the same, she didn't even like calling them that for the same reason. The truth was she practiced the way she battled, full force and Theo did the same. No stepping back from that. If either of them gave an inch in their contentions, it would have been the end. And he was getting a lot better thanks to her training, she wanted to add with a flourish of pride. More so than him getting better, it had forced her to look at some of her own techniques and tweak them.

If she was honest, she couldn't see a world where he lost in the final in a few days. It sounded way too overconfident, but she had a feeling he'd have more than Scott Taylor could deal with. He'd be able to stroll over the line and shock the crowd. He didn't look to be struggling with nerves, she just caught the wave of quiet confidence and smugness radiating from him. That and the urge to gasp for breath. He was in ridiculously good shape and sometimes it felt like he could run all day given the chance. They'd started running together in the mornings and the evenings when it was cooler underneath the Vazaran sun. If he'd suggested it midday, she'd think he'd lost his mind. Today, the evening was warmer than normal but still tolerable. Even so sweat caked her entire body, dust clinging to her legs. Only another few miles and she'd be able to climb into the shower...

She didn't know which halted her first, the sight or the sensation. The tall man up ahead in their path, immaculate suit, resting on a cane or the sudden deluge of revulsion that tore through Theo like a monsoon of distressed anger. He skidded to a halt, hands already skittering about like nervous pale spiders as he sought something from his pockets. Already the man stepped forwards, hands held up in a gesture of supplication, but it didn't stop him. It went on a few seconds more and then his smile vanished from his sharp features. She didn't catch much from him but what she did sense made her feel dirty. Unclean even. Here was not a nice man, she could tell immediately.

"Calm yourself Theobald," he said derisorily. "You're making a fool out of yourself in front of your friend."

"Shut up!" Theo almost snarled. "You... You shouldn't even be here." She could hear the worry in his voice, she turned to the other man and tried to work out why he seemed so familiar. Not just to her but to Theo too. Maybe it was that they looked a little alike, the same scowl, the same way of walking... and the eyes. They were intensely cold and emotionless. Everything Theo once had tried to be, everything parts of him remained. He'd finally found his summoner, drawn it, even if he hadn't moved to activate it. Anne glanced around their surroundings, not many people about. The fewer the better if it came down to a fight. This part of the parks on Carcaradis Island wasn't busy this time of day and that was a blessing.

"You don't need that, boy." There was a hint of amusement in his voice. "I'm not here to fight with you."

"Yeah sure!"

His mouth curled up in the corner. "I'm not about to fight with one of the finalists of this fine competition." Anne thought she heard some sarcasm there. "I doubt I'd win for a start. I know there's a point where every son bests his father, but I'd prefer it not to be so devastatingly public."

This time he smiled at Anne. "The name is Cyris, my dear. John Cyris. Since you're wondering where you've seen me before. Everyone does. I'm afraid I'm rather famous, you see."

John Cyris... JOHN FUCKING CYRIS! She reacted with a start, not quite able to stop herself. She knew that name of course. There'd been flyers with his picture on all over Unisco buildings at one point.

"Despite whatever my son insists his name is, of course," Cyris said acerbically. He glanced sideways at Theo who was still scowling. Okay, that was strangely uncanny now she saw it. The family resemblance was strong between them.

"My name is Theobald Jameson," Theo said, his voice surly. "I'm not having the Cyris part anymore. I don't want people knowing I'm related to you!" He said the last word so harshly, Anne was surprised.

"Okay, I deserve that," Cyris said. "But I still think you're overreacting, son."

"Don't bloody call me that!" Theo snapped. "You're not my dad. Not in any way that matters."

That scowl… she was trying to think of it as Theo's but now she suspected he might not have been the progenitor, flashed back across his face before he pushed it back into the depths of his being. "You really shouldn't lash out at the people who love you. You should know that by now!"

"You don't love me!" In a heartbeat, the old Theo filled with anger was back, rising from the depths of his seclusion. The Theo who'd been broken slowly shattering again b she worried for him. She honestly thought he might leap on his father for a moment. "You're not fucking capable of it!"

"Don't swear at me!"

"You're not bloody capable of love!" Theo insisted as if Cyris hadn't spoken. "You only use those you need and throw them away if they don't live up to your expectations."

"Your point is?" Cyris studied him with an impassive expression. "Everyone does that, my boy. Me, you, her, everyone. Don't make me out to be the villain of this. It is a picture you cannot paint."

"Screw your damn picture you bastard!"

No love lost between them, Anne thought dryly.

Cyris nodded sagely, ending with a head bow, almost apologetic in its expression of supplication. On the surface, that's how she interpreted it. Beneath the surface… She didn't know. Below his mind felt murky, foggy, his intentions clouded. That was a surprise, she blinked several times. First time she'd experienced that phenomenon. Some people had that level of self-control. Everything she'd ever heard about Cyris, she'd have probably guessed he wasn't a slave to wild emotions.

"I probably deserve that. Theobald, you can't keep staying wildly angry at me like this…"

Theo cut him off with a bark of harsh laughter, his shoulders shaking with the efforts. "You want to bet that I can't? You're having a laugh, right? I intend to!"

"I just wanted to offer you my congratulations," Cyris said. She might not have been getting anything from him, but she did catch sudden surprise from Theo. He would have turned and walked away had those words not halted him mid-step.

"What?" He couldn't keep the bemusement from his voice.

"I'm proud of you, son. I've probably never told you that enough, but you've done good with your life." Cyris took a step forward towards them, hands outstretched in front of him. Still keen not to prove himself as any sort of threat, Anne guessed. "I know I've not been an ideal father. We never were a good family. When your mother went, we never really had much to keep us together. Blood only takes you so far, wouldn't you say?"

"You're not bloody wrong there," Theo growled.

"I can't change that now," Cyris said, almost apologetically. He shook his head sadly. "If I could, I would. But it's beyond any of us. The past is the past. I've done what I've done and..."

"Is this your way of apologising?" Theo asked, not quite sarcastically but still with an effort of disbelief in his voice. "Because I think it needs work."

"And what, pray, am I apologising for?" Cyris demanded suddenly. "Because of the way I brought you up, you're in the final of this bloody tournament?! Whatever my failings might have been, they can't have been that bad!"

"You think this justifies it?" Theo said harshly. "Fifteen years of horrible fucking abuse and now 'oh yeah, look at you now.' You know who didn't have that? The other finalist. The other semi-finalist. There's more than one way to skin a pepper-pear."

"Perhaps. Perhaps not. We'll revisit that theory whether you triumph or not," Cyris said, folding his arms loftily.

"You shouldn't," Anne said suddenly. She could sense Theo getting angrier by the minute, wasn't a pleasant sensation having him stood next to her. Like resting next to a kettle threatening to explode at any given second. She locked her eyes on Cyris, never wanting more than to be able to read someone than right now. If he was being sincere, then she'd feel bad. If he wasn't then it'd be Theo who'd suffer in the long term. But better Cyris than his son be hurt by what came next.

"I shouldn't, what?" Cyris said, condescension in his voice, silky like a luxurious scarf made into a noose. "Do tell, my dear."

"You shouldn't revisit that theory," she said, not quite sure what she was doing. This was out of character for her. "I don't know the story between the two of you, but your son hates you and really I don't blame him!"

Cyris' face curved into a smirk at her words. "Oh, I wouldn't..."

"NOT FINISHED!" Her shriek cut through the air, surprising even herself. She calmed for her next words. That smirk had pissed her off though. "He doesn't want anything to do with you. You've broken him inside, cut up any chance of him ever being normal and I don't bloody blame him from wanting to be as far away from you as possible! Funny how you show up just as he's on the verge of making history."

"I've wanted to find you for a while," Cyris said quickly, looking at his son with a beseeching look. "But..." He sighed. "I didn't know where to look." Those last few words sounded a little too pathetic for Anne's liking. And she didn't believe them either. There was always a way to find someone.

"You know what I don't quite understand," Anne said, glancing sideways at him. They'd found a secluded bit of the island, looking over the ocean in the shade of a couple of great boabke trees and they'd sat down. She'd gotten the impression he wanted to talk but he in his own time without being rushed. He looked like there was nothing more he wanted to do than forget the whole thing but still he cocked his head to the side and raised an eyebrow. The smell of salt in the warm air left her feeling relaxed. More so than Theo anyway. She rested a hand on his shoulder, could feel how tense he was, saw he'd been chewing his lower lip for the last moments, his hands balling in front of him as he finally spoke.

"Go on?"

"Okay I get why you changed your name. I mean I would as well. Everyone's heard of your dad..." She saw the flinch at that word and made a resolution not to mention it again. "And I wouldn't want that hanging over my head either. But where did Jameson come from?"

He visibly softened and rubbed his chin thoughtfully. She sensed the hostility leaking from him rapidly and that was a relief. He'd been nothing but a big ball of angst since the encounter and it worried her. "Jameson was my... Ah, it was my mother's name."

"Bit of a masculine name for a woman." She grinned as she said it. He looked at her like she'd spat in his food. His mouth twitched as if he was trying to fight the expression. Then he smiled.

"Funny," he said. "Hand me some emergency skin because I'm about to break out laughing." The sarcasm in his voice was just so strong she couldn't help but laugh. And then despite everything he was laughing with her. "That was pretty cool the way you chewed him out."

"Well I couldn't let him get away with that, could I?" she asked. "I mean, what did he honestly expect was the best thing to come out of this for him?"

"He's a snake," Theo said simply. "He'll appear when you least expect him, he'll strike for the heart and him showing up usually doesn't mean anything good. If you come out unscathed, it's usually a good day." He paused for a moment, looking out at the ocean in silence. "There were more bad days than good growing up, I know that much."

She reached out and squeezed his hand. "It's over now though, right? He's not coming back?"

"Shouldn't do. He doesn't like failure. He'll give it a few months skulking on his own, bitching about how the world is against him or the Senate are trying to frame him or how Unisco are trying to slip tracking devices into his coffee. Then he'll try something stupid. And because he'll do it badly, he'll get fail and get caught. I know how he works and it's usually routine." Theo went silent, just craned his head back to stare at the sky. "And I suppose you could say I'm his biggest failure of the lot. Whether he sees it that way I don't know. He wants to be a lot of things, but he's never quite worked out why it never happens."

"When you say failure…"

"I never wanted to be his son. Changed my name and everything as soon as I could. Got out of there. Didn't want him to be a part of my life. His ego couldn't take that."

Anne said nothing. It wasn't uncommon for names to be changed these days. In fact, it felt like it was becoming a more and more common practice. But for that reason, she'd never heard of it before. Hatred of a parent.

"He was a bastard growing up. Unreasonable. Cold. Emotionally shut off."

Who does that sound like? She almost asked it, held her tongue. It probably wouldn't go down well. Theo scuffed the toe of his shoe against the grass absentmindedly. She caught a flush of frustration rippling from him, curiously strong in the evening light. "He's right though, you know," she said. "You can't change the past. You can't. He can't. What's done is done."

"And I'm supposed to forgive him for it?!" That tiny seedling of frustration started to swell in him, not yet anger but it felt capable of developing into that tree.

"Well maybe not right now," Anne said placidly. "I'm all about forgiveness. You should know by now that people aren't perfect. They tend to be bastards. But maybe, you ever think there's a chance he might be genuine?"

Theo shook his head without hesitating. "No. Absolutely not! He's not genuine. Don't trust him. Absolute bastard."

"But at least you're willing to give him a chance," she said dryly. "He's your father…"

"And is that supposed to mean something to me? Because it sure as hells doesn't to him." She could hear the conviction in his voice, the belief he was right and everyone else wrong on this subject. In a way, she admired that. In a lot of others, she wanted to slap him for his pig-headedness.

"I'm not saying believe him," she said. "Just... I don't know. Listen to him. Give him the benefit of the doubt for the time being. If he lets you down..."

"And he will!"

"Then he lets you down, you were right, and I was wrong," she said. "And I'll apologise for that, but you only get one family."

"No, you don't," Theo said. "You can't choose your family, but you can choose your friends. The people who you desire to spend time with rather than being forced to. And eventually they become your new family."

"I'm not quite sure it works like that but go on. I mean, you already lost your mother..."

She saw the flash of anger in his eyes. "Yes. I did. And look what's happened since. She was... She didn't deserve it. And bloody Cyris carried on living. Where's the justice in that?"

"Hate to disappoint you but justice doesn't exist the way you're thinking," she said. "You want those who are good to live and those who are bad to die horrible deaths. It's not going to happen. You know what they say about the good dying young."

He looked at her with a rueful look. "That's probably you going to die before your time then."

She felt her cheeks burn at his words. "That's either really morbid or really nice. Can't decide which." Still she felt a warmth in the pit of her stomach, acknowledgement of a nice thing to say. Today more than ever she felt on the path to understanding this strange anti-social man slowly becoming a part of her life.

"Meant to be nice," he mumbled. "Sorry. Not got a lot of... Compliments don't come easy to me. I..."

She patted him on the shoulder, an almost reflex gesture he didn't flinch from to her relief. "It was nice. Sort of. I appreciate what you were trying to say."

He stayed silent for several long moments, she let him keep his tongue to himself. If he didn't want to say anything, she wasn't going to force him. Silence could be nice.

"You know, this is not how I pictured my day ending," he eventually said with a sigh.

The third day of Summerfall.

They were here.

Cyris knew the moment he strolled into the hangar, one hand in his pocket, one on his cane. He didn't need the cane, but it had become a public affectation he'd employed. People saw him with the cane and underestimated him. They thought him lame, a cripple and felt pity. He wanted to laugh at that notion. Plus, it was lined with cadameenium, a metal so densely strong they lined aerofighters with it. It made one hells of a weapon, you got hit with it, you stayed hit.

He limped towards the aeroship in the middle of the hangar, aware of the eyes in the dark but kept his eyes straight ahead. Don't show any sign of weakness or they'll be on you. He didn't think they'd turn violent, but you never knew. Already he was forming a plan in his head. The way to use this situation to his advantage. He didn't want to be arrested on some trumped-up charge and never seen again. There had to be some way to do it.

And then it hit him. Something so simple anyone could have thought of it. And it wouldn't be too much of a stretch until it came to the simple act of telling the truth. John Cyris knew he had told so many lies over the years it would be hard for the truth to be believed. But regardless, he needed to make them see. He stopped, cleared his throat. The little signs were there that someone was here. The lack of people about, just in case it turned violent. No mechanics or maintenance staff, no pilots milling about or even security. The aeroport on Carcaradis Island was not the busiest, but still he'd seen all of this before. Barring his cane and his summoner, Cyris had no weapon. Nothing illegal. The way parts of the hangar fell unilluminated didn't bode well. Darkness was something to hide in, at least in a physical sense. On a philosophical level, getting in was sometimes easier than getting out.

"You know, if you wish to ask me something," he said, pleasantly loud. "Then please do. Let us not skulk around with each. It's unbecoming for one thing. Rude is another. I know you're there. I know how you work."

They came down out of his aeroship… Madam Coppinger's aeroship… weapons out if not pointed at him. Three of them, faces blanked out with those damn mufflers they wore. He'd been trying to score up schematic plans for those things for years but no dice.

"There we are," he said, resting his weight on the cane. "So much more civilised than you grab me and force my head into a bucket of water, wouldn't you say?"

"John Cyris," the figure in the lead said, voice suitably distorted. He got the hint it might have been male but very little beyond it.

Certainly nothing to identify who was beyond the mask. "Former leader of the Cyria criminal organisation."

"Cyria never dies," Cyris said, the pleasantries still in his voice. "It's just dormant. But I've done my time. Society has judged me reformed. You can't arrest me for dormancies, thankfully. Someone else will pick the idea up sooner or later."

"We don't care about Cyria. We've got bigger things to worry about." This second voice was more than likely female, the speaker's body also added that impression. Something familiar about her, Cyris couldn't quite place it on the moment. An unusual sensation but not one he cared about implicitly. It was designed to hurt and although it might have been a stab in the ribs, it missed his heart.

"That's my benefit then," he said loftily. "Sorry boys and girls got nothing to say on Cyria. If you're harassing me, then you've got nothing."

"Good thing we don't want to talk about that then," a third voice said, suitably different to the other two, Cyris guessed at it being male. All of this was starting to both unsettle and annoy him. It made him want to look over his shoulder to check nobody was behind him. This was how it started. First there was idle chatter, then a bag over your head and knockout drugs in your system with them determined to make you talk no matter what. It was an experience he very much wouldn't like to repeat. Of course, nobody admitted they did it, but everyone knew. Everyone was complicit. And when you'd done some of the things John Cyris had in his life, it was a bit much to ask for the public to cry out on your behalf.

"Well Cyria is about all I know, if you want anything else…"

"Want to tell us about any association you might have with Claudia Coppinger?"

Okay, that threw him, he had to admit he hadn't been expecting that to be the next thing he heard, he laughed out loud, unable to suppress the grin. "Okay, you've got me there. Who?"

"You think this is a joke?"

"I'm just wondering if you do," he said innocently. "Never heard of her. Should I have?"

"You came in on a Reims-registered aeroship," voice number one said scornfully. "She's the top dog at that company. She's someone we'd very much like to talk to."

"Wow, the inner workings of the most secret bunch of bastards across the five kingdoms. Is there anyone you won't go after?"

"So, you don't know her then?" voice number two, the probable woman asked.

"I didn't say that."

"Yeah, you just did. You said you'd never heard of her."

"Oh yeah…" Cyris said. Inside he was smirking. On the outside, he gripped his cane a little harder. It wouldn't do much good if they opened fire, but it'd put one of them down if they came closer. Broken bones minimum. A touch of defiance would do wonders for his story. He also knew if he came out with it all straightaway, they wouldn't believe him on principle. They were expecting him to lie and be as evasive as the hells. In that regard, he couldn't bring himself to disappoint them. People overall were an easy to manipulate when you knew how. "Did I say that?"

"Yeah. You did."

"Right well, yeah maybe I know who she is. Pretty woman. Nuttier than nutkin shit, I think is the term. But she's definitely got something going for her." He smiled at them. "Kind heart to let me come here. Shame she didn't know how quick Unisco were off the bat."

"Where can we find her?" voice number one asked.

"Well it's not that easy, is it?" Cyris replied, stretching his arms out lazily. "If it were, you'd have done it already. Take it you tried her homes and her offices?"

"That's classified."

"Don't give me that, boy! I asked you a question!" His hackles were up suddenly, and he fixed a glare on the three of them. In his peripheral vision, he could see two more doing their best to look dangerous.

"She's not there."

"I know she isn't," Cyris said, taking a perverse delight in the way voice number one came out with that crestfallen revelation. "You won't find her. You can't. Not without my help."

Here it was. His gambit. His moment of truth.

"You're going to help?"

"I didn't say that," he said, clasping both hands on the top of the cane. "I really didn't. See she's got a grand vision for the future and I think she's determined to follow it through to the end."

"So are we!" voice number three said. "Her end, preferably. We don't know what she's doing but it's probably not good. There's a trail of events on this island leading back to her and it needs to stop now before it gets worse."

Cyris knew all about it. Of course, he wasn't about to reveal that information. It probably would have helped them, but on the other hand he was asking them to believe a lot already. The entire truth would shatter his credibility. Better they found out on their own. He nodded in agreement. "She wanted my help. She wanted everyone's help. The big guns. The Montella family, the Fratelli's, me, Mazoud, Kenzo Fojila, the Regan's, a whole bunch of enterprising bigwigs in the underworld. She wanted an army and she had plenty to offer in exchange. As I said, she has a vision. A good one."

"What is it?"

They had to ask. He'd have been shocked if they hadn't. He gave them a sweet smile. "Nothing less than total domination and subjugation, of course. Already got the first piece of the puzzle. She's on a ship."

"That narrows it down then," voice number two said. "Must be thousands of ships in the five kingdoms."

"But," Cyris said, wagging a finger at her. "Not ones outfitted with Divine-class cloaking devices. She won't show up on radar with it. Any radar. So good luck finding her without my help. She could be sat a few hundred miles above us right now and you'd never know."

"What's it going to take for your help?" voice number one asked. There was just the right note of defeat in his voice to satisfy Cyris.

"Well I'm glad we might be able to do business," Cyris said gleefully. "Since you do… How about you make sure you put the bitch down!" He almost spat the words out, he saw them recoil in surprise. "Nobody tries to put me on a leash and I don't bloody follow! You understand me?! You kill her, you forget anything you have on me and I'll give her to you. It's a good deal boys and girls. They'll give you all medals for a job well done."

He smiled at them and felt the glee rush through him. If they went for this, it'd be a good day. It'd be a good day indeed.

"It's when it's calm that you need to worry. While there's the potential for improvement, there's an equal or greater chance things can grow worse with the passing of time."
Wim Carson to Claudia Coppinger in a private moment.

The third day of Summerfall.

Boredom was slowly working its way into every fibre of Nick's being, the irony not lost on him how he'd gone from one cell to another. If it wasn't for being released to take meals with the staff here, he'd have probably gone crazy staring at the four walls. A gilded cage, he reminded himself, was still a cage. And though the bed might be comfortable and the reading supplies more substantial than on the island and fresh water on demand, he still felt like he was waiting for the other foot to fall. Something had to give sooner or later. He hadn't seen Claudia Coppinger since those first nights, hadn't had the chance to subtly probe her for more information or even go deeper. More than once he'd proclaimed out through his cell door that he wanted to speak to her, but they'd fallen on either deaf ears. If he squinted through the bars on the peephole on his door, he was sure he could see one of the Taxeen strolling around outside, keeping a tight guard.

Still he'd tried to occupy mind and body, a few hundred push ups every morning, alternating with sit-ups, he'd found himself running through a dozen possible scenarios for escape or attack in his head. He had to do something soon, the inaction probably the worst experience, even if there wasn't much he could do about it. It all boiled down to the Taxeen outside as his first great obstacle. He remembered what Tod Brumley had said in unarmed combat practice about facing an opponent both armed and skilled with a knife. His first words?

'Try to avoid a fight with someone with a knife. If they're any good,' and the Taxeen undoubtedly were, 'they'll cut you into shreds before you can take it off them. If it's a fight you can't avoid, hit them hard and early. You'll usually get one free shot, depending how fast they are. You hit them right, you can gain an upper hand.'

It was one thing to think about it, it was one thing to practice it, it was entirely another thing to go out and do it against a knifeman whose reflexes had been honed throughout the years, whose bodies had become part of their armoury. They'd adapted themselves to suit the weapon, not the other way around. They were serious, dedicated individuals. It might not come to it. Nick liked a fight as much as anyone, but he'd prefer to walk away from it at the end.

The rattle in the door told him the bolt was being pulled back. In this era of high tech security, a simple bolt might have felt out of place, yet all it meant was they had faith in the guards. To withdraw it by hand and let him out, they had to get past the Taxeen. A security lock could, admittedly a pretty big could, be hacked. As the door swung back with a scrape, Nick saw two of the Taxeen staring unblinking at him with those large eyes set against dark skin. He smiled at them.

"Good... morning, is it?" he asked. "You'll have to excuse me, I'm a little lost on when it actually is."

Neither of them paid any heed to him. Nor did they enter the cell. They were professional, considering they dressed like desert rats in their robes. One gestured for him to follow them and the other moved off. Nick sighed, made to follow, his steps bordering on skittish as he walked past the gesturing guard, not entirely comfortable exposing his back to him. The knife he half-expected to come never did and still he followed the first Taxeen. He saw several other cells on the way past, just as he always did, never quite able to see inside them. Except this time, he saw a face up at the bars of one of them, a pretty Vazaran face with close cropped black hair wearing...

Huh...

Unless he was mistaken, that was a Unisco flight suit. He could only see the edges of the sleeves and the tips of the shoulders, but it sure looked like one. Weird that. If he was going to get out, he'd have to investigate this first. If there were Unisco people aboard, he couldn't leave them here without at least trying. On the other hand, Arnholt had been very specific he was supposed to make bringing back the information his top priority. But he couldn't have known about the woman. Maybe she wasn't alone. Maybe there were more. Decisions. This had started off so simple, now it felt like it had taken an ugly complexion. He swallowed hard and continued to walk, ferreting away at the problems at hand.

They'd gone a different way this time, one he hadn't experienced before. He'd have remembered this view, found he needed to stop and look as they passed the great window, saw the sky outside. Clear blue cloudless sky for as far as his eyes could see and his heart fell, as beautiful as it might be to experience. His chances of escape had just grown slimmer. They had to be miles in the sky nobody knew this was here or there'd be investigations. Nobody liked to have strange unidentified ships hovering above them. Especially not ones armed like this.

Shit, Nick thought as he glanced at the semi-ring down below him, high powered lasers rimming the surfaces. In the distance, he could see a strange brand of aerofighter he hadn't encountered before, six out on flight manoeuvres and flying like they had no small amount of experience. The thing was huge, easily bigger than some of the dreadnoughts the five kingdoms could call on. He stumbled forward, had to rest his hands against the plastiglass to steady himself, the sudden enormity of his task at hand stunning him. This... This was so much bigger than he'd imagined, than any of them could have, and yet here was the proof in front of him. They were in so much danger right now and nobody knew. One of the Taxeen pulled him away roughly, he fought the urge to strike back. It'd be a good time, he wouldn't expect it, but there'd be another chance, no clear advantage to revealing his cards here.

Always when not to act as much as when to act. He let out a sigh and shrugged the arm off him, giving the Taxeen a glare. "Okay, sorry," he said grumpily. "It just took me by surprise though." Out in the distance, the aerofighters swept past the setting sun, light reflecting off their wings and he couldn't help but be awed by the sight.

They didn't linger long after, he had to move quickly to keep up, much to his chagrin. There was barely time to take in some of the more interesting details of their surroundings, about all he could do to keep track of their movements. He figured he could find his way back to the cells from here. Now he understood why they sent guards every time. It'd be easy to get lost if you didn't know these corridors.

The door they led him to was heavy and wooden, it looked expensive and he gulped as he took it in, not entirely sure why. He caught just a hint of foreboding from it and it unsettled him. Couldn't explain why, wasn't sure he wanted to. The faintest smell of scent lingered, something he couldn't place from somewhere else. One of the Taxeen knocked brusquely and he heard a voice from the other side. Female. Familiar. He ground his teeth as the permission to enter came and the door slid open.

Claudia Coppinger wasn't alone in the room, rather there was a scruffy looking Vazaran man who looked in his fifties stood next to her, his face rough and wild. When he smiled, what few teeth he had were uneven and broken in his mouth. He looked like a campaign poster for battered wolverines. Claudia rose to her feet; he was sure she was wearing the same clothes as when he'd last seen her. She looked tired, worn down by unseen weights and Nick wasn't sure what to make of it. Dark bags rimmed her eyes, she looked haggard and weary. He chose not to mention it, just smiled politely. "Miss Coppinger," he said, strolling into the room. He didn't give the Taxeen a second glance, just kept his eyes on the woman and her associate. The man wasn't the biggest, he looked thin but dressed casually, his clothes almost exercise-like underneath a heavy poncho that split aside at the front to reveal the utility belt wrapped around his waist. Twin silver cylinders glistened, hooked to the belt. He fought the urge to look closer. There was something about one of them, the very presence of it stirred something in his memory, chiming like a klaxon bell. Something he was sure he'd seen before, but where. It was starting to annoy him now, scoured through the recesses of his mind as he sought to recall its origin.

"Mr Roper," she said. "Good morning. I have good news for you. President Ritellia no longer wishes to press charges against you. Full retraction of any attempts to press charges, he even apologised for intruding in your time of distress."

"That doesn't sound like something he'd do," Nick said breezily. He lazily brushed a speck of dust from his shirt. "Who twisted his kidneys up into his lungs for him to accede to that demand." Her face threatened to break into a smile, but she held herself.

"I like your metaphor. Ritellia is an overgrown slug made fat by those he should serve. Stand up to him and he slithers away to find someone else to bully, someone less... disagreeable"

"But a powerful slug regardless," Nick said, glancing sideways at the impassive face of the Vazaran. There was something off about him he couldn't place.

"A potent slug is still easy to squish," she replied nonchalantly. "It's just about finding the right place to apply pressure."

"I'm sure it is." He left an edge to his words, gave her a smile.

"You won't have met my associate, Wim Carson," she said, jerking her head towards the man. "The one who has made all this possible. He has been my guiding light since he entered the picture." Carson nodded his head at Nick, Nick returned the gesture, his mind still musing over where he'd seen that metal cylinder.

"Sounds like you've made a big impact then," Nick remarked. "I didn't know we were on a ship."

She laughed. "This is more than a ship. This is a life raft, if you want to look at it in practical terms. Everyone here has been selected for a pure purpose. There is a war about to come, I don't want it to be prolonged, but it may be so. Plenty will be killed. Knowledge and skills will be lost, if they need replacing with my own people then it shall be so. When all is said and done, this will be the capital beacon of the five kingdoms. People will come from miles around for my favour."

Cuh-razy! Nick kept his face blank, saw Carson's eyes narrow curiously at him. They were beady and small, one of them bloodshot, the other an electric blue but still they gave the impression they could pass straight through you. It was very much in keeping with what some people had said about Anne Sullivan, the thought occurred to him with a jolt. They all knew what that meant. Everyone who'd worked for Unisco past a certain amount of time had heard the stories about some of the stuff she could do. He straightened himself up, gave Carson a sardonic smile and fixed on Claudia.

"Sounds like a plan," he said. "I want to be a part of this, I've given it some considerable thought. And I ask what you would have me do, ma'am." Idly he wondered if he should bow, show the proper decorum.

"You can start by calling me Mistress," she said primly. "That is my chosen mark of respect and you will adhere to it."

"Of course," Nick said. He wanted to roll his eyes but fought the urge. "You've got a lot of guns on this life raft, uh Mistress." The word felt unfamiliar in his mouth, but he put his all into it. It wasn't at all arrogant to call yourself that.

"There's a lot of people out there who will fail to acknowledge my new world order," she said. "I've always believed that the best form of defence is a good offence. Our guns are powerful, our shields are strong and the best thing of all is that nobody will ever know we are here until it's too late."

Huh... This already was starting to look like a problem for anyone on the ground. They could easily repel an attacking fleet with the armaments he'd seen lining the body of this ship. Maybe if they didn't have the advantage of surprise, it'd be different, but the chances of a successful assault from the front reduced their chances. "What's that mean?" he asked curiously. His note of confusion in his voice wasn't entirely faked. Wim Carson hadn't taken his eyes off him. "You got one of those cloaking device things on here?"

"Divine-class," she said proudly. "You know what that means?"

Truthfully, he didn't. He'd never heard of it. The top bracket of cloaking device in his previous experience had been labelled at kingdom class. That meant that there was no chance of spotting them on any sort of scan, no radar would pick them up, no satellite could track their path, computerised targeting systems would be useless. "No."

"It means nobody's finding us. We're all alone up here and it's going to stay that way. Some of my top people managed to perfect on the cloaking device. Previous iterations were flawed in that some of the air disturbances around it could be tracked to a fashion, if you knew where to look... Not this. The cloak extends out and..." She paused. "I'm boring you, I know. Don't want to drown you with technological jargon. We're invisible. And unlike some inferior models, we can see and hear outside our shields as well. I love technology. Isn't it marvellous sometimes?"

His heart fell, he tried to recover from it almost immediately and only partially succeeded. She seemed well protected up here, if what he'd seen and heard was anything to go by. And the sinking feeling wasn't helped by the knowledge of what he might have to do to leave.

"I'm sure you'll be a just and fair ruler," he said thoughtfully. She narrowed a brow at him, apparently not happy with his choice of words.

"Ruler?" she asked. "I'm not satisfied with that. I want to be adored. I want to be feared. Mister Roper, I want to be worshipped. Godhood beckons. And when that happens, the only option is to accept it with open arms. Few are chosen but all must accept." She sighed wistfully. "And it is a burden that I am willing to accept. When you have gone so far, turning back is not an option. The only choice is to follow it all the way. I have moved so much to get this far; the last ten years have been the groundwork to arrive at this moment and it is coming."

There had been more of what she'd had to say, mainly her outlining what his roles were to be in the world she was building. She'd mentioned he'd have to undergo training and orientation, he wasn't entirely sure he wanted it to go that far but he'd enthusiastically agreed, all to keep up appearances. She'd told him how she thought he was leadership material and she wanted him for a prominent role given she'd gone to great effort to recruit him. She'd mentioned some spirits she wanted him to look at, some very special ones indeed and she'd laughed as she'd brought them up. Nick wasn't entirely sure what she meant, but it couldn't mean anything good for the five kingdoms below. The Ista Neroux, she'd called them, an ominous title if ever one had been heard. At the end, she'd offered a hand and swallowing down disgruntlement, he'd bent and kissed it. It seemed like the sort of thing she'd have expected, the sort of thing she'd have swallowed, and he applauded his genius. Her cheeks flared with red and she smiled, he half expected her to giggle.

"You know, I might have to make that protocol, Mister Roper," she mused. "You're a charming man."

"I do my best," Nick said gruffly. "Mister Carson."

"Master," the dark man corrected almost instinctively. The muscles in his face tightened as he looked Nick up and down. "Master Carson."

"Master of what?" Nick wondered aloud. The broad mouth split into a toothy grin and he knew for sure that he didn't like that smile. There was something shifty about it which hinted at so much potential for death and destruction. The only sort of Master he looked like was a Master of Nothing.

"This and that. Some of the other."

Evasive answer, he noted. That didn't fill him with confidence. "I'll remember that then," Nick remarked. "Nice trinkets by the way." He inclined his head down towards the metal cylinders at the man's waist. "Been to Serran recently?"

The expression that came back at him was one of bemusement. "Serran? Not for a good few years. Why?"

He wasn't pure Vazaran, there was plenty in his accent that gave that away. There was some southern Serran in there. It wasn't an uncommon mix, south Serran wasn't very far away by boat from northern Vazara. Children of inter-marriages kept on appearing and Carson was one of them by the looks of things. The name Wim hinted at that. He'd known a few across his life.

"Saw a few just like them when I was there not too long ago," Nick said. "Hand warming devices, right?" It was bullshit, he knew that, he had a feeling Carson did as well. There was just something too spooky about him to avoid playing games, but at the same time, he needed to know. He had the horrible suspicion and letting it go didn't feel like an option.

"Something like that." Carson's face remained inscrutable. "I picked one up in tragic circumstances. It belonged to someone who met an unfortunate end." His voice cracked a little as he said it.

"Yeah?"

"Someone who didn't deserve to die. I wish it could have been avoided." It sounded like there might have been regret in his voice.

"We all know someone like that," Nick said, his thoughts drifting towards Sharon once again. Wasn't the first time since he'd seen that cylinder on Carson's belt "World's a bitch, right?"

"It is," Carson said. "She was one of a kind all right." Nick didn't hear the words as he glanced down at it again, taking in the silver sheen, the heavy rubberised grip, the pearl-like growth towards the tip of it. He could picture it now, the memories of it resting against so many clothes. He'd never known what it was for, Sharon had always told him it was a memento from the past. She'd said it apologetically, as if daring him to inquire for more information and at the same time firmly as if to say he wasn't getting an answer if he did.

"Where you get it?" he asked, hot rage boiling inside him. If he'd had a weapon, Carson would be dead in a heartbeat. As it was, it was taking all his control to avoid jumping over the table and strangling him. Any hint of downplaying his feelings was lost as he leaned back and swallowed. The mission. The mission. There's a mission and he needed to follow it through.

"Picked it up on Carcaradis Island," Carson said. "You seem distressed, Mister Roper. Are you perhaps having second thoughts about what the Mistress is attempting?"

Nick smiled painfully at him, the simple act of curving his lips an effort. It was a false one, it lacked any sort of warmth or passion.

"No," he said. "My heart is as clear. I know the path I must take, and I intend to follow it to the end. I know that more than ever now."

"A troubled man," Wim Carson said after Roper had been escorted away to his new quarters by the Taxeen. He'd been less than impressed with the choice of guards, informing Madam Coppinger on more than one occasion the Taxeen were vastly inferior to the Vedo that their subculture had loosely been inspired by.

It wasn't a lie either. He'd always been a student of history; he probably knew more than the two silent men did themselves. The Taxeen had been created some hundred years earlier by a crippled Vedo and although many weren't Kjarn-sensitive, they could still fight. The kjarnblades had been cast aside in favour of the poisoned knives made from sharpened versions of their own removed finger bones. How fucking primitive, had been his reaction at the time and he hadn't seen anything since to make him retract it. They were thugs rather than noble warriors. Scum. Expendable. A blight.

Jerl Taxa, their founder had lost most of his fingers in a duel, he'd fashioned their method of killing by himself. For a time, he had served as the Vedo executioner until his mind had finally gone. Wim shuddered at that thought. It happened with all executioners. Every generation needed one, to cut down the Cavanda should they raise their heads, and ultimately the stress got to them and they were removed by their successor.

In the case of Jerl Taxa, the successor had failed badly, and Taxa had fled into the night, forsaking the Kjarn forever or so the legend went. It was one he'd heard many times before, one that troubled him. To forsake the Kjarn disgusted him. Anyone who willingly did was nothing in his eyes, they were worse than cowards, they were traitors.

Madam Coppinger had smiled at his assertions of inferiority and pointed out that she didn't have Vedo, she had Taxeen and she intended to use them. "Troubled?"

"Oh yes," he said. "I sense much anger and sorrow in him."

"What about duplicity?"

Wim hesitated. He couldn't say for sure. His use of the Kjarn was still tenuous at best, still a fragile thing to grasp and while the raging emotions he'd heard were impossible to fake, he couldn't say for sure. "I get the impression there is something he's not telling us," he said slowly. "But nothing more. I don't sense any overt duplicity; I didn't sense a lie in his words. But that doesn't mean there are untruths there. He might just have supreme control. Some people are harder to read than others."

"It's perhaps better not to take chances though," she said. "Perhaps he should be questioned more thoroughly."

"Of course, I can't be sure," Wim said hurriedly. "If you believe he is of value, then perhaps he should not be tossed aside. You have a purpose earmarked for him, I assume."

"Better dead and guiltless rather than living and traitorous," she said. "We shall see." She reached into her pocket and withdrew the key he had found for her. Wim was still amazed by the phenomenon privately. He'd sensed it, once his abilities had returned, it had all been just a matter of pinpointing it, no easy task but one accomplished. "Either way, we have a trip to make, I assume."

"We do," Wim said. "I will take you to the door, but I can go no further. That way lies madness for those not worthy. It is a path you must walk alone."

"If it is a road I can't traverse alone, then I have no business walking it," she said with a smile. It had almost as much emotion as the final one Roper had given him. There'd been something about the way he'd acted and spoken that felt wrong, like there was some piece of the puzzle he'd been missing. "Roper gets a reprieve until we return. Maybe then I can pass judgement. For now, I say he shall survive. Head says he's a risk but it's one my heart is telling me to take. He can be a strong asset for us."

She rose to her feet. "Gather your things for we depart soon."

He couldn't hold it in. Nick had taken everything into consideration and now he judged it the time to act. He either needed to get to a communications post, or even better the cloaking device controls and disable it. If someone on the ground could see this ship, they'd investigate. Secrecy was Claudia Coppinger's greatest weapon, blow that secret wide open and she'd be exposed. He exhaled sharply, glanced around his surroundings and sought out something, anything to give him an opening to deal with these two guards. Taxeen were raised to fight with the knife almost from birth, they were lethal with it.

Not for nothing had he been trained by Unisco. He'd never stepped away from a fight before and he sure as hells wasn't starting now. Nick grinned, flexed his knuckles as he kept walking. There was a doorway ahead, that looked promising, it was already sliding open as the three of them moved towards it. Both the Taxeen looked bored at their duties, babysitting someone they considered barely a threat. In a way, he enjoyed that, wasn't often he was underestimated.

"Hey, guys," he said, glancing around at them. The one on the right was bigger, his eyes less alert than the one on the left. Neither of them was really anything less than intimidating. The left one had eyes like an overgrown weasel, they skittered across the corridor, seeking out anything and everything. He'd be the faster to react, Nick guessed. If there was going to be anything to do, then it'd need to be done to him first. Of course, it was all a matter of inches and split seconds. Deep breath. "Any chance I can catch a break while I'm here. Bathroom?" He let a pleasantly hopeful look flash across his face, walking backwards all the way to the door. Neither of them responded, other than a slight smirk across the face of the smaller one. He understood, Nick guessed. He just didn't care. They weren't going back to the cells now, he'd already guessed, he got the feeling he didn't want to go where they had in mind for him next.

"Please?" he said, allowing a pathetic note of pleading to enter his voice as he carefully stepped back through the door, halting on the other side. "Give a fella a break, yeah?"

If the smaller guy came through first, it'd be better. If the bigger guy came first; Nick'd be in trouble. By the time he had him down, the smaller guy would be all over him.

Fate smiled for the smaller guy came first, and Nick was already in motion, throwing one of Tod Brumley's patented love taps towards his face. He'd always thought the name was amusing, a rare piece of wit on Brumley's part. Land it properly and they'll be swept off their feet, he'd said with a smirk. It was completely out of the blue; he shouldn't have seen it coming, even so, he'd very nearly dodged it.

Nearly. Not nearly enough. The little guy staggered, Nick's blow bouncing off the side of his skull, it took a snap kick to his side to send him smashing off the frame of the door and out for the count. No time for a breather, he was already at the big guy, knife was already sliding out of his sleeve and into his palm. No time to be gentle either, Nick sprang and delivered a crushing palm straight into his windpipe, all his weight behind it. One free shot, Brumley had always said and he'd made it count. The big guy bellowed like a bull, fell back and hit the ground, scrabbling at his throat. Amidst his frenzied struggles, a wet burbling broke from him as he unwittingly buried his own blade into his chest. His eyes went wide, his struggles slowed but Nick didn't have time to wait for him to die. Places to be and all that. He was grateful this Taxeen hadn't lived up to the reputation.

He'd barely made it more than several feet when the alarms went off and he froze stock still, just for a moment. It sounded like they were echoing through the ship, he cursed his actions. Someone must have seen him act and pushed the button.

Without a choice, he ran.

"Yeah, I see it, Director."

With Jacques Leclerc and Alvin Noorland behind the controls of the aeroship, they'd made good progress towards the coordinates given to them by John Cyris. In a way really, he'd been more than helpful. David Wilsin just wasn't sure it was a good thing or not. People were very rarely that helpful unless they had an ulterior motive. Granted Cyris did want to be free of them minus any sort of charges levelled against him. And he did want them to stop harassing him. Having them walk into unnecessarily dangerous situations was not a good way to get that done.

He'd told them everything, or at least he claimed to. Wilsin wasn't quite inclined to believe him, even if Arnholt had been very interested to hear it all. He'd taken it straight to the Five Kingdoms Senate, had managed to get approval for a task force to converge with them in record time. Word had it he'd called in every favour he had. They'd be here in hours. Enough time for the team to get in, get Roper and deal with Claudia Coppinger before the airbase was blown straight to the hells. It was a simple plan, maybe that was what worried him. Everyone was here on the ship, barring Arnholt and Okocha. Even Brendan had deigned to come along, sat there in armour and muffler just like everyone else, weapon resting across his lap.

"Guess Cyris wasn't selling us a pony on some levels," Fagan remarked. "How easy is this going to be?"

"Put it this way," Derenko said. "Going to make our last mission to Cubla Cezri look pleasant."

"Fuck me, it's huge!" That came from Mel Harper. Wilsin had to agree. It sat like a fat bloated spider amid the clouds, thick chunks of metal resting against fluffy white background with an aura of menace. "It's going to take most of the fleet to knock that thing out."

"Guess we best work fast then," Brendan said. "I don't want to be caught on that thing when they start to hammer it."

The large size hologram of Arnholt sat in the middle of the floor nodded sagely. "This is not going to be easy by any stretch. We all have our tasks, we all need to perform to the best of our ability. This action has been sanctioned, with great difficulty, I might add, and a task force devoted to it. We are the advance wave, we need to get Roper out and deal with Claudia Coppinger. Our intelligence hints at more personnel than we can deal with, so we'll be the advance guard in one of their own vehicles before the task force shows up. Hopefully we can use that as a distraction to make our move through the facility. Lethal force. Our sources tell us we can expect a hostile reception. Chief King will lead the force to find Coppinger, Agent Derenko will take his team and search for our missing agent."

The projection sighed, looked tired for a moment. Wilsin felt a brief stab of sympathy for Arnholt. Then he remembered he wasn't the one who was probably about to start getting shot at and the sympathy faded. Both him and Okocha were far, far away from here, well out of danger.

"You've studied the data. Everything we have, everything we could take from John Cyris. It needs to be enough. You've all been well trained, known a day like this would come where your lives will be put on the line for the sake of freedom. It is a cost you may have to pay but know that with what you do today, others may live."

"Bravo," Lysa said dryly. "We don't need an inspirational speech, Director. We know what we got to do."

"We just need inspirational music!" Wilsin quipped. "Preferably nothing by Ulysses Forty or Premesoir Dreams."

"I like Premesoir Dreams," Noorland said. "Bit of Rock All Night does it for me."

"Really?" Fank Aldiss asked, raising an eyebrow. "That's your song of choice for banishing pre-mission nerves?"

"Yeah. We can't all like Tamara Wise."

"Hey, I don't..."

"You do, Fank. You claim not to like her, but I've seen your playlists."

"Hey, she makes me feel things!"

"She makes a lot of people feel things. With me it's nausea but hey ho." Noorland grinned as he said it.

"I'd hit Tamara Wise," Wilsin said, glancing around. "Right in every single hole. Am I the only one who'd do that?"

"Nah," Lysa said, giving him a thumbs-up. Towards the back of the aeroship, Anne Sullivan had sat pensively, deep in thought, not saying anything so far. She'd only shown up for the briefing, unavailable to interrogate Cyris. She looked like something was troubling her, but for the life of him, Wilsin couldn't work out what it was. Privately he didn't care, too busy thinking about Lysa and Tamara Wise. A nice image.

"Anyway," Noorland said. "Pilot normally picks the tunes, so on the way back, I'm blasting out Rock All Night all the way home." He sounded confident, Wilsin noticed, unsure if that was a good thing or not.

"Damn, almost hope we don't make it now," Tod Brumley said. For him, it almost passed as a joke, the silence that followed painful as they approached the ship.

"We're going to make it, you know," Brendan said, breaking the quiet as Noorland and Leclerc guided the aeroship down towards the docking bay, Leclerc bluffing his way through with someone on the other end. Cyris' details had turned out to be accurate on that front, he'd provided them with authorisation codes and proper procedures, based on what he'd managed to glean from his pilot, the man currently in Unisco custody.

"This is it though," Derenko said as the hologram of Arnholt faded away with assurances that the fleet was on its way. "This is how it starts."

"Just because something sounds too unbelievable to be true doesn't necessarily mean it is, just that you should reserve your opinion until you can be sure."
Ruud Baxter to Sharon Arventino, a long time ago.

The third day of Summerfall.

It felt eerily quiet minus the presence of the other Unisco agents on the island. With just him and Okocha remaining, Arnholt settled into his seat and studied the feeds around him. He wanted to know as much of what was happening up in the air as possible, mainly if it was going to blow up in his face or not. He wasn't going to lie to himself, there'd been moments he'd truly doubted what John Cyris had to say. The man was a proven liar, a cheat and one of the worst criminals ever to hit the five kingdoms, no crime too depraved for him to avoid, except perhaps maybe this. His tales of a woman seeking ascension to godhood might just have been too ridiculous to believe, except it tied in with what they had, did explain a lot of things. Too much had happened for it all to be coincidence. He couldn't just let it go now. Sometimes you had to take a chance, a big one it turned out. If everything had been proven false, it might have been the end of him as director of Unisco. But the audio confirmation from his team high above had lifted some of the weight from his shoulders, leaving him feeling vindicated. He just needed the mission to be a success now.

He'd moved wheels within wheels to get everything into place, called in favours and although not quite reached the point of begging, there'd been moments when it had almost approached that. Cyris' story of a flying airbase, heavily armed and exceptionally dangerous belied belief, he was aware. Hence the need for confirmation before the fleet came in, a delicate balancing act. Cyris had told them the airbase carried several compliments of fighters and enough on-board personnel to cut down any force sent against it. Hence, Arnholt knew the fleet was not only key to blowing the base to smithereens, but to draw as many of the enemy out as possible for his team to do the job.

Eliminate Claudia Coppinger. Retrieve Nick Roper. Two simple objectives with so much potential for going wrong. He'd struggled with the first, elimination seemed a little harsh for a first step, but orders had come from above. He couldn't do anything but have them followed. People who weren't in the know about Unisco often brought up how their remit seemed to fluctuate wildly from case to case, that those who should be killed were often spared in the line of duty and the reverse.

Every mission every agent took part in had its own parameters. A good complement of agents around the world did focus more on the domestic side of things, just as an even smaller complement needed to function as little more than assassins. another balancing act. This mission was no different. Dead was preferable. Of course, if she could be taken alive…

He dismissed the thought immediately. Deviating from orders would do nobody any favours. They had to just hope that casualties were kept at a minimum. The fleet had been given their conformation to department. They would already be converging on the coordinates and within moments, the two forces would meet.

"Divines help us all," he said. Across the room, Okocha fiddling with a control panel, glanced over. "Because only you can judge what we do here today."

"Might be a little late for prayer, Director," Okocha said softly. He'd opened a can of soola and put it down on the desk next to him. Arnholt could smell the peppermint from across the room. "But I guess every little bit helps, right?"

"I think we're going to need every little bit of help we can get here to avoid our team being wiped out," Arnholt said. "I'm not normally a religious man. Today I think I can see the benefits to it."

They came flying out of the midmorning sun, most of the advance guard spotting their objective moments before it appeared on their sensor boards. Aboard his flagship, the Wild Stallion, Allied Kingdom Admiral Gary Criffen had a bad feeling about what lay ahead. Yet stood alone in his command post aboard the great dreadnought, he tried not to show it. Whether they be ill-advised or not, he had his orders and he would follow them. The Senate hadn't scrimped on the task force under his command. They were taking it seriously.

He'd heard the transmission from Unisco played back. It had sounded serious trouble in every sense of the word. Enough for them to throw together everything they had at hand. Not only his Wild Stallion, but the medical freighter the unfortunately-named Sitting Target, the carrier ship, the Lost Lucie, as well as the Bounty Snatcher and the Carrion Crow, both smaller, deadlier, more modern versions of his own ship. He'd grown attached to the Stallion though. All ships carried enough firepower to repel any threat, because he knew if things weren't resolved here, it could be war. Nobody wanted that. He needed to oversee the job here properly. Twenty fighter squadrons were docked aboard the Lucie including five donated by Unisco for the duration of the mission. He felt confident this would be another successful engagement. If there was a threat their mustered firepower couldn't deal with, he didn't want to meet it. Likely he wouldn't survive the engagement. His thoughts drifted more to the positive, at least until he saw the target ahead. He felt sweat drizzle on his face as he stared out the view port. Divines, the thing was huge. Words failed him as he gripped the armrests of his seat. The bad feeling felt justified, its size was monstrous. It hung like a great eye in the sky, staring at them and although he didn't feel terror at its presence, it didn't do much for his confidence.

"Technical officer, I want scans of their offensive and defensive capabilities," he suddenly barked, jerked into action. "Communications officer, open a hailing frequency to them, see if we can talk this out without firing a shot." He paused. If they were lucky, this would be the case.

The part of him that was human wanted this to be the case. In his life, he'd seen enough death and destruction to hope that they'd back down. The part of him that was a soldier knew better. They were trying to make a point. They weren't going to meekly go to the table when they could march up with weapons in hand. "And open up channels to every ship in this task force. I want them to hear what happens." He said nothing else, silent with his reasons. If he was going to make them give up their lives, he wanted them to go to their deaths knowing he'd done everything to avoid this end. It helped him sleep better at night.

For a few moments, nothing. Privately he doubted they could end this amicably. Criffen had always been an optimist though, even when faced with tragic odds.

The alarms went off as their aeroship flew through the disabled energy shield and into the hangar, and just for a moment, Wilsin thought they'd been rumbled. He half rose to his feet, nerves threatening to overcome him, expected the automated guns to turn towards them and engulf them in a big fireball. Dead before the whole thing had even started properly. Anne put a hand on his arm before he could make a further fool of himself.

"The fleet just arrived," she said. "They're panicking. Nobody's supposed to know they're here, right?"

Wilsin cleared his throat. "Excuse me," he said, apologetically. "That was unprofessional of me." He managed a nervous grin.

"Bit jumpy, Agent Wilsin?" Brendan inquired, more amused than impatient by the reaction. Leclerc was the one who chuckled loudly, the sound echoing in the cockpit.

"Tenterhooks, Chief," he replied. "Skulking around doesn't suit me."

"It doesn't suit any of us," Lysa said quietly, her hands running a quick check over her weapon. "But it's got to be done."

"Speak for yourself," Fagan quipped. "I like a bit of skulking around, me." It brought some faint laughter, Wilsin sat down and tried to relax. He'd never done that before; he couldn't help but feel like he'd overstepped somehow. He tried to control his breathing and regain composure as the two pilots brought the ship towards a landing berth.

Outside, he saw scenes of flurried of activity, men and women in jumpsuits scurrying about in a hurry to ready equipment for a type of aerofighter Wilsin hadn't seen before, they resembled posing eagles with the wings curved in arcs across the body.

"Hey," Noorland said. "There's something you don't see every day." He sounded appreciative. "Eaglefighters."

"Eaglefighters?" Fagan asked, getting a better look. "Seems a bit on the nose for a name."

"Based out of Premesoir now, think they're a Sandoval model originally. Not seen any like these before. Maybe they sold the rights to the design to Reims, I don't know. No mistaking that design."

"There's a lot of them," Derenko remarked. "They could invade a kingdom with what they have here." Already pilots were getting into their eaglefighters through a hatch in the belly of their ships, some already taking off, leaving the way they'd entered.

"Not our problem," Brendan said. "There's still going to be plenty of hostiles, so stay sharp. Noorland, when we get in there, I want you to get to a terminal and hack in, see if you can find some schematics. We need to know where to look. It's huge, we get lost, we could be searching for days until we find what we came for."

"Roger that," Noorland said, the aeroship finally coming to a gentle halt. Already people were moving towards them, some of them carrying weapons although they didn't appear to be ready to use them yet. "Guess I get the easy job, huh?"

"There's no easy jobs up here, son," Tod Brumley said, giving his Featherstone one final once over with his eyes. "Sorry to say."

"That's not true," Aldiss said dryly. "We could die Tod. That'd be piss easy."

Kyra twisted her kjarnblade and deflected a trio of blaster bolts back into the jump-suited grunts up ahead, trying to block out the sensation of their lives slipping away from them. The hits had been good, lethal fire turned back into upper bodies and throats, the shock palpable on their features. Nobody ever expected it. They'd probably put more effort in if they did. She blamed the Vedo for it, if she was honest. Everyone should see that glowing laser blade and know it meant certain death. It was a fearsome weapon but the Vedo had chosen to hide it away, use them for ceremonial purposes and training toys. That very notion was an insult.

Her blade hissed as she deactivated it and took in her surroundings. Another corridor, only a vague idea where she was going. She'd made it out of the maintenance corridors into the ship proper courtesy of the key she'd removed from... Yeah, she wasn't going to think about him now. What was done was done. The alarms had been going nonstop for what had to be ten minutes now, made it hard to think but not impossible. Letting the Kjarn move once again into her footsteps, she sped through the corridors, blazing past anyone who might have seen her. They might have noticed a blur out the corner of their eyes but beyond that, she was moving too quickly to track. Needless bloodshed wasn't always a good thing despite what some said, she only wanted out of here, she wasn't on a crusade to punish them unnecessarily.

Truthfully, they'd done her some favours, she was closer to the Kjarn today than ever before. In hardship, she'd been forced to swim against the current in circumstances nobody should find ideal. Her master would be proud, she hoped. What had Cobb ever done to warrant something like this? He hid in his labs and preached progress when really, she knew he was just... a... coward. He didn't have the balls to do what she was prepared to.

She was gritting her teeth together so hard she thought they might crack, suddenly aware of the pain. Kyra exhaled sharply, slowed down and felt the exertions creep up on her. To use the Kjarn like that wasn't an absence of fatigue, it was merely a delay. A helpful one but everything had a cost and sooner or later she'd need to pay it. And when she'd gotten off this ship and was safe on the ground, she'd sleep for a week but now she had to keep going. She'd suffered worse than this. Back in the first days of training, her master had refused her sleep for days on end, all with the intent of preparing her for times like this. At the time, she'd hated him for it. Now, she was glad that he had.

He hadn't managed to find the cloaking device but looking out a window, he had seen a fleet approaching, ready to start an assault. Nick guessed it was an Allied Kingdoms fleet, he'd seen some of the ships before, even if he couldn't name them off the top of his head. But it just meant he was running out of time. Someone had tipped them off, he needed to get out of here. The cloaking device wasn't an issue now; it'd be taken care of when the whole thing blew. It'd prevent automatic targeting, but if they could see it, their gunners in that fleet could hit it manually with enough ordnance to blow it out of the sky.

Nick gulped. So that left two objectives. The prisoners and Claudia Coppinger. As much as what he suspected about Wim Carson, it wasn't something he needed to do. He couldn't prove Carson was involved with the death of Sharon, beyond him owning something that Sharon might or might not have possessed. No, it was more a hunch, one that he couldn't drive from the forefront of his mind. Whichever he came across first, he'd need to deal with. He turned and ran, almost straight into an armed guard who didn't have time to bring his blaster rifle to bear before Nick hit him with a flying elbow to the face which put him on the ground. Putting the boot in next, he was out cold, and Nick had retrieved the weapon in one swift motion.

He should kill him. And yet he couldn't bring himself to shoot the unconscious man dead, he'd been disabled, he posed no threat, Nick might need the charges in his weapon. It was all the convincing to himself that he needed. He was closer to the prison block, he guessed. This corridor looked familiar, the same picture he'd seen earlier. An artist's rendition of the Divines in their glory, or at least as much glory as their meagre ability had been able to convey. He'd seen better paintings. The artist's use of colour was severely lacking, if he was being generous about it.

Yep, everyone's a critic.

They were in motion, the moment the door open, they hurled some of Noorland's special credit grenades out of the hatch. They'd been developed over months of testing, the shell containing a small motion sensor, the interior holding well over a hundred spiked ball bearings each smaller than the average fingernail. Upon detonation, they'd sense out the nearest source of movement and shoot their load in that direction, range about good for a dozen feet, control chips in them preventing an overlap of targets and upon six simultaneous detonations, they hurled themselves from the aeroship, weapons blazing into wounded men and women. Bodies dropped by the dozen, even as one of the eaglefighters was already reacting, moving to turn its weapons on them.

Brendan King moved faster, hit the button on the summoner on his belt and a pair of humanoid golems emerged in a burst of light, one made of steel, one from stone and brought uniblasts to bear on the eaglefighter before it could do the same to them. Most summoning devices could easily support two spirits at once, some of them even more, it was just a considerable drain on power when they did. Two by two, they filed out of the ship, more shots finding the surveillance devices in the hangar, shattering lenses and destroying recording equipment. Those few enemy combatants left behind fell under the second wave, taken by surprise against a more heavily armed onslaught.

Within moments, they had it. The area secured, although Wilsin knew it was just one small part of a truly enormous task. Still, most plans failed within the first few seconds of combat so for this to still be working with all of them unharmed was a bonus. Brendan was barking out instructions around them, weapon still held to his shoulder.

"Watcher go find a sniper spot," he ordered. "Team two, you have your objective. Team one, form up on me." Noorland and Leclerc had been ordered to remain with the aeroship, along with Anne Sullivan making up the threesome. She hung her Saga over her back and immediately made for one of the elevated areas, determined to seek out a good position. Her skills as a sniper weren't much use in the corridors and the close-range combat they were about to see. Wilsin formed up on Derenko's team along with Mel Harper, Fank Aldiss and Pree Khan. Their team was smaller than the other, everyone they could spare for the secondary objective. Find Nick Roper. He had to be somewhere. Dead or alive. Wilsin really hoped he wasn't dead. It'd kinda put a whole downer on the mission if he was. He slipped his summoner tight to his belt, checked a crystal was loaded. Just in case.

This wasn't the time to try and get artsy with his kills. Those who did that wound up dead. A spirit could make a difference in crowded areas, especially when they were as lethal as his veek. But trying to direct it at the same time as trying to duck shots required an uncanny amount of focus, the sort of levels that were difficult to teach, if not impossible. It didn't stop them from trying to impart it at the academy though.

Right now, he was glad they'd at least made the effort.

"Madam Coppinger, the five kingdoms fleet is trying to hail us."

The voice came through her earpiece, Wim could hear it as he moved items towards the small ship. They were getting out of here, although the timing appeared to be terrible. He shook his head and stretched out his arms. Physical labour wasn't his forte but moving them with the Kjarn felt disrespectful. It wasn't something to make life easier. It was something to co-exist with. A way of seeing the world.

"Ignore them," she said simply. "Have you despatched the eagles to meet their attack?"

"Of course, Ma'am. We're preparing to engage."

"I'm about to leave," she said. "Not because I don't have faith you'll rout them but because I have places to be. Keep them away from my departure point. I want no survivors. We've been found up here, I mean to make sure they don't send a second party any time soon. You're in charge, Commander Folson. Win this battle and the rewards will be great."

Wim could almost hear him swallow with pride on the other end of the line. Folson... Folson. The name rang a bell, but he couldn't picture the face. That undoubtedly boded well for them all. Idly he extended his senses out, hoping to see if he could catch a glimpse of which way the battle might turn if things carried on the way they did but either the Kjarn wasn't willing to reveal it to him or the future remained clouded. Either way, it was a failure on his part and he swallowed it down angrily.

"Our place isn't here," Madam Coppinger said, glancing over at him. She'd changed out of her working clothes into a pilot's flight suit, not dissimilar to what others wore in the hangars. The only difference he could see was hers bore no rank insignias. He also had to admit she cut a fine figure in it. "Unfortunately, we have places to be. More important tasks."

"I quite agree. I hope you can pilot us out of a firefight," Wim said.

"Well someone has to," she said. "My shuttle only holds two people. I'm a competent pilot. And I'm sure you'll let me know if someone gets a little close for comfort. That remarkable danger sense of yours."

He let that go. She had a point. That had been the first thing he had sought to recover upon his regaining his ability to touch the Kjarn. That and the telekinesis. Through those two skills, the fine control would eventually return, then the pure power he'd once held at his fingertips. Knowing when something was coming was always a handy skill, especially around here when one never knew if a knife was coming towards his back.

"Maybe you won't have to deal with the issue of Roper after all," he said. "Him and his conflicting emotions. Maybe he'll be killed in this attack and it'll cease to be a problem. You won't have to worry about his loyalties."

She smirked at him. "You know, it never occurred to me before I saw him look at you. But maybe there's a reason for that." Wim didn't like what he was feeling from her. "He recently suffered a bereavement. The woman he loved died."

"Yeah?" Wim felt disinterested at hearing that. People died. It was the way of the world. No power could change that.

"Sharon Arventino. They were engaged to be married."

That brought his attention, almost sent his hand to the second kjarnblade he now wore on his belt. The one that had belonged to her. She was right, it did explain much. He raised an eyebrow at Claudia, saw her smile. She'd seen the twitch in his hand. She knew. Wim got that impression in the quickest moment and he hid a shudder. He regretted it but that didn't change what had happened. "Interesting," he said. "A small world." She didn't push for what he meant. Still the feeling only grew that she knew and inside he recoiled.

"A lot's interesting about the whole thing," she said. "Now come on, let's get this show on the road. We don't have long."

It looked like it was to be battle then. Criffen sighed, saw the eaglefighters coming towards them and he looked around his crew on the bridge of the Stallion. "So, it starts," he said. Their attempts at contact had failed. They didn't want to talk. The Lost Lucie was still spitting out its own fighters, ready to engage the eagles at close range, HAX's and Kingdom Chargers flying out in tandem. At first glance, they looked to be matched for numbers. The Sitting Target had moved out of range, behind his own ship, while the Carrion Crow and Bounty Snatcher moved up on him in a three-pronged formation. Already he knew they'd be readying probes to try and pick up on any downed ships, recover any pilots lost in the engagement. A thankless task but one that he wouldn't deny them.

"Gunners! Focus firepower on that thing!" he barked. "Aim to disable. Try to avoid hitting the central node for the time being." He knew Unisco had their own mission, they were to wait before going for the kill, even if it was easier said than done. All through the three capital ships, the guns were lighting up, white hot bursts of plasma screaming through the air to crash against the eye-shaped ship.

"Several confirmed hits, sir!" one of the tactical officers offered. "Their shields held. Showing strong still."

"Repeat fire!" Criffen said. It took a few seconds, but the guns sounded again and again, dozens upon dozens of blasts peppering the shields to little effect. It'd soon be time to take more drastic methods. On the field of battle, he could see furious dogfights ongoing as eagles and HAX's and Chargers spat deadly plasma at each other. "Snatcher, do you copy?"

"Copy Admiral," the voice of Captain Adetouni growled through the comms. "What would you have us do?"

"Snatcher, I want you to move into an advanced position and hammer that thing with your gravity bombs. See if we can suck that shield off them. Carrion Crow, attack from the other flank and overload them with your unilasers. If we can get that shield off them, we'll hit them from three different angles, compromise them. Fighter squadrons, one through six, keep the eaglefighters busy. You…"

He looked at the readouts, more eagles were joining by the minute, threatening to tip it to Coppinger's favour. "You might be outnumbered but you're the best. Keep your wing-mates close, keep your enemies in your sights. Seven and eight, nine and ten, eleven and twelve, keep on the capital ships. Run interference in case any of those eagles get through." Even enough mosquitos could bring down a mighty beast. One eagle on its own wouldn't have much chance against a dreadnought like the Wild Stallion but fifty would pose a serious challenge hammering away at their shields with repeated rapier assaults. "The rest of you, move in on that ship for the time being, hammer it with slasher missiles. Do not use your laser cannons against it, it will not penetrate!"

He paused for breath, smiled grimly and tried to brush down the adrenaline assaulting his system. Bounty Snatcher was already moving into position; he could imagine gravity bombs being readied for launch. They'd been intended to be used against something with a potent shield generator, they'd suck at those barriers, leaching power until it overloaded, a process that would be made swifter by the Carrion Crow hammering it with laser fire from the other side. Normally, shields sensed where a breach was imminent and focused maximum defensive priority to that area, reinforcing and holding up at the expense of others temporarily. Enough pressure in different areas and they'd overload. Military issue shields were considerably more powerful than civilian but hitting them in multiple places was still a considerable drain on the ability to sustain it. Slasher missiles weren't especially potent against bigger targets, the projectiles split into multiple smaller blasts after being launched, but they'd do the job here. Especially in greater numbers.

He smiled. For all those credits and its size, this airbase couldn't hold out against them for long. Maybe, just maybe they'd be able to take it intact. And wouldn't that be another medal just waiting to happen?

They'd waited a few moments longer as Noorland had moved to the consoles in the hangar, starting the process of breaking into them. Although it wasn't his forte, probably Will Okocha would have been a better choice, Al Noorland wasn't too bad at it. Nobody would dispute his skills. Wilsin had been there when Arnholt had forbidden Okocha from going on the mission. Too important, he'd said. The rest of them probably should have been insulted but in a strange way, Wilsin felt proud he was here. To say this was important was understating it.

Brendan's golems continued to patrol the edges of the hangar bay, crushing the bodies beneath their giant feet rather than walking around them. Noorland slipped an automated hacking tool out of his pocket and into the console, tapping a series of rapid quick commands into it. Wilsin could see his brows furrowing, breathing quickening as he leaned over to the console and clucked his tongue. It wasn't a good sign, rather one of frustration and Wilsin found that unnerving, perhaps more than anything else.

"Few moments," Noorland said, glancing around at them with an easy grin. His discomfort had faded. "Tricky system to break, but I'll get it. Just another..." He hit a key, they all heard a faint beep. "Damnit! Hang on, hang on..."

"Damnit Agent Noorland, quit playing around and work it out," Brendan said angrily. He didn't like theatrics, Wilsin remembered, Noorland did tend to showboat when people were watching his performance. He loved playing to the crowd, he was a master at it. "This isn't a..."

"Done," Noorland announced cheerfully. "I'll guide you all to your destinations, see if I can track down the objectives." He jerked a thumb towards the exit, a thick sliding blast door already opening even as he did so. "Over there. That's the start. Hurry back, yeah?"

They were still here and with them another Taxeen stood half at alert, ready and waiting. This one, Nick couldn't help but open fire on, sending a triple blast into his upper body and watching him go down, knives drawn but dry. He exhaled sharply, swept the stolen weapon around to check he was covered, before moving back into the cells. Now that the shit had hit the fan, he was almost feeling nostalgic for the prison cell. There'd been no doubt that was what it was, no two ways of looking at it. He found the right cell immediately, the woman in the Unisco flight suit had retreated to the back of it. She wasn't alone in there, another guy sat down on the bed.

"Who are you?" he demanded. "How did they get hold of you?" He scrambled to unlock the door, searching for the controls. Somehow, he'd work it out. "Unisco?"

The man didn't react. The woman, the Vazaran did, rising to appraise him coolly. "Perhaps."

He decided to take a chance. "I'm going to get you out of here."

"Do your best," she said. Still amused.

"Don't rush to thank me then," Nick said, fiddling with the controls. Idly he considered leaving her in there for a moment. The man on the bed finally looked up, grinned at him.

"She likes her jokes," he said. "Anything to keep the spirits up. You one of us?" He was also wearing one of the flight suits.

"Not a pilot," Nick said. He knew how to fly but he'd never had an aptitude for it. He could get from point to point with minimum fuss, Unisco made a point of insisting as many of their agents as possible could manage various vehicles, but there were some who were a lot better than others. Some belonged in a cockpit, looked more comfortable in them than they did on the ground. These two looked like pilots, the suits their badge of office. "Not a career one anyway. But a friend." He hit the switch, the door ground open with a screaking sound that hurt his ears. He got the impression it hadn't been opened for a while. "After you."

"You with the agency?" She finally looked interested. "How will we ever thank you?" Interested but still no mistaking the sarcasm.

"Well," Nick smirked. "I could use someone to fly me out of here. Soon. Got something I need to do first." He clutched the weapon tighter to him.

"Reckon they still got our HAX's in storage?" the Vazaran asked, her companion shrugging at the question.

"Hells if I know. I'd have slagged them first chance I got. Remove the evidence."

"What squadron?" Nick asked, curious. One way to work out if they were genuine. Things could be faked, given enough prior knowledge. And just because it wasn't common, didn't mean it wasn't available.

"Remnants of Wolf Squadron," the man said, throwing a salute. "I'm Sergeant Ross Navarro, that's Lieutenant Alexandra Nkolou." The woman rolled her eyes.

"And that's why people call me Alex," she said in a tone suggesting he should too. He wasn't entirely sure why she resented being called Alexandra, but he'd humour her for now.

"But I'll oblige you," he said. "Wolf Squadron? I heard you all got wiped out."

"Not all of us, clearly." Nkolou wasn't having it. She reached down to the fallen Taxeen, snapped one of the knives away his wrists, broke it off with a ruptured crack, Nick nodded in appreciation. She looked like she knew how to handle it, he said nothing. "You got any other weapons?"

"Nope." It wasn't a lie. "Hangars are…" He turned back towards the doorway, trying to work out where they were, based on what he'd seen so far. "Back that way. Find a ship, wait for me, I'll be as quick as possible." He gulped, saw the looks on their faces and felt the weight of his conscience on his shoulders suddenly. Things were getting hairy out there by the sounds of it. Nobody knew how much time they'd have on here, all it'd take would be one lucky shot and the whole thing could go up. "Fifteen minutes. If I'm not back in fifteen minutes, or if you don't hear from me, get out of here. No point you…"

"What's happening?" Navarro asked.

Just for a moment, Nick felt lost for words. "Outside, there's a five kingdoms fleet. They're here to beat the bad guys. The bad news is…"

"We're right in the middle of the enemy?"

"That's about the sum of it," Nick had to admit. "So yeah, we're one lucky blast… or unlucky, depending on how you want to look at it… from being blown up. I'll understand if you don't want to stick around."

"So, what are you going to do?" Nkolou wasn't going to let it go.

"Got to try and kill her," Nick admitted. "Claudia Coppinger. The brains behind all this. If I don't make it, you got to find Arnholt, confirm that. Maybe he already knows, maybe he doesn't but he needs to hear it from me." He threw them the Unisco salute, fist clenched and tapped it to his temple. They returned it quickly and he felt the buzz of reassurance. "Divines be with you."

"You too," Navarro said. "You got a name?"

He smiled. "Nick. Nick Roper. If we all make it out, rendezvous on Carcaradis Island, we'll celebrate it. Sound good?"

"Sounds fantastic," Nkolou smiled. It was the first time he'd seen it. Probably a sight many'd consider worth waiting for. "Don't dawdle, yeah?"

"No intention of it," Nick grinned. "Good luck."

"Just get the fucking job done and survive!"
Terrence Arnholt's silent prayer to Unisco operatives before any dangerous mission.

The third day of Summerfall.

They'd run into trouble almost immediately, the enemy resistance might have been trimmed but still there were enough to outnumber them, David Wilsin could testify. It felt like they'd hit every possible group in their push for the cells, under Noorland's directions. He had to constantly reassure himself Al wasn't doing this deliberately, that he couldn't help where the patrols were based. That would have been massively unfair on their eyes in the system. They were pushed for time, he had to get them there as quickly as possible.

He jerked the Featherstone above his head, fired blindly from behind cover, Derenko and Aldiss moved out under his support, he heard their own weapons erupt with the sound of fire. Muscle memory and instinct took over, he continued to point and shoot, any sense of higher thought lost as more came running towards them, all eager to shoot, all eager to kill.

He didn't know how many he'd done for personally, just that the body count was racking up and nobody had gotten hurt. At least not badly. Mel Harper had screamed when a stray shot had punctured her shield, grazing her shoulder, but she was still moving, if not freely. Wilsin allowed himself a glance at her. She'd live. Blood stained her armour, her face contorted in pain, yet still she continued to fire, if erratically. One combatant came out a side door nearby, weapon raised and Wilsin clubbed him to the ground with the butt of his weapon. He went down, a quick survey telling him he was the last. For the moment, silence, bar the ragged little gasps coming from Harper.

"Wilsin," Derenko called down at him. "Take care of Harper, catch us up in a minute. Get that wound patched." By the sound of it, he'd noticed the erratic shooting as well. Wilsin reached for the pack on his waist, digging out some numbing agent and a patch. It wouldn't be a perfect job, but it would mean Harper enjoyed a little less discomfort.

"Roger," he said, throwing him a nod. Derenko, Aldiss and Khan moved off, he noted the direction they'd gone before turning back to Harper who'd already peeled off her armour with great discomfort. It hit the ground with a thump, she staggered back to lean against the wall, her face screwed up with pain.

"Damn," she said, looking down at the wound. Her eyes were glazing over, her breathing laboured and the blood running freely down her arm. "That really, really hurts, yeah? Fuck me!" She spat the words out viciously.

Wilsin said nothing, just moved closer, broke open the numbing agent and sprayed some into the wound. Her eyes went wide, she bit down a scream as the agent worked into the wound, he saw her leg spasm involuntarily as she clutched his wrist tight as she continued to swallow down any audible reaction. Screaming now wouldn't be the best idea, there were still hostiles active out there. He could hear blaster fire in the distance, the rest of the team had run into opposition by the sound of it, even more outnumbered than before.

"My hero," Harper murmured as he started to apply the patch. At least the trembling had stopped, some semblance of recognition returning to her eyes with the absence of pain. Still she favoured her shoulder when she moved but it was manageable for her now. Or so he guessed, given she didn't look like she was struggling. "Thanks, Dave." If he'd looked down at her, he'd have seen her eyes go wide with fear. As it was, he muttered it was nothing, moved to put away the medical items. It was when he closed the clasp on his pouch that he realised the lights had dimmed in the corridor. David Wilsin blinked several times, not exactly sure why until he looked up. He blanched, swallowed a very deep breath and clutched his weapon tight.

He'd seen him before. The big fellow. The missing link. The blank slate. Whoever he was, he looked a whole lot bigger up close. Especially with the fixation on Wilsin in his eyes and his arm coming back to hurl a punch.

"Oh crap!"

It was like getting hit by a mag-rail carriage, suddenly he was airborne, blinding pain rupturing through his chest as his armour was compromised and he hit the ground in an untidy heap.

Unilasers and gravity bombs hammered into the shields from two different angles, Criffen could see they were having a gradual effect, if a slow one. No shield, no matter how strong could take abuse like this, continuous bursts of bright blue fire ripping into the shields side by side with the blinding white boom-blast from the gravity bomb that were followed by a sudden temporary absence of sound. Gunships swooped to follow up with slasher missile bursts, each of them sending pretty scarlet sparks over the shields and Criffen smiled at the report the shields were slowly being compromised. Let the Bounty Snatcher and the Lost Lucie deal with the shields, pound away until were no more and then his own ship would start to shred the airbase below with fire when they went down. It felt like the perfect plan. Getting past the shields would take all the firepower of those two ships, they'd withdraw and recharge while the Stallion moved in for the kill.

Across the battlefield, eaglefighters and HAX's and chargers were engaging each other furiously, blowing up as many of the enemy as were taken with them, the numbers rapidly thinning out by the second. Already they'd lost twenty percent of their attack force and the numbers showed no sign of slowing down. About the only saving grace was that they were taking them with them, eaglefighter numbers reduced by the same amount, no wait, more, twenty-two percent, twenty-five percent...

The shields went down, not with a bang but with a whimper, he'd privately hoped for more of a show as the announcement came they'd been disabled. Airbase was no longer a defended target. He fought the urge to rub his hands together in glee. That was exactly what he wanted to hear. "Stallion move in for the kill," he commanded. "Snatcher, Lucie, proceed to move out of range. We're going to light this thing up now."

"Sir!" one of the analysts shouted, cutting off his train of thought. "The airbase's weapons are powering up."

"What?!" Before now, they'd had no indication of weapons. Just that they were hiding behind shields. Scans had failed to pick up any sort of weapon systems on board and suddenly he rounded on those analysts. "Where the hells did those come from?"

The weapons lit up like a firework display, ten, twenty, thirty, forty... more than he could count... all erupted simultaneously, weapons systems easily on a par with the unilasers pounding the shields moments earlier but outnumbering them by a comfortable few dozen and suddenly they were bombarded with calls from the Lost Lucie, the dreadnought's own shields rapidly overwhelmed and suddenly it was the hull being breached by corrosive fire, missiles suddenly launched into the fray. No ship could take that sort of abuse for long...

Criffen had never felt so impotent as he watched the Lost Lucie explode in a fireball, a lucky shot hitting their fuel banks, hundreds of men and women lost forever. He exhaled sharply, collective gasps heard around the control centre. To be up against such firepower was unheard of. "Impossible," somebody muttered, he was almost in agreement with them. For a few moments, the control centre resonated with stunned silence and then he remembered himself. He remembered where they were.

"Nothing's impossible. Get back to them now! The shields are down, we need to take these risks! Squadrons move in! Bombard them with all your firepower, you'll be harder to hit. Watch out for eaglefighters on your backs. Bounty Snatcher continue to assault, back those fighters up. Sitting Target, do you record any survivors?"

"Negative admiral." The words came like a hammer, he tried to block them out. The important thing would be to not get caught out by the same trick twice. It did absolutely nothing for those already killed though.

The metal ring flashed to life in front of them and Wim was momentarily surprised by it, only for a few seconds though. The portable projector on the floor of the shuttle winked into action, producing a tiny holographic figure, just a head and shoulders but one he didn't find familiar. Madam Coppinger did though, it would appear.

"Mistress," they said. Certain features were distorted, the voice electronically altered. It was difficult to even tell what gender they were. Not his business. "Unisco are here for you. I regret I was unable to tell you earlier…"

"What the hells do I pay you for?!" Claudia snapped at him. If there was any sign of distress in the figure's demeanour, it didn't show.

"They're here for you," they continued. "I didn't find out until the last moment, haven't been able to get the message to you. I'm here with them, but don't worry. I'll ensure you get out. They won't take you alive."

"That's reassuring." Some of the anger had faded from her voice. "Where are they now?"

"All running through the ship, looking for you. I've managed to split away from them to send you this. I can't stay but always remember I'm looking out for you."

She said nothing, just pursed her lips thoughtfully. Wim was suddenly bemused by the whole thing. It figured that she'd have someone from Unisco in her pocket but for them to be brazen enough to contact her in the middle of a war zone spoke of loyalty to the credits she could bring to bear. And who was it who said finance couldn't be turned into a weapon?"

"What can you do for me?" she asked.

"I've reprogrammed your automated guns to cover you as you leave, see if they can keep the fleet off your back. The rest's up to you. I'm sorry I can't do more, but I don't want to arouse suspicion."

"You've done enough," she said flatly. Granted she was still irritated he hadn't told her earlier but better to know late than to have his cover blown unnecessarily. The past couldn't be changed. "You've earned your bonus today, Subtractor. Proceed as you would normally. I need you to remain in place. You're too valuable to be thrown away. Thank you."

"Oh, it was my pleasure, Mistress," they replied. Wim thought they might have had a smirk in their voice by the sounds of it. It was hard to tell. "Be seeing you."

Wilsin pushed himself up, his entire body aching. He looked down at the front of his armour, blanching as he did. The punch had shattered it, torn a great rend into the material, shards of it sticking into his ribs and he let out a groan. If it hadn't been so good at absorbing blows, he'd be dead. He saw the grinning figure stood watching, take one ponderous step in his direction. And suddenly he had the Featherstone in his hands again, raising the weapon and squeezing the trigger. He kept it steady despite it threatening to leap from his hands numerous occasions, didn't let up until the power cells ran dry and the sound of blaster fire died away. The hulking man reeled under the blast and he felt a momentary surge of triumph flush through him.

Their eyes met, and the man winked at him. That triumph slowly bled away as the smoke cleared, he saw the holes torn in his body from the shots knit back together, great chunks of flesh reforming. David Wilsin stiffened, knew it was impossible! He'd just emptied enough firepower into him to kill an elephant, but he'd shrugged it off.

"That was your free shot," the man growled. "Now it's mine!"

He started to move and suddenly he looked a lot less ponderous than before, thundering across the floor with rapid steps, moving like a locomotive. Wilsin readied himself, swung out with the useless blaster rifle like a club, aiming for the face. He ducked around, took the weapon from him with ease, tearing it from his grip. Any attempt he made to hold on was useless, felt it ripped from him despite best efforts, the weapon hitting the floor with a clunk and suddenly he was on the defensive, ducking under hammer blows belying the apparent languidness of the man, all previous visages of clumsiness forgotten. Wilsin struck back, hit him hard in the side and he just shrugged it off, laughing with manic glee. He didn't even try to counter back, just let Wilsin hit him three, four, five more times to little effect. It was like hitting a side of meat, he'd struck with fist and elbow alike and he thought he'd done more damage to himself than to his opponent. He even smashed a kick into the big man's knee, fought the urge to cry out in pain as his foot met hard bone, like kicking a metal post. He looked up, scowled and suddenly had to jump back to evade a punch. He had the feeling if he was tagged by one of those blows, he wouldn't be looking too clever afterwards.

It wasn't a punch that caught him, rather a flailing palm that sent blinding pain through his system, a flat hit that pushed him back onto the ground, his ribs on fire again. He'd felt something snap and now it hurt to move. Shots in the distance, he allowed himself to sneak a look past and saw Harper on her feet, her own Featherstone in hand and doing as he had, emptying her power pack into the big man. Unfortunately, it looked to be having the same lack of effect. Wounds were already healing, skin and flesh and bone knitting back together. About the only sign remaining of the damage was the stink of burnt flesh and muscle in the air, mixed with the exhaust odours of the Featherstone, his clothes ruined.

This wasn't good.

Alex Nkolou had been having that sort of day as she and Navarro bounded into the hangar, immediately finding a pair of Featherstone rifles and a laser dot trained on them from somewhere above them. She didn't dare move, she'd spent weeks expecting to be shot by the enemy. She wasn't going to be killed by friends.

"Don't shoot!" she yelled. "Friendly, friendly!"

"Who are you?!" Everyone knew Alvin Noorland at Unisco, he was one of the ones giving them the look. The weapon wasn't lowered though, kept trained on them.

"Sergeant Navarro and Lieutenant Nkolou," Navarro offered quickly. "Unisco. Last remnants of Wolf Squadron."

Leclerc... Jacques Leclerc, possibly one of the few agents around who might recognise them both nodded in agreement. "Is true. I remember them. Him not so much. Her, she's hard to forget."

She felt a stab of amusement in her gut. "What do you mean by that, Jacques?"

Leclerc said nothing, Noorland instead took over briskly.

"Where the hells have you two been?" he demanded. "Wolf Squadron was last heard from weeks ago..."

"They're all dead," Navarro said. "Wolfmeyer, Hasigawa, everyone. They were killed by a big guy riding a vos lak and the Black Wind. Ambushed when we were delivering Harvey Rocastle to containment."

"How did you survive?" Leclerc asked. There wasn't quite suspicion in his voice, but there was something there suggesting suspicion.

"Not sure why they didn't kill us," Alex said. "They sucked our ships into theirs along with Box and we were locked up."

"Good break for you then," a third voice said as a petite woman appeared out of nowhere, a huge sniper rifle strapped to her back. "I think they're telling the truth, Alvin."

"Nice of you to join in, Agent Sullivan," Noorland said waspishly. "How come you got let out now then?"

"Nick Roper let us out," Navarro said. Both Leclerc and Noorland looked at each other at that. "Killed a couple of Taxeen in the process."

Alex tried to hide how impressed she still was by that small fact. Weapon or not, Taxeen were not easy opponents to disable. She'd seen the bodies of more on the way here. He'd undoubtedly employed the element of surprise, but it had been enough.

"Oh, he's running around loose, is he?" Leclerc asked, sounding annoyed. "That's not good. We've got a team looking for him. He came here undercover to find out what was going on. I think that's probably gone to hells then."

An explosion rocked the airbase and Alex looked around in bemusement. "Take it the battle's going well then?"

"Not from what I hear," Noorland said. "I think they could use reinforcements, but they'll not get here in time. The ships are getting pounded by this place's laser grid. I've tried hacking into them but Will's better at this stuff than I am. So far, no luck."

Alex glanced around, hoping to see any trace of something she could take into battle. It was a frustrating feeling, she'd been out of the cockpit for far too long and she needed to be back in one. Sitting in a cell had left her almost going crazy for it, she knew it was like an addiction, but she didn't care. Not until she saw it in the far corner of the hangar, something that made her heart leap. "What the hells is that?!" she asked, trying to sound nonchalant. Her stomach was doing somersaults with glee at what she saw.

Hello baby.

Into a hangar, Nick noticed, still clutching the blaster rifle close as he ran through the doors and there they were. He saw them immediately, Claudia Coppinger and Wim Carson preparing to board a Hope-Standard shuttle, a pointed nose two-person vehicle with a narrow wing span. It was probably the ideal vehicle to leave in, it gave the impression of being something that was ideal for falling but also it packed a surprising range of manoeuvrability. They'd just finished loading some stuff aboard, he didn't see what and he didn't care. He brought the rifle up, sighted the two of them and squeezed the trigger, two, three, four, five times, single shots driven straight at the two of them.

Wim Carson reacted superhumanly fast, spun on the spot and suddenly a stream of light shot from his clenched fist, sword-like. He... No way! Nick couldn't quite believe it, he fucking parried the blasts down into the ground and swept the blade up in a challenge.

"Mister Roper," he said cheerfully. "It's so nice of you to join us."

Claudia stiffened at the sight of him but said nothing. Maybe she'd been lost for words. That'd be nice.

"Pleasure is all mine," Nick said. He flipped the switch on the rifle to fully automatic fire and returned the grin. "All mine." He opened fire again, the rifle dancing in his arms as he started to strafe sideways, suddenly certain he didn't want to be stood in the same spot if Wim could turn aside laser blasts. Already he was running through the options in his mind, determined not to be caught out. More shots he aimed in Claudia's direction, if he could take her out, it'd be mission accomplished. But Wim blocked them all, deflecting them either into the ground or harmlessly wide. None came back his way, thankfully, he wasn't sure if he could evade them forever. But he knew his power pack wouldn't last, and when it ran out, he'd be in trouble. Wim's face never lost its serenity as it was bathed in the glow of the weapon sweeping in front of him.

Finally, Nick's weapon ran out of power and he saw the savage look of triumph on his opponent's face, the expression of a man who knew victory was imminent and he was trying to savour it before applying the final cut. He couldn't help it, Wim jerked a hand in his direction and the useless rifle flew from his grip. The surprise momentarily threatened to overtake everything else. He had no other weapon, bar his reclaimed summoner but he wasn't about to send a spirit against that energy blade. It'd cut them to pieces in no time at all.

"I suppose that this is the way it would always have to end," Wim said softly. "And for that, I am truly sorry. I wish there was another way."

Nick's head jerked up, he heard something to the left, one of the hangar doors opening noisily. As did Wim and so did Claudia, all of them looked towards it as something fizzed and burned angrily at the controls before the doors slid lazily open and a young girl, reaching the end of her teens with coffee-coloured skin and rusty red hair came running through. Wim's face lit up, Nick was more preoccupied by noticing that she had the same sort of weapon as him, a bright energy blade clutched in her fist. She looked up, saw the three of them and blanched. Her lips moved in a silent curse and Wim threw both arms up in a mock sign of welcome.

"I knew you hadn't died," he said warmly. "I knew you'd find your way back to me. Why chase something that will eventually return. I could feel you all this time."

She rolled her eyes, held her weapon out in front of her. "Lucky me," she said sarcastically. Nick could detect a trace of bile in there. "Don't suppose you're going to step aside and let me leave, are you?"

"Well I didn't before now, did I?" Wim said. "That's really up to the Mistress. I suppose if you swore loyalty to her, she might let you live." His face hardened. "I wouldn't though. Any word out of your mouth would be a poisonous lie. The only thing I'll believe is your dying breath." He swept his weapon up with a flurry, a battle stance Nick knew that much. He wasn't entirely sure what was going on here, but it looked like some sort of family tiff. Her own weapon hissed back and suddenly Wim had another weapon in his hand, a second one.

Sharon!

He'd never known that was what it did before but seeing the weapon erupt into life, it felt almost like a nail in Wim Carson's coffin. It was a hard feeling to explain, like he could see so much of the previous owner within it. Everything about it screamed Sharon, too many memories suddenly threatened to overcome him. He'd seen that thing so many times he'd almost taken it for granted. Now to see it in the hands of another...

"You know I didn't kill her," Wim suddenly said, glancing over towards him. Nick reacted with a start, not expecting it. "I really didn't, I'm sorry she died. That wasn't my intention. I wasn't the one who shot her." What?! Nick didn't know what to say, wondering at the same time, if he wasn't involved then how did he know she'd been shot.

Anything else he might have said was lost as the girl raced towards him and suddenly the two of them were engaged in combat, lightning fast and beautifully deadly, three blades hammering away at each other.

The blank slate was tough, Wilsin had to begrudgingly concede that. There was no other way to go about it. He was fighting two highly trained Unisco operatives simultaneously, taking blows that would have crippled any normal man, instead he just shrugged them off, didn't react beyond a few scant signs of discomfort across his features momentarily. How do you beat someone who apparently couldn't be harmed? They were tag teaming him now, the other hitting him hard when he was focused on one of them. As tough as he might be, he couldn't keep his focus on twin targets at the same time. He came after Wilsin, he made to evade every powerful blow thrown his way while Harper went at him from behind, throwing punches and kicks to every normally sensitive area, the knees, the solar plexus, the neck, anything she could hit. None of it had any visible impact. Not until he rounded on her and threw a punch which might have taken her head from her shoulders had it landed. She ducked with a grunt, tried to tackle him to the ground with limited effectiveness, her shoulder bouncing off his stomach.

Having been hit once, Wilsin had no desire for a repeat performance. With him turned, he took a run-up and sprang onto the huge broad back, wrapped both arms around the powerful neck, bringing all his strength to bear on trying to twist it. He heard a deep chuckling laugh building from deep down in the man's body, all efforts to snap the neck coming to naught. It was like trying to snap a stone wall in two. Only his reactions saved him as the blank slate hurled himself back at the wall, hard. Wilsin flung himself free, heard the crack as the man hit the wall. He hoped it was his spine but somehow, he doubted they would be that lucky. There definitely was a twitch within those craggy features, he hoped he'd hurt himself. Indeed, he was proved right as the man stepped away from the wall, he saw a huge dent within the metal. If he held any discomforts from hitting it, he wasn't showing them. At the same time, Wilsin mentally blanched about what would have happened had he been caught between man and wall.

Okay, so I don't do that again.

The blank slate was on the attack again, this time facing them head on, he didn't charge, didn't run, just moved slowly and deliberately. Almost like he intended to intimidate the hells out of them. And that was just too bad, Wilsin thought. Unisco agents don't intimidate. This time they attacked from the front, ducking under the first blows thrown at them by the ham-sized fists and landed their punches simultaneously, the same locations. The blank slate stiffened, a sudden expression of pain shooting into his eyes, just for a moment. And in that moment, David Wilsin dared to dream. Maybe, just maybe the two of them had managed to do together what one couldn't alone.

He'd underestimated the blank slate, the man recovered all too quickly, swept out a huge palm and shoved Wilsin back. Shoving wasn't giving it enough credit, it was like being hit by a tractor, it drove shattered armour back into his aching ribs and he hit the ground with a yelp of pain. All the breath was forced out of him as the blank slate rounded on Mel Harper, a Harper who looked so very tiny stood alone in front of the monolith of fury before her.

Credit to her, she did fight, managed to land another three or four good punches until finally he tagged her with a brutal punch to the jaw. Wilsin heard something snap, saw her jaw bent at an awkward angle. Suddenly unsteady on her legs, he saw her wobbling, desperately tried to force himself to his feet. He needed to get back in there…

Too late. Blood was running down her face; the blank slate was upon her. She tried one final time, threw an unsteady kick and almost toppled off balance. She'd have hit the floor if the blank slate hadn't caught her by the hair and snapped her back towards him, catching her a tremendous punch in the face as she flailed helplessly. No mistaking that crack, Wilsin realised as he watched her fall to the ground, her head bouncing hard off the floor, her neck at an awkward angle.

Son of a bitch!

Fresh fury filled him as he rose to his feet, all previous pain a distant memory to him. How he was going to put him down, he didn't know. But put him down he was going to do. Not just for him, but for Harper. She'd deserved better than to die like this!

"Get away from that ship!"

The accent was broad Canterage, not altogether removed from Fagan's, but the men coming into the hangar weren't as friendly. Alex Nkolou turned, pointed her borrowed blaster at them and fired, getting one shot away before a flurry came back her way. She ducked down under the landing strut, heard the blasts shatter harmlessly against the ship above her.

What a ship it was. She'd never seen curves so sleek and streamlined, even if she wasn't keen on the emerald piping adorning an otherwise silver sheen. No time to admire it now, Navarro and Noorland were shooting back at the previous owners unless she was mistaken. Leclerc spun from cover, firing from the hip and scattering them into fractured groups while somewhere far above them, Anne Sullivan's saga boomed three, four, five times. She heard yells, imagined them falling. The borrowed X7 felt heavy in her hands, she'd never much been one for blaster play. It felt... wrong, for want of a better term.

Still she was nearly in through the hatch, nearly aboard the albus-class ship. A lot larger than a fighter and packing increasingly more firepower, they were still incredibly manoeuvrable and could take a lot of damage should the need arise. The classing marked it as a smuggler's runner, or at the very least the source of a great many wet dreams for those who aspired to the profession. The shots were still coming although they'd slowed to a few paused flurries.

The front of the ship was disc shaped, the rear more of a squat square shape that curved up at the top, a single chunky outlook sticking out the top of it, a mirror image of the same design at the bottom. Top and bottom mounted manual cannons, unless she was mistaken. Until she got aboard, she wouldn't be able to fully assess its attack capabilities, but those cannons looked powerful. Easily strong enough to blow an eaglefighter into tiny pieces.

It was an Elki model unless she was mistaken. One of the T-J500's, straight out of Serran. Not many of them still around, they'd long been upgraded into the, in her opinion, much inferior T-K600S. The upgraded ships had been much more popular, plenty of them had been sold to the Allied Kingdoms Army over the years. For the first time in her life, she thought she was in love. Even from behind cover, she couldn't stop staring.

Noorland's hacking tool was doing its job, slowly but surely. She could see it cycling through the numbers on the tiny screen, searching thousands of combinations for the right code to unlock the hatch. Then she'd need to hardwire into the control system, find out what she was dealing with. That she might not be able to fly it didn't enter her head. If it was air-worthy, then she'd have it off the ground sooner or later.

By the looks the battle outside, the fighters were tearing each other apart, while the base itself hammered at the dreadnoughts, preventing them from getting too close. A ship like this could just about change the flow of battle, if she'd read the situation right. Whoever was commanding the five kingdoms fleet had erred in their tactics, they'd elected not to bring cruisers into play and it could cost them dearly. The entire fleet looked like it had been thrown together at minimum notice and they'd gotten what they could. Wouldn't have surprised her in the slightest if that was the case.

At least coming out of the airbase, she'd be able to get close to those guns. Noorland had already filled her and Navarro in on the deal from what he'd been able to pull from the computers. Every onboard defensive cannon functioned as part of a chain reaction protocol, they'd fire one after another, all in a row, the combined force of over a hundred blasts enough to deal with anything. One dreadnought had already found that out to its cost. She'd looked out onto the battle, had seen the last traces of smouldering wreckage vanish out of sight.

That had been the point she'd known she needed to get out there as soon as possible. In here, it was marginally safer. Out there, she'd be taking a huge risk. She was tired and hungry, would be rusty behind the controls of a ship. But at the same time, Alex wasn't about to stand by and do nothing.

She was going to make her contribution, one way or another.

"Sooner or later, everyone has to take a running jump into the unknown."
Amalfus to Kyra Sinclair and Gideon Cobb about the unpredictability of situations.

The third day of Summerfall.

Kyra hissed inwardly, felt one of the blades flash just a little too close to her face, light searing across her vision and involuntarily, she felt herself recoil and surrendered a little of her position. He was on her immediately, both blades hammering down at her own. She reacted as she needed to, defending desperately for her life. Fighting against two weapons when you only had one was a desperate gambit, you needed to be twice as fast to avoid being cut to pieces, especially if the opponent possessed more than a modicum of skill. Already she was tiring, drawing more and more on the Kjarn to supplement her movements, her blade leaving faded imprints of colour in the air. She was lucky, very lucky her opponent's moves and motions seemed rusty, out of form. Were he any sort of practiced sword master, this fight would already have been over. As much as her confidence in herself was justified at times, she held no delusions she was the greatest kjarnblade wielder ever. She was young, she lacked experience her opponent might possess, given his years on her. Holding her own against him was commendable, but it'd count for nothing if he cut both her arms off.

Of course, there was more than one way to fight. One of his blades came down, she pushed it back and then jumped back several feet, throwing out a hand to strike him with an invisible wall of force that sent him staggering. He hadn't expected it and with both his hands full, his ability to counter it was nullified. The hand gesture wasn't necessary but, as she'd always been reminded, it was useful as a focus. With just that simple piece of motion, you knew exactly what you needed to do, and it was easier than doing it without. The vigour behind the motion helped as well, push forward hard and inevitably some of the aggression bled into it. Just a little nudge and it was controlled, placed. The thinking was sound. She'd seen those who could throw someone across a room just by looking at them, but she was a kingdom from being able to.

Somehow, she doubted right now he had the control to fight back with the Kjarn minus a free hand. She smiled at him, not ashamed to admit quietly to herself she was loving this. As one of the possible heirs to the Cavanda, this was one of the things she'd been trained for since she'd been inducted into the group. To face the Vedo should they ever return, to ensure they stayed extinct.

Being bisected would probably remove that enjoyment. But she went in again, once more traded a flurry of blows with him, this time trying to force him onto the defensive. She heard him grunt, saw his nostrils flaring and his chest rising and falling with the exertions. He didn't like it. He wanted to kill her, he was going to make every effort to, but he was slowly realising, and she could see it in his face, she wasn't going to make it easy for him. She kept her breathing level, kept her form firm and continued to strike at his two blades with vicious thrusts, alternating between rapier fast slashes that he struggled to halt, and hammer blows that rained down on him, each of them threatening to break through his defence.

With Wim distracted, Nick turned his attention to Claudia. If he had a weapon, it'd be so easy, just point and shoot, click, boom, dead, no more trouble. That wasn't an option. He tried to move towards her, saw her eyes narrow in his direction and she raised a hand. For a moment, he half-expected something bad to happen until he saw the slim silver remote in her grasp. He relaxed, not sure what he'd been expecting but it didn't do to jump like at the first sign of danger, before he saw a slim finger deliberately push a button on it.

That might not be good!

He saw movement in the background, over at her shuttle and hurled himself out the way as a flurry of lethal cannon fire obliterated the spot where he'd been stood. They continued to track him, he lunged behind some overturned supply crates, praying to whichever Divines might be listening there was nothing explosive inside. That'd make the story a short one, the title being Unquestioned Failure. It wasn't something he wanted his epitaph to be.

He lay there several seconds until the fire faded into silence, raised his head to sneak a glance. They hadn't retreated. Wim Carson and the girl still fought, moving around the full area of the hangar now, the girl looked almost primal savage in the rage stamped across her features, her hair blowing about and caked in sweat to add to that look. Wim Carson looked like he was struggling, his footsteps slowing, something about his movements suggesting fatigue. They bore under the exertions, weaker, wearier. Just another missed chance. He regretted shooting at him all those times now, if he still had some shots left. Maybe the girl would kill him. He could live with that. Whoever she was, she might do his job for him. It wouldn't be as satisfying but he didn't care. Across the way, she sprang up and hammered her sword onto Carson's two, the effort requiring both to rise block. And then with her free hand, she swept out a vicious punch, one that didn't quite connect but Carson reacted as if it had, his body doubling over, swords cutting a groove into the ground beneath his feet.

The girl kicked out, hit him in the wrist with a boot as he tried to block, and Nick was sure he heard the crack as one of the swords died and was thrown clear. It landed somewhere in the distance with a faint 'clink' on the metal floor. That was Sharon's, unless he was mistaken. He was still trying to wrap his head around the idea of Sharon owning a laser sword, but there was no time for that line of thought right now. It'd have to wait.

Alex Nkolou wasn't impressed.

"You know who this guy was?" Noorland asked, she heard him over the earpiece he'd given her. It wasn't directed at her; it wasn't directed at anybody, but she got the feeling he was talking for his voice to be heard. "Sammy Regan."

"Who?" Navarro sounded about as disinterested as her from the higher gun emplacement, it sounded like he was far more impressed with the potential of the new toy he had to play with. He wasn't the only one, she thought with a smile.

"Boss of the RCE. Regan Community Enterprises? Major player in the Canterage criminal underworld. Guess Cyris wasn't bullshitting us about Coppinger getting all these criminal hard cases on board with her plan."

"Mmmm-hmmm." Alex still wasn't impressed but she'd stopped listening now, instead running through her pre-flight checks. Of course, they'd been locked, the controls had needed to be over-ridden and quickly. The battle wasn't going well outside, there were going to be mass casualties by the looks of things and this... This felt right, being in a cockpit again. If Regan was who'd they'd just gunned down, and this was his ship, she wasn't impressed with the levels of security he'd employed to make sure nobody flew off in it. He had had one of those Canterage accents that made the speaker sound like they were permanently on something that befuddled the senses.

First day of Unisco flight training, she'd had to crack into the ship she was due to fly. Because, as the instructor had primly pointed out, you're not going to always have a ready-made ship available for you to pilot. Sometimes you need an unfamiliar one. Sometimes you might have to appropriate one and you need to know how to get in, how to make the computer dance to your tune.

Noorland had given her a transponder beacon to announce their presence as friendly to the fleet. She'd hesitated over the idea of turning it on, wondering how long she could run the surprise on the enemy, before she'd gone ahead and activated it. Better to be shot down by an enemy than an ally. At least you could shoot back at the enemy.

The cockpit was small, suitable for one pilot and the seat tilting back at an awkward forty-five-degree angle, her feet locked into restraints at the base of the seat for added security. She wasn't sure she liked it. If she could find the override, she already would have disabled the feature. But there wasn't time now and if the ship was shot down, being able to run for it wouldn't make a difference.

She'd wanted someone in the belly gun. Both Leclerc and Noorland had declined, citing their presence as being more important here, Noorland especially. Then Anne Sullivan had volunteered. How she felt about that, she didn't know. The woman was a sniper and the job basically involved shooting. But still, taking the time to line up a shot, watching and waiting was very different from the frantic pace of aerial dogfights. This could get very messy. Still what was life without a little risk. And the cannons did both need to be manned. From here, all she had was a pair of solitary forward lasers, powerful but not tremendously effective when surrounded from all sides, as well as torpedoes. They weren't military issue, but they'd leave a nasty hole in a target. Regan had obviously had some contacts capable of supplying him with something illegal. The T-J500 was living up to its reputation as the ship of a desperado in this instance. The transponder ID she'd picked herself. Whatever the ship had been called before, it was now the Wolf Rose. Why, she couldn't say. It had felt right.

"Guess this is it then," she said.

"May you die before people forget your name," Leclerc said through the earpiece solemnly. "All of you."

"Not great sentiments, Jacques," Sullivan replied. "I'd prefer not to go at all."

"You might be going into the wrong engagement then," Navarro said, the Wolf Rose already airborne. She did handle well, Alex had to admit. Whatever the faults with the security, there could be no complaints about the maintenance of the engines and the controls. It felt good to be back in the cockpit, she thought, as she gently directed the ship towards the exit. Ready to hit the thrusters in three, two and a half, two, one and a half, one and...

She punched them, and the Wolf Rose shot out the airbase like a cork from a bottle, straight into the fray.

Here we go!

Strangely, she didn't feel worried by what came ahead. Either they'd die, or they wouldn't. Couldn't fight what would happen. Only fools didn't accept the future for what it was, something that would happen when it happened and there was no changing that.

Fresh shots rang out above Nick and he chanced a look, grimacing as he did. Someone else was approaching, several fresh blasts crashing into the shuttle's automated gun. He heard a shatter, an eruption of sparks and allowed himself a second look to confirm his suspicions. The gun turret hung limply, useless. The bad news was he still had a pair of blasters trained on him, the wielder heavyset and roughly the same age as Coppinger albeit someone who looked like they'd fared not as well in the constant struggle that was life. There was also something dreadfully familiar about him. He'd seen the guy before, he'd been a contestant in the Quin-C. Nick had even been to see him fight a few weeks earlier. How times change, he thought with a dreadful sense of irony clasping at his stomach. Where once there had been unquestioning friendliness in that expression, now his face bore a look of determined concentration.

"Ah, there's the scallywag," Connor Caldwell said jovially. A pair of black eyes protruded from his hands, pointed firmly in Nick's direction. "Come on out Mister Roper and join the fray. Plenty of fun to be had by all."

"Do you mind if I decline?" Nick asked, pushing himself up onto his feet. Both blasters were pointed at him, Caldwell had moved to stand next to Claudia.

"Be a bit rude, I feel," Caldwell grinned. "But I won't hold it against you. Hands up please, my friend. No sudden movements."

"You see, Mister Roper," Claudia said and there was just a small hint of unbearable smugness in her voice. "It pays not just to have friends around but family. There's a certain sort of loyalty there you just can't buy."

"Family?" Nick tried to sound offhand, he didn't want it to sound like he knew more about Coppinger than he should. It was probably too late to explain stuff away without mentioning Unisco but no point showing all the cards. Now she mentioned it, he recalled the files on her did mention Claudia Coppinger had an estranged brother. "What is he, your dad?"

"Cheeky bastard," Caldwell said. "That's the funny thing about family. You can't hold a grudge forever, y'see. Someone eventually wants to bury to hatchet. And sometimes you need to be the bigger man and go to fix things. See, I love my sister for that when she could have done all this on her own."

Who shot the gun out then? Nick wondered, not entirely sure what had just happened. Still he raised his hands above his head and glanced around, looking for any sort of way out. There had to be one somehow.

"You can't stop progress, Mister Roper," Claudia said. "It's sad but true. What is going to happen is going to happen and nothing you do will stop that. Nothing the five kingdoms can do will save them."

"I'll take your word for it," Nick said. "I probably won't be around to see it, right?"

"Maybe, maybe not," Claudia said. "You might still be…"

"I think you will be," Caldwell said, cutting her off. Her eyes narrowed, and she turned to look at him with bemusement.

"Collison…"

"Connor," Caldwell grinned. "You know that thing about loyalty? You can't just turn it on like a tap, forget everything you already knew."

The look on her face as he pointed both weapons at her was priceless. He quickly underhanded one weapon to Nick who caught it, fought the urge to point and shoot the woman the moment it hit his palm.

"I didn't tell you everything I did while I wasn't talking to you," Caldwell said quietly for a moment before the friendliness came back to his voice where some might have sounded sarcastic or cruelly triumphant. "But things have an astonishing way of working out, sister."

"Five kingdoms fleet," Alex shouted into the comms system. "This is the Wolf Rose, requesting permission to join in the fray."

"This is the Wild Stallion, Wolf Rose, identify yourself immediately." The voice on the other end of the line was taut, harsh and stressed. "Who is this?"

"Lieutenant Alexandra Nkolou…" She grimaced, still hated the way her own name failed to roll off the tongue even after all these years of practice. "Formerly of Wolf Squadron. I have an albus class ship and… Damnit!"

She jerked the Rose to the side, still grinning like a little kid at the way the ship responded to the deftest of touches, a hiss of laser fire streaking past their prior position. She continued to weave the ship down through the fray, letting loose with the forward lasers every time an unlucky eaglefighter happened across her bow. Above and below her, the turrets continued to blaze away as Navarro and Sullivan pumped high powered blasts into anything hostile that happened too close for comfort.

"What is your identifying number?"

"Ah... Four-alpha, three-six-two-eight-bravo..." She furrowed her brow. Yeah that was right. Alex jinked the ship up between the gap left by two eaglefighters, saw them both explode in the periphery of her vision. "Seven! Sorry there was a seven on the end of that. Also have Sergeant Ross Navarro on board and Agent Anne Sullivan, all of Unisco."

"Well it appears you no longer require permission to join the attack," another voice said dryly, something familiar about it. "Lieutenant, this is Admiral Criffen. You're closer to that damn thing than any of us. We've had data forwarded to us by your team on the inside. Targets of convenience in disabling those guns. Can you take them out?"

Alex didn't hesitate before nodding to herself. "I can start the run on your mark, Admiral." She flicked several buttons, found the data packet he'd mentioned. "Requesting fighter support on my six."

Criffen looked across the deck at one of his aides, already holding out his hand for the data file in her hands. He wanted a quick look at Lieutenant Alexandra Nkolou before he gambled more ships to join her. Already this engagement was turning out to be most irregular. The Sitting Target was bombarding the airbase with long range shots from its cannons, but they didn't look to be having an effect from range. The more craters they tore in the outer shells of their target, the more vigorously it was shooting back, shots pounding impotently against its shields.

Nkolou... Wolf Squadron Lieutenant... Unisco pilot for five years, several classified missions in her native Vazara and in Serran... Graduated her class with top marks... Exceptional reflexes and cool under pressure... Great judgement in crisis. Presumed dead.

That last one was a little surprising but if she'd been on that airbase, it made sense Her last assignment had been to escort a high security prisoner to mainland Vazara from Carcaradis Island, a transport that had vanished on the way there. There'd been some evidence of an attack. The presumably late Richard Wolfmeyer, commander of Wolf Squadron had left in his notes that she was an exceptional pilot and potential command material. Her code did match. Voice pattern analysis had matched. It had to be her. And he'd watched the first few moments of her entering the fray, straight into the midst of the largest concentration of eaglefighters...

She could fly. It had been many years since Criffen had entered a fighter cockpit himself, but she was handling the much large albus class ship like a HAX. That took some special skills.

"Lieutenant Nkolou," he said, glancing down at one of the screens. He tapped on three separate squadrons that had taken severe depletions to their numbers, Five, Nine and Seventeen. "For the duration of this engagement, I'm giving you a field promotion to Commander. Squadrons Five, Nine and Seventeen, gather your remnant numbers and converge on Commander Nkolou's ship."

There it was. Another gamble, one he hoped paid off. Tactically, it made sound sense on every level. Five, Nine and Seventeen had eight fighters left between them. Forming them up as one unit would hopefully give Nkolou's potential suicide mission more of a chance of success. And the temporary increase in rank would hopefully get them over the line, glue them all together enough for one final push. Those guns needed taking out.

"Thank you, Admiral," Nkolou said. She sounded both surprised and grateful. He took that as a good thing. "Over and out. Join up on me, squadrons. Keep your call-signs."

A general chorus of acknowledgement came up over the communications system, voices of all kingdoms and genders. This was happening. Her time to shine. He hoped she wouldn't let him down.

"Let's win this thing."

David Wilsin hit the wall and just for a moment, his vision went black. He couldn't keep this up for much longer. His knuckles were raw, red and bleeding. He was sure he'd broken some of them, but he had to keep on going. His entire body felt like one big bruise and worse still, his giant opponent still looked fresh and healthy.

"When you get to the hells," the big guy growled, striding over to him. "Tell 'em Domis Di Carmine sent you there in the name of the glorious Mistress."

It hurt but he managed to roll his eyes, pushed himself to his feet. He was unsteady, tottering and just about able to keep his balance. Maybe he should just give up, let it all go and let death take him...

No!

It was only a quiet voice, but it cut across his subconscious like a blaster shot, burning deep into his pain fogged brain. You never surrender, you never give up and you never die on the job until it's complete. It had been years since he'd been through the Unisco training, but those words had never left his mind.

He turned, threw a punch that the blank slate... Domis... caught one handed and raised a craggy eyebrow in bemusement. As if to say 'really'? Wilsin tried to jerk his hand back away from him, found it caught tight in the vice-like grip. Domis wasn't even squeezing, just holding him at arm's length, appraising him like a butcher appraised a fine cut of meat. Those dark little eyes studied him as he tried to jerk himself free, efforts cut off when Domis brutally kicked out at him, the blow catching him in the side and he felt something give, at least one rib snap and fire shoot through him. He'd have fallen had Domis not still held him up, gradually applying more pressure to his hand.

"I always heard Unisco were something special," Domis said in that slow deliberate voice. "You are nothing and I am going to show you that. You will be broken."

His face split into a grin and then everything changed, just a little too fast for Wilsin to realise what had happened but suddenly it felt like he was sat on top of a miniature explosion, the bang, the light and the heat and suddenly the cold sucked at him, threatening to draw him in. For a moment he thought he was dead, but he could still feel the pain. He blinked through the blood gushing in his eyes, saw light rupturing through a hole in the wall. Domis was distracted, he jerked his free hand back, desperate to ignore the screaming pain and went for the X7 holstered at his waist.

As Domis turned back towards him, the shots were perfect, two straight between the eyes. But he didn't stop there, for they'd been marginally more effective than the previous attempts to shoot him, Domis was in pain, blinded and staggering. Some brain function had to have been affected, Wilsin took a deep breath and tried to ignore the pain before lunging towards him. It was like hitting a brick wall with his shoulder, fresh pain tore through his body, but it had the desired effect. Domis fell back, off-balance again at the lips of the hole.

One more step and he'd fall. The wounds on his face were already starting to close again and Wilsin didn't hesitate. He pulled the X7 and fired again and again, emptying the power pack into him, taking a step forward with every shot until he was shooting at point blank range. More than one hit him in the face, he reached out with one giant arm and clasped at the ragged edge of the wall, still desperate to hold himself up.

The final shot hit him in the hand and that was enough, strength in his fingers faded catastrophically and suddenly they were scrabbling at empty air. He couldn't hold himself any longer and then he was gone.

He slumped down, suddenly relieved, all the exertions and the pain catching up with him. David Wilsin felt his back hit the wall, felt fresh stabbing sensations creep through him and yet that was fine. He'd done a good job here, he'd done something he'd thought impossible moments earlier and he'd come through it. He was chalking this one up as a win. A very big win. The cold air continued to buffet him, threatening to drag him down and reluctantly he got to his feet and shuffled away from it, reloading his weapon. Several feet away, he found his Featherstone, bent down to pick it up with some difficulty. Close by was Harper, he didn't want to look at her, but he couldn't help himself. It was something he needed to do, needed the reminder. He wanted to take her out of here, make sure she got the proper burial, but sometimes it just couldn't be done. It might just be a sacrifice she'd have to make in a war that she'd never started.

"Damnit," he said softly. He looked at her, then the hole in the side of the station, the air still blowing in. Be better just to kick her out here than let Coppinger and her lot get their hands on her. He didn't even want to consider doing that, he felt dirty for thinking it.

The anger on her face was noticeable, she'd screwed it up like old paper and Nick was sure she was just seconds away from a full breakdown. Already she'd gone crimson and it was slowly turning purple. He hadn't known Caldwell was a Unisco agent. Nobody he'd spoken to had either. And privately, he wasn't prepared to take his word on it until he heard from either Arnholt or Brendan King in relation to the matter. If anyone knew, then one of those two had to. Still, it looked good odds he might be. He had the feeling all of this was just some twisted game to someone and, if it was Claudia Coppinger, then she'd just been dealt a massive blow. More than that, she already looked like she was set to take it personally.

"You…"

"Unisco," Caldwell corrected, looked a little sorrowful as he said it. "Sorry, sister. But things happen. Family is what you make of it. One family kicked me out, another took me in. I was so pleased when you got back in touch. My superiors will be pleased with me when I report what you've been up to here. I suspected you were up to something when you got back in touch. This was just the perfect opportunity for them to find out for sure."

"You betrayed your blood!" She spat out each word as if they were poison. "There's going to be a special place in my new hells for you, Collison!"

He shrugged. "You know it's not going to happen, sister. I'm sorry to tell you that and if you still believe it will, then you might be able to get away with an insanity plea."

"You know I'm not insane!" she hissed. "You two both are if you think you'll stop me achieving my destiny."

"Do you have any idea how ridiculous you sound right now?" Caldwell asked. "I'm sorry, it's embarrassing. There is no grand destiny for you. All you've set out to achieve is what you sewed yourself. That should make you proud, but it should also disgust you."

"I'm beyond petty emotion like that," she retorted. "Morals, ethics, decency, disgust... They're just words and what are they compared to power."

"Words can have power, just as much as actions, Claudia," Caldwell said. More and more, Nick was starting to feel like a spare part. He wondered if he'd be better off just shooting her, one in the head and spare the five kingdoms a lot of time, credits and pain. It'd probably be for the best. Even if it wasn't the right thing to do. And he had previous for doing this. Nah, he'd let the two siblings play out what they were doing, it was what they seemed to want to do. Let them. There were some real issues here, it was almost entertaining. He glanced around to where the fighters were, both had vanished and one of the hangar doors sliding shut. If he focused, he could still hear the distant clash of their weapons meeting with.

"You're right," she said. "The type of power that needs to be backed up by actions. Words are cheap, they are the tools of governments and pawns. My rule..."

"You do know that you can't be allowed to rule," Nick said, cutting her off. "Don't you? I mean, you're insane for a start. That's usually a pretty destabilising factor when you want to be in charge. It makes long term planning erratic at best."

"If the two of you insist on pointing those weapons at me," she said, her face splitting open into an awful grin. "I in turn have to insist you use them. I'm either walking out of here or I die. I'm not going with either of you. I have too much to do, submitting to your notions of justice doesn't appeal."

"You sound like you think you have a choice, sister," Caldwell said.

"No," she replied. That grin grew wider. "You think you do. But you haven't realised just how wrong you are yet."

Derenko's team hadn't found Nick Roper, but they had found something just as good, if not better in the context of the greater mission. A lot of it had to do with them being taken by surprise but you just went with it and claimed the victory. They'd found the heads of most of the great crime syndicates around the five kingdoms sat together in one great room. Some of them had been armed and had tried to resist. They'd been killed immediately, as had their bodyguards who had made the same choices. The others had been held at gunpoint as Derenko had stepped forward.

"Listen, ladies and gentlemen," he said. "I really don't care about you all now. Your people shot first, that's why they died. But we've got bigger fish to deal with and so I'm giving you a limited time choice. You can surrender now and come with us when we leave, submit to Unisco justice, we'll even put good words in for you about how you did the right thing when it came down to it. Showing signs of contrition and all that, how you were clearly in over your heads and all that stuff. You were taken in by someone who managed to fool you all as to what you were getting into, maybe even coerced you." He gave them all a friendly grin, as if to remind them that shit happened sometimes.

"Or you can leave and none of us will stop you, you can take the head start and sooner or later we'll remember what we saw here and devote all our resources to hunting you down at a tremendous waste of time and manpower. It's going to annoy everyone involved. And when we do find you, you'll likely be killed resisting arrest because we won't be doing it gently. So, it's your choice. Leaving will be considered a sign of complicity and I really don't think you want that. Because we're probably going to have to name a bunch of new crimes after your boss and I really don't think you want to go down with her."

He gave them a few seconds to think about it. It wasn't technically proper procedure but as he'd said, they weren't the reason they were here. Bigger fish and all that. Coppinger was the mission target. These would be a nice bonus. Some of them did surrender immediately, once Anthony Fratelli stuck his wrists out and sighed. Of all the faces in the room, he was perhaps the most well-known. Maybe even the most wanted.

"It is in my best interests," he said reluctantly. "None of us wanted this. She's crazy, I don't truck with crazy. Not her kind of crazy. She's like fire, she'll burn up all before her."

"Thank you, Don Fratelli," Aldiss said. It was slow at first but most them did make the same gesture, a sign of deference and surrender, choosing to give up. Doubtless most of them had seen the battle going on outside between the two fleets, they'd felt the pounding the airbase was taking from long range weapons and they figured being alive gave them a chance. That was something you could always rely on with these criminal types, they had an incredible sense of self-preservation. Derenko grinned to himself. Even if they didn't get Coppinger, it'd be a good second prize consolation.

Now where the hells were Harper and Wilsin?

"Okay, everyone, form up on me!" Alex shouted. "You've got your targeting data, go in groups of two and hit them hard. First fighter draws the weapons fire, second one hit it with your missiles. By the way, you're now Makeshift Squadron. Make the name proud." She hit a few buttons. "Keep your numbers from before." Her radar shifted to display the change in ID's, just so she knew where everyone was.

"Right away Commander," Makeshift Two said quickly. She had Two, Three, Five, Six, Eight, Ten, Thirteen and Seventeen, knew nothing about any of them, who they were beyond the call signs, but she was relying on them. Plus, commander had a nice ring to it.

Apparently, Navarro agreed with her.

"Check you out," he said. "Commander. Straight out of captivity. Nice work, Alex."

"Appreciated, now keep shooting!" she ordered. Eaglefighters were everywhere, she didn't want to take a stray shot in the rear because Navarro was too busy trying to have a chat. She jerked the Wolf Rose straight down into a dive, cut across the bow of two onrushing fighters and saw them both explode under a barrage of fire from the twin turrets, shrapnel and shards buffeting her shields until she hit the thrusters and accelerated away from their remains, Navarro cheering in her ear.

"Boom! Have some of that!" he yelled.

"You do know there are people in those things, don't you?" Sullivan asked mildly. Her voice betrayed disappointment, almost sternly so.

"Yeah, they're trying to shoot at us," Navarro said, more than a little indignant at her reaction. She knew when he was pissed, his voice took on a higher pitch.

"Doesn't mean you have to like it."

"Hey, each one you put down is another few seconds you get to live," Navarro shot back. "Not getting killed works for me in a big way."

Alex tried to block them out, focused only on the flying, spinning the Wolf Rose almost on the head of a pin, a tight manoeuvre in a HAX, she could feel the sides of the albus straining as she pulled it in this. Controls squealed in defiance, she couldn't do this again. It'd be a real strain on the systems, she didn't want to blow something, yet it had come off almost flawlessly. Now she was locked back on the airbase, the Eye of Claudia or whatever she'd overheard it being called in her cell. The defensive guns were firing again, she could see them starting their chain fire, one, two, three, four, all going for the Bounty Snatcher. Five, six, seven...

"Full thrusters ahead!" she barked. "We need to get on an intercept course, cut those guns off before they build up full power." Eight, nine, ten, eleven...

"You want us to speed on ahead and wait for you?" Makeshift Seventeen asked politely. Somehow, he managed to make it sound sarcastic as well and Alex bit back a retort. Now she was holding the rank of Commander, however temporarily, she had to conduct herself with a little more decorum. She'd find out who he was and kick his ass when they made it out of here. What she did instead was divert even more power into her thrusters and felt the sheer force of the movement plaster her back into her seat, shooting straight past all the HAX's that had moved to overtake her, suddenly she was straight on a collision course with the hull.

Not quite. She would have had she not reacted, shoved the controls straight up and it was tight, oh so tight, she could almost feel the hull scrape against the belly turret, could hear Anne Sullivan swearing angrily, but the upside was during the sudden rise, the twin turrets did flash furiously, she saw three, four, five of the guns explode. The fire halted for several seconds before starting once again. Depleted. She punched the air. Now if the rest of them could do their job, they'd be sitting pretty. More eaglefighters were closing in on them, she could feel shots raining down on her shields and she twisted the Wolf Rose away, saw the flashes of laser screech past her viewport and she accelerated away, daring them to chase her. The guns were firing, two of them exploded into fireballs but more were coming. Makeshift Squadron were already heading for their targets, she was on her own for the moment, no wing support...

She didn't need it. This ship was fast, way too fast for the enemy and so she swung towards the cannons lining the exterior of the airbase, a determined grimace locked across her face. See if you'll follow me down here...

The cannons were slowly building up to a head again, the faint glow spilling from them revealing their time was near, and she punched it once again, hitting her thrusters to maximum...

Here we go again!

She swept straight past the open mouth of the cannon, three, four, five fighters following her as the cannons fired. Two of them exploded instantly, one of them lost a wing and spun out of control until it was hit by the laser fire of another HAX. She couldn't think of a worse way to die. The others lost altitude, crashed hard into the hull to a crescendo of fire.

"Commander, we have arrived at our targets, preparing attack runs now," someone said in her earpiece.

"We could talk all day," Caldwell said. "But I'm afraid we have to get going. There's a nice private cell with your name on it, dear sister."

"You're no brother of mine," Claudia said, narrowing her eyes. "Not now. Not ever again. I renounce you as a traitor to the name Coppinger. When the new world comes, you'll be the first to be dragged before me and I promise you a very unpleasant death." She bared her teeth at him as she said it. Caldwell brushed it off without so much as a retort.

"Did she always go on like this?" Nick asked suddenly. Connor Caldwell craned his head over towards him and gave a half smirk.

"And you!" Claudia said, jabbing a finger towards Nick. "Don't even consider where you're going to be. It's not too late for you to join me though. Shoot him." She jerked her head towards Caldwell. "Shoot him and join me and I'll make you everything you ever wanted to be. I'll give you anything you want."

Nick looked at her long and hard, sighed sadly. "Sorry, there's only one thing I want, and I doubt you're able to give it to me."

A smug smirk replaced the frown. "Oh, you never quite know. You never know when you might see her again."

That caught him with a start, she flexed a hand and hit another button on the remote control. Somewhere in the distance, they heard a roar and a clang, something either way too close or way too loud. They both turned their heads and in that split second, Wim Carson was there, minus a weapon and looking ragged. He brandished a hand at them and suddenly both Nick and Caldwell were airborne, hurled back by invisible force, hitting the ground hard. That moment to recover themselves was all it took, the two of them aboard the shuttle and the engines firing up. Nick cursed, grabbed the blaster pistol and started to fire at it, emptying the power pack into the fuselage but to no avail as it gently rose from the ground and made for the doors at the end of the hangar. More blaster fire behind him, he glanced around and saw Brendan King and co making their way in, all weapons blazing. But even their combined weaponry couldn't do what his blaster had been unable to, laser bolts bouncing off it. One of Brendan's golems even launched a uniblast to no avail, the attack narrowly sailing wide, singeing a wingtip but nothing more.

"Fuck!" Caldwell swore, beating his fist into the ground as the team made their way over towards them. "Where were you twenty seconds ago?"

"Calm it, Agent Caldwell," Brendan said dryly. "Stand down, the pair of you."

"Oh, he is with us then?" Nick asked. "I thought he was bullshitting her."

"Really?" Caldwell replied. "I know all about you. I've been running cover for you since you got up here. Really good plan by the way, Roper. Get yourself captured and brought up here. That's not at all suicidally reckless, is it?"

"How is that any different to what you did?" Nick inquired. "We haven't heard anything from you…"

"Yeah but I wasn't a captive. How were you planning on making your report from here? How were you planning on leaving?"

Nick smirked coolly at him, somewhat aware that the rest of the team was looking at him. "I'd have worked it out."

"Wow, that's reassuring," Caldwell said. "Some real tidy undercover work here and you all come in threatening to blow it all."

"Okay there's a lot of hostility here," Tod Brumley said. "Let's calm it down. Lot of people didn't tell a lot of other people about what was going on."

"We didn't even know where you'd gone," Lysa said to Nick, smiling at him. "We thought Ritellia had had you carted off to some… My Divines! You did it deliberately, didn't you? Took a swing at him to get locked up and hope you'd get dragged up here."

"They seem to like people who hate it the way it is," Caldwell said. "Weird like that, but hey, it almost worked."

Brendan wasn't listening at this point, still engaged in communication with someone else, a frustrated look on his face.

"Listen to me, Admiral," he said angrily. "You need to intercept a shuttle that's departing this airbase. Shoot it down, kill everyone aboard! Yes, I'm aware you're fighting a battle, but the battle is pointless if those aboard get away…. Yes, that couldn't be helped. You can't control every piece on the board, Admiral. It'd be an easier job if we could."

"Err…" Lysa suddenly piped up. "What the hells is that?"

Something scarlet was coming through the open hangar door, prising huge metal slides aside with bare hands, the sound cutting through Brendan's voice with a wicked screech, the being not so much walking as floating, closing in fast…

"And what of life after death? Who's to say the dead don't remain with us in our memories? Because if someone is there to remember them, can they ever truly die?"
James Michael Tan, five kingdoms philosopher.

The third day of Summerfall.

The entire left side of Kyra's body had gone numb. She tried to move it, felt uneasy about the whole thing and hissed in pain as fire coursed through her. Lucky bastard, just…

No, a calm voice somewhere amidst the hurt and the rage rationalised to her. She didn't want to admit it sounded like her in some of her more serendipitous moments. Not luck. You were sloppy, you thought you'd won and he punished you. Which is still less than the master will do if he finds out about this whole damn mess. She gulped at that thought. It wasn't a pleasant one. Few regarding the master were. Sometimes she was sure that voice in her head, calmness personified, was something he'd implanted deep into her mind to ensure he could always monitor her, influence her no matter how far away they might be.

It was ridiculous of course. He didn't have that kind of power…

That you've ever seen, that same voice reminded her. Maybe it was a side effect of the electrical surge that had struck her. She had only just stopped convulsing; he'd had her dead to rights, just as the reverse had been the case moments earlier. Minus one blade and the one he was using flickering badly like it had been poorly constructed, Kyra had taken the offensive and thrown a flurry of attacks at him he'd struggled to keep from touching him. He was tiring, she'd seen that for a while, his movements growing sluggish and all it would have taken was one false step, one which had come, granted but not perhaps as fatal as she had hoped for. He'd tried to push her blade back, overreached and she'd danced around it, feeling the potent mixture of both the Kjarn and exhilaration flowing through her as she'd sheared through the top of his weapon, cut the energy flow through it and rendering it little more than two useless pieces of metal, good only for scrap. She'd had him, fresh joy bursting through her like fireworks as she'd raised her weapon to finish him off, she was going to be the first Cavanda for a good few years to kill a Vedo before the bastard had sucker-punched her, pulled her trick back on her from earlier. She'd tried the lightning, so had he. She'd screamed as it had thrown her back, sent her muscles into spasms, leaving her on the floor in a pile of blood and sweat and the contents of her bladder. All he'd need to do was summon her weapon to his hand and bury it into her face and that'd be the end of Kyra Sinclair. Her story would have been closed.

But he hadn't. She still couldn't work that out as he'd studied her thoughtfully, just for a second and then he'd turned to run, straight back into the hangar. Already she knew what it meant, failure on her part. She could already picture herself bowing before her master, explaining how it had all gone so badly. She could hear the coldness in his voice. So, he'd say, not only did you get yourself captured by powers unaligned to our own cause, but you revealed said powers to those individuals. And with those individuals having a Vedo amongst them, you have also revealed yourself to them. Now they may be few, but it doesn't mean they're gone. Never underestimate an enemy faced with extinction. We might be many, and they might be few, but things change. Once the reverse was true. How long before they now work out we are still out there? Align themselves together once again to hunt us down?

That voice was cold and all too real in her mind, nor was it pleasant. She really didn't want to go back to him but at the same time, what choice did she have? If she ran, he would find her sooner or later. And if it was later, Divines help her. At least if she went back to him, he might find it somewhere in his black heart to grant her a quick death for complete and utter abject failure. Dress it up however you like, that was what it was and that was probably what it would remain. No way of redeeming this situation.

Gingerly, she flexed her muscles and though they were still horribly sore from the current that had raced through them, she was lucky to be in one piece. She'd seen people rendered horribly deformed by pure Kjarn lightning, seen bones contract and flesh melt from the muscles, they looked like nothing more than huge candles by the time the full force of energy had been ripped into them. Those that were lucky died before the pain became indescribable. She'd never forget the screams of those who were still alive, hoarse and cracked through sheer power of a force they couldn't hope to stand against. The man had been a Vedo and a poor one, no doubt. Not a killer instinct in him. A Cavanda wouldn't have left her alive. It probably wouldn't have been a quick death either. Excruciating most likely.

Any threat her master might be able to bring against her wasn't worth considering, at least not for the moment anyway. As she stood up, she realised that, taking in her surroundings. She still had to get off this damn ship anyway before that could happen. If she died doing that, at least it'd solve her problems of dying sooner rather than later.

"Wolf Rose, Commander Nkolou, do you receive?"

That was Criffen's voice again and Alex subconsciously sat up a little straighter in her seat, wishing he'd picked a better time to get in touch. The bombing runs were going well, the newly fashioned together Makeshift Squadron doing their jobs across the killing fields the outer rims of the airbase had slowly become. Before, there had been many guns across a plateau of supposedly unassailable metal. Turned out it wasn't so unbreakable after all. You just had to focus your firepower.

She knew this for she'd blown a hole in it with one of her missiles earlier, something telling her that it was important to hit that precise spot. Who or what or why had remained a mystery but she'd flown by, fired the ordnance into it, watching as the hole had been blown into it, not as grand or majestic as she'd have liked but satisfactory. Several moments later, she could have sworn someone had fallen through, but she couldn't be sure. Still her feelings told her the situation was resolved. After that, she'd given the whole thing no more thought.

"Copy, Admiral," she said. "Reading you."

"There's a call come in from that thing, there's a shuttle out there that needs intercepting. Bring it down. Just tracking it… Data should be on your screen in moments. Unisco high command demands that it be shot down."

She nodded. "Understood. Makeshift Squadron stay on the mission here, I'll be back in a…" She frowned at the data, saw the shape on her tac-reader and flexed her fingers. Two of the Makeshifts were closer, they could swoop in and blast it from the sky without a need to deviate from her course. That was the beautiful thing being in command, she could delegate the task. It was something that felt alien to her, she liked to do it herself, but at the same time she could get used to it, given the chance. "Makeshift Five and Six, deviate from your task and shoot down that shuttle. Now!" She added a touch of authority to her voice, aware it might need it. The people in those gunships didn't know who she was, they didn't know what she could do or that she had apparently only gotten her temporary rank because of her positioning in the battle. But they needed to be professional. If she gave them the order, she expected it to be obeyed. And obeyed it was, the twin HAX's moving away from their bombing run and towards the shuttle.

Alex would have been lying if she said she wasn't enjoying this whole thing in its entirety. People might be dying but being back in the cockpit meant she could do something about it. If they failed, how many more would die? She honestly didn't know. Maybe she didn't want to know.

"And here they come," Claudia said, glancing out the viewport at the two incoming ships. It wasn't a surprise. She'd been expecting them, surprised it had taken this long for them to notice her. Next to her, Wim Carson was piled untidily into his seat, soaked in sweat and stinking the place up something rotten. Shuttle was handling a little sluggishly, no doubt a result of that attack that had clipped them before she'd gotten them out of the hangar. Still that Unisco team and her... No! She wasn't allowing herself to think like that. He was no brother of hers. She'd disowned him. She wouldn't even think his name any more. Only when it came to kill him, would she acknowledge him as what he was. Traitorous bastard.

Maybe he was already dead. She'd set the unialiv on them, it should already be tearing into them right now. Nothing could prepare them for that creature, one of her synthetic spirits. Letting it free had been a tactical gambit, one she'd needed to make and one she would again in the same circumstances. It could have backfired, it still might but if she remained alive, her decisions were sound ones. Death was not an option she'd have to regret.

She heard the computer trill out a warning a weapons lock had engaged, that the two aerofighters were moving into position for the perfect shot.

"Don't you have weapons?" Wim groaned. He looked more than just tired, he looked both physically and mentally exhausted, his clothes burned and torn, his wrist bent at an unnatural angle. He'd lost his weapon, she smirked at that, he was one to talk about them.

"Only automated cannons for repelling boarders," she said. "We're not going to win a fight with those. Can't do too much here and now about that. I was hoping you could."

He stared at her long and hard for a good few seconds, his eyes narrowing deeply suspicious at her. "And what exactly would that be?"

"I'm sure you'll think of something," she said breezily. "Given we're going to die in the next thirty seconds unless you do." She leaned back in her chair and crossed her legs, fighting the urge to whistle jauntily. Now the end could well be imminent, she was surprised to find herself not sad or scared but rather tinged with regret at what could have been.

His glare at her grew but she couldn't find it in herself to care, not as the weapons lock warning turned into a missile incoming warning, she blew on her fingernails and wondered if she had time for a last drink. And then Wim Carson rose with a look of deep loathing on his face, craned his head about, narrowed his eyes and then threw out a hand. She imagined it must have looked exceptionally strange to the naked eye, on the tac-reader the missiles simply ground to a halt themselves and then exploded way short of their target. Looks like she might have time to put those regrets right after all. "And the pilots," she said. "They need removing from the equation. Unless you want them to keep on trying to kill us."

Alex saw it and couldn't believe her eyes as the two Makeshifts she'd despatched towards the shuttle were flying normally for a moment and then everything changed, one of them suddenly jerked wildly starboard-side and crashed hard into its wing mate, both fighters going up in a sudden eruption of fire and debris. First the missiles, an unexpected occurrence in isolation, and now this?

"What the hells just happened to them?!" Navarro yelled. "Never seen any idiot fly like that before. Straight into the side! Some people just shouldn't be allowed in a cockpit!"

Either way, it looked like her mind had been made up, regardless of Navarro's rantings. She jerked her control stick about, drove the Wolf Rose after the shuttle, already plotting an intercept path in her head. At this rate, she'd be on them in moments and then they'd be hers. It was something that needed to be done and she was going to damn well do it right.

"What the hells is that thing?!" Brendan barked as the creature closed in on them, flying without wings, gliding gracefully through the air until it came to halt just ahead of them.

Caldwell took one glance at it, then blanched, all the colour draining from his face. "Oh fuck!" he exclaimed. "Not that thing! She wouldn't have!"

"What is it?" Nick growled out the corner of his mouth. Lysa had gone for her summoner, Brumley still had his weapon pointed at it. Fagan looked like he was caught between those two options and the third of making a run for it. The creature was big, easily taller than Nick and it studied them with bemusement through three slit-like eyes, humanoid but something distinctly unnatural about the way it held its body, sort of stooping and weirdly elasticated, to the red-blue flesh. Now Nick looked closer, he could see the skin was little more than pure muscle covering its internal organs. It had four ears, each shaped like a miniature antenna, while thick spines emerged from its legs like thick crimson hairs.

"It's one of her patented spirits," Caldwell moaned. "It…"

The creature moved, sprang towards him with an almost electric motion, crashed a clawed fist across his jaws and sent him to his knees. Already Brendan's golem was moving to intercept, the steel behemoth towering over the creature. The two stared at each other before the trio of eyes began to glow vengefully. Any hint of an attack building inside the golem was quickly lost as the energy took hold of it and Nick saw it go hurtling through the air, straight through one of the walls. He winced, that had to hurt.

The second golem, the stone one turned towards the new creature, broke off bits of its anatomy and started to fire the rocks at it with crushing force. At least, it would have been had any of them even come close to landing. It was fast, way too fast, it shot into the air as if fired from a laser cannon and came back down again like a swoop bat, crunching its body into the golem. The stone spirit staggered backwards, the unfamiliar creature swung out a fist brimming with energy and…

Holy shit!

The sound of bored rock broke through the room, there was a moment of resistance and then the punch went straight through the great stone body. Nick could see Brumley on the other side, he sent a spray of fire towards the creature from his Featherstone. He almost shouted a warning, realised even then it would be too late and a futile gesture. The thing was just too fast for Brumley, it was around the remnants of Brendan's golem and on him in an instant, a great hand reaching out to grab him by the neck. Brumley was big and Brumley was strong but even he was dwarfed by the size and menacing strength of the otherworldly creature. He flailed out, kicked it in the stomach with a satisfying clunk but if it did anything other than annoy it, Nick couldn't see it.

Lysa entered the fray, sending one of her spirits for it, a gold-and-black striped lynx landing on its back and digging in deep with razor sharp claws. That did get its attention, it let go of Brumley who hit the ground, neck covered in blood. Before it could get to Lysa and her lynx, Fagan's Cantish wolfhound sprang in and bit down on an extended leg, tried to tug the thing back away. It was a futile effort; Nick saw immediately as the strange creature immediately pulled it a dozen feet across the floor before kicking it with its other foot. Still the hound hung on despite the crack of breaking bones rupturing through the hangar. With the attention momentarily off it, the lynx lunged back in and went for the throat with toxic-backed fangs, Nick thought it had succeeded for a moment as well, just before it was halted in mid-flight, flailing helplessly with claws and teeth as the alien spirit continued to hammer away at Fagan's spirit, eventually kicking it away from its leg. It didn't bleed, Nick noticed, grimacing as the hound hit Brendan in the face and knocked him out cold.

It was dealing with them one by one, he noted, not entirely sure he was relieved by the realisation. Not just the spirit but the caller too. Most creatures when threatened, went straight for the most obvious threat and dealt with the next one when it emerged. Not this thing. His theory was reinforced as it sprang in a two-pronged movement, sending the lynx back towards Lysa, it hit her in the stomach and sent her doubling over in pain before snapping away into the opposite direction, looming over Fagan like a muscular monolith.

That was when Nick burst into action, brought out his own summoner and sent Empson into the fray. Some might have been surprised by his failure to act until now, he rather thought of it as seeing how the thing moved and attacked. Everyone else was going in blind and it wasn't doing them any favours. The penguin shot forward, steel edged wings held in front of him like a knife, ready to impale the thing from behind. Nick winced again as he saw the creature knock Fagan out with a brutal slap to the head, he went down and hit the floor with a vicious crack and then it rounded on Empson.

Lysa wasn't unconscious but everyone else was either there or close and that just left him. It was a sobering thought, but he smiled at the spirit, knew Empson was closing in and he had plans to see it didn't wriggle its way out of getting hit here. The trio of eyes started to glow, it tried to halt Empson just as it had Lysa's lynx, but Nick smirked as he saw his penguin grind slowly to a halt. The beak opened, and a torrent of water erupted out, hit it square on in the face and suddenly Empson was moving again, all trapped momentum let loose, moving even faster than he had before and the steel tipped flippers tore into its stomach, ripped through muscle like it was paper. The alien spirit looked down at the wound and at the penguin with bemusement in those strange eyes. Empson attacked again, swung out a flipper that would have decapitated anything else. The strange spirit blocked it with an arm, the blade-like flippers cut deep but didn't separate the limb, Nick thought he saw a flicker of discomfort flash across those eyes, but he was through trying to work the thing out. He just needed to put it down. Or…

Well that was just a crazy idea. He smirked to himself, urged Empson to keep fighting on, raining razor sharp hammer blows down onto the creature. Sooner or later it'd cut off something vital. The two continued to trade their attacks, Empson occasionally mixing it up with a beak slam or a blast of water. In retaliation, the foe's eyes glowed bright and invisible force cuffed the penguin about the face and body, rapid blows threatening to break the bird's concentration. Fair play to Empson, he never wavered, never gave in, never looked like falling. All while Nick ran through further plans of attack in his mind, a dozen different plots rejected before he decided to go ahead with his initial idea. He needed an opening.

The alien creature swung out with a fist although Empson wasn't there any longer, replaced in the fray by Carcer who swept down onto its back, dug claws and teeth in viciously. Still the wound didn't bleed, just great empty holes gaping through the skin. Nick watched it flail around, trying to shake the shark-lizard off but Carcer held firm, digging the claws in deeper, biting down with needle pointed teeth, ripping and tearing against hard skin. Just in the right position, he noted, it couldn't reach Carcer from there and if his spirit hung on then it'd all be good. One more spin, another desperate lunge and he could tell it was struggling. He caught a glimpse of its broad back and saw it looked a real mangled mess.

"Closing in on target," Alex said, guiding the Wolf Rose in on the same vector as the shuttle, aware it was doing its best to flee. She wasn't going to let that happen. "Gunners prepare to light that thing up we…" She paused, her train of thought suddenly lost to her. For a moment, she wasn't quite sure where she was. She… She'd just been about to do something…

Instinct kicked in and she jerked the control stick to the side, evade a blast of laser fire from an oncoming eaglefighter, one who in her momentary reverie had managed to sneak up on them. Sullivan took it out with a well-placed blast of turret fire, she saw it explode on her tac-reader.

"Sorry, we need to take it out and quickly. Admiral's orders," she said, turning her attention back to it. She couldn't dwell on what had just happened. Not now. Back on target, closing in fast, finger on the trigger of her forward bound laser…

It hit her just as she was about to let it fly, the sudden wave of confusion, she involuntarily juked the controls and lost her course again, turret fire scattering wildly all over the place.

"Are you losing the fucking plot Commander?" Navarro yelled in her ear, but she was a little distracted, couldn't quite make him out. Who was Navarro again? "With all due respect," she heard the distant voice add hastily. By the time she'd forced her mind back onto the job, she was furious. Something weird was going on here and she didn't like it. Nobody made her look like a bad pilot. For the third time, she righted her course, pivoting the ship down on a cred-coin and found the shuttle. It was doing its best to get away from her, but she wasn't going to allow it. Setting her face in grim determination, she pushed forward, all thrusters on maximum as she went for it. She was going to get it; this was it…

And that was when her controls locked up, suddenly finding herself unable to move them, as if invisible forces were resisting her every effort to right them. Alex swore angrily, pushed at them but no joy. At least not until the pushing started in the opposite direction. And suddenly she was facing the airbase again.

"Come on, come on, come on," she growled, hitting buttons with her free hand. One of them remained locked to the stick, she couldn't move it even if she wanted to, unable to even wiggle her fingers free. Worse, her hand pushed forward to move the Wolf Rose in that direction, speeding straight for the side of the airbase. Her heart leaped, the yelp died in her throat. She couldn't adjust course, couldn't shift off the vector. All warnings on the system told her a crash was imminent, there was the admiral on the comm system demanding to know what she was doing. At least if she hit it and the ship exploded on contact, she wouldn't have to live with the shame of trying to explain. Of course, there were other people on board. They shouldn't have to pay for her mistake. Neither Navarro or Sullivan deserved to die. But die they would unless she got this thing back on course and out of trouble. Hitting the shuttle might be a mistake from this point.

She had to let it go. It had already cost two fighters and it might take her out yet. She couldn't divert more fighters from their bombing runs on the airbase, not when their attacks were taking their toll. The Wild Stallion and the Bounty Snatcher were already moving into advanced positions, starting to pound the airbase from long range, the armour starting to show signs of attrition. "I don't have control," she admitted quietly, not broadcasting, but just so Sullivan and Navarro could hear her. "Something's wrong. I can't get it off this course."

"You want me to come down and do the flying for you?" Navarro asked sarcastically. "Pull your head out of your arse or we're going to die. I don't mind being shot down, but I draw the line at getting killed by you! Are you a damn good pilot, or aren't you?"

Well, that was a little uncalled for, she thought. The first part at least. The last part was just about damn right. She smiled to herself. Yeah. Yeah, I am and I'm not getting killed by a ship error. She set her jaw and pushed back against the controls, willing herself to do it, not content with dying here. They responded. Just a little but it was enough to give her hope. Again, she gathered herself and pushed. The albus made a little groaning noise as if protesting. Less than ten seconds to impact and closing fast. This really was her last chance. With her free hand, she punched the stick, felt her muscles complaining as she pushed against it with all her strength, determined to force it skyward.

Just let it go, a little voice said in her head. It'll be a quick death at least. Which is more than can be said will happen if you persist this foolish course of action. That little voice felt calm and reassuring, just for a moment she was almost convinced it was the right thing to do, maybe she should just give up and let whatever happened happen. After all, it was supposedly one of the fastest ways to die, even if it was horrible for just a few seconds...

But why?

That was all her, that. Asking the question as to why she should just let it happen. Why should she? She wasn't about to die. She didn't want to. More than that, she didn't desire to be remembered as a pilot who died by smashing her ship into the thing they were trying to blow up. Not least without it being a blaze of glory suicide so that everyone else could live type of thing.

Because it's easy?

It wasn't the answer she wanted, and she berated herself for even thinking it. All this went through her head as she still fought with the controls. Navarro said something in the background, even Sullivan was starting to sound worried. Still all the possibilities began to run through her head, all of them offering the same little message about how she'd worked so hard and how it'd be nice to finally let it all go. Just let it all go and relax. The message felt almost hypnotic in her mind, so soothing and calm, sinking in deep and letting her know just how easy it'd be to give up and die...

Screw easy! I'm not dying here! Get out!

She didn't know where it came from, or where she'd found the will to say them, but with those final two words, something released, like a pressure she hadn't known was there in her head and suddenly she felt free and liberated again. More than that, the stick had freed itself and she was able to push it up and evade the impact.

"Thank fuck for that," Navarro said. "Thought you'd fallen asleep then."

Alex ignored them, glanced down at the tac-reader. The shuttle was almost out of range, she guessed maybe it'd be possible to catch it up. But it'd be a struggle. And right now, the airbase looked like a bigger problem. Makeshift Squadron was getting buffeted by laser fire and the eaglefighters were starting to retreat towards their home, thickening the air with plasma. Trying to blow this thing up had to be a bigger priority. Plus, given her last two run-ins with this thing, including what had happened to the HAX's she'd sent after it, she wasn't keen for a third go at it. It might come across as cowardly, but she was still unnerved by the way her controls had locked and she'd been unable to deal with it, almost as big a mystery as the way those two HAX's had crashed into each other with no discernible reason why. More mysteries she wasn't at liberty to deal with as she pushed the Wolf Rose down through the smallest of gaps, between two eaglefighters, watched them both explode as the guns turned on them, Navarro whooping eagerly in the background.

Nick jumped, a container crystal flat in his palm and he smashed it against the back of the alien creature, praying this would work, otherwise he'd look a massive, massive idiot. And it'd probably be a painful few minutes that followed if it didn't. The creature's skin felt grainy and hard, like wood but there was some warmth and the faintest trace of something slimy. He focused up his will, started the process of claiming, only for something hard to kick him out almost as quickly as it had started, a mule-kick to the face that sent him reeling. Hot sticky fragments remained in his palm, he looked down dazed at them and saw the blood and glass all mixed together.

It destroyed it...

Supposed to be impervious...

The creature hit him, hit Carcer with the other fist and the shark-lizard was thrown far across the hangar, heard the clang as he hit a shipping container. Nick was too busy being thrown on his arse to care, rolling to an ungainly stop against something solid and hard. He couldn't think, his mind was all messed up, never been hit so hard before. Incredibly, it hadn't broken anything, he didn't think, the pain tolerable but constant.

Something scarlet broke through his vision, he saw the thing coming towards him, hovering maliciously and he scrabbled around for something, anything he could use to defend himself. A toolbox went flying wide as he flung it in the direction of the strange creature and then his fingers scrabbled around something cool and metallic, something cylindrical. Nick's eyes went wide as the realisation dawned on him, he pulled it closer to him and almost laughed. Wherever Sharon was, he privately thanked her as he drew the weapon closer to him and held it out sideways at arm's length. There were a few buttons on it, but only one prominent one, he remembered her love of crystals and he pushed it down.

It was an unusual weapon, he had to admit, lacked for any sort of weight to it as the blade burst into life, flickering wildly but strong. Holding it, he felt at peace, a sense of calm that he hadn't felt since Sharon had...

That thought struck him and he pushed himself to his feet and lunged towards the creature, swinging out with the blade. More than once he had to be careful on his backswing, he'd seen how it could cut through solid objects and he didn't want to accidentally bisect himself. It wasn't like any sort of weapon he'd ever used before, it felt unfamiliar, alien and he didn't want it in his hands any longer than he needed it. The creature blocked the first strike, but badly, Nick saw the blade scrape the length of its forearm and remove a ten-inch sheath of flesh that hit the ground with a splat. It didn't make a sound, didn't register any pain but looked at him with a puzzled expression. Some callers did do it this way, drove a creature down with weapons rather than their own spirits before they made the attempt to claim it. He'd always considered it a little cruel if he was honest. There were more noble ways to do it. Besides if you wanted the cool credits, then you'd be using your spirits to fight somewhere down the line anyway, hence the idea behind using them to claim others. Practice. Not quite the same thing but close enough.

Still the groove in its arm didn't stop the creature from attacking again, if a little warier this time. It was stalking him like a giant crimson predator, watching and waiting for any hint of weakness. Maybe it knew he wasn't familiar with the weapon. It had a point; fencing training hadn't been part of the Unisco curriculum. Using a smaller bladed weapon had however, yet he got the feeling if he tried some of that stuff with this, someone would end up cut in two. Bit of a difference between training with blunted knives and fighting this fucking thing.

He grinned at it, held out his free hand and jerked two fingers forward, beckoning it in a casual taunt. Nick saw the eyes light up and he realised that there had to be some hint of intelligence at work deep inside that mind. Not just innate animal cunning but a spark of something complex and capable at work. It didn't make a difference as to what he had to do but he could appreciate there was something magnificent at work close by.

The same hand dropped to his waist, slipped another crystal into his summoner and Froak appeared, the toxic frog hitting the creature from behind, the same way Carcer had earlier. It reacted with surprise, turned to face the new arrival and Nick struck, sprinting in and ramming the weapon through the creature's side, all the way to the hilt, saw the shock in its eyes, pain and surprise, as if to say, 'this wasn't supposed to happen.'

It had to hurt. It really did. When it reached around and grabbed his hands, crushing down on both them and the hilt of the weapon, he was a little surprised. He couldn't pull away, they were clamped down too hard, he could hear something shattering and he hoped it wasn't bone.

And then something weird happened.

This was the capture trance; he'd heard every experience of it varied from caller to caller. That moment of calm when caller and spirit could become one, some found it easy, others found it hard. Him, he'd never had any real problems with it, not really. It was all about willpower. Now he was here, he found himself wishing he wasn't. The creature… The creature as it was inside stared at him, all knots of fear and rage and angry loathing, not actually a physical shape but more a web. "Sorry," he said. "But you were trying to kill me."

"Laws of the jungle."

He stiffened, almost lost his focus. He knew that voice, saw her stood there barefoot and in a pretty white dress. Nick turned, saw her as he wished to remember her. Not with the way her face had been smashed in but radiant and beautiful… He didn't want to remember the way her eyes were wet now, her makeup streaked down her face.

"No," he whispered. "Don't cry, Sharon."

"How can I not?" she replied. "You're in so much pain. And it's only going to get worse."

Nick shook his head. "You're here now."

She mirrored the gesture. "No, I'm not. Not forever. Soon I'll fade like the memories. You won't remember the true me, you'll just remember what you want to remember. I'm just a shade."

"I'll remember I loved you," Nick said, his voice breaking just a few octaves. "I'll remember I was willing to spend the rest of my life with you."

"And I did spend the rest of my life with you," she said. "It just wasn't as long as either of us wanted." It was a sad smile but at least it was a smile. "I know I loved it."

He'd loved it too, truly had. Her smile grew. She knew, she reached out a hand to him. He took it, couldn't help it. Her skin was just as soft as he remembered, if a little weird. Like she wasn't entirely there, spongy even. If he squeezed, his hand might go through hers. For the moment, he forgot where he was, threatened to forget who he was, everything and everyone, even the unialiv. But it couldn't last, wouldn't last. It was gone, just like her.

"So why are you here?"

She sighed. "Always so keen for answers. You're messing about with power you can't even start to understand. And that thing…" She pointed to the creature. "It's poisonous. You're tripping badly lover. Maybe I'm not even here. But you're close. You'll survive this. You know how! It's what you've always done. While we're on that subject! Can't believe you never told me you were Unisco! Bastard!"

"Yeah like you didn't have secrets either," Nick said dryly. She laughed wryly at that and clapped her hands together.

"Okay, I'll give you that," she said. "Maybe this isn't the last time we'll see each other. The ways of the world are mysterious indeed.

But you shouldn't seek me out. That way lies true heartbreak. Now I'm dead I see it all, I see how it all fits together and how we're all a small part of something greater. It's sobering. Everything I ever wanted to know and some things I didn't." She reached out again, gave him a sorrowful look. He took it, this time she didn't feel of anything as she moved to embrace him, something that hurt more than anything the creature could have. When she shoved him back into the tangled messy web that was the opponent, he found he was already coming to accept it.

It was weakening, either he'd conquered it, or the wounds were killing it but there was no crystal. The creature… the unialiv… now he was this close to claiming it, close to becoming a part of him, he could see it in horrible detail spasming repeatedly, parts of its body fading and reappearing. The weapon's blade faded, and the metal casing of the hilt cracked beneath his hand and the unialiv vanished from sight through the cracks.

Seconds later it all came to pieces and Nick saw something small and shiny hit the ground amidst metal fragments. A crystal, larger than most he'd ever seen but now containing the spirit of something that had regardless managed to nearly wipe out an entire team of Unisco operatives. Sighing, he fell back and let his head rest against the floor of the hangar. Somewhere, his eyes had gone wet, he tried to blink them away, but his heart wasn't in it.

"I have firmly always believed a strong relationship with women like Claudia Coppinger, women of integrity and power, of unquestioned business acumen is good for any kingdom where she decides to set up shop. It's good for the people and for the kingdom."

Premesoir Vice-President, Thomas Rogan singing the praises of Claudia Coppinger.

The third day of Summerfall.

Prideaux Khan had found herself with probably the worst part of the mission but in a strange way, she was relishing the challenge. Find the vital systems of this damned airbase and disable them. She worked alone. She always did. While the rest of them had gone off in their teams, she'd taken a bag of high-yield explosives and set out to deal with the engines, the weapons, the life support, anything she could take out. All with the intent to make the fleet's job that little bit easier. She'd trained as an infiltrator, a saboteur, she might have made an exceptional assassin in another life.

For now, she wasn't thinking about that, rather about the whole mess this damn thing had resulted in. Because it was a mess. Assuming everything went to plan, then there'd still be the hells to pay with what came next. Heads were going to roll, Cyris had given them enough information to be assured of that. Noorland was already going through the system to see what he could dig out, they'd already been warned Ritellia had been, if not aware, then at least complicit in this whole affair. That'd be a pretty big worm to dangle at the best of times, not least when you also considered people like Mazoud and Thomas Rogan himself had been named. Thomas Rogan, a name she'd not thought about for a while. And if a man like that had been in the pay of Coppinger, the catch got bigger. Thomas fucking Rogan. Vice-president of Premesoir and the inventor of the ghost containment particle barrier, a tool of a merciless criminal organisation capable of unknown levels of destruction and deceit. Through him, they found themselves close to the ear of one of the most powerful men in the five kingdoms. Oh dear.

She had a Featherstone, but she hadn't fired yet. Those occasions when she'd come across Coppinger grunts, she'd either slipped past them or dealt with them silently. Her instructors back at the academy had always said she had an uncanny knack of slipping in and out of shadows you hadn't quite expected to be there. Master of concealment and all that. Of course, there were things that they didn't know about her. About her childhood… She couldn't let them know. At best, she'd be considered a security risk. At worst, they'd probably feel sorry for her. And she didn't want that. Didn't need it. Sympathy was a useless emotion. Only the for the weak. And she wasn't weak. Far from it. She was the Spectre, the nickname she'd been apportioned a long time ago. She'd considered it from every angle and had decided she approved. If she hadn't… Well someone had tried branding her under the name Spooky once. He'd been proof that human teeth don't grow back. And that eating mashed-up food for the rest of your life doesn't do much for your disposition.

The next grunt she let see her, strode in front of him and watched him react almost painfully slowly. His weapon was almost locked onto her heart before she hit him twice in the throat, hard and true. His neck jerked back, he began to gag, she wrapped a leg around his and twisted him to the ground, watched him land with a dull thud and died amidst tragic little moans threatening to break her concentration. She frowned, kicked him again just to be sure. This time he went quiet. Hint taken.

Still moving silently like a deadly jungle cat, she continued to stalk the corridors in search of her quarry. Al Noorland was there in her ear, guiding her when she needed it, but she was tuning most of what he said out, bar the stuff with value. Blow something important, sabotage this whole thing, be a hero. She had to admit, she found that last one a quaint notion. So many of the things Unisco agents did were as faceless men and women. If she was to be a hero, it wouldn't be gaining the recognition and admiration of the public. It'd be a few frank words from the director, warned not to take so many damn bloody risks again, followed by a handshake and several warm words of congratulations. The sort of thing that made her blood boil. When you did good work, you wanted to be rewarded. Something for something, nothing given for nothing, nothing taken for takings sake. It was human nature.

Not that she hated her job. Far from it. Unisco as an organisation had given her something she'd been lacking in her life for as long as she could remember. Not just a chance to make a difference, but a chance to let out what lay nestled inside her to let the demons come out and play. Here, alone and surrounded in the enemy territory, she felt that she knew who she was truly. That some good came out of it all was just a happy side effect.

Wim Carson wasn't satisfied. Perchance he was still rusty with the Kjarn, you couldn't undo five years of atrophy in a short space of time after all. But he'd felt something when he'd tried to work his power on that second pilot. That bigger ship had come chasing after him, following his previous efforts in slamming the control stick of one of the fighters into crashing into his wing mate. And he'd gotten into her head, he'd put her out of it once, that should have dissuaded her. He knew it was a woman. But she'd fought back and come at them again.

The second time had been harder, he'd had to pull out more of the stops to try and put her on collision course with the Eye of Claudia. And he'd nearly succeeded only to once again have her thwart his efforts. It rankled. Still things were looking up. She might have broken free of his influence but at least she was keeping her distance now. Interesting developments to say the least. It was unusual to find someone with the strength of will to resist influence as she had. It wasn't unlikely she had some potential. It was also entirely irrelevant right now. He'd never find out who she was. And at this moment in time, he had other things to focus on. She wasn't important.

"We're almost clear of the fire zone," Claudia said, breaking the silence and his concentration. "Almost free. Good job."

"I told you I'd keep them off your back," Wim replied thoughtfully. "How did this happen?"

"Someone had to have talked," she said. He heard a bit tinge of regret in her voice. "No other way to explain it. And as for my brother… Did you really never sense any deception from him?"

"It doesn't work like that," Wim said, a little annoyed at her accusation. "It's not an exact science and I'm not fluent. Signals can be misread. Muddled. I sensed nothing but absolute certainty in whatever he said or felt. He avoided me a lot. I wonder if that was the reason why."

"Perhaps," she said. "It's irrelevant now, I'm afraid. Things have gotten a lot more interesting. We have to move up the schedule." She sounded excited by what she said, unless his ears were telling him lies. But her emotions told him she was giddy, gleeful.

"Mistress Coppinger! We're losing the battle, our eaglefighters are being taken out by the dozen. We're outnumbered, our guns and shields are failing, we need to retreat!"

She sighed at hearing Folson's voice. And the excitement faded away to be replaced with malice. "You mean you've failed me, Commander?"

"Mistress, my life is yours to do what you…"

The sound of laser fire broke across the comm system and Wim winced at the sound of it, followed by the slump of a body hitting the deck. "As he wished, Mistress." He recognised that voice. Rocastle. "Am I in charge of the retreat now?"

"Rocastle." He could hear the malice in her voice. "Where is Domis?"

"Nobody knows. Am I in charge now?"

An audible sigh. "Yes," she said begrudgingly. "Harvey Rocastle, I promote you to temporary commander to oversee the retreat. Shed the damaged outer layers, bring the control centre in. They won't expect that. Remember, you'll be incredibly vulnerable once you shed it, so you need to wait for them to get off your back before running. We cannot afford to lose that station, Rocastle. If we do, I'm holding you responsible."

"At the risk of sounding unfaithful, Mistress," Rocastle said. "Am I going to ask them nicely to do that?"

"No, arrangements have been made," she said. "Just pick your moment."

She closed the comms, grimaced. "Why am I surrounded by morons? No offence, my friend."

"None taken," Wim said. "So... Set a course for Burykia, I guess. That is where we must go and the sooner the better."

"That's the plan."

"Admiral!"

Alex heard the shout across all the channels, at roughly the same moment the tac-reader screeched out a warning of its own. She had a horrible feeling she knew what Criffen was about to be told even before it came, the sight of new ships entering the fray.

"Enemy ships in sector twenty-eight! They're coming right for us!" That was the captain of the Sitting Target, unless she was mistaken, though she couldn't remember his name. "It's the Dark Wind!"

Alex couldn't help but laugh, even as she knew she'd been right in her assumption. This was about reasonable for her. This whole thing had started for her where the Dark Wind had been concerned, that felt like such a long time ago now, and here they were to finish it. That was their plan. And, she gritted her teeth together hard, if she had anything to do with it then it wouldn't be a success.

"Taking heavy fire! We need air support now!"

She should have guessed it sooner as debris and smoke tore through the air around her cockpit, the blasts taking their toll on the outer hull of the Eye. In the heat of the battle, she had other distractions. For a moment, she felt a complete lack of envy for Criffen's position. He had a horrible choice to make right now, press the attack and complete the mission, or lose another capital ship in a wildly escalating battle he'd done his best to control but ultimately come up short in. She glanced at her tac-reader, saw that the number of combatants were falling by the minute. It had turned into a war of attrition that had gone against them. They'd tried to cut down enemy numbers, they'd succeeded but so had the enemy in reverse.

On the other hand, this airbase was a danger to everyone else in the five kingdoms. Although its armaments were depleted, it could be rearmed. Rebuilt. Taking it out had to be the priority.

She saw the first wave of Dark Wind fighters buzz across the Sitting Target and she had a horrible feeling what was going to happen even before she was proved right. Criffen's voice cut across the comms, he didn't sound convinced he was doing the right thing. "All squadrons move to defensive positions and attack the Dark Wind," he said. There was an aura of regret in his voice, but it held steel. Like a man who had decided to throw the consequences to the hells but still knew the fire might roast him in the end. "They picked their side. Now show them what happens to traitors. I repeat, all squadrons."

That meant hers. Alex sighed, threw the Wolf Rose around and nosed it out the way of a spattering of fire coming from one of the guns they hadn't destroyed. If Navarro and Sullivan had anything to say on the matter, they held their tongues. Good, she didn't want to hear it. And she needed to concentrate, keep her mind on the job. Going in here, they'd be heavily outnumbered, and she didn't want to get blindsided. Just focus on the flying, let your gunners do their jobs. Easier said than done. She had faith in them, they'd earned that much for getting her this far. They'd probably already be a fireball if not for their efforts.

"Affirmed, Admiral," she said. "Pulling out and ready to engage." She hid her frustration well as a flurry of more such sentiments filtered across comm systems from other ships. After all the time she'd spent a prisoner on that thing, she'd been looking forward to seeing it go up in flames. "Makeshifts let's get them." All the remaining fighters converged on her tail, it felt strange flying at the tip of the formation but at the same time she realised she could get used to it. It wouldn't do to get too comfortable in the role, but it'd be nice to one day hold it for real. Not just for one engagement where the admiral had done the best with the cards he'd been dealt.

Too many ships, a ragtag mismatch of models, just like before. She'd always had a theory it was what made the Dark Wind such an effective force to fight against. Some of those ships might be old but they were maintained well. And the older a ship was, the longer out of general use it probably was. Some of them had to be ten to twenty years old but their equipment and weaponry was doubtless top of the line, constantly upgraded to the best stuff. The longer it was out of use, the easier it was to forget exactly what they could do, to forget an old dog could still bite.

"Makeshifts do not underestimate any of those crates," she ordered. "If you do, you'll die, and I'll be waiting to kick your ass in the afterlife." It was something Wolfmeyer had said sometimes and maybe it had worked for him, but it felt wrong in her mouth, uncomfortable. They probably didn't take her seriously with it, she decided that it had been a bad thing to do. She just hoped it wasn't going to turn out to be an omen for the battle.

"It's a psychic poison," Caldwell said, looking across at Nick. He'd been sat for several long moments, the crystal in his hand as he tried to fathom out what was going wrong with it. For those moments, he'd felt it grow hot and cold many times over, it had vibrated and thrummed in his grasp as if trying to escape but it had never quite managed it.

"Huh?"

"The unialiv," Caldwell said. "My dear sister designed them all from the genetics up, didn't she? I saw some of the specs for them. She decided to take biological weaponry to a whole new battlefield. That one you caught, it emits a psychic poison. When it touches you, it drains you mentally, you lose stuff slowly." He sighed. "That's how it disabled most of us so quickly. It's a giant emotional leech basically. In the heat of battle, we look like a buffet. All you can eat."

"Oh." Nick said. "Nice to know when you put it that way. I just claimed a giant emotional leech. Yay."

Brendan, still bearing a woozy look from the blow he had taken, regardless stood up straight and cleared his throat. It was a hollow sound in the echoes of the hangar. "Okay," he said. "We've failed in our mission to capture Claudia Coppinger. We need to get out of here while we still can. Back to the ship! That's an order."

Nick couldn't help but notice the sense of solemnity around the group as they filed out, weapons at the ready. Just in case. They'd cocked it up, they all knew that. He should have killed her when he'd had the chance. Caldwell should have. Both should have been ready to pull the trigger and they'd failed to do so. Now she was still out there, she'd gotten away from them and whatever happened next, it was their fault.

"You can't think of it like that," Caldwell said, falling in beside him. Nick jerked out of his thoughts with a start, he hadn't seen him coming. "It's been bugging me too. But it's not going to be our fault."

"Excuse me?"

"My bloody sister. She does what she does because she's crazy. Always has been. Nuttier than squirrel shit. Look, I'm not happy that she got away. But I don't regret not killing her. She needs help…"

"You're not convincing me," Nick said. He was grateful that Brendan couldn't hear them, although Lysa and Tod Brumley looked interested by what they were saying.

"No, I'm saying killing her wasn't the answer. It shouldn't have been. We were never specifically given a kill order on her, it was never part of your orders or mine, take them alive unless ordered otherwise. It's protocol, we obeyed it. We're in the clear."

"Apart from the knowledge that we could have stopped her and didn't," Nick said. "How do we live with that?"

"Guess we're going to have to find a way," Caldwell said. "I regret what happened in that she got away. I regret that she's going to be out for my blood now. I regret there's likely a whole lot of trouble it's going to cause. But you can't change it now. Not should you be able to."

"You've both killed before, right?" Tod Brumley asked. "So, what stopped you here?"

Caldwell opened his mouth to protest, Nick got in there first with a sigh. "Hot blooded kills are different to cold. In a fight, the adrenaline is pumping, and you can go through with it on pure emotion. To snuff someone out when they're not a threat, you've got to look at them and think do they deserve to die for it? She probably did. But you know what. There, when she was defenceless, not a threat to me and I had the blaster on her, I wanted to take her in. I couldn't pull the trigger. Probably wouldn't have unless my life depended on it."

He managed a weak grin. "Can we drop the subject?" Especially before someone brought the Jeremiah Blut killing up again. It wasn't entirely the same thing and he had no desire to justify it as such.

Still, at least they found themselves in for a nice surprise as they reached the ship.

"All the baddest men in the kingdoms," Derenko said loftily. "Came across them, thought it'd be rude to leave them here to get blown up." He managed a weak grin, stood there leaning against the side of the ship. Nick could see one of the faces at the back of the aeroship looking ruefully out the window. It wouldn't be pleasant sharing the way back with them, restrained and secured as they may be. But at the same time, he was just glad to be out of here.

As plans went, it hadn't been a complete success. He couldn't consider it that. Doubtless there'd be those who disagreed with him. It was his own opinion, not something he could really put a finger on but at the same time he felt the bitter taste of failure. Claudia had gotten away. Wim Carson had managed to get away with her. He was no closer to his goals. And although he had sort of seen Sharon again, it wasn't in the way he'd have wanted. He wasn't even sure if it was really her he'd seen or just some crazy hallucination. Psychic poison Caldwell had called it. Made some sort of sense. Not much but some. As excuses went, it was pretty limp, and he couldn't lean on it. He didn't know what had happened.

Lysa was looking around at the team, Aldiss and Derenko the only two out there. He could see Fagan and Noorland bustling around someone up in the ship, someone who looked in bad shape, they were being strapped down. Of course, he reasoned, it might be rough getting out of here. "Hey, where's Mel?" she asked suddenly. It wasn't Harper who was strapped down, Nick noted. Too big. If he'd had to hazard a guess, based on who hadn't been there in Brendan's squad, it had to be Wilsin. Simple process of elimination. Wilsin fit the profile.

"She didn't make it," Aldiss said. "I'm sorry." Silence pervaded the area, a moment for a fallen comrade.

"And Agent Sullivan?" Brendan asked.

"Riding shotgun for Lieutenant Nkolou," Leclerc said. Brendan looked like he'd been slapped at that comment, his eyes going wide with surprise.

"What?"

"Yeah, two of our pilots were being held here," Leclerc said. "They took Sammy Regan's albus and went out to join the battle. Crazy. But my sort of crazy."

"It's true, Chief," Nick said. "I let them out the cells myself. They were caught when they took back Harvey Rocastle. Remnants of Wolf Squadron."

Brendan snorted. "Humph, how about that." Nick had thought he might sound more pleased about that than he did. "How's the battle going?"

"Not good, Chief," Leclerc said. "We were winning and then the Dark Wind showed up. They're currently laying hammer to the capital ships. Not a good time to run for it. We won't have any cover; we'll be a target. They pulled all fighters off this base to go fight the Dark Wind."

"Then I suggest you and Agent Noorland fly both rapidly and skilfully," Brendan said. "Where's Agent Khan?"

"Still not reported in," Derenko said, before right on cue, a series of distant explosions rocked the station, the reverberations threatening to topple them all over. Nick had to reach out, grab something to steady himself.

"If she doesn't in the next two minutes," Brendan said grimly. "We get ready to leave. If anyone can get out on their own, it's her. Either she makes it or she's dead. Everyone aboard!"

It was getting very cosy aboard the aeroship, Nick had to note, what with the crime bosses all handcuffed to their seats in the back of the passenger area, none looking pleased about it. He was impressed that Derenko and Aldiss' team had managed it, especially considering they'd lacked the numbers Brendan's team had mustered. He went and sat down next to David Wilsin, the man looking like he'd seen better days. His eyes were closed, he wasn't conscious by the looks of it and his breathing was ragged and shallow.

"Keep an eye on him," Noorland said, moving towards the cockpit. "Don't let him swallow his tongue. He took one hells of a beating from the big bastard. I recorded it all, be something to play at the celebrations." He grinned weakly, not really believing what he was saying. "Hells of a damn mess huh?"

"Just a bit," Nick said. Idly he wondered where Khan was. It wasn't unusual tactics to turn her solely loose on the enemy in a mission like this. The woman could be chaos in the field, had a knack of surviving the odds no matter how hopeless they might be. Brumley came and sat down the other side of Wilsin, nodded at them both. Seats were becoming a commodity, last frantic bits of activity underway as Aldiss and Fagan shifted crates of weapons away from where the criminals had been secured. They had a point. Last thing they needed was someone getting loose and firing a weapon in here. Brendan himself went around, checked the restraints quickly, his muffler still active so nobody could ID him.

"Okay, estimated time of departure," Noorland called back. "A few minutes' time. Running final checks, fuel supply looks good, I'd just find something to hold onto. This is not going to be a pleasant run."

"Get on with it!" Lysa called up towards him. "If you're going to get us killed, at least be quick about it."

"I love her attitude, don't you?" Fagan quipped. "Some people are just in so much of a rush to die. Me, not so much."

"Nobody's dying," Leclerc said. "Not today, anyway."

"Save it for when we're on the ground, why won't you?" Derenko offered pleasantly.

This was turning into chaos, exactly the sort of battle Alex had always wanted simultaneously to be both involved in and avoid like the plague. It was a strange conflict of emotion, she had to admit, she loved the thrill of rushing through the gauntlet of enemy ships, aware that all it'd take was one good shot to rip through her shields and that'd be all she knew about it, exhilaration and fear mixed in together in one draining cocktail. They were all over her, starting to focus on her, but that was good. At least she had the manoeuvrability to evade their fire, unlike the dreadnoughts which had already taken a beating under their blasts. Sullivan and Navarro continued to pour fire into anything that came too close, the sound of their guns a constant companion by now. She'd almost forgotten a time she couldn't hear them, such was their song in the heat of battle. They were running hot, but the two of them couldn't let up. The Wolf Rose had a kick to her engines, it didn't mean she should let her take one in exchange. And it was better than flying a HAX, although not by much. For such a much larger ship, she had an excellent range of movement and she'd used it on more than one occasion to surprise someone who'd gotten on her tail.

The Dark Wind pilots were good, but she'd already proven herself against them once and come out tops. Sweeping through the firestorm, she skimmed her ship along the surface of one of the dreadnoughts, rolled the ship out of the shadow of the Wild Stallion and watched one of them explode trying to match her move for move. He failed, room to manoeuvre just too small and one of his wings clipped the hull of Criffen's flagship and spun out of control. A stray laser blast took him out, superior firepower shredding through shield and ship with equal disdain. Easy target, easy kill.

I'm taking the assist for that, she thought sardonically.

"All ships," Criffen said over the communication system. "We've just received word that the extraction team is ready to leave. Ensure they make it out unscathed. Keep any enemy fighters from them. This is paramount!" A glance at her tac-reader confirmed that he was right. An unarmed aeroship was sneaking its way out of the airbase and slowly making its way onto a flight vector. From here, it looked small and frail.

Don't try and fly through this melee, don't try and fly through this melee, she urged quietly. Only a suicidal idiot would try it without any weapons or shields. She had both, for now. She added the last part as a flurry of shots clipped her shields, causing her to frown. Upper aft fading was the warning she got, the last thing she needed. She tapped a few buttons on her console, trying to get them back up.

Mission accomplished. That was what it felt like.

When Prideaux felt the buzz of energy suddenly close to her throat, she felt a little trickle of irritation flow through her. Mostly because of the presence of the girl holding the blade to her. She gave her an annoyed look, would have folded her arms impatiently had she not been aware moving probably wouldn't have been the best thing to do right now.

"What do you want?" she asked, more than a little sulkily. How dare this little bitch hold her up.

"I want out of here," the redhead said. "I want to go home. I've been here too long. You're going to get me out of here."

Prideaux raised an eyebrow. "I'm going to, am I? And how do you propose I do that?" She supposed the genuine absence of fear was something to worry about. Not just for her, but for the girl. With a weapon like that, it was useful for intimidation. And here she was, not caring.

"Can you fly a ship?"

Prideaux nodded gently, still aware of the blade. "I can. But unless you've missed something, there's a battle going on out there. I'm not flying into the middle of it. There are better ways to die."

"Look!" the girl exclaimed, letting an authoritative note slip into her voice. It hinted at obedience, threatened the notion of defiance. "I need to get out of here. You do too, I take it. Let's help each other out."

"What's in it for me? Because the fact you're trying to coerce me into helping you suggests you can't fly yourself. Therefore, if you cut my head off as you're threatening to do, you'll be screwing yourself over first," Prideaux said. This time she did fold her arms and raised an eyebrow. "Save the theatrics for someone who gives a shit. You don't scare me. This place is going up any minute now, I've got higher worries than you. So, if you want a lift, you ask me nicely."

Big sweet smile at the girl who looked furious. Baiting her like this probably wasn't the smartest idea but at the same time, it felt so enjoyable. Prideaux genuinely wasn't afraid of death here. Not from the oncoming explosion, not from this child. Whatever happened would happen and nothing she would do could change that. She could tilt the odds in her favour, but ultimately her survival was already a foregone conclusion, a matter of factors she had to consider, an array of options that should she choose wrong would be fatal for her.

No pressure then.

The girl lowered the blade and she let out the breath she hadn't even been aware she was holding. "Please," she said. "Help me."

Prideaux beamed sweetly at her, the expression dripping with venomous sarcasm. "Of course. If you'd asked me nicely in the first place, we might already be on our way. Consider that a lesson for the future. Jam and vinegar, all that sort of stuff."

It took very little time to find a ship, an old Saravejo SS-1 freighter that had seen better days. What it was doing here, Prideaux didn't know. It looked massively out of place but as she bypassed the controls and stepped into the ship, she knew it'd do. Provided they weren't shot down. Always a risk.

"What a hunk of junk," the girl said. "How we going to get out of here in this? We probably won't make it past the hangar doors."

"Shut up," Prideaux said pleasantly. "I can deal with negativity but not your bleating. Have faith. Isn't that what you're all about?"

"No, I prefer…" She tailed off, suddenly glancing at Prideaux as if seeing her for the first time. She could see the cogs grinding away in her head, the sudden wonder forming and blooming deep inside. "What do you mean by that?"

Inside Prideaux smiled. "You've made some strange decisions most people wouldn't have, faith seems to have gotten you this far so far. You're not behaving like a rational person would. Maybe you're desperate but you're following your heart in what you believe is the right path. Sounds like faith to me." She worked away at the controls, wincing to herself at the way they failed to respond adequately to her attempts to power up. Always a handy ability to break into a ship. She'd taken those classes in Unisco training, always figured they'd come in handy one day. It appeared that day was today. Of course, that had been military grade hardware they all practiced on back at the academy. Hard to break but at the same time, there was always a readable pattern to the system. Once you figured it out, you could break it. This was a civilian one, not wired up in the same way. Once you worked one logging pattern out, the next one would be entirely new and fresh. Perhaps. Depended how much someone wanted you to avoid stealing the ship. This piece of junk, she didn't know how secure it would be when they took to the skies.

Maybe she was just rusty. That was possible too.

The entire station suddenly jerked around her, almost hurling her from her seat. A warning alarm sounded outside, though she couldn't quite hear what it said. Whatever it could be, it probably wasn't good. Turned out that was just the sort of incentive she needed to work harder until she broke the final code, heard the reassuring 'cling' of success. All systems lit up, she became very aware of the girl stood tapping her foot. Resisting the urge to turn around and slap the bitch, she instead settled back in her seat and strapped herself in.

"Here goes nothing," she said, firing up the engines. They let out a cough, a low pained hum and then threatened to fire into life, before dying. Prideaux swore, beat them with a fist.

"I don't know what you're smirking at," she said aloud.

The girl let out an indignant sound. "I wasn't…"

"Talking to the engine," she said, moving to reroute power. Things couldn't possibly be a bad as they looked. This thing couldn't just be... The station shook again. "Damnit, I wish they'd pack it in for the time being, let me think!"

Divert power from all non-essential systems... Interior cooling, don't need that. Sure, it might be hot, but it'll be even hotter if this thing blows up while we're inside it. Weapons, shields... Nice to know they were optional in the first place. Guess we really will be a sitting duck when we take off. Thrusters, working. Landing controls, ouch, they look dodgy. That might be touch and go.

"So, what are our chances?" the girl asked. Prideaux didn't realise she'd spoken out loud during her diagnostic.

"If we get into the air, about fifty to fifty," she said. "We fail to get off the ground, probably about... Yeah zero. No chance. We'll die here."

The girl closed her eyes and just for a moment nothing happened. Then the ship shuddered, threatening to rise off the deck. It stuttered and then crashed back down. She opened her eyes, suddenly panting. "Too heavy," she said. "It's too heavy."

Useless little bitch... "And completely useless as well," she said, still working her fingers away over the controls. "All we need is a spark..." She paused as inspiration struck, she rerouted power down through the secondary diffusers, caught it on the rise and then flooded the spare back through the primary. This time when the engines kicked to life, they stayed alive. "Oh, you little beauty," she said, already working the stick back to guide it up off the ground. "Let's get the hells out of here."

Bits of the ceiling were starting to fall away around them as they made their way to the hangar doors, she had to be quick on her feet to evade the debris, last thing she needed was to be crushed like an egg. Prideaux swore as one came down in her path, had to nudge the ship to the side to avoid crashing. That would have topped an already stressful day.

They'd just about made it through the hangar doors when the airbase collapsed around them.

Total collapse might have been an exaggeration but at the same time, the wing of the structure they'd been in was crumpling, the twin outer structures falling from the central 'eyeball' part of the base. They'd jettisoned the damaged parts, Prideaux realised, the destruction clear to see from up here. Smoking craters and long trails of destruction had been painted all over the surface of the twin outer hulls, fires dying as they fell away through the air. At least there was nothing but water below. No chance of a small town being wiped out by them hitting it.

For a long moment, the orb hung there in the air, dwarfing even the dreadnoughts in the distance. And then it turned to run, hitting maximum acceleration in a matter of seconds. No time to track it, no time to guess where it might be going. One moment it was there, the next it was a speck in the distance. Out of sight but not out of mind. Prideaux swore. This mission had to have been the biggest bust ever. All for nothing. She'd been interrupted from her own task by this little bitch and all left now was what to do about it. The girl looked relieved. Time to see how long she could make that last for.

"I've always been a firm believer that if you want to hide a door, the best way to do it is in plain sight. It helps if it doesn't look like a door, of course. Some people display an almost chronic inability to see beyond the surface of things."
Almer Rushford, former Vedo to his apprentice.

The fourth day of Summerfall.

Nobody was saying anything much and certainly nothing more than they had to. An aura of pervasive silence filled the makeshift Unisco office as everyone present found themselves crowded around the viewing screen, watching the ongoing speech. Six people were present in the pictures, all widely known throughout the five kingdoms. Ahead of them all was Cosmin Catarzi, Chancellor of the Senate of Representatives, the nominated figurehead in charge of it all. Behind him were the rulers of the individual kingdoms, Adam Abbot, First Minister of Canterage, Joseph Christopher McCoy, President of Premesoir, Luisa de Alcacer Giminez, High Queen of Serran, Masahiro Nakamura, Emperor of Burykila and finally Leonard Nwakili, the Premier of Vazara. All wore expressions of solemnity, a show of unity. A dozen or so prominent senators stood behind them, all part of the fabric of the government that made up the five kingdoms, all stood together in one space at one time.

Nick couldn't help but think it was a tremendously bad idea. If things went south, as it felt like there was a pretty good chance of them doing, a lot of them would be in danger. Arnholt had told them as much, Catarzi had pushed it off. He'd refused to bow to the threat, saying they'd show the solidarity that had formed the kingdoms initially. They'd live together, and they'd die together if it came to it. He couldn't help but wonder what some of the senators would have thought given the choice. Most of them weren't renowned for having a strong centre of fibre when it came to statements like that.

"From here on out," Catarzi intoned deeply, drawing on every word as if his life depended on it. "There is no way to mistake it as anything else, we are at war. And yet our war is not with our neighbours abroad, it is a war with an enemy within our midst. Yesterday, the first shots were fired in the skies above the Vazaran ocean. Many lives were lost, plenty of servicemen and women who devoted their lives to peace will not be returning to their families. It is a war of interests, a clash of ideologies. The enemy is none other than a woman many of you may have respected or liked or even taken credits from over the years. Claudia Coppinger. Vital Unisco intelligence acquired at great risk has shown some of the truly sinister nature of her plans, including building a battle station and a fleet of warships. And although a five kingdoms taskforce managed to deal serious losses to her, she escaped. Most of her lieutenants escaped. Her station escaped, the limits of her armies remain unknown."

He looked more and more stressed out the longer the statement went on, Nick felt a little sorry for him really. It wasn't the sort of news anyone wanted to deliver, the sort of thing that anyone wanted to happen in their lifetime. And here he was, telling the entire five kingdoms they were about to descend into civil war. Whatever happened, whichever side won, history would remember Catarzi as the man who had let it happen. His legacy was already tarnished, he probably wanted it over as quickly as possible. Something everyone in this room had in common.

"Poor bastard," Derenko voiced aloud. It was hard for him to look too sad, Nick noticed. Derenko had been buzzing ever since they'd returned from the mission, his Unisco stock at an all-time high with the capture of every major crime boss in the five kingdoms, barring Cyris of course. He'd been told all about how the pardon for the man was already winging its way to Catarzi's desk, urgent priority and highly recommended to be acted on. There were even rumours Derenko was about to be promoted off the back of it. No wonder he looked way too pleased, despite everything that had happened.

"He's not wrong though," Caldwell said, still checking out his surroundings. To the best of Nick's knowledge, this was the first time he'd been here, and he was still treating it like there was an enemy around every corner. Still it paid to be suspicious, for if Claudia Coppinger had a kill list, Caldwell was probably the top name on it. That wouldn't just be business, it'd be personal as well. Right now, Nick didn't envy Caldwell one bit at all. "It's going to be a mess. You know how many people Reims has employed over the last ten years? You know how many people their feeder companies employ? Any of them could sympathise with my sister. A lot of people will. It's probably how she accrued so many armaments in the first place without anyone noticing. Credits and charisma account for a lot. What you saw upstairs wasn't the entire thing, it was just the start."

"As chairwoman and owner of Reims Incorporated, Claudia Coppinger has proven to be a truly shrewd mind in the business world," Catarzi said. "We can only hope for a swift resolution to the situation and that her talents do not run as prolifically to warfare as they did to the business world. All Reims assets left in the five kingdoms are in the process of being seized and held in Senate acquisition."

"That'll be the investors running for the hills," Lysa said. "Maybe this'll bring a quick resolution to the whole thing."

Caldwell shook his head. "I doubt it. That's just the company. It won't make a difference. She's been bleeding the books creatively for years. It's worthless really, little more than a pretty shell. The real credits from it have long been siphoned into personal accounts under a dozen different names in a dozen different offshore islands, some of which don't even appear on maps. She's smarter than that, she didn't want it to happen this soon, but she knew as soon as it came out into the open it'd explode into one unholy mess. My sister might be many things but unfortunately, stupid has never been one of them."

"So, no quick resolution then?" Aldiss said hopefully. He echoed the thought passing through all their minds. The longer this went on, the more danger each of them would be in individually. The number of dangerous missions on offer would go up, all of them would be vital and there'd be a greater chance of being killed. Of course, it was what they'd been trained for. They'd all just prefer it if that wasn't the case. If you were going to die, perhaps it was better to die for a just cause. What felt like a better one than this?

"Not likely," Brendan said.

"In addition to this shocking act of treason," Catarzi said. "Another has already been spawned out of it. The Vazaran Suns were tolerated by everyone despite the element of lawlessness that runs through them…" He shot Nwakili an annoyed look out the corner of his eye, Nwakili who continued to stare determinedly into the camera. His face betrayed no emotion, "chose to join Coppinger in her treason. Dark Wind ships rushed to join the engagement in the skies yesterday, their involvement was key in ensuring she could escape with most of her assets intact. Therefore, as is traditional in these times, I am posting bounties on everyone involved."

"This never helps!" Wilsin exclaimed. "I don't know why he thinks it does!"

As he'd pointed out, it was traditional at times like these for bounties to be posted in hope those unfettered by the law might be able to end it all quickly. Nick had always thought it displayed a contradictory message but there was always someone willing to try and get the credits. Offering a million credits for the head of Claudia Coppinger certainly had its attractions. It was a shame none of them would be able to claim it if they killed her. The theory put to them being that since they were already employed in a profession that meant they were being paid to pull the trigger on her when it came down to it, they were not about to be paid twice to do the job. Those putting the credits up weren't completely stupid.

Of course, it never quite went as planned. So many would-be bounty hunters sprang up out of the woodwork at times of crisis like this in hopes of striking it rich. It meant there'd be a lot of bodies piled up in the streets before long. Semi-retired soldiers, blaster nuts, medicated psychopaths, they all suddenly seemed to lose their sense and go after the men and women the bounties were posted on. Very few of them lived to claim the credits.

Claudia Coppinger, a million credits. Fair enough. Phillippe Mazoud, eight hundred thousand. Arguably a much harder target to deal with. Had he been in the shoes of those bounty hunters, Nick wouldn't have touched that one. It was pretty much a suicide note left unwritten. To remove Mazoud, one would likely have to fight through the Vazaran Suns as well. Connor Caldwell had already told them about Coppinger's right hand man, a man named Domis who David Wilsin had already claimed to have killed. Noorland had even shown them video footage of some of the fight. Nick hadn't quite been able to miss the smirk on Caldwell's face when he'd heard him say that. He'd even voiced his disbelief out loud, pointing out how hard to kill Domis was allegedly. In fairness to him, Wilsin had agreed, telling them all how he hit like a wrecking ball and had a stupidly unfair ability to heal wounds dealt to him. Hence the confusion as to whether he was dead or not. He'd told them of Jake Costa who Nick remembered all too well from their encounter in the Carcaradis Island jail, the bounty had been placed on him at a paltry hundred thousand credits.

Then there was Harvey Rocastle, Caldwell had informed them he'd been instrumental in recruiting callers disillusioned with the current state of the competition to the Coppinger side of the coming conflict. He told how they'd been subject to conditioning, trained, battle hardened to ensure that they were of maximum use. Unfortunately, he'd been unable to provide a complete list of names but had told them that Weronika Saarth and Reda Ulikku were on the list. Nick had felt a brief sensation of vindication at being proved right. Most of the names were ones he'd already pulled out in his investigation. New ones would be good but being proved right wasn't to be sniffed at. It was the small victories that made all the difference.

Rocastle's bounty held at fifty thousand, on top of the twenty thousand that was already set out for him for escaping Unisco custody. He'd also named Doctor Dale Sinkins for them, a bounty listed at the same number as for Rocastle, fifty thousand. A preposterous amount for someone whose role had been research at most, still that was their choice. That was what taxes paid for apparently these days. Pay for us to hunt your enemies. And by your enemies, we mean our enemies. The final name on the list, Nick noticed was one Wim Carson. He couldn't find it in his heart anywhere to agree with the bounty posted for him. Fifty thousand for him was massively undervaluing him. Caldwell had made him out to be some sort of guru slash advisor who Coppinger had plucked out of obscurity and kept his value to her secret. Even from her brother. A shrewd decision it would appear on her part. Nick wasn't convinced as to the ease of the kill. He'd faced down Carson, he'd fought him and with that laser sword of his, he'd not just survived, he'd come out the better. If that girl hadn't appeared, he'd have been dead. No doubt. It wouldn't be some amateur bounty hunter who dealt with him. That bounty would go up and up and up, it'd either be someone like him or someone immensely lucky.

"Makes your mouth water, huh?" Noorland said. "Makes you wish we'd all gone private before this whole thing, huh?"

"It's not too late," Fagan said. "Reckon we can still form our own mercenary company, go after them and share the profits."

"Not worth it," Leclerc said quickly. "Unless you want to hit Coppinger or Mazoud. Rest of them split fifteen ways wouldn't be worth getting out of bed for."

"Fifteen of us could hit Mazoud easy," Derenko mused dreamily. "Eight hundred grand, fifteen ways… Just over fifty thousand each. Not bad for a morning's work."

"Nice to see what sort of loyalty we have from our agents when the times get tough," Brendan said sarcastically. The room went silent, an ugly undertone to the quiet. He might just have crossed the line with his joke, even Arnholt and Crumley glared at him. Only Nkolou and Navarro, the two captured pilots remained unmoved by it, Nick noticed. They'd been kept around for now, they were down numbers after Harper had been killed in action and still minus Wade and despite their rustiness in field action, they'd survived the enemy camp for a good few weeks. They had information, potentially. They would be useful. They'd already proven themselves heroes in what was now being dubbed the Battle of Red Sky by the media after the explosions had stained the sky temporary shades of red and orange. It hadn't been easy to miss; everyone had been forming their theories as to what happened. Catarzi confirming it was the best thing possible given some of the rumours.

"Just a thought, Chief," Fagan said. "We're all on the same page here." Maybe because he was feeling ire at the suggestion, he also added, "as if you have to ask." Brendan let it go, even with the hint of challenge in the words. Maybe it was just Fagan's accent. Everything sounded like it was bordering on insubordination at times. When he was annoyed, it sounded like he was about to set off on outright mutiny.

"I know it's a terrible situation," Arnholt said. "But hey, we all know the score. We know nobody on our side is going to come out a winner in this. We might have to do terrible things and live with the consequences." He sighed sorrowfully. "Can't do anything about it. Goes with the job I'm afraid. This is the greatest catastrophe to hit our lives, certainly our working careers. We need to step up or be stepped on. Sad truth I'm afraid to say. Everyone here is needed to be ready, willing and able to do what needs to be done. I'm told the Senate is voting to relax our regulations, maybe even restructure the organisation for times of crisis."

"Fuck me!" Nick said aloud. "It must be bad then." His reaction brought a few titters from the group, mainly Leclerc and Fagan, Arnholt rolled his eyes. Brendan looked like he wanted to say something but bit down on it. His jaw muscles must have been aching badly, Nick noted, the Field Chief had a face like it was hewn from stone.

"And it has been dutifully summed up by Agent Roper there and then," Arnholt said. "Relaxing the rules that we must follow to do our jobs to an efficient standard of enforcement. To say the least, it would appear they are desperate for a quick resolution. They have apparently arrived at the conclusion the ends justify the means. The reality is so very different. I don't have to tell you what a delicate situation this could turn into."

"I don't follow, sir," Alex Nkolou said, piping up for the first time. "If the regulations are relaxed, then surely that's a good thing. We can do our jobs easier…"

"And it's a can of worms," Pree Khan replied to her. She'd shown back up not too long ago, unwilling to talk about how she'd gotten back. "Where's the line? If we don't know where it is, how the hells can we avoid crossing it? Your view is what the Senate believe, if suddenly we don't have to follow their regulations and can trample roughshod over whoever the hells we want, we'll have the job done in five minutes. It's not that simple…" She paused suddenly, aware of the look Arnholt was giving her. "Sorry, Director."

"Oh please, go on," Arnholt said. "You're putting it very succinctly. Don't interrupt me next time, Agent Khan."

"Apologies," Khan said. "Anyway, the reality is different to what the Senate believes will happen. Think about it. Claudia Coppinger is fighting a war based on change, correct me if I'm wrong, Agent Caldwell. She wants to go out with the old, bring in the new and she has to tear down that old before she can build on top of it."

"Sounds about right," Caldwell said, stretching out his arms behind his head. "She wanted to find people disillusioned with the current system…"

"Currently that extends as far as the ICCC and probably us, but it could move towards the Senate as well. Chances are that it will go towards the Senate in time. Can't do anything about it," Khan said. "What we absolutely don't want to do is give her weapons to use against us. If she's going on about how the Senate are corrupt and want to safeguard their power and will do whatever it takes to ensure that happens, and then it comes out that they're telling us to do whatever we must to do just that, it could give her fearmongering a new angle…"

"See," Arnholt said. "Knife edge. I still expect all my agents to use their judgement as wisely as possible in any given situation." Nick thought it was a touch ironic given what had happened just a few weeks earlier in the whole Jeremiah Blut affair but didn't bring it up. Under new rules, he'd have probably gotten away with it. Irony. He rolled his eyes at that thought. "This is all just hypothetical anyway. The Senate are voting on it later in the week." He lowered his voice. "The rumour I hear is that they're waiting until the Quin-C final. They want to bury it amidst a bigger story in the media. It's not a decision that's going to make them popular. A lot of people already don't like what we do. The Senate might not even vote to approve it."

"I think we all appreciate your optimism, Director," Okocha said wearily. "But the general feeling is that the senators are terrified by everything going on. If Coppinger goes after them, they're going to want to do everything they can to get her first."

"Where you hear that?" Tod Brumley asked, curiosity in his voice.

"What, you've not got sources on Five Point Island?" Okocha asked dryly. "I know a few of our guys who work down there. There's that much terrified chatter in the air, it's screwing with the auditory detectors. Some of them are already finding excuses to leave their homes on the island and return to somewhere a little less exposed. Seriously, not lying."

"I think what Will's trying to say," Noorland said. "Is that scared people do desperate things. And those senators sound scared, by what he's saying." He grinned around the room. "Because whoever heard of a politician ever leaving luxury accommodation willingly?" Nick knew what he meant. Five Point Island was the home of the Senate building, a huge colosseum of a structure opened to the sky but protected against the elements by use of a protective shield like those employed around spirit battling fields. Surrounding it for most of the expanse of the island were private accommodations, each of them easily as luxurious as the best hotels on this island. The only reason the media didn't absolutely slate them for living like that was perhaps because they truly didn't know the extent of the decadence present. The only journalistic presences on the island were limited to the Senate building, they had their own landing pad, passes were only available on a strictly vetted availability. Anyone caught outside the approved zones was arrested for trespass. It had happened many, many times and each time the journalist in question had been dealt with under the full force of the law of the island. Suffice to say exposing the lap of luxury had been the last thing on their mind when faced with the trial for their supposed crimes.

When you thought about it like that, it wasn't hard to see why Claudia Coppinger had decided to do something. Granted maybe she was going about it in an excessive way, but maybe she had a point. Nick sighed to himself. This was all going to be a horrible mess before too long.

"Okay then, we have a building of terrified senators, we're going to be ass-deep in bounty hunters wanting to make a name for themselves, we've got a sociopath ready to really fuck things up and we're allowed to do whatever we want to stop it before it really descends into chaos?" Lysa asked. "Any good news to throw at us, anyone?"

"Just that while they might be wrong to go about it the way that they are," Arnholt said, "It doesn't mean they're not right in thinking this needs to be resolved quickly. If we fail to do so…" He didn't need to finish his sentence. Everyone knew. They didn't like it, but they knew. Just as they knew that the stakes were higher than they'd ever been for them.

Burykia.

The fifth day of Summerfall.

The town of Hoko stood silent in the night, the only sounds of life beyond the crickets being the crunch of grass beneath her boots as she and Wim Carson made their way through the fields. She looked around under the faint lights that lined the streets and found herself if not at peace, then definitely more relaxed here than before. Now she was away from it all, things felt good.

Since they'd landed in Burykia, she'd heard from Rocastle, had been pleasantly surprised to hear he'd done some good for her. Finally, and not without good timing as well! The man was a liability and the potential for buffoonery but maybe she'd misjudged him. Perhaps he could hold some further long-term use. His role in her plans had initially been a small one, yet it had turned out to be key. He'd had to jettison parts of the Eye, but she'd ordered him to do it, so he couldn't be faulted for following orders. Not this time. When she returned from this trip, she would have to run an inventory, see what had been kept and what had been lost by the efforts. What had been up there wasn't her only stockpile, she had others around the kingdoms, but it was still a blow. Silently she cursed her foul run of luck in the recent days. What had brought Unisco and the five kingdoms army to her doorstep? She never knew but she suspected Collison had something to do with it. The absolute fucking snake! She stopped for a moment, let the rage flow through her, hot white anger brushing against her vision. She'd trusted him! Let him back into her life when he'd tried so hard to get away from it and what had he done? He'd betrayed her. Admitted to conspiring with her enemies against her. The bastard would have to be dealt with at some point. A message to all those that might go against her when it mattered.

Still revenge could wait for now. It was a dish best served freezing, but she wasn't intending to leave it that long. Not if she could help it. He knew stuff about her plans that could be fatal, she was just grateful she'd chosen never to reveal the identity of her source within Unisco to him. If he was with that group of malcontents, then it would have been disastrous to have the leak plugged. Perhaps she could arrange for her man to deal with her traitorous brother.

As an idea, it was rejected the moment it entered her head. Drawing suspicion on her mole wasn't the best course of action, even if it could be explained away. The unialiv had failed as well, though she wasn't sure how. Rocastle had reported that there was no sign of it on board the station and no bodies in the hangar. If they couldn't find a body, it wasn't dead. They had recovered the body of one of the Unisco operatives, someone who they'd identified as a Melanie Harper. The name meant nothing to her. It meant that there was one less of them in the kingdoms. Either way, her remains had been disposed of.

"I've never been here before," she said aloud, anything to draw her out of her thoughts. Wim Carson had halted, arms folded and looked at her with a cocked eyebrow that made him look way too reckless. She'd noticed he'd been unarmed since his encounter with that troublesome little girl back at the base.

"You seem troubled," Wim said.

"You know what?!" she said, anger suddenly rising in her gorge and she couldn't stop the bile spilling out. "I am! I'm trying to heal these sick kingdoms, and everyone seems intent on stopping me! I didn't expect them to lie down and die but their resistance is becoming tiresome. I had a plan and it's all been blown to shit before we even started! Now I'm trying to get it all back on track and I'm worried where the next screw up is going to come from."

"They say every plan is sound until it comes into action," Wim remarked evenly. "In my experience, it is perhaps not the ability to formulate a plan that defines the ability of an individual but rather the ability to adapt once it all falls apart. You cannot plan for every eventuality. To try and do so is a waste of effort. And you're not doing too bad. You're still alive. You still have most of a battle station. You still have most of the Ista Neroux."

That was a sore point. Two of them were unaccounted for right now. Not only was the unialiv missing in action but the sabuyak had never been retrieved either following that mini-breakout they'd experienced weeks ago. It was rather hard to track a ghost at the best of times but to have completely lost track of it irked her to say the least. It hadn't been the most powerful of what they'd put together but still that it wasn't where it was meant to be annoyed the hells out of her. It was her property and how dare it wander off!

"You still have most of your facilities! You still have your vision," he continued. "You know the medicine this place needs and you are in the position to ensure you acquire it. I can think of nothing else that you need. You perhaps are too critical on yourself."

She let out a bitter laugh, more for show than anything else. If Wim was half as sensitive to moods and emotions as he made out, it wasn't going to fool him. But she didn't care about that. Fooling him wasn't part of the deal. "The thing is, if I'm not going to be hard on myself, who else is? If I fail, it's all been for nothing and I can't let that happen."

"Then don't fail," Wim said simply. "Do or do not. If you die, then at least you died making the effort. It's more than most of the people in these kingdoms can say. If you die, your name will be mud. Everything you have done will be regarded with scorn and disgust. You will have lost everything, and it will be beyond you forever." Then he smiled at her, a warm almost fatherly expression that made her think of days long gone and times that weren't going to come back to her. "But what if you win?"

Exactly. What if I do win? She was sacrificing so much in this venture with so little appreciation right now. She was set to be a pariah and her list of friends and allies she could count on was growing smaller by the minute. Rocastle had reported the crime bosses she'd invested so much effort and time in bringing together had been taken by Unisco. Phillipe Mazoud still had her back for now, he was throwing his lot in with her, but his organisation was limited outside of

Vazara. If she was caught here in Burykia for example, he wouldn't be able to do a lot to help her. No, she needed more. In recent months she might have been hesitant about this decision, but she had no other choice. Even had she the means to put it into play before, still she might have shied away from it.

It was the statue. Of course, it was. She'd never been to Hoko before but everyone who knew anything about Burykia always said that the biggest brightest statue of Gilgarus was to be found here. It was, Claudia had to admit, damn impressive as she stared up at it from paws to collar to crown.

"I remember the first time I saw this," Wim said thoughtfully. "My master brought me here, told me the legend of how this thing came into being."

"Gilgarus?"

"The statue. Although the two are linked. I believe you know the story. I believe your Doctor Jeremiah Blut did as well, not that he knew how to prove it or not."

"You always seem to know a lot about this stuff," she said. "And yet you never share how you came about this knowledge."

He did that thing with his eyes, smiled without smiling. He had the look of a man smug beneath his secrets and privately he loved that feeling of superiority. "I wasn't always a man of the streets. I did used to be someone. Before I got it all back, I lost it. And before I lost it, well who I was should have been feared. At least if people were in the know, they would have. I was the archivist for the Council of Nine."

"The what?" She wasn't even a little bit ashamed to admit she'd never heard of them. The sense she got from him said he would have been even more surprised if she had. The supercilious way he'd been talking and acting since he'd brought them up, almost preening with his own foreknowledge, she got the impression she wasn't expected to know them.

"The rulers of the Vedo," Wim said. "The nine strongest to govern them all. I was one of them. As I'm aware, the only survivor. Though that wasn't without its cost. A life left living is worth more than a death dealt dead. There are others but by right I am the heir to the empty throne."

"Fascinating." She only half meant it. Perhaps better to deal with Wim sooner or later. He could be a problem if he had thoughts like this.

"You speak with scepticism?"

"Perhaps," she said. "I still find it hard to believe an organisation like yours existed for all this time and nobody ever found out about it."

"Well of course they did," Wim said. "People found out about us all the time. Hence the need for our Buffers. They were always needed to be heavily employed whenever we announced our presence to the kingdoms. Always the circumstances would be great and our greatest Cognivites would be out there to fog the recollections of those who saw us, to make us as ghosts. We prided our secrecy. Anyway, enough about people long dead."

He cleared his throat, rubbed at his chest with the scruff of his fist. "In my role as archivist I found so much out, more than I could possibly ever remember. Information is the greatest weapon imaginable, I believe you would agree with me on that score. I always remember the rumours about this statue though. It's built above a nexus of power; the fabric of reality is ever so slightly thinner here than anywhere else in the five kingdoms. Hence, with a place like this, you need something to mark it. And what better than a great statue of Gilgarus? It makes sense when you think about it, do you not think? More than that, people come here to worship. All that belief, all that faith, into an area where reality is weaker than everywhere else. Belief is a powerful force, Mistress."

"I think it's big," Claudia said. "It doesn't surprise me that there's a legend like that floating around. But if you're telling the truth, if that is the true story then how come nobody has managed to get through? How come nobody could prove it one way or another? How come it's just a legend?"

Again, that smile. She fought the urge to slap him. It wouldn't do anyone any good, as much as it might make her feel better. "Because anyone with the ability to open it by force should know better," he said. "And those without the ability lack the key. Punching a hole through the fabric of reality is not a task taken lightly, it's a dangerous undertaking and only someone truly desperate would do it. The consequences would be disastrous, even if as the stories say, the rip is the back door to Gilgarus' own kingdom. Just picture about what might lie there? The items. The artefacts. The potential power."

"We have both here," she said. "You could do it by force, couldn't you? And we have the key." She was grateful utterly she'd had the foresight to keep it with her always since he'd first smashed that statue of Melarius. "So why do you want to open it up?"

"My dear Madam Coppinger," Wim said sorrowfully. "I believe we're both desperate individuals here. I believe this is the only course of action left. I do not wish to rip my way through it, but I will open the door for you. We had a deal. Once the deal is honoured, then I am free to engage in my own pursuits."

"Is this dangerous?" she asked. "I mean, it's not going to cause irreversible damage or anything, is it? Using the key?"

"Shouldn't do," Wim said. "The truth is I have no idea. There are stories of those who endeavoured to open it up. Their fates ultimately remain unknown. Perhaps the first thing you will see on the other side is the bones of those who have fallen. Or perhaps you will join them." There was no emotion in his voice as he spoke, just a statement of fact. It might have worked to put a lesser person off. Claudia only felt the desire to find out for herself.

She held out the key, the shiny stone and Wim raised a hand, calmly gesticulating with his fingers and she felt the kiss of it on her palm fade away. Slowly she watched it rise into the air, fighting against gravity and the wind but ultimately powerless against Wim's mental touch. "There's an indent on the wheel of justice," Wim said softly, his face screwed up with concentration. "Missing a jewel. They always think it's an aesthetic design flaw. An oversight. They never assume it's actually meant to be like that because of..." One final flurry of his arm and even over the distance, she heard the slight click of the gem slotting into place. "Perfect."

For several long moments nothing happened. She folded her arms, tapped her foot on the grass. If this was the big finale, she wasn't impressed. Not until the grass beneath her boot started to shimmer, faint at first to be confused for moonlight until its brightness eclipsed the lunar illumination. Wim jumped back several feet, well out of the way and for a moment she felt betrayed, until she realised he was watching her with an expression of utmost serenity. If she listened, it was like she could hear his voice in her head.

This is your journey, Madam. It will make you or break you. It will be hard but everything worth doing is. You walk alone, and the world will still be here when you get back. Do not fear, just let the light take you.

Those words continued to echo through her head as she pushed away all thoughts of hurt betrayal and tried to do what they'd suggested, just relax and let them take her. How she was supposed to do that, she didn't know but it was warm in the light. It tickled her exposed skin, it made her felt safe, even as she found herself sinking deep into the glow...

"The return of old friends is an occasion that should always be savoured. When they have been kept from you for a long time, you never know when next you'll see them again."
Matthaus Tammer, Serranian author.

The eighth day of Summerfall.

To say security had been massively stepped up was perhaps an understatement, Wade considered as he and his travelling companion stepped off the boat and felt the dry land of Carcaradis Island underneath his feet. It felt good to be back. Even though his eyes still hurt a little behind the dark glasses shielding them from the afternoon sun, he didn't realise quite how much of the atmosphere he'd missed of this place. If anything, the sudden increase of potential danger had sparked it back into life, even with the added security.

Far from being cowed, people had set out to show they were going to enjoy the last few days of the tournament before harsh realities kicked in. There'd been a big thing a week or two earlier how Ritellia had promised to bring in a Vazaran Sun presence to help ensure the peace was kept. Considering recent revelations, that presence had been quashed, removed from the island and replaced with a fresh influx of Unisco agents and local Vazaran cops from the mainland.

Not even Ritellia was stupid enough to fly his own flag in the face of something like this. Things weren't looking good for him; rumours were rife that he was being forced into stepping down when the tournament concluded the following day. Being associated with Claudia Coppinger by proxy looked like it might have done for him, especially given her role in ensuring the locale for the Quin-C as well as certain allegations about his private life.

Thomas Jerome was already playing up to the media, to get in as the front runner for the next head of the ICCC, a move Wade personally found distasteful but in well keeping with the man's prior behaviour. Whatever happened over the coming months, it was unlikely the spirit calling governing body was going to be much towards the front of it. People would have more important things on their minds. It was quite incredible really, by the sounds of it Ritellia had fought tooth and nail just to ensure that the final was held. There had been calls for it to be cancelled and rearranged for a later date, or even declare it a draw and split the prize money between the two finalists, something Wade had to concede would probably have been for the best. But no, it wasn't to be, and it had gone ahead. Just as planned.

271

It was finally here, Wade had noted. Just six short weeks after it had started, the final was fast approaching, and, in a way, he was relieved. He'd come here with the intent of dominating, he felt himself grow anxious with thoughts of what could have been. What wasn't to be, wasn't to be. He couldn't complain. He'd done what he felt was the right thing, about the only thing he could do; he'd been way too ill to compete. Always there'd be regrets but he couldn't let them paralyse him. There was too much at stake for indecision.

"Remember, a regret is an opportunity missed, but an opportunity missed leads to an opportunity taken down the line."

It was largely because of the final being held the following day that the figure with him had arrived. One of Wade's oldest friends, they'd come through Unisco training together, been partnered up on their first assignments. He hadn't seen much of him over the last five years but the last fortnight in his presence had been eye-opening, figuratively. Of course, he did have a lot of those insightful statements to add to every situation. The older he'd gotten, the more he believed his wisdom had grown. Wade wasn't sure about that, but he was bloody glad to have him at his back. After all, Ruud Baxter had a certain reputation. Not just as the man who was about to hand back the trophy, a sign his reign as champion of the Quin-C had come to the end. A lot of people didn't believe he was still alive for one thing; five years of solitude would do that to a man's public image. Of course, Wade knew the truth. The two of them hid few secrets from each other, at least to his knowledge.

"We all have regrets," he said softly. Getting through customs was a slow process this time, the guards insisted on searching everyone individually. Vazaran police from the mainland clad in sweat stained uniforms, Wade winced at the sight. If they didn't like you, you weren't getting through. And even all things considered, they were probably still less reliable than the Suns. At least the Suns were notorious for being incorruptible beyond their high doctrine. They wouldn't take bribes to avoid doing their job. Idly he toyed with flashing his badge and moving past the searches, but it wouldn't help his companion.

"Don't worry," Ruud said. "I'll be through faster than you, I'd imagine." He was a slender man in his late thirties with a fading tan, almost dapper in his built and of averaging height, unremarkable but for the thick black hair dropping down to his lower back, growing wild on his chin. He still carried the cane, although as far as Wade was aware, he'd never actually needed it. He was just a notorious eccentric where it was concerned, about the most physical use he had for it was occasionally whacking the shins of those in his way.

That aside, he had a sense of an easy-going nature about him, one that suggested he didn't take life too seriously. Clad in a sapphire blue suit and jaunty hat with a cream coloured rim-band, he cut a dashing figure on the docks, easily standing out amidst the tourists. Very few recognised him, largely Wade guessed down to the fact he'd been clean shaven and short haired when he'd won the tournament.

"Want to bet, my friend?"

He'd overheard some of Ruud's exchange and mentally kicked himself. There was always the lesson about gambling, never knowing how the cards were stacked or might fall for you. Out the corner of his eye, he saw Ruud display his pass card with its wildly incomparable photo and the security official studying it pensively. Ruud smiled at him. Two people behind him in the queue, one of them a redheaded girl studying her summoner, her foot tapping against the ground. She looked... If not unnerved, then definitely agitated. Wade smiled as he saw her. They must think his eyes worse than they were.

"Need to search your bags," the official grunted. "Official procedure."

That smile only grew. "Of course, I understand. But it isn't needed here, you see." Those eyes locked on the officials, there was more than a bit of a twinkle in them. Ruud could be quite charming when he needed to be. He remembered back in the day, women had thrown themselves at him.

"I see. It's not needed here."

"Thanks. You've been most helpful." Eyes still locked, grin still plastered across his tanned face, Ruud clapped him on the shoulder. "Have a nice day sir."

"Always here to help. Have a nice day, sir."

Wade had beaten him through. But not by much and he still had to contend with Ruud's smirk as he slipped the credit over. He was careful not to look him in the eye, he knew that much. Looking him in the eyes was always an interesting experience. Ruud's eyes were mismatched, one a dull brown the same shade as mud, one a brilliant sky blue. No matter which one you met, always you got the impression he could see through anything you'd say, pick out the lies and then play you at your own game.

"You know, you should really inform people these guys are very susceptible to that trick," Wade said thoughtfully. "It's quite worrying."

Ruud shrugged. "I've got nothing to hide."

"What about the two young men who've been watching you ever since we got on the boat?" Wade asked, keeping his voice neutral. "Have they anything to hide? What about the women? And what about you, dear cousin!" He raised his voice, the redhead behind them reacting with a start. "You must be slipping if you think I wouldn't notice."

"Okay so I didn't come alone," Ruud grinned. "An entourage is always nice." He held out his hands in front of him, a gesture of mock surrender. "Besides, you never know what's going to happen, do you?" Something about his voice made Wade straighten up and take note. Ruud might be an annoying bastard at times, he might have a layer of extreme self-confidence bordering not just on arrogant but obscene, but he had reason to be. He could back it up, knew what he was talking about, and you disregarded it at your own peril.

"I wondered how long it'd take for you to notice me," Clara said, moving in. Wade grinned at his younger cousin. "Thought you'd forgotten."

"And then the hells froze over," Wade replied dryly, stepping over to embrace her happily. "Not about to happen. Not going to forget my favourite cousin. I'll play my part and Baxter'll play his games. We all know how much he enjoys those."

"Only because you failed utterly to win this one completely, my friend," Ruud said. "I knew you'd noticed I wasn't alone on this trip. But I doubted you'd notice everyone I had with me." His grin was just about unbearable. "Safety in numbers, double that for the unknown."

"Do you know something?"

"I know a lot of things. You could too if you just believed…" Ruud trailed off his voice, raising an inquisitive eyebrow at Wade. "You need not fear what you do not understand. That path leads to hatred and anger. It's not a dictate to live by, it's just good advice for living a good life."

"I've told you before…"

"Your cousin embraced it, the power is strong in you and yet you choose to let it atrophy like a useless limb. Very few people in your position would turn it down. We've told each other a lot of things before."

Wade glanced back and forth around them, narrowed his eyes and folded his arms defensively. Clara had fallen in alongside him and Ruud, he shot her a disparaging look and kept it on her until she fell back several steps. She didn't need to hear what he and Ruud were talking about. "And perhaps that's a better thing for the world that I do. I'm not afraid of what I might do…"

"False." He said it quietly, but it still had all the emphasis of a whip crack.

"I'm not!" Wade insisted Once more he glanced about them, still too many people on the docks, still a chance their private conversation would not remain so for much longer. "There's a great deal of difference between fear and respect. I respect power enough to know maybe it shouldn't be used."

"You're not going to change his mind, Master," Clara called forth. A few people looked at her, she brushed them off as if they weren't there. Both Ruud and Wade looked back at her, stern looks urging her to quieten down. She did but didn't look happy. The two men Wade had spotted earlier fell in with her, soon they were out of eyesight.

"Your cousin is headstrong," Ruud said wearily. "A chore indeed."

"Always has been. You didn't grow up with her." Wade smirked to himself, before adding. "You didn't know her when she was a teenager. Or when she discovered guys. That! That was an interesting time. My uncle never quite recovered from it."

"There's not many challenges I'd turn down," Ruud said. "But that part of parenthood is something I'm really not ready to face."

"Don't you need another person for that?!" Wade's smirk said it all. Ruud gave him a sardonic look in reply.

"Your wit remains as dry as ever."

"Some things don't change, I think you'll find," Wade said. "You didn't answer my question. Do you know something?"

Ruud said nothing for a moment, instead choosing to look over at the ocean with deliberate thoughtfulness. He cleared his throat, rubbed the edge of his sleeve against his mouth. "Hard to say," he said. "The future is always in motion, snake-like. Always weaving one way and another, every choice brings about something new, it's almost impossible to predict accurately. Beyond me to get it right every time. The seers of the old Vedo order went mad very quickly trying to get it right. It burns out the mind. I'll take a murky future and relative sensibility over knowing what's coming and drooling at the mouth, thank you very much. About the only thing I know for sure is I desire a shave."

"The old Vedo order," Wade said. "I remember all the stories you told me about them once upon a time. I didn't believe half of them."

"Well therein lay your mistake," Ruud said. They were rapidly approaching the second set of customs officials, so far twice as many present when Wade had come here the first time. "Your fault is not that you don't believe, rather you don't believe enough. Most of them weren't true to start with, being fair. Time has greatly exaggerated the deeds of the long dead. The truth always was the Vedo of the past were victims of their own insularity."

"And this is a group you're trying to rope me into joining," Wade said sarcastically. "And then you wonder at the same time why I'm not keen."

"The Vedo of the past are all dead to the best of my knowledge," Ruud said. "Those of the future won't repeat those mistakes. I'll see to that."

"And what of fresh mistakes? In avoiding those of the past, is there not a risk you might inadvertently create worse ones?"

Ruud said nothing. Wade knew he'd scored a point but perhaps it wasn't the best time to bring it up. "The old order had many advantages, many decades to grow and become the behemoth it did," he eventually said. "The new one won't be built in a day. Five years since the old one fell. The wounds are still fresh; the healing process is a slow one. Every venture has its risks and you cannot in any sense of reason, avoid them. Risk is what makes it worth it in the end."

The first thing he'd wanted to do upon leaving customs was go to the small cemetery out in the very centre of the island, just a few minutes' walk from the stadium where the final would take place tomorrow, Wade noticing he was shaken as he entered. If he'd been unflappable walking through customs, then he was struggling now as he strode towards the one solitary grave. He'd brought flowers. Vazaran lilies, he'd seen him drop a lot of credits into the hand of the vendor. More than enough. The old man had looked like all his birthdays had come at once and even some of his Winterheights'. He hadn't hung around as Wade had scooped everything up and walked away, his arms full of the blooms. The lilies were a mix of pure whites, sand tinted creams and even some dull pinks, none too shabby. They were intended to grow in these conditions, Wade guessed that much. He wasn't a gardener, probably wouldn't ever be. Nor were they the only flowers that would lay across the single grave, the headstone hadn't even been laid yet.

The dirt was packed solid, a large photo of her stood at the head of it. A few other people stood around in silence, none of them gave either of them a second glance. One person had a picture box out, was taking a photo. Ruud craned his head around to look at him as they passed, locking a long lingering gaze on him and the Burykian quickly lowered it. He almost walked into someone else in his hurry to leave.

"It's too damn bad," Ruud eventually said, turning his attention back to the grave. He'd laid out the flowers on the dirt amidst the already considerable array of blooms, careful to make sure he didn't disturb those left by others. "I wish I could have gotten out here for this."

"Me too," Wade said. "She was special, wasn't she?"

"Just a touch," Ruud agreed. "Just a touch. Never met anyone like her." He was shaking properly now, Wade noticed, arms folded about himself and knuckles clenched white. "I felt her die you know. Wasn't a pleasant thing. She put out a real kick when she went. Wouldn't have surprised me if everyone sensitive for a hundred miles around felt her go. Either sensitive or close to her. She had a way about her. Can't teach that. Real warm and receptive. Everyone loved her."

"Except Maddley Junior," Wade said, he couldn't even bring about a grin. It was grim out here, depressing, threatening to wear him down, would do it to them both if they stayed here much longer. And yet they needed to be here, all because of a senseless war invoked by a woman with an outlaw complex who should have known better. Sharon Arventino had died senselessly and painfully. "But I think she even won him over in the end."

"You know who did it yet?" Ruud asked. "Any leads?"

"Roper says it was Wim Carson. You might have seen there's a big bounty on him... Well a bounty. He's on the kill list. And there's strong evidence to suggest there was a second person involved. They recovered fibres and hair from the room that hinted Harvey Rocastle was involved in some way. He'd definitely been in that room at some point."

"Rocastle?"

"Spirit dancer and probable sociopath. He has a history with women, not in a sexual way but in a potentially abusive way. Tried to kidnap the director's daughter right from this very island, if you can believe it. He was working for Reims while he was here, recruiting several disillusioned callers for what Agent Caldwell called Rocastle's Angels. They were believed to be forming an elite spirit combat group, sort of like their own version of Unisco."

Ruud frowned. "Or to counter you, perhaps. Secret warriors to face you on your type of terms."

"Maybe."

"He really tried to kidnap the director's daughter?"

Wade nodded. "I stopped him myself. Fought him, beat him, slapped the cuffs on him. He escaped from custody when we were transporting him to the mainland. The convoy was attacked by Vazaran Sun fighters and we never saw them again. At least not until the whole battle when some of our pilots were retrieved."

"You're remarkably in the loop considering your sick leave."

"Well I like to stay in it," Wade said. "I'm surprised they haven't tried calling you back up to active status given how bad it looks like it might get."

Ruud laughed. "I might do it under the right circumstances. Which there undoubtedly aren't any right now."

"You don't get the right circumstances during war," Wade said before sighing heavily. "I think Arnholt wants to see you while you're here. I believe he's going to ask you about Wim Carson. He had what Nick claims was Sharon's weapon."

"Her kjarnblade?"

"Yeah. That'd hint he was, if not responsible for her death then at least involved somewhere along the line. I don't think he's going to be as easy to deal with as people think."

"He shouldn't even be a part of this," Ruud said. "Wim Carson was a Vedo, he swore certain oaths and everything he does now he's involved with this woman breaks each one of them. Last I was aware; he didn't even have his powers…"

"I didn't know you could lose them," Wade interrupted. "I mean…"

"Well it's not impossible but it is rare. If they're foresworn away and you stop using them, they can atrophy completely. If they're never developed in the first place like you seem so intent on doing, it gets harder and harder. My sister went the same path, rest her soul, she trained and eventually just lost her faith it was the way forward. Didn't save her. She and her husband died, her daughter lost, her son oblivious because of my intervention. The events that preceded the Fall did untold damage not just to the Vedo but to the Kjarn itself. It affected people in different ways, some went mad, some lost their power, some died. Some had all the above. And yet if Wim managed to get it back, it's not impossible he could have. There's always a way. The Kjarn will always triumph over any adversary."

"You talk about it like it's alive."

"Well of course it's alive," Ruud said softly. "Just because you can't register a heartbeat on it, doesn't mean it isn't. The Kjarn is life, it is the parts that make life, the two are intimately connected beyond rationale."

"It did her a whole lot of good," Wade said, looking down at the grave. "I spoke to her a lot, I was going to be best man at her wedding, I never got the impression she was one of you."

"She wasn't," Ruud said. "I trained her, she was my apprentice way back before the Fall. She was never raised, she only got as far as ascendant, she had the potential, but her heart was… It was never in the role, she always wanted to be a spirit caller more than anything. She had a gift and she was happy to learn how to use it but at the same time I always got the impression she'd have been happier if her father had never forced her into it. Canderous Arventino I remember only too well. He was not a good man, a bully and a bastard."

His face took on a nostalgic look, tinged with regret and recollection. "I killed him, you know? I never told Sharon that, but I always got the feeling that she knew. I didn't want... Yeah I didn't want her to be disappointed."

"If he was that bad..."

"He was still her father and one of the highest of the Vedo, perhaps the only reason she wasn't allowed to leave. If her father had been a nobody, a journeyman with no significant skill or status, she might have been able to slip through the cracks, nothing but a memory. Still Canderous went the way of the rest of them, brain-fried by the Kjarn and..."

"That's actually a danger? And you're training people in this?"

Ruud rolled his eyes. "It's not a danger with the right training. The Fall... It hurt the Kjarn because it made it just so damn addictive. It dulled the senses, made your judgement slacken... Soon you were little more than a puppet. Your brain was gone, mind shattered and your body animated by the Kjarn. It was exceptional circumstances. I hope to all Divines above it is never repeated." Wade said nothing, found it a lot to take in. He was vaguely aware more had joined them around the grave, men and women he didn't recognise beyond a solemn looking Clara. All of them bore the same look, tired regret, heads bowed, arms together.

"Sharon Arventino," Ruud said. "One of us. In life and in death, a noble heart, a kind spirit and a ferocious combatant. A woman who..." He let out a long sigh, a choked breath caught in his throat. Just for a moment, Wade thought he saw his friend's eyes glisten, but he clamped down on it just in time. For a moment, the façade had nearly cracked and what Ruud was really feeling had almost shown through. "Excuse me. A woman who we'll miss. Those of you here may not have known her. But you'll feel the loss in generations to come. We all will. The stars in the sky have one more in their collective now, she is one with the Kjarn and through the Kjarn, her memory will live on, join the names of those fallen in the past. She lived a Vedo, she died a friend. That is all we can ask for of life. May the Kjarn embrace those who mourn her. May her spark join the blue flame of the Vedo evermore."

He didn't remain, turned tail and walked away. Wade found himself turning to follow him, suddenly glad to be away from the permeating aura of sadness filling the immediate area around the grave. Ruud was right, he didn't know any of the people here barring Clara and maybe Sharon had known them, possibly, but the feeling had been there. Unavoidable, genuine regret. And he'd felt it too, a sensation that had simultaneously overawed and unnerved him beyond belief.

"Ruud," he said. He saw him slow to a stop, crane his head back across to meet his gaze.

"Yeah?"

"You loved her, didn't you?"

"Like the daughter I never had," Ruud said. "The bond between teacher and student... She was beautiful, I knew that, and she knew that, but I never felt the need to violate that bond. I loved her equal parts daughter, equal parts little sister. She'd been trusted into my care. They wanted me to have her, they thought it'd calm me down, stop me wandering off on Unisco business and give me more of a tie to the order. Unlike her, I didn't have any such high ranked father." A bitter grin burst across his face. "They always thought I'd leave, just not come back one day. I think that's the reason I never did, you know. I didn't want to give them the satisfaction of knowing they'd been right about me. Like her, I never really felt comfortable in that order. And look at me now, in charge. The Kjarn has its own funny ways." He turned away, cleared his throat. "I don't think Terry's going to wait forever for us now, do you?"

Wade smiled, made to follow him. He was right, of course. Ruud likely would be here, if he wasn't required by the ICCC. He was surprised even then that he'd shown up. Ruud never gave the impression he'd be overtly bothered if they pursued legal action against him. And yet he'd brought his entourage with him. There was obviously something going on, something Wade couldn't quite see just yet. It was an infuriating feeling to be infinitely aware there was some piece of the puzzle you couldn't place and if you could just see it, then all would fall into place.

The moment they'd knocked at the hotel room door and waited to be admitted entrance, Ruud's entire demeanour had changed, the sorrow had gone and been replaced by the same consummate professionalism with which he'd carried himself all through his years as an active Unisco agent. Arnholt gave them that permission, allowed them to enter and he'd embraced Wade like an old friend. When the two of them had started at Unisco way back in the day, Arnholt had been their immediate superior. Twenty years later, here they all were again. The irony wasn't lost on Wade. Time had a funny way of coming back around on you when you least expected it.

"Ruud," Arnholt said warmly.

"Director." Still referring to him by his title, Wade noticed with a grin. "You're looking well."

"Not sure if that'll last," Arnholt said with a weary grin. "I could say the same to you, retirement suits you. Not sure about the beard though, I think it makes you look like a vagrant."

"I think it makes me look wise. And knowledgeable."

Wade smirked at that, bit back a remark. None of his business. "Plus, hard to find razors where I've been. Wasn't so bad growing it after the first six months."

"Fascinating." Arnholt gestured over to the cool box in the corner, a big corporate logo stamped on the side of bright blue plastic. "Drink? Water, iced coffee, soda beer? Wade?"

"I'll take water," Ruud said softly, the same moment Wade chose to get a soda beer. The stuff wasn't alcoholic, no danger of it interfering with his meds. It just tasted as if it was, which he liked about it really. The cans of iced coffee remained untouched, he noticed. Wade took the offered can, put it on the table but didn't open it. Ruud unscrewed the lid of his water, took a deep draw.

"It's a bad time, Ruud," Arnholt said. "I don't think anyone realises just how bad it might get right now. The Senate wants it resolved quickly…"

"I imagine they would," Ruud replied. "But I agree with you. Based on my admittedly limited understanding of the situation, mainly what I see in the media, I don't think this is going to go away without one hells of a fight. Not just a fight to win, it's going to be a fight to hold on to everything held dear. The future rests on a pivot, what happens over the coming months is that pivot. You will win it or lose it in the next several weeks, the lines will be drawn early."

"I knew there was a reason I wanted to talk to you," Arnholt said. "You have an uncanny knack for telling it how it is in as poetic a manner as possible. Unfortunately, that's not the reason. Wim Carson. Talk to me about him."

"I already told Wade… Agent Wallerington… everything that I could. He was a scholar more than anything, a man who sought out knowledge. When the Vedo fell, he lost everything but his life. There were few survivors of that cataclysm, him, me, Sharon Arventino, one or two others sadly no longer with us. I would have done more for him after what happened but well, we all had to deal with our own problems. By the time I could help, he'd slipped through the cracks, his mind broken and beyond me. How he's walking around again, I don't know. I wish I did. It might explain a lot of things."

"Caldwell… we had him on the inside, right in Coppinger's ear, yet he couldn't get anything on the subject beyond the two of them had some sort of deal," Arnholt said. "Coppinger and Carson, I don't know what they'd be able to do for the other. She's a billionaire industrialist turned international terrorist, he was a mystic with a magic sword..."

"And formerly in charge of the biggest library in the five kingdoms," Ruud said. "I wouldn't underestimate anything he could have brought to her table. It must have been something she needed. What's her endgame? What do we know? As Carson likely proves in this situation, knowledge is the true power in the kingdoms."

"It's a we now, is it?" Wade asked. Ruud gave him a sarcastic look in reply.

"The adage that it's easy to fall back into bad habits is truer than you might believe," he said thoughtfully. "Well I say we for a reason. The director is going to try and get me back into the mix."

Arnholt said nothing, kept his face neutral. Wade wouldn't have liked to have played Ruin with the man. He wasn't giving anything away to his true intentions."

"And I'm going to have to decline. I'm afraid the constraints on my time are as such that I wouldn't be able to function as a field operative."

"You're wrong, you know," Arnholt said. "I wasn't going to ask you to come back. Not permanently. You got out, I was happy to let you go your own way. You'd done a lot, more than returned our investment in you. No point making you keep on going until you died. And it appears that very little has changed with you in this regard."

"I have people who depend on me," Ruud said. "Like you. People I'm responsible for, people who I've invested a great deal of time and effort in. I'm not abandoning them right now. I absolutely will not do that." His hand twitched, like he wanted to smack it against the table to emphasise his point. Wade leaned back, cracked open his can and took a swallow of the amber liquid inside. It fizzed in his throat, he was grateful to feel the bitter taste against his tongue.

"Is there anything at all you might be able to do to help us locate Wim Carson? Any sort of hideout, safe house, anything you know of that might lead us to him?"

Ruud's laugh was sarcastic. "He lived in a cave up in the Fangs before the Fall. After the Fall, I believed he went from respected scholar to homeless, credit-less vagrant bumming around the five kingdoms. He went from everything to less than nothing. I'm not entirely sure where you think he got the resources from to get a safe house. You won't find him like that. I think he'll be with Claudia Coppinger, personally. It's about the only place he'll have to go. Plus, he always did like charismatic women. One of his weaknesses. Should have seen him with the leader of the old order. She couldn't have had him on a leash any more if she'd tried. Think he'd have eaten out of her hand if she'd let him."

"Then you've got nothing for us?"

Ruud stroked his chin thoughtfully. "I'll meditate on the matter, see what I can find. Perhaps I can divine some sort of location for him although I doubt it'll be much use. My particular talents don't lie in that area; it has been left somewhat neglected over the years. Our Cognivites are untrained, potentially fantastic but inexperienced I'm afraid to say." He straightened up though. "Any useful information I find though, I'll be sure to pass it on to you."

"Thank you. And I'm sorry that you're unwilling to come back to us. The agency hasn't been the same since you left. You were one of our best operatives. A lot of the recruits these days can't hold a candle to you," Arnholt said, nodding his head as he said it. "Still, if you're unwilling to change your mind, no point in regrets. Are you sure I can't get you a better drink than that water?"

Ruud shook his head. "I'm good, director. And I thank you for your compliments, but this is one time that flattery won't get you everywhere. I'm just passing through. I've got places to be in a few days' time."

"You caught any of the Quin-C so far?" Wade asked. If Ruud wasn't coming back, there was little point in carrying on the discussion. Their information was classified, it was kept that way for a reason, no point Ruud knowing more than he was meant to for now. A lot of the tenseness faded in the room with that, all professionalism gone and suddenly they were just three old acquaintances left together, chatting about old times and the impending futures.

"Everybody loves that final day, a time of hope and expectations, a time when you can dare to dream. For one of these two callers, their dream is going to come true. Neither of them expected to be here, they've defied all odds... In a way, you could say they're both winners. At least until that final spirit falls anyway and then one of them actually is."
Terrence Arnholt.

The ninth day of Summerfall.

Scott couldn't sleep. Small wonder really. He rolled over, looked to the timepiece on the bedside and saw there were still another three hours before it was reasonable to even consider getting up. He let out a little sigh, the sound lost amidst the delicate little snores coming from Mia, her head on his chest. Her breath was warm, she was a comforting presence, being this close to her made everything feel so very vivid. Somewhere out in the night, Permear was floating around but Scott didn't know where.

Part of him really didn't want to know. The ghost had been acting more than a little strange recently, as if he knew something weird was going on but unwilling to share it with the rest of them. If it was something, it might not have been, but at the same time, he couldn't shake that weird little feeling he was going to have a very bad time sooner or later. He just hoped it wasn't going to be during that small event coming his way. The Quin-C final.

Weeks ago, he could only have dreamed about being here and yet it had become reality he couldn't quite believe had come to pass. He let out another little sigh. The past few days, well ever since the semi really, they'd all gone by in sort of one big blur, they'd been a mix of research and practice, sparring with a mix of Pete, Mia and Matt, none of whom were any sort of substitute for what he'd face against Theo, but it was good to keep practicing. He'd faced Theo once already, in the semi and he'd failed miserably to even come close to beating him but that didn't matter now. He'd researched him even more thoroughly now than he had then, he'd had Kitti Sommer to worry about at the same time, but with that barrier out of the way, he'd thrown all his attentions towards Jameson. More than that, he knew Anne Sullivan had been training him, so he'd looked at some of her styles as well. When being trained one on one by another spirit caller, it wasn't uncommon remnants of their style would creep into the process.

More than once, he'd considered even asking Terrence Arnholt for some sparring practice, the man infinitely more skilled than either of his children, a lot more experienced than himself or Pete. It would have been the smart thing to do and yet at the same time, Scott had refrained from doing so. When he'd met him for the first time, when Mia had introduced him as her boyfriend, he'd been more than a little uneasy about it, felt like he was looking right through him with those emotionless grey eyes. There was something more than a little off-putting about Terrence Arnholt, Scott got the feeling he didn't entirely like him.

Or maybe he just doesn't like what I'm doing to his daughter, he'd thought later. That was entirely possible and not at all unreasonable. He smiled a little at that thought, even as Mia coughed in her sleep, an adorable sound. He closed his eyes, settled back and once more tried to let sleep overtake him. No use. He shifted underneath her, tried to get a little more comfortable. She coughed again, three little hacks in a row this time. Something wet hit his bare chest. Nice, she was drooling on him. He'd have to remind her about this in the morning, see her squirm a little. More droplets hit him. For some reason, he could smell the ocean. The scent of salt and the sound of ocean birds, the lap of waves against rocks…

That coughing turned into choking, more water touched him, Scott jerked bolt upright in bed and Mia fell off him, spasming helplessly amidst the choking, water flooding from her. Suddenly the bed was soaking wet, puddles forming on the carpet, her hair billowing out around her head like she was submerged. Slowly her flailing turned violent, her foot caught him in the chest and kicked him off the bed, he hit the carpet with a soggy squelch and he saw her movements slow as the chokes died away, her head falling listlessly against the bed, water still streaming from her mouth, one final harsh breath slipping from her.

He was immensely proud of the fact that he didn't wake up screaming. He'd never done it before after bad dreams and he wasn't about to start now. Not even close. Not even Permear stood floating above his head, if that was the right word was going to put him in that frame of mind. The ghost glowed eerie bright blue in the darkness, his tongue out in front of him listlessly in the air as if he were trying to catch bugs. "Hey, bagmeat," he said nonchalantly. "That was a doozy of a dream, I think. Why you all damp?"

Acutely aware he was sweating, Scott ran an arm across his brow, saw it had plastered his arm hair flat. It was warm in the room, but he didn't think that had much to do with it.

"Is that the most drastic bed wetting example ever?" Permear continued. "Or is she part mermaid? No wait, she wouldn't drown, would she?"

Scott looked up at him, raised an eyebrow. "You saw that?" He didn't know why he even made the effort to sound surprised.

"Yeah," the ghost said. "Was tasty shit that dream. Little dreary."

"Wait, what?" He'd heard rumours of that but never actually met anyone who'd been able to lay proof to it one way or another. "You ate that dream right out of my head?"

"Well duh, bagmeat. Can't live off what you don't feed me." Manic laughter broke through the room, somehow still not waking Mia up. Scott glanced down at her, shifted his hand under her nose just to feel her breath on his fingers. He wanted to check she was still breathing. It was there, no mistaking it. He wasn't ashamed to admit he let out a brief sound of relief.

"The more messed up the dream is, the tastier it is. Angst? It's pretty good shit seasoning, yeah?" Permear said, carrying chattering on as if Scott's actions were of no interest to him. "Not quite as good as fear. That's a good one. I don't like lusty dreams though. They leave a sour taste. That's why I stay out her head." He pointed at Mia. "She got some freaky shit in her head. Ask her about leather. That's all I say. I a traditionalist. I believe it look better on the animal. Which I not that far removed from. Six degrees of evolution. And life."

"Fascinating," Scott said, though he didn't mean it as Permear burst out into raucous laughter at his own joke. Just because the ghost could talk, didn't mean he was always worth listening to. And yet at the same time, sometimes there was gold amidst the shit. He glanced once again at the time, still too early. His head hit the pillow, he wondered if there was anywhere still open on the island he could get a drink.

It wasn't so much the dream itself that bothered him. Everyone had nightmares every now and then. No changing that. And he'd had some truly freaky ones in the past. No, there was something different about this one. The fact that he'd suffered through it every night for the past week didn't help settle his mood where it was concerned. Though it was the only time Permear knew he'd had it, there were six he wasn't aware about. Maybe. More than that, Scott was worried.

The second the bout was over, they were out of here, already making plans to leave, no matter the result. He wasn't staying on this island longer than he had to. It felt like he'd outstayed it. Given everything that had happened and looked like it was about to happen, he wanted to be as far away as possible. All he knew was what he'd seen, some crazy woman had declared war on the five kingdoms. It had been all over the media the previous days, shouts of outrage and fearmongering, how they were all going to be murdered in a bloody tide of retribution for some imagined slight. It brought about a troublesome problem. Where would be safe? Nobody knew where she was so therefore how did you get as far away from someone as possible without knowing where they were to start. It felt a little difficult.

These were problems still troubling him hours later when Mia let out a small grunt, a result of her having twisted her face into his chest and bolted awake with a start. Her eyes were red and fogged, her hair stuck to the side of her face. Not an attractive look by any prospect of the imagination, yet he guessed she pulled it off in a messed-up way. "Morning," she muttered. "What time is it?"

"Too bloody early," Scott said. At least she hadn't started leaking salt water out of her mouth, he knew he was awake that way. He couldn't even grin at that, was just too bloody weary. A good start to the most important day of his life, to be sure. "Wake me up ten minutes before I'm due on the field, yeah?"

She playfully hit his chest with her fingers. "I'm sure you're not... Bad dreams again?"

That got his attention, he hadn't... "What makes you think I've been having bad dreams?"

"A little ghost told me."

"Sorry bagmeat," Permear said from somewhere in the room. His guess, the ghost was under the bed. The sun was up, he didn't like that, as much as Scott had been able to infer from conversation. "But it slipped out."

"How?!"

"Well I sort of told her to stop having mushy dreams, they were giving me cramps and..."

"Why do I ask him," Scott muttered under his breath as Mia giggled quietly. "Why don't I just let it be? Thumbs up and smile, that's all it takes, and we need say no more."

"And well she got all pissy, women eh and..."

"Perm!" Mia said loudly. Scott winced at that. How and why Mia had suddenly developed the ability to understand Perm, he didn't know. Or perhaps it had been Permear who had found a way to make himself understood. Either way, it had been causing no end of trouble so far. Two ways of looking at it, one, it was good she knew he wasn't imagining it. Two, it was a little more awkward when the ghost went off on a tangent. "Who taught you to say stuff like that?"

"Your mother!"

"See, I think it's a lesson you need to learn as well," Scott said, twisting around to look her in the eyes. "Just let it go."

"Anyway, when you two are done bitching, I sort of let it slip you were having these bad dreams like a scared little bitch and she got all worried. Surprised she couldn't keep her mouth shut about it."

"He's definitely getting more eloquent," Scott said, ignoring the look Mia was giving him. Passive-aggressive curiosity really didn't suit her. "I'll give him that. Not exactly sure that's a good thing."

"You look terrible," she said. "I mean it."

"Bit candid, aren't you?" Scott said. "I mean I know honesty is supposed to be good for a relationship…"

"No, it isn't!" Permear said loudly. "Lie! Keep lying!"

"But that was a bit brutal for my liking. I can't help what keeps rattling around my head."

"What do you dream of?"

"Believe me, you don't want to know."

"Well it's obviously distressing you. They're just dreams, Scott. Nothing special, nothing ominous, just your own subconscious telling you something."

"That really doesn't help me with the problem, you know." He held his breath for a moment and then sighed. "It's about you. Every night this week, I'll get to sleep, and I'll still be in bed, or on a boat, in a restaurant, even on the battlefield once and you'll be there. And you'll look damn fine and all that because hey, I'm not aware it's about to all go south." Deep breath, he saw her look more than a little mollified by what he'd just said. That look wouldn't last. "And then you drown. I'm not joking. Not a drop of water in sight and you're suddenly choking it up. It's horrible."

Theo had already been awake for an hour and in cooler morning temperatures, he'd taken his early jog around the resort, keeping a steady pace and focusing on his breathing as he went around his second lap. Anne had been right, he hadn't believed her at first when she'd told him it was surprisingly therapeutic, good for focusing the mind. He'd slept well, he was just building up his appetite before breakfast. A good few hours before it was all due to start yet and while he wasn't looking forward to the various bits of window-dressing they insisted on at the start and the finish of these events, ones he'd no doubt be close to, he was looking forward to the battle itself. What wasn't to look forward to? He'd beaten his opponent once, not that that had a bearing on anything. He wasn't about to take him lightly, but if he performed to his maximum then there wouldn't be anything he could do.

Already he was running through various tactical outlines in his head, possible combinations to lead off with, anything to confound his opponent. Doubtless he'd have done his research; Theo had done the same. To fail to prepare was to invite failure upon you. No more distractions. It had been bad enough having his father appear again, the first time he'd seen him in many moons. Not that he could really describe him as a father. John Cyris had many qualities and none of them were applicable for a good stab at parenthood. He'd made Theo's childhood miserable, an absolute horror to recall and yet at the same time, he had a point. Those trials had hardened him to the point he was ready to drive home to victory today. He could win.

More than that, he was going to go tooth and nail to ensure he absolutely did win and nothing would stop him from claiming that title. He had his coach in his corner, he wouldn't have done it without her, a realisation that gave him mixed feelings. He'd wanted to do it under his own steam, not ask for help. To the best of his knowledge, his opponent hadn't sought out any help. He'd done it all by himself, and Theo found it a little galling. Because he, Theobald Jameson, wouldn't be here if he hadn't lucked into getting some help he'd never asked for and yet wound up with anyway. It was a strange feeling, a maelstrom of conflict inside him, the knowledge that what he'd done had turned out to be right, or it would be if he won, and the feeling he should have been able to do it under his own steam.

That was all he'd ever wanted. To be able to say he'd done it by himself.

"And we're here outside Carcaradis Stadium, live above Yeboah Walk where the fans are streaming into the stadium. We've got people from all over the five kingdoms coming to see this event today, billions more watching from afar and it promises to be an absolute cracker of a final."

"Yeah, we've seen a lot of competitive spirit calling over these past few weeks, we've seen some absolute quality on show, we've had excitement, we've had brutality and it's all about to come to a head today, Tom."

"You're listening to the Tomani Lister and Mike Ellis show; we're building up to the final of the Competitive Centenary Calling Challenge Cup where two relative unknowns before the start of the competition are about to face off against each other for the highest honour in the sport. Nobody would have predicted it before it all kicked off, Theobald Jameson and Scott Taylor have stuck their middle fingers up to the predictions and both are going to be remembered by the annals of history today. Come win or lose, each of them will probably

go onto have a sterling career after this, it can only be the start of something incredible."

"And we've got a special guest just walked by us, we'll pull him in…" A few moments of silence and then the speech returned. *"None other than the former Quin-C defending champion, here to make the symbolic gesture of handing back the trophy, Ruud Baxter, how are you Ruud?"*

"I'm good, thanks, Tomani, Mike. Good to be on the show instead of just listening to it. Big fan."

"Ruud, you probably get asked this question a lot, why didn't you defend your title this year instead of just showing up at the end to hand it over?"

"Because I chose not to." It was a tone of voice suggesting the speaker didn't want to go into further detail. *"I'm effectively retired as a competitive spirit caller these days. And today isn't about me."*

"Okay. Who do you think will win today?"

"It's too close to say but I think it's going to be a memorable final, I think that there's going to be a lot of drama and I genuinely can't pick a winner. I think they both have their strengths, they both have their weaknesses, I think the one who capitalises on both his own strengths while undermining his opponents the best will be the one who takes home that trophy. I think… Jameson to shade it. Narrowly. I think the longer the battle goes on, the better he'll cope. But I wouldn't be surprised if it goes the other way. Taylor has some interesting qualities of his own and he's the sort of caller who'll never give up no matter how hopeless it looks. Never underestimate just how important that is. I saw that fight against Steven Silver earlier in the tournament, it was the single most impressive performance I've seen in a long time."

"Thanks Ruud. So, what does the future hold for you if spirit calling isn't an option?"

"Well I've not fought competitively for five years now so it's a bit late to be asking me about my future…"

Scott stood up and switched the radio off, he didn't want to hear another person come on and say how he thought Theo was going to win. It seemed to be a recurring thing, it hurt a little bit and more than that, he didn't know where it had come from. Neither of them had been favourites for the tournament before it had started, anyone who'd claimed they'd known the two of them would reach the final was a liar. If they'd known that, they'd known a lot more than he did. They'd also be a lot richer than him if they'd put their credits where their mouth was.

He'd been in the locker room for half an hour now, just waiting for the signal to get out onto the field. Any sort of fatigue he'd felt was long gone now, he just felt wired, restless, he wanted to get out on the field and give it everything he'd got. And if it wasn't good enough, well that radio presenter had been right. It was still just the start of his career really. Most callers never even got close to winning this tournament, he'd done well. Runner up at his age hadn't really been done before. He could even be the youngest ever winner yet. He heard a sound at the door, looked up and saw them. Mia, Pete, Matt, even the crystal tech Sam N'Kong who'd done so much to help him with Permear. The friendship had stuck, surprisingly. He and Mia had already promised to go see him in Vazara at some point down the line, all four of them were wearing t-shirts with his face on them, a sign of showing their support for him which he appreciated. The vendors outside the stadium were doing a roaring trade in them, he'd heard. A few contestants had tried to get him to sign their shirts earlier, which he'd obliged with. He'd never been asked to sign merchandise before, it was a surprisingly good feeling.

"Hey," Matt said with a grin. "Are you ready?"

"Oh yeah," Scott said, standing up. It was all he could do to stop himself jumping on the spot. Right now, he had so much energy it was spooky, he could feel it rushing through him, all thoughts of fatigue truly gone. "I woke up ready."

"It's true, he did," Mia said. "He was arguing with Permear at an undivine hour earlier. Really unsettling. Believe me on that."

"Good luck, Scott," Sam said. "You're going to beat this guy, I know it."

"Yeah," Pete agreed, striding in to pump his hand. Scott took a deep breath then pulled him in and hugged him, much to Pete's surprise. "Oh hey, what's this! We hugging now? I don't do that, bud!"

"Told you I'd make it. Way back in Burykia right before it started, I said I'd make it, didn't I?" Scott couldn't hide his grin. "Only you seemed to think I'd be facing you in this match."

"Yeah well, I miscalculated with my guess, didn't I?"

"No, you were wrong," Scott said, almost singing it. "I had a little dance and everything. Not going to do it though. Not unless I win."

"You've got to win," Mia said. "If you don't, I'm leaving you… Kidding! Kidding!" she finished, seeing the look on his face. "Nah, I'll love you win or lose. And don't worry," she added with a wink. "I'm staying away from deep water." Pete furrowed his brow, looking first at her, then at Scott as if the answer behind it was going to present itself. When none was forthcoming, he let it go.

"Good luck, Scott," Sam said, walking over to grasp his hand firmly and pump it twice before squeezing the fingers in a vaguely Vazaran style. He'd never gotten it, but he'd heard it symbolised affection or something. They had a whole range of gestures like it, you needed to have grown up with it or something to understand them all. If his dad hadn't fucked off, he might have gotten it. That was weird. He hadn't thought about his dad for a very long time. It was a difficult task given he knew very little about him in the first place being honest. His mom had never talked about him, even before she'd passed on.

"Thanks, Sam," he said. "Nice to see you come out."

The tech laughed. "Seriously, as if I were going to miss premium seats for this on my own. Nice for you to invite me as your guest."

"Well you did a lot to help me when I needed it, you're a good guy and I had a larger allocation than I needed," Scott mused. It was true, he'd gotten a message from the ICCC telling him he was entitled to five free premium grade tickets for his entourage. He'd almost laughed at the idea he had an entourage, but he'd handed them out to those who'd been there for him when he'd needed help. Already the four of them were wearing their VIP passes, looking very smug about it in the process. He was keeping that last ticket, determined to hold onto it as a collectible in hopes its value would skyrocket in the years to come. Especially if, as rumoured, this was the last Quin-C for a while, what with all the stuff going on. It felt like only time would tell. "Wish me luck, guys," he said, managing a grin. Ten more minutes until he had to be getting onto that field for the preliminary announcements and suddenly his stomach was starting to feel like the bottom had been yanked away. "I might just need a little bit extra to get me over the line."

Sam shook his hand again, a different style this time, five pumps and no squeeze but there was a wave in it, he hoped it was good luck or good fortune or something, Matt just gave him a normal high five. Pete hugged him again, the two of them embracing a few seconds before awkwardly splitting, their eyes not meeting. At least he'd avoided making a quip that'd have made them both uncomfortable.

"Good luck, bud," Pete said. "You'll do it."

Mia kissed him, kept her lips locked against his to the point time seemed to have no meaning to him, everything else beyond little more than a blur. All he knew was her eyes as the two of them held each other.

"Hope you weren't expecting that from me, mate," Pete quipped as they broke away. Mia playfully hit him on the arm.

"Go," she said. "Be fabulous. Win. We'll all be cheering you on."

"Better be," Scott grinned. "Bye guys. We'll have big celebrations after, yeah?"

Oh Divines! Theo stepped out onto the field, saw the podium was all set up and the great and the good of the ICCC already milling about waiting for their cue. The great and the good part meant entirely ironically. He rolled his eyes, stuck his hands into his pockets and made a conscious decision he wasn't going to share the limelight with them if he could help it. Instead he strode to his caller area, mindful he wasn't going to do it anonymously as a great cheer broke out to greet him as he strode across the field, a hundred thousand people screaming his name. It wasn't unpleasant. He'd already made up his mind he was going to savour every moment today, no matter the result.

The battlefield itself was bare, not a hint of grass or ice or stone upon it as there had been in previous rounds. It didn't matter, a battlefield was a battlefield, he'd conquer it. He'd left Anne behind in his locker room, she'd given him a small kiss on the cheek which had felt nice, her breath warm on his neck, her lips soft against day-old stubble. In the excitement, he'd forgotten to shave. Too much on his mind. Most of the ICCC delegation he didn't recognise, he knew of Ritellia and Thomas Jerome, no mistaking those two men, little and large stood side by side at the podium, chatting with each other as if they didn't have a care in the world. If the rumours were true, he was surprised by how stress-free Ritellia looked. He also recognised Adam Evans stood behind them, a serene look as he examined the arena around them, focusing on the crowd. Evans always gave the impression he knew exactly what was going on, more than that, he looked like he cared about what was going on.

His opponent had emerged, closer to the stage than Theo was, but that was up to him. He'd looked it up, there was nothing in the rules saying he had to pander to the dignitaries, that he was aware of. If he could avoid the slimy piece of shit, then he gladly would. Ritellia had that look about him that given the chance he'd be able to offend all five senses. Theo had no desire to even speak to him.

The klaxon horn broke out over the stadium, having the sobering effect of silencing the crowd, making Theo jump and he cursed the idiot who'd decided to play it. No doubt they were killing themselves laughing somewhere at the way their action had gotten a reaction. He clenched his fists, kept them at his side but secretly wanted to go for his summoner. Ritellia broke away from Jerome, a big sickly grin on his face if the giant screen atop the stadium was accurate. He bent down, picked up the microphone and turned his great body to look at the crowd, one part of the stadium at a time. Someone booed him, a few ripples of laughter broke out. Theo was close enough to see the flash of annoyance on his face. Still he didn't let it put him off as he started to speak. Far in the crowd, another one yelled traitor. That garnered even more of a reaction but still he stayed professional.

"Ladies and gentlemen of the five kingdoms," he said, his voice hoarse. He didn't sound well, Theo noted. Maybe he'd gotten off his deathbed for this. Everyone could only hope, to say that Ritellia wasn't well liked was an understatement. The master of self-interest and all that. "Has it really been six weeks since I first stood before you to announce this magnificent tournament was about to get underway? I can't believe it has, how quickly the time does fly when the good times are rife. We've all enjoyed it, I hope, we've seen some exciting moments and some sadness as well. I can only hope the good outweighs the bad when it comes to remembering this landmark event. We can never wholly forget those who have been lost to us during this time, nor should we. But…" It sounded insincere even to Theo who folded his arms and rolled his eyes, aware even now a picture box was probably picking up his reaction. He didn't care. His disrespect wasn't to the dead but to the hollow words given out by Ritellia. "But that was then, and this is now. In a few short hours, it'll all be over for another five years, five years of uncertainty and strife. I can only hope our prestigious entertainment provides solace in the hard times to come, that the memories of what we produced can be a reminder harsh times come and go but we all endure.

Endurance is the only way to describe our two young competitors. Nobody had ever heard of them before the start of the tournament, indeed one of them only came in as a wild card entry and while some of us might have hoped for two more established names to be fighting it out to the finish, I'm sure these two combatants will give their all and make it a final to remember. Neither of them has anything to fear. Except defeat." His face split into a smile, as if he were expecting laughter from the crowd. If he was, he was to be sorely disappointed. Deathly silence followed his quip. Eye rolling had turned into head shaking now from Theo, how dare the fat bastard criticise him and that Taylor kid for daring to make the final ahead of someone with a bigger name. Reading between the lines of what he'd said, it was all he could do not to stride on the stage and whack him upside of the head. But that'd create headlines for all the wrong reasons and being arrested would probably mean he automatically had to forfeit the match. It wouldn't be the first time someone had taken a swing at

Ritellia during the last few weeks, he could remember Nick Roper doing it at Arventino's funeral and he'd laughed himself stupid.

"So, I'm sure that's what we all want to see, and thank you for humouring an old man with the time to speak," Ritellia said. "I give you Scott Taylor and Theobald Jameson. But first, a song for the brave and the departed, a song for the young and those whose desire burns hot in their hearts. A prayer and a memory. I give you Teri-Lyn Quick."

Theo almost choked. Now he'd seen it all, the president of the ICCC introducing a singer to the stage. Then again, he remembered it was standard, now he thought about it. Always happened. Always they started with a song. His thoughts had been elsewhere the last several hours, this couldn't have been further from his interest if it'd tried.

Teri-Lyn Quick was in her mid-twenties, her ice blond hair a sharp contrast to her coffee coloured skin. She wore a white dress that shimmered with blue and green as she strode out to the centre of the battlefield, Theo's eyes following her every high-heeled footstep. Overall, he wasn't a great fan of music, but even he had to admit she had a great voice. Figures they'd get someone local to sing the tournament's closing song. On the big screen above, it showed a close-up of her thick sensuous lips lined with a scarlet gloss and her perennially innocent-looking grey eyes rimmed with black, the silver stud in her nose glinting in the afternoon sun. "Hey, y'all," she said in an accent not entirely local. Theo was surprised. There was some Premesoiran in her by the sounds of it. "Got this for y'all to hear. The last chance I'll ever take. Enjoy and peace out. Love each other." The crowd went wild for her, more than they had done for anything Ritellia had had to say. And then she started to sing.

> *"Fire walk with me*
> *Come save me from the days*
> *Take me home, take me high*
> *You and I, we'll see the sky*
> *Drift so high and spread the sun*
> *Feel it burn against our skin*
> *You'll say my name, I'll melt away*
> *Save the passion for just one more day*
> *The nights are cold and you're burning hot*
> *Your memories are all I have*
> *The good, the bad, the not so cool*
> *Reach in and spread the word*
> *Him and me, you know we're through*

Divines smile, they want me to
But you, you're all I need to set me free
The last chance I'll ever take."

A lot of the crowd were on their feet, forming a sea of waving arms, Theo found he was tapping his foot along with it, surprising him more than he wanted to admit.

"Battles come, and battles go
Women cry, and men bellow
Fires burn, passions hot, you and me
We just keep firing, ashes in the sky
All we want, we just can't have
Because baby, we're just passing through
Through life, through love, through ecstasy
Better believe, you won't take the sky from me
It's our time to be so young and just so old
Freak like me, monster like you
The last face I'll see when the lights go out
The way it should be.
You can do it if you really try.
Take everything I am, make it your own.
Divines smile, they want me to.
You're all I need to set me free
You'll be the last chance I ever take."

It was an abridged version of the song, Scott noticed. Not that he cared. If it was meant to psych him up for a fighting mood, it had probably had the opposite effect, he'd found it rather sobering, truth be told. Still that was it. Time to go. Ritellia and the dignitaries had already made their way off the battlefield, a few dozen locals moving the stage and the podium. It'd be where the trophy was presented to the winner. Baxter had given it back, Theo had missed that. He wanted to be stood up there so badly, it hurt like he'd been stabbed in the stomach. He couldn't leave anything behind. Scott looked out into the crowd, out to the area where Pete and Mia and his friends all should be sat but he couldn't see them individually.

This was where it ended. He found his poise and made his choice. A strong start from a spirit that had never let him down yet. No regrets. He stared across the plain floor of the battlefield and drew a deep breath. The video referee had gone through all the rigmarole; they were giving him the all clear to make his first choice. He had to pick first. Of course, he did. Hopefully the only setback he'd face. "Okay Palawi," he muttered. "Let's get this party started."

"Finals are usually tense, cagey affairs. It's very important not to lose early on and fighters pick up on it, adjust their tactics accordingly. I don't expect this one to be different."
Prideaux Khan before the Quin-C final.

The ninth day of Summerfall.

His opponent went canine as well, bringing out a huge one-eyed wolf that dwarfed Palawi in size. The dog immediately bared his teeth, small needles compared to the giant knife-like fangs filling the wolf's mouth, the first of six spirits he had to knock out to get the trophy. Scott had seen this beast before, he remembered the semi-final when Theo had used it against Kitti Sommer and her svartwolf. So therefore, in theory, he knew what to expect. Of course, he reflected as the buzzer went, knowing what to expect and dealing with it were two different things. The one-eyed wolf tore across towards Palawi the moment the starting buzzer went, and he grit his teeth. If it was going to charge at them like that...

Charge away!

That last part went out to Palawi who obliged with a blast of electricity straight into the wolf at point blank range, the charge rupturing through the lupine and Scott held his breath for a moment as he saw its legs buckle. Surely it wouldn't be that easy.

It wasn't. He shouldn't have expected it to be. Even with spasming muscles and burns across its pelt, the wolf managed to get back up and bare blackened teeth at Palawi in anger, its one good eye twitching. Theo looked furious, maybe not with Palawi but most likely with himself. Scott let his breath go, already turning over strategies in his mind. He wasn't about to go rushing in, not against something bigger and stronger than Palawi, he held no illusion it couldn't rip his dog apart given a chance. Maybe best just to hold back, hit the thing with counter attacks. It wasn't immune to electricity, but it was going to take a fair few blasts to down it. The one-eyed wolf continued to growl, jaws half open, Scott felt the hairs rise on the back of his neck, his instincts telling him one thing.

Move! Now!

Palawi lunged to the side, the split second before a uniblast ripped from those jaws and shot across the arena, tearing a huge gouge in the ground where the dog had been holding position. Scott swore under his breath; immensely grateful he'd caught it just in time. He'd seen the faint glow on the wolf's breath, he'd expected something like it to come, relieved he had. He couldn't let it slide, a blast of electricity swept back towards the one-eyed wolf who nimbly skipped out the way and then charged again.

It took a few moments to build up that charge, Scott knew, maybe another half second to direct it. He'd dug himself into a hole here. Palawi had spent a blast of electricity towards the opponent and was now defenceless until he could go again, Theo clearly had some idea of that, making the most of his chance to attack. His wolf bore down on the dog, jaws opening impossibly wide. It almost felt like he could swallow Palawi without the need to chew if he had to. At Scott's mental command, Palawi lunged out the way in one uneasy motion, felt the jaws snap. The dog sprang back in, ducked under the muzzle and landed a series of bites across the wolf's stomach, scarlet staining his head and back as the wolf snarled, twisting to try and get him. Palawi leaped, bit down on the wolf's tail and twisted hard, bone breaking and flesh ripping away. Scott winced as the pained howl broke through the air and a fresh spray of crimson spurted through the air.

Nice one, Pal, he thought. I think you just pissed it off even more.

His spirit spat the tail out, saw it bounce away and then the one-eyed wolf was back on him, jaws snapping ferociously to try and get any sort of purchase onto him. It was all Scott could do to keep urging the dog to keep running, tire it out, don't let it bite down onto you or you will be in trouble. Running away wasn't the manliest way to win a tournament but at the same time, it made it very hard to lose in a stupid manner which was infinitely more important. No spirit caller alive would have sacrificed a victory at the expense of style. Winning pretty was one thing but only one of those words was the key one. The stump where the wolf's tail had once been still bled bad, crimson spurting from the wound, maybe he could wait it out. The more it ran, the faster its heart pumped, the more its heart pumped, the more blood went rushing around the body and straight out again. Not pretty but effective.

It looked like it was slowing, looked fatigued and out of breath. It came to a halt, one front leg buckled underneath it and Scott paused, suddenly wary. This could be it. He felt a surge of glee rush through him. Oh yeah, this was the way to do it. Palawi turned, rocked about and fresh sparks of static ran through his fur making it stand upright for a moment before he unleashed another thunderous blast of electricity straight towards the wolf who howled in anguish as the blast ripped through its body.

Incredibly the lupine was still standing as the glow faded and the crowd went silent. They couldn't believe it, Scott couldn't believe it. It appeared the only one in the stadium who could was the wolf's caller,

Theo stood with a smug expression on his face. What exactly he had to be so smug about, Scott wasn't sure. It wasn't as if he could do much more from here. Either way, he still had Palawi moving on tippy claws ready to spring aside if a uniblast came his way.

It didn't. Apparently staying upright for those extra few seconds was more than the wolf could stomach and it hit the ground dead, fur charred and smoking.

Yes! Scott fought the urge to punch the air, even as the crowd cheered the first knockout. This might go his way after all.

Emotionless.

That was the best way to describe his opponent as he stood impassive in the afternoon sun and for all intents and appearances, he didn't have a care left in him. Theo looked calm, even restful and just for a moment, Scott wondered what he had up his sleeve. The videos he'd seen of him in the past showed him angry and twitchy on the battlefield but there was none of that here. Here, he was the picture of serenity.

His next spirit towered over Palawi and even the two callers, Scott blanched as it rose to its full height and stretched out two powerful arms. This one was new to him; he knew what it was, but he'd never fought one before. Its body was squat, dumpy even despite its great size, but the skin couldn't be called dull, not with the rich gold and black fur covering the powerful muscles. Thick claws extended from the end of each limb, the ones on its standing legs tearing into the turf of the battlefield like it was water while it bore not one, not two but three individual tails, each stringy and whip-like. Its face was feline but in a decidedly ugly fashion with more teeth than it needed spilling out the mouth. The ears were small and pointed, the eyes a brilliant shade of golden grey but watery.

A tiger-troll. These things weren't common, were hard to find in the wild and where Theo had gotten it from, Scott didn't even know where he'd start. As it was, it stood between him and another victory. Plus, he had faced a troll since he'd gotten to this island, although the less said about it the better but he knew what to expect. Sort of. That desperate clash with Harvey Rocastle felt a very long time ago. He wouldn't make the same mistakes now as he had then. On the other hand, the conditions were very different here.

Inwardly he formed a plan, he could feel Palawi's reluctance but pushed it aside, tried to shore up the dog's confidence, you can beat this, Pal. It's big but how fast can it be?

He shot Theo a sweet smile, desperate to break that façade of calm before the buzzer got them fighting. Anything to get under his opponent's skin. And as it did, he didn't waste any time, Palawi broke loose with a blast of lightning straight into the troll's chest.

If anything, it went even worse than he'd expected it to, it didn't just fail to affect the troll, the thing absorbed it without flinching, held out its arms and bathed in the blast the way Scott might have stood in the shower. Skin glimmering with an effervescent energy, it charged from the ground and shot towards the startled Palawi. Scott couldn't believe it either, reflexes kicking in before he knew they had, mentally screaming at Palawi to evade. The dog did but just barely, two great fists slamming down into the space where he'd stood a moment earlier. The troll didn't let up, going on the chase, beating fists hard against the ground with no apparent ill effect, cracks forming spider-webs across the battlefield at their touch. Once Palawi got close enough in to land a bite and Scott winced as he heard the crack of teeth breaking against skin. Troll skin... Hard. Yeah, he already knew that. He'd never seen one as hard or fast as this though, Palawi was still ducking and diving, leaping and lunging to escape the blows raining his way and it was only a matter of time before he caught an unfortunate one where it hurt. Claws were useless, teeth were broken, lightning attacks even worse.

Yeah it looked bad.

There was an unproven but not entirely disproven theory in the world of spirit calling that every opponent had a weak spot which any attacker no matter how bad the circumstances were would be able to target and thus given a fighting chance. In situations like these, great callers survived them, anything less and they forfeited their spirit for the round. Scott wasn't entirely sure he was ready to give up on Palawi yet but at the same time, he couldn't see how the hound was going to get out of it.

Observe. React. Attack.

Always a good plan to fall back on. Why exactly weren't the lightning attacks working? Obviously, the creature had some sort of imperviousness to them, it surely couldn't be natural. It wasn't just resistant, it had absorbed it. That clearly wasn't natural. He winced, mentally congratulated Palawi on avoiding another attack. Now run up its arm next chance you get. Stay in close to it, but not on the ground. If Palawi tried running between its feet, chances were that he'd get stamped on, a broken spine would be the end of it. At least on its body, he had a fighting chance. Unless the troll was willing to whale on itself to try and dislodge Palawi.

Hmm. In lieu of a better strategy, that might work. These things weren't smart. Next attack that came, Palawi sprang up and landed on one broad arm, digging stubby claws into fur and flesh unwilling to yield. If he'd tried to stay still, it might have been an issue. As he carried on running, he didn't stay in one place long enough to fall, not until the tiger troll spun its arms around suddenly, a vicious twisting motion that left Palawi scrabbling at thin air and falling. He never hit the ground, the other arm swept around and caught him a vicious punch in the side that sent him flying across the arena like a rag doll, eventually the hound hit the ground near Theo and didn't move. Knocked out. Dead. Either way, he wasn't getting back up, Scott had heard shattering bones and it wasn't pleasant. A wave of sadness flushed up through him, tinged with regret. "Thanks, Pal," he muttered. "Good job."

Who next? He had to make the next spirit count. Something who could hit this thing hard and take an attack in exchange. With armoured skin, power counted. Palawi had been a completely inappropriate matchup in hindsight. Still he had five more, as did Theo. And although Palawi hadn't really hurt the tiger troll, the exertion the thing had spent to nail the hound had to have done something to its stamina. If he wanted pure power, then there had to be only option. Sangare or Sludge might be apt choices, but he wanted to keep the dragon in reserve for if it got bad and although Sludge might be able to take the blows, there was no guarantee the poison would get through that skin.

He went with Snooze, the giant sloth-bear flopping onto the field and giving a big yawn. This time the two were matched in size, two heavyweights sizing each other up. Theo looked impressed, a smug smirk crawling about his features as if to express his amusement at being given what he no doubt considered a challenge. More than anything, that pissed Scott off. Not considering Palawi to be a challenge was more than just disrespect, it was adding fuel to the fire. What didn't help was Snooze had faced Theo in the semi and lost. Maybe he thought it was going to be an easy victory.

He wasn't making the first move this time, not after what had gone before. This time Scott was letting Theo make his attacks and he was going to counter them. Snooze couldn't go after the troll the way it had gone after Palawi. Best thing to do was hunker down, mount a defence and then retaliate hard. Except anyone who'd ever fought a sloth bear knew that was the standard way to get the best out of one. Their size made speed impossible, it was playing to their strengths in every single way. Best way was to pick them off from a distance with an elemental attack, preferably one aimed at the head. He didn't know if Theo's troll had that capability, best to keep on his toes and try not to be taken by surprise.

First sign he got of the troll charging, Scott gave Snooze the order to hit it hard with a uniblast, the beam ripped out of the bear's giant maw and caught the troll powerfully in the chest, hurling it several feet through the air. Incredibly the skin hadn't been broken though it had left a serious of painful looking burns prominent across it, the fur burned away leaving dull grey smoking patches. It leaped to its feet bellowing angrily and struck back, generating its own lightning and sending the shockwave into Snooze who let out an agonised howl and fell onto his back, muscles going into spasms. Having dealt out plenty of those attacks throughout his career, the irony wasn't lost on Scott. With Snooze down, maybe Theo assumed he was good to attack, the troll lunged, sprang up into the air and prepared to bring both fists down into the bear's head, hammer style.

Now he was just playing into Scott's hands, Snooze rolled back even further, brought both stumpy hind legs up and kicked out, putting all his considerable weight behind them and suddenly the troll was airborne again, this time involuntarily, arms flailing helplessly. It was a good kick, Scott was sure it hit the roof of the protective shield and bounced hard into the ground, face first. The crowd let out an appreciative sound and the exterior of calm broke again once more, a snarl flashing across Theo's face for a split second.

"Zap," he said calmly but coldly. "Stand up."

It took an effort and Scott was pleased to see that, but the tiger troll did manage to rise, which he wasn't so pleased about. Its legs looked unsteady, he was sure there were some cracks forming across that skin, but he'd seen spirits look worse with less. At the same time, Snooze scrambled back up with just as much effort though he could see a giant sweat stain on the ground where the bear had lain. Deep breath, they'd be at it again in a moment and he was proven right as Zap lunged in, fists flailing in gracefully clumsy motions, blows bouncing off Snooze's ample gut. The bear's eyes widened, and he flicked out a front leg of his own and swatted the troll away, sending it staggering in the same way Zap had hit Palawi with the death blow.

Both caller and spirit looked irritated, Theo because maybe he was realising just how much he'd underestimated the strength of Snooze and Zap because maybe it wasn't used to being pushed around like that. Still he wasn't one to deny an advantage, this time both of Snooze's fists swept out to crush Zap between them and his heart soared as this time there was the distinctive cracking of bones breaking and suddenly the troll looked like a shattered tube of toothpaste. The top of its head had nearly been blown out by sudden twin impacts of pressure to its sides and that had to be that. Nothing could survive a hit like that, not on top of everything else it had suffered.

Scott hadn't been expecting it to still be conscious, by all rights it should be dead, so the sudden eruption of lightning caught him by surprise, the electricity ripping from the shattered body like an enormous storm, ruptured through Snooze, tearing a ragged entry wound through the thick layers of furred fat on his stomach, coursed through his great girth and ripped out through the top of his head. Though the wound cauterised immediately, the internal damage was too great to overcome, the sloth bear clutched at his chest, scrabbled wildly in panic until the pawing faded. Scott felt every second of it through the connection and winced. Ouch. Not pleasant. His own chest felt tight, sore even and if he never felt like this ever again, it'd be too soon. That was it for Snooze. For both him and for Zap. Neither of them was continuing, the scoreboard showed the naked truth, they were drawing two defeats for two. Four more each for regular battle. There was still an outside possibility of sudden death, Scott really didn't want it to go that far.

His next choice was to unleash Becko upon his opponent, the leaf lizard swarming into existence with a flourish of the blades on his forearms. They spread out like fan blades, the lizard covering his pointed face with the extent of them. Scott had taught him that pose recently, just a little something Mia had pointed out about psychological intimidation. Appearances can be deceiving, she'd said. It was a spirit dancer's trick; one the average caller might not recognise.

Theo went with a huge fucking spider and he mentally kicked himself, realising intimidation wasn't going to work against something that big and ugly. His skin began to crawl as he stared at it, saw many more little bristles of hair covering those spindly legs than he could ever count. Eight eyes blinked at him, the mandibles clicked in anticipation. The fangs that grew from them were easily the size of his arm. He was starting to notice a pattern with Theo's spirits. All big so far. All intimidating. They did say the spirit was the extension of a caller's personality. What did that make him? He'd never stopped long enough to consider it before, wasn't entirely sure that he wanted to. Scott heard the buzzer and the first thing he had to do was scream mentally a command for the leaf lizard to evade, a thick glob of poison sailing towards him from the spider's maw. Becko sidestepped it, hissed angrily.

Engage at close range with your speed! Do not let it bite you!

Simple instructions, the best kind. That second one was imperative. That spider had already displayed the deadly poison it could administer. He didn't doubt the bite was just as potent. A second command and Becko's jaws snapped open, a flurry of razor sharp seeds fluttering towards the spider as he ran towards it. Some sailed wide, most didn't, and they cut shallow gouges across the arachnid body. Scott's experience of spiders mainly extended to that they were supposed to be stood on, not be big enough to do the standing. They were supposed to be squishy, this thing looked anything but. No blood, that didn't surprise him, just a clear grey substance that stank like hells. It made him want to wrinkle his nose in disgust.

In close, Becko swept the blades with razor quick impunity, slashing with rapid manoeuvres almost too fast to keep track of with the naked eye. Two of the front legs were hacked off before the spider could react, the crowd cheering loudly, their applause and cries reaching a crescendo as the arachnid skittered back in surprise, several fresh new gashes torn across its body. Something akin to rage fluttered across its eyes, Scott saw it and suddenly it charged, surprisingly agile even on only six legs and tore across the ground towards Becko like a runaway mag-rail car. The lizard tensed the muscles in his legs, gracefully sprang up and over the oncoming spider, dropped and dug in both blades hard to the rear, something giving by the sounds of it. Its giant behind looked like it had suddenly deflated quite a bit, Scott's spirit rose. This might be over very quickly.

Becko suddenly roared angrily, not a loud roar but a hissed one that embodied every venomous emotion in the lizard's array, he saw why as the spider spun around, something glistening white lay over the lizard's feet, Becko's efforts to pull away failing miserably. Three...

Scott cursed himself. What do spiders do, Taylor?! They spin bastard webs! Trap insects and stuff so they can eat them! His own stupidity amazing him, he pushed it aside for a moment and tried to figure out a way around it. Hacking at the stuff with the blades didn't do a whole damn lot of good, it clung to the blades themselves and left Becko struggling to pull free in two separate places.

Two...

The eight-eyed monster was almost on the lizard now, bearing hungrily down, jaws opening wide and Scott felt something snap inside him, a moment of cold horrible inspiration he'd never quite expected to find within him. His skin felt grimy even considering it. If you can't win, the important thing is to ensure that you don't lose. He'd not known just quite how far he was willing to go to ensure the coveted trophy had his name on it at the end of the bout before now. Yet even as he gave the order, felt the wave of shock, he realised he'd not wanted to consider it before because it made him feel dirty. Regardless Becko obeyed and he squeezed his eyes shut to deny himself the sight. He couldn't block out the screech, the sudden silence of the crowd and the stunned spluttering's of the stadium announcer, nor even what the radio commentators were probably describing for the benefit of those around the five kingdoms who didn't have viewing screens.

Blood was gushing from Becko's ruined limbs, he was free of the web, but he wouldn't last long. Somehow, a supreme effort on the part of the lizard, he leaped, landed hard on the head of the spider, claws digging in while at the same time he dug his blades hard and fast into the body, ripping and sawing away with no thought of his own safety, ichor and other gunk sputtering out under the cutting force. Scott tried to shut out the stunned silence, already aware what people were probably thinking about his desperate gambit, but it looked like it had worked. So why did he feel so worthless about doing it? Already Becko's movements were slowing, he couldn't keep it up and he could see the shattered body with the stumpy ends of the hind legs sliding down the great hairy body. As he landed in front of the dying spider, it had to be on its last legs, Scott groaned inwardly at his own pun, it skittered forward in its death throes and trampled over the stricken lizard, six legs leaving great puncture marks across green scales until it finally collapsed, legs curling up uselessly.

Another draw. Three defeats for three. So far, they were proving evenly matched. Either that or Theo was fighting a war of attrition, wear away at him, ensure he didn't get defeats and just go stronger as the bout went on. He couldn't be sure, not just yet. The remains of Becko's bloody feet, still stuck in the web vanished along with the lizard, sucked back into the container crystal. Still evenly matched. So far neither of them could claim domination. It could still swing either way and yet he knew it was important that he take some measure of control over the situation.

Otherwise the circumstances could be dire for him.

He let Theo pick first the next time, saw a bear of his own materialise into existence. It wasn't as big as Snooze, just a plain old nasty looking grizzly who dropped to all fours and let out a bellow, a cacophony of pride and anger. Claws dug into the turf and Scott tried to ignore it. He'd faced it before. In retaliation for that defeat, he chose Herc, the stag bug fluttering to land. The patch of web had already dissolved; one less thing to worry about. The two combatants faced each other, the stag bug emotionally passive, the grizzly frothing with barely controlled rage. Herc's arms swung loose at his side, the two pairs of eyes locked on each other, bear and bug desperate to see who would flinch first.

The buzzer went, and it was the bear, deceptively quick as it moved across the space between them, raking claws down Herc's front. Wings snapped out and Herc shot backwards swiftly, a deep gouge left in his carapace, but it wasn't serious. The bug's features broke into anger and Scott tapped into it, gave a command the bug could get on board with. Lowering his horn, Herc shot forward, propelled by his wings and landed the blow hard into the grizzly's kidneys, breaking the skin. A sudden release of jeering escaped the crowd as crimson exploded out, covering Herc's carapace. The bug wasn't bothered, he spun and threw a punch upwards, an armoured fist connecting with the grizzly's jaws. The roar that erupted in response startled even Theo by the looks of it, pain and absolute white fury ripping from that maw as it suddenly charged, checked Herc with its greater girth and weight, pushing the bug back hard. Scott tried to get him to push back, to no avail, the difference between their sizes and weights just too great, the bear had momentum and getting Herc to fight against it was an uphill task. All he could do was run and evade once more, a similar pattern.

In moments, the two of them were at the edge of the field, the bear biting viciously at the armoured shell, still pushing hard. They went past the outlines of the field and through the advertising hoardings, he could almost hear anguished ICCC officials bemoaning the inevitable complaints from companies who'd paid good money for sponsorship, and hard into the energy shield protecting the crowd from harm. Herc hit it with a sickening crunch, Scott winced, the bug had been caught between an immovable object and a seemingly unstoppable force. Not an ideal situation for anyone. Even now, his arms, previously held in place made several false starts to move and then went limp.

He reacted badly, he knew it with the way his eyes went wide, and his mouth dropped open, words failing him for the first time that day. He just... Herc! Four defeats to three, advantage Theo. That bear was powerful, he'd not guessed at just how strong. Herc wasn't a slouch and he'd cast him aside like he was nothing.

A scowl crawled across his face, a deep feeling of bitter resentment rushing through him. He might have been smiling, he couldn't tell through the numbness in his face. Oh, you're going to pay for that, Theo! He could feel the anger bubbling underneath his surface, he knew it was a slippery slope getting like this, but he felt pissed, not just at Theo but just as much at himself. Permear! Now!

The ghost appeared almost before Herc had vanished, stretching his arms out and yawning. "Oh, is it I? About bloody time, bagmeat. Hey, a bear!" The ghost waved at the bear who at least looked confused enough to halt appearing perennially pissed off, Scott noticed with a smirk. Probably not the best time to be caught smirking really. It might give the wrong impression.

"You got this, Perm?"

"Oh yeah, it be fun. I got this," the ghost said confidently as the buzzer went off. He cocked a hand to the bear and gesticulated, wagging his fingers in a taunt. The bear went for him, bundled straight off towards him and brought back a clawed paw for a powerful swipe that passed straight through Permear's body leaving him looking bemused. "That supposed to do something? Kinda tickled. And not in a fun, hey this is where he touched me way!"

"Perm!"

"Oh yeah!" The ghost spun, threw a shadowy uppercut straight into the bear's nose and the crowd let out a surprised jeer as it was thrown backwards, landed in an untidy heap, eyes glassy and unfocused as the huge body hit the ground. "Think I broke something," Permear quipped, hovering a few feet off the ground. The wound in the bear's abdomen was still bleeding, Scott noticed, gore spattering the ground beneath its feet. It looked slippery. "Now, as for my next performance."

Hit it in that big bloody gash! Scott bellowed mentally.

"You a big bloody gash," Permear muttered unhelpfully but reciprocated anyway, hurling himself away through the air to tackle the grizzly, tearing at the wound with claws formed out of his own smoky substance. "Come on, bleed for me!"

Bleed it did, Scott noticed with a barely suppressed sense of glee. The ghost might be intangible but when he wanted to reach out and touch the world around him, he could do it in tremendous fashion. The bear roared, tried to beat Permear away but failed utterly on every swipe, even fired a uniblast into the ghost at point blank range yet to the same little effect as the smoky blue body was everywhere around it, untouched by every attack. Gradually they faded away, the attacks losing their vigour as the bear continued to bleed to death, Permear not letting up at damaging the wound, Scott was sure he was even mauling at the organs inside the bear. That'd account for the agony on its face as it collapsed face first with perhaps the final intent of landing on the ghost. Nimbly Permear stepped out the way and kicked it in the head as it lay in a big pile of fur and gore. The foot bounced off with a dull thud, left a deep groove in its skull.

"Nice one," Scott muttered. See, it all works out when you do what I say... When you take my advice. Not that I'm dictating to you.

"You got lucky, bagmeat," Permear said as the bear was summoned back into a crystal. Any hint of serenity felt by his opponent before was fading, Scott noticed, a frown etched into Theo's forehead for minutes now, fists clenched at his side and he looked ready to kill.

His next choice ramped up the temperature even more, sweat beading onto Scott's forehead the second it appeared, something he had to shield his eyes to look at directly. Was that thing made entirely of fire? It left burning footprints in the ground, smoke rising from wherever its footsteps met bare ground, he couldn't entirely see what it looked like through the flames, but it stood on two legs, had two arms, maybe a head.

"Shit dude, that's just nasty," Permear commented.

You know what that is?

"Yeah, it's on fire!"

Ha, I'd never have guessed.

"Well you know what you feeble humans are like, I got to tell you this stuff or you might miss out on it. Fire ghost."

Wait, that's a ghost?

"Ah, maybe a spectre or an elemental is more accurate. I don't fucking know, do I? I do you a solid, bagmeat, tell you what it is, not its damn life story."

Fire elemental, Scott thought. He'd never recalled anything about Theo having one according to the data files on him. So maybe they were incomplete. The buzzer brought him back to his senses, told him how much it really didn't matter right now. He snapped to attention, fired off an order to Permear, adding he needed to be careful.

"I don't need to be careful, I..."

You do know that it can hurt you, don't you? It was true as well, elementals, spectres, ghosts, they were all cut from the same genetic material. They could interact with each other without any problem.

"Yeah, I'm... Oh shit!" The fire elemental was suddenly on top of Permear, swung back a fiery fist which he barely avoided, swung back with one of his own that thudded into its chest. The ghost's features twitched, his knuckles smoking, Scott privately amazed he hadn't complained about it. "Hey, I heard that."

Permear flung an orb of shadowy gunk, struck it hard in the chest, enough to double it over, the elemental retaliated with a stream of flames the ghost had to dodge, executing a series of surprisingly nimble dance moves that had cheers emanating from the crowd who hadn't been expecting it. Scott hadn't, for that matter.

"What, you think I don't listen to what Mia tells HER spirits?" Permear asked, once more attacking from distance under Scott's behest, the shadow blast hitting hard but not hard enough. Rather than reply, Scott was too busy thinking about what he knew on elementals which wasn't as much as he needed. They were stronger than ghosts, wouldn't have surprised him if Theo had brought it in specifically to counter Permear.

The two of them continued to circle, Scott sure it was getting hotter, the fire elemental was continuing to ramp up the heat. Any hotter, it'd be dangerous for him and Theo to be in this space, never mind Permear. The protective bubble stopping any stray attacks from going into the crowd would keep the heat enclosed, just making it worse. He gulped, gave Permear his orders, told him he needed to knock it out quickly. The response was just as sarcastic as he'd expected.

"Well, gee, I thought I talk it to death."

Still the ghost did obey, shadow blast after shadow blast landing as he advanced on the elemental, each burst countered with a ball of fire which had the unfortunate effect of nullifying it. It didn't matter, Scott just needed an opening, he needed to get close enough to land a decisive blow. He heard screams from the crowd, yells about the heat and spun around. Normally you couldn't see the barrier, but you knew it was there. Like the Divines themselves, yet now he could see it winking out of existence, glowing bright just before fading into nothing. Theo looked just as confused, the stadium announcer screaming about a systems failure before a shadow cast across the arena floor grew prominent, growing and growing more by the second. A winged shadow.

Scott glanced up, saw it looked like a big leathery bird, something prehistoric but what wasn't up for debate was how nasty it looked as it soared down, opened its jaws and let loose a series of sonic blasts from its jaws which made him flinch. Both Permear and the fire elemental took the main brunt of the blasts, both went down defeated before she landed, the mount putting a clawed foot atop the downed elemental. Minus its flames, it looked small and frail. The woman on its back looked familiar, it took Scott a moment to remember her name and why he should even know it. Then he realised, she'd been in the media most of the last few days. Most wanted in all the five kingdoms. She cast an eye down at Permear, there was something there he didn't like in her expression. Claudia something-or-other.

What the hells?! He got the feeling things had just gotten infinitely worse and he wasn't going to like where they ended going here.

"Wait, there's someone down there on the battlefield... Most invaders just run on the pitch, they don't fly down on... What is that, you know what that is? Some sort of bird, I think... WOAH! She just knocked out the combatants' spirits! Both ghost and elemental have fallen, they are down, I repeat they are down. What the hells has just happened here? Oh, this has suddenly turned nasty, security is running to apprehend her. Maybe we'll be able to resume... SHE KILLED THEM! Things have taken a sudden ugly turn here at...!"

Last few seconds of commentary at the Quin-C final before the power was lost.

The ninth day of Summerfall.

It was Claudia Coppinger. Claudia fucking Coppinger here in the flesh, smugly stood basking in the surprise of the crowd, as if she were minus any sort of worry in the world. Managing to look as suave and sophisticated as ever, despite being the most wanted woman in the five kingdoms, not a hair out of place and a big grin of confidence about her features.

Some boos and jeers rained down on her as she raised a head to the crowd, taking it all on the chin, letting them get it out of their system. Her smile grew. It was cold, the self-satisfied smirk of someone yet to let others in on the joke. Maybe she did have something left yet to offer. Already security was making their move, uniformed guards making to take her off the field. She turned her head left, then right, nodded to her spirit. The great toothed beak clacked open, Nick somehow knew what was going to happen even before pure golden light erupted from within. Not even ashes remained of the guards, the act had precisely two effects. One, the crowd suddenly shocked into sobered silence and two, Theo Jameson erupted in anger.

"How dare you!" he said. "Who the fuck do you think you are!?" Thousands of viewing screens around the world heard it uncensored. With what followed next, the dozen complaints to the networks over the bad language, were likely the least of anyone's problems or cares. All complaints went ignored. Nobody held the companies responsible.

A videocam focused on her as she stared him down with two red-gold eyes, narrowing them until they were little more than cat-like slits. Nick was sure they hadn't been that colour before as Theo tried to hold her gaze, failed miserably as a trickle of blood gushed down his cheek, his eyes widening in horror. Nick didn't even want to think about what he might have seen, the last thing he saw before the giant screen in the roof of the stadium flickered and died, any magnified view of the battlefield lost to them. It didn't dull her voice though, she remained as clear and concise as before. "Quiet!" she hissed. "And you!" She rounded on Scott Taylor before he could say anything, keeping him stunned into silence. "If you speak, you will be injured. If you continue, you will be hurt further. It doesn't matter to me. You're all here to listen, not to speak!"

With that, she turned back to the crowd, drinking in the atmosphere around her, the air suddenly fetid with fear. Around the stadium, men in black body armour, big boxy assault weapons clutched in their hands were starting to materialise out of the crowd, menace hanging overtly from them. They didn't look friendly, they moved with purpose and Nick already had a horrible feeling he knew what was going to happen. A statement was going to be made. There had to be dozens of them, it didn't sound like a lot amidst a crowd of a hundred thousand-ish, but a lot of people would still get caught in the crossfire.

"People of the five kingdoms," she said. "Hear me now and hear me well because I have something to say and I can think of no better platform for it to be heard. Because well, I paid for all this. I made it happen. I've given you the last few weeks all out of my own pocket. I brought it here, I suppose the least you can do is give me five minutes of your undivided attention."

Nick glanced around, trying to see where the closest guard was. Three rows back, seven seats away. Not close. Couldn't do anything. Not yet. And he wasn't carrying his weapon either. He cursed silently. Not that it might have made much difference. Right now, he was outnumbered and outgunned, best to just hold tight, see what came of it. People had to know about this outside the stadium, backup had to be on the way. No point overplaying too early. It was always about picking the right moment to act.

Below on the battlefield, Claudia continued speaking, apparently the most relaxed person in the stadium, like she was talking in the mirror to herself. It was a little unnerving, Nick had to admit. "Of course, I can't claim that my intentions were all truly benevolent. Anyone who claims themselves for sainthood is a liar, a charlatan and often should not be trusted on general principle. People lie, they see themselves as better than they truly are. Trust not your fellow man for they shall lead you down a dark path if left unchecked. Everyone takes their own path to self-destruction. It is best if you evade following others. Rely on yourself and not others. Are these not the teachings of the book of Gilgarus? You know who else that you shouldn't trust? Divines."

Nick rolled his eyes, paused mid-way. He'd seen too much to discount her as a complete fanatic, was too in control for lunacy. If she walked a fine line, she was going to fall off sooner or later. In a way, that was infinitely more worrying. A frothing at the mouth psycho would blow up under their own machinations, start ranting and raving. There was nothing like that about her. He'd heard the gist of it before and he wasn't really interested in what she had to say. "You know, recently I engaged in an endeavour. I wanted the answers to the questions the same as everyone else. This island is a fantastic nexus, an absolute veritable fountain of mystic rivers all flowing into one same source. The natives knew that. That was why they refused to leave. And that was why we needed to have it here."

Her smile grew. "Well one of the reasons anyway."

Silence had fallen in the makeshift Unisco headquarters, a dozen pairs of eyes glued to the viewing screen, not quite able to believe it. Any thought of decisive action had been momentarily kicked out of them by the appearance of the woman. She shouldn't be here, hadn't had the nerve, surely. Ultimately, it took Okocha to rouse them into action, banging his fist on his desk several times to grab their attention. "Guess we know who killed them now then," he said. "I mean, that's pretty much a confession, right?"

"Assemble," Derenko said. If he'd been shocked into inaction before, he'd snapped out of it. He rubbed his eyes and stood up. "Let's gear up. Get everyone we have together, Okocha, Noorland, you stay here, I want you monitoring the situation. Everyone else with me. We might have to put her down. Scratch that, we need to put her down."

"No arguments from me," Leclerc said, already moving over to the weapons cabinet. In a matter of moments, he had it open, already starting to hand out blaster rifles.

"Clearly not," Tod Brumley said. "You know; I think this is one time we should ask questions later."

"He's right," Derenko said. "Fuck questions. Meet at the speeders in five minutes. We can't afford to waste any time. We got in heavy, we go in fast. Priority is protecting the people, there are too many innocents for there not to be any sort of casualties, but we need to minimise them. The odds are high, but that's okay. I've got the best here. We have people in there. Second priority is supporting them. Arm them if they need it, take a second weapon. Or a third if you like." He sighed dejectedly. Always he'd known he might have to give an order like this, but he'd privately wished it would be in better circumstances. "Third priority. Show these fucks that you don't mess with Unisco or you go out in a body bag." He glanced around the room then banged his fist abruptly on the wall. "Now what the hells you waiting for?! We've lost enough time! Go!"

"Now I like the nexus theory. I like to think of it as one big boiling pot simmering on the fire. All that pent-up energy flowing through it, through the soil and the stone and the ocean, I wanted to poke it to see what would happen. And what better way than having all you people here. Human beings are the most naturally destructive creatures in any world, not just this one. If there's something to be done, you'll do it. Introducing a couple hundred callers to this environment, well I thought something would give."

Her face lit up as she rubbed her hands together. "And boy oh boy, wasn't I right? See, like everyone, I sought answers about the great mysteries of the world. I didn't want to know who or what the Divines were. I knew all that from the stories, the legends and the tales, from origins to Cradle Rock. Instead I wanted to know why and how. Maybe I even wanted to know a little of the where. Because to see the natural habitat of something, you can learn so much, you can be on the inside. Sort of anyway. A little. I wanted that knowledge, just a little bit more than anyone else. But that's not entirely true. It wasn't the only thing I wanted. I wanted to see the wonders of the world from a different perspective."

Someone at the opposite side of the stadium yelled something at her. She ignored it with a cool indifferent arrogance.

"Of course, there always will be those willing to shout you down. I've gotten used to that. I heard it as a child and as an adult. I always thought the official motto of humanity should have been, you can't do that. And yet, if everyone had that attitude, where would we be? Some of our greatest inventions have been fashioned by people who were told that they couldn't do it. And of course, they did it. Like anything, it's perseverance, effort, determination. The qualities everyone believes they have. Yet when push comes to shove, how many people step up to shove for them? For the most part, people are happy to let themselves be corralled like cattle, keep shuffling towards an oblivion of our own making. Well a long time ago, I decided that I wouldn't be one of them. I would bring change."

"You actually get what she's going on about here?" Noorland asked, suppressing a yawn. He knew it made him look callous. He didn't care. You needed a certain level of black humour to survive this game. They'd both being doing it a while now. It was probably closer to the action than Okocha liked, but hey, live and learn. "I mean; I think she's going to start ranting soon."

"Soon?" Okocha said. "I think she's ranting now. I mean, I'm a genius and you're not the dullest apple in the barrel..."

"Oh, how you've summed my entire life up to this point up there nicely," Noorland said sarcastically. "I was worried I'd wasted everything up to this point."

"But I don't get where she's going with this. Doomsday stuff... I wish that guy would shut up. He's going to get himself killed."

The heckler had gone again, yelling abuse at Claudia, unconcerned for his own safety, just determined to get his vehement point across. She shook her head, sadly, crossing her arms. Already two of the armoured men were moving towards him. Too late he saw them, realising only as they closed in on him what was going to happen. He tried to run, scramble away from them. Their weapons rose, a flurry of shots caught him in the back and he went down, toppling down the stairs across the centre aisles until he came to rest in an untidy bloody heap at the bottom.

"I detest rudeness. Now, where was I?" she asked. The silence had suddenly turned ugly. "Ah yes, our oblivion. I had no desire to trundle aimlessly towards the end of a pointless life. I sought the answers, opened the doors that shouldn't be opened. I found out why we were told that they shouldn't be opened. I did what I could because I was able to. Because for once, I wanted to put one over all those people who always said it couldn't be done. And you know what?"

Her smile was back, wider than ever. Truly it was a creepy expression, Roper decided as he watched her stood there like a statue, only the barest hint of animation except when it suited her. "I did it. I found the Divines. Well, most of them. I found my way into their home, found their secrets and well, it made me realise one thing. There's all that knowledge, all that power and a truly shocking lack of desire to use it. I concluded being human might not be all it's cracked up to be. But divinity, well that surely has just as many drawbacks. I detest apathy and I saw it in spades up there." She threw out both arms and her smile threatened to crack open her face. "Truly, I desired to be something more. Not one or the other. Something new. Something worthy. This little interruption, well I suppose you could say it is to announce my ascension. Worship, I don't expect that. Not yet. One day, you might worship me as you might Gilgarus or Melarius or Griselle. But you know what you should do? You should fear me. Starting today, I'm the new boss."

"Is she serious with this?" Okocha asked. "Is it even possible what she's on about here?" He sagged back in his seat, shaking his head. "I miss the simple life."

"You and me both," Noorland agreed. "I don't have a buggering clue anymore. This whole world isn't what it used to be."

"Al."

"Yeah?"

"What if it's not rubbish? What if she's telling the truth?"

Noorland said nothing. Just stared at the screen, his eyes flickering back and forth. Finally, he sighed. "If she is, then we really are so screwed, I can't even imagine it. Who's already on site?"

"Roper, Montgomery, Wade, Sullivan, Caldwell, Khan... Oh and the director. Brendan as well. Hopelessly outnumbered." He sagged back in his seat, shaking his head.

"Shit, this is going to turn into a bloodbath," Noorland said. "Hopefully she keeps talking until Derenko and his team can get there."

Neither of them voiced the fears they were both privately feeling, knowing even with Derenko's team, the numbers might still be too great for them to counter effectively. Instead, Okocha studied a screen in front of him and hissed angrily. "Reinforcements have been delayed," he said thickly. "We're trying to get other Unisco teams on site, but these fuckers are in the streets as well as the stadium. It's turning into a bloodbath out there. This gets better and bloody better!"

"You should fear me," Claudia repeated. "Because you don't know what I'm capable of yet. You should fear for your lives, for your families, for your homes and your livelihoods, everything you hold dear. Because there will be no respite. I am going to change the world. There will be a remaking. And you might just live through it. Remember, as far as you're concerned, I'm the ultimate authority now. There is no other. I trump your kings and your presidents, I trump those unworthy for your worship and your love." Some people did start to jeer again, and she let out a cruel laugh. "Of course, I understand some of you might reject that notion. After all, the faith is strong. It wouldn't have survived this long was it not. And I realised that even though I make the offer of the carrot to you, some of you will inevitably prefer the stick. That's what you are. Stubborn, arrogant, unwilling to accept change. So, a warning, shall we?"

All around the stadium, flashes of light were appearing, spirits forming into existence. Somehow Nick knew what was coming even before they were fully formed. Those slathering jaws, the three curved horns protruding from the canine heads, the onyx black fur and the muscular bodies, dozens upon dozens and dozens of the same identical spirits. Doom dogs, everyone knew about them, though some people called them devil hounds instead. They were supposed to only be a myth.

Oh, we're fucked!

"But that is just the appetiser," Claudia continued. The hounds hadn't attacked yet, maybe they were awaiting her order. She looked ready to give it, her eyes now manic and her hair wild. Something had snapped in her, maybe it was the idea of an audience, maybe something hadn't been right to start with. Either way, she was lapping all the attention up, the fear and the hatred, the pure nervous shock emanating all around the stadium. "For those who truly doubt my claim as the ruler of the new world order, I show you this. The main event. I will show you fear as for the first time in millennia, a god walks these kingdoms." Beneath her feet, the ground had started to crack and splinter, smoke billowing up around her. Scott and Theo moved to bring back their spirits, they'd already started to edge away from the battlefield. Both looked understandably worried about being closest to Claudia as a great head poked out of the ground, lizard-like and coal black with a scarlet patterning across it, pushing through the earth like it was water. As it pulled its body up out of the hole, it continued to grow and grow, from the size of a speeder, to the size of a house, to almost the size of one of the huge island hotels.

"I give you Cacaxis!"

She was out of the way in no time at all as giant clawed hands ripped away at the earth, tearing at it like it was paper, this time the panic was real and people in the lower rows of the stadium were starting to flee, the threat of the doom dogs and the men with blasters suddenly a very distant second place to the giant spirit in front of them. And that was when everything went to absolute madness, laser fire and flames suddenly everywhere, found himself amidst a maelstrom of activity, he could hear spirits forming into existence, he should have guessed some people would run while some would fight and before he knew it, he had one of the armed men in his sights, close enough to reach. Nick moved, gave him a brutal left-handed punch to the throat putting him down on the ground, hard, a boot to the face and he found one of the weapons in his hands. BRO-60 assault rifle. Just what he'd always wanted. Good enough for despots, not good enough for Unisco. Irony, if nothing else.

Beyond that, he didn't think, just put two of the closest guards down with well-placed shots neither saw coming. Somewhere around the arena, he heard in a dozen different places the hiss and roar of something vaguely familiar and as he allowed himself a second to look up, he saw a dozen different blades of light and energy light up around the stadium.

Fuck! This could be good, or it could be really, really bad. He'd seen those weapons before. Memories of his encounter with Wim Carson were still in his head. Either way he couldn't worry about that right now. Cacaxis was roaring, swiping at the structure of the stadium with front legs the size of mag-rail carriages, each bow shattering stone and metal. It let loose a uniblast into the higher echelons of the stands, punching a ragged burnt hole straight through. The thing stank like sweat and steel, smoke and smog and no matter how much he tried to ignore it, it was permeating into his head.

Hmm… He continued to fire, trying to pick off any guards close by, trying to keep out an eye for any of the doom dogs. Get swamped by them and he would be in trouble, some of the crowd had stood to fight around him and their spirits were keeping them at bay, but always there would be more of them.

He grabbed his summoner, slipped a crystal in, a very distinctive crystal and activated it. Unialiv appeared, springing into action immediately at the command and grabbed one of the dogs by the scruff of the neck. Nick jerked his head towards Cacaxis and the spirit pitched it neat, hurled it straight towards the giant lizard. Perfect throw, it hit Cacaxis and bounced off its shoulder, sliding into the abyss below its feet.

"Unialiv," Nick said. He might need to give it another name, amidst everything that had happened, it had been the furthest thing from his mind. This was the first time he had even unleashed it, not even thought of modifying it, but he had a feeling it might be immune to it. As it turned to him, he could see the hole in its chest that had failed to heal where he'd stabbed it with Sharon's weapon "See if you can do something about that big lizard. Anything. Just try and distract it for a few moments."

Two roars rang out, the first proud and loud but ultimately drowned by the second one as the great black dragon swept down and sprayed Cacaxis' back with orange energy, leaving burns on the scales but doing little other damage.

Bakaru!

Nick glanced up, saw Wade stood on the upper tier of the stands, pistol in one hand, other at his ear barking out orders, summoner hung around his neck. He fumbled his own earpiece out of his pocket, just as he saw Wade's arm rise, his X7 bounce three times and one of the Coppinger soldiers went down. All the way across the stands, small pockets of resistance had broken out, any Unisco agents among the crowd, any callers with the stomach for a scrap; all of them doing what they could to survive. He shoved his earpiece in and caught the back end of a conversation.

"… Down here, need a wider entrance," Derenko was yelling. "Beresutzky, take that wall down. Everyone, please remain calm!" He heard a trumpet, followed by crashing and screaming, roars and bellows. It sounded just as bad outside as it did in here.

"You here, Roper?" Wade asked. "You want to double team this big son of a bitch?" Even from a distance, he saw him jerk his head towards Cacaxis.

"Think that's blasphemy?" Sullivan. "Where's Brendan and Arnholt?"

"Last I heard, they were in the studio with Khan!" Somewhere in the stadium, Montgomery was panting heavily. Laser fire spotted the sound waves around her communication. "I'm going to try and get to them."

"Wade, it'd be my pleasure," Nick said. "Anyone who can take out these damn dogs, get on it. They're the real problem." He ducked a shot, let out a flurry of return fire one-handed over a cluster of melting seat. "Don't let them swarm you or you're done for!" Above him, Unialiv shot into the air, both arms out in front of him and struck hard into Cacaxis' throat, a blow which brought a hiss from those huge jaws as it staggered backwards. If it fell and hit the stands, there'd be even more trouble. It was easily heavy enough to crush anyone beneath it.

He had to hurl himself backwards, jump over some seating and come to a painful landing on the hard floor, a hot fire jarring up his ribs as he caught it against a sharp-edged step. Still the alternative had been getting shot so he couldn't complain too much, he'd seen the blaster fire out the corner of his vision and reacted accordingly. Fighting on two fronts was hard, very hard. Being honest, it was almost impossible, especially when your life depended on it.

Deep breath, Nick heard a crash and a more muted roar, temporary silence from Cacaxis, the metal around its great head ringing as Unialiv smote it a great blow to the face. A mental cheer, he soon found himself flinching as the giant lizard let loose a burst of iron tinged fire towards his spirit. Perhaps he shouldn't have worried. Unialiv spun away gracefully, formed a blade of pure green energy and struck at the face, the air thick with smoke from its great mouth. Wade and Bakaru were still circling, hitting the giant lizard with attacks with its attention elsewhere, keeping out of range of any counter-attacks when its focus turned back to them. Now Theobald Jameson had entered the fight against Cacaxis, Nick could see him and his great green anklo stood several tiers down, firing barrages of razor sharp leaves and forest-based attacks against it. Roots grew from the shattered ground, locked around its feet and prevented it from moving, at least for the moment.

Go for the eyes, go for the eyes, he willed silently towards Unialiv. If you can! Slowly, he allowed himself to peep over the seating, trying to spot the guy who'd been aiming for him, weapon aimed first. He needn't have worried, one of the people with the laser swords had cut him down, Nick saw him… He thought it was a him… throw a salute. That was all the cover he needed, he rose to his feet and emptied the BRO-60 in the direction of several doom dogs nearby, cutting them down, allowing a group of cornered spectators the chance to flee. Some of them were burned and bloody, they'd need to be able to make their own way out though, he was needed here. By the sounds of it, the rest of Unisco were trying to organise an escape route, the people just needed to survive long enough to get to it. He scooped up a new rifle from a fallen corpse, turned and saw Lysa Montgomery running towards him, unarmed and a trail of shots following her, three of the black-clad figures locking in on her. He raised the weapon, fired again and again. Then it was two. Then one.

She came to a halt, out of breath but still with a defiant look in her eyes. She reached down, scooped up a discarded BRO-60 and ran a quick check. "Bastards," she said. "They're taking liberties here, aren't they? They're not going to be allowed to get away with this. I mean, the whole five kingdoms pretty much just saw this…"

Lysa tailed off as Nick shook his head sadly. "Think that…"

She fired behind him, he ducked down instinctively, saw one of the attackers fall under the blasts. A dozen new wounds filled his body. "Oh, look out," she added. "By the way." He rolled his eyes, shook his head. He'd have rebuked her, didn't have the heart to do it right now. Too much else to worry about.

"Think that was the whole point of this little exercise," he said. "Cover me, I'm going to find the director and Brendan. They were in the studio." Nick drew a deep breath, glanced around then started to run, sprinting up the stairs. Behind him, Lysa's weapon started to fire again. At the top, a trio of doom dogs came running to greet him, slather prominent in their smoky pointed muzzles, he activated his summoner and sent Empson at them, the penguin gracefully darting into existence, cutting two of them in half with razor-edged flippers before crushing the third hard against a wall with a torrent blast of water. Summoning the bird back, Nick continued to run. Cacaxis was in issue, but not his any longer. He'd left Unialiv the instructions to keep attacking. It might be a fool's errand, but it was all he could do right now. That spirit would have to look after himself for the time being.

Bakaru caught a glancing blow, suddenly the two of them were going down and Wade found himself stood back to back with Theobald Jameson, his anklo still attacking the apparently invulnerable foe.

Nothing is invulnerable, he told himself. And we don't need to win, just drive it away.

Jameson looked ragged, a streak of blood running down his face, clothes ripped and covered in dust. But still his eyes burned with fury and defiance, Wade could almost feel it radiating from him like fire. He was more than angry, he was incandescent with rage and Wade could see it in the way he was fighting. He wanted to put it down, more than that, he wanted to hurt it in the process. Whatever else might happen, he wasn't to be upstaged by a youngster when it came to deal the hurt. He withdrew Bakaru, sent out Thracia. As sea serpents went, this one was decidedly on the large side, blue and cream scales covering a huge body that scraped over seats, crushing them down. Thracia's mouth was so large, she couldn't even close it, filled with needle sharp fangs. Her face looked like one of those ancient Burykian masks, all frills and frippery, the basis for the masks in fact he believed. He'd found her in the seas around the Burykian mainland a long time ago, she'd been one of his first spirits.

Aiming for the eyes, she curled her neck back, strained upwards and fired a uniblast straight at Cacaxis' face. Always nice to let a fresh fighter into the fray. Cacaxis wasn't invulnerable, it just wasn't falling. So much damage had been inflicted upon it, great sheaves of skin and flesh torn away, sometimes it gave the impression of wobbling although Wade wasn't sure if it was his imagination or not. Either way, it had to be doing something. They'd pumped enough attacks into the damn thing to win an entire tournament, yet still it stood.

Nick's spirit continued to buzz about its head, still distracting it, still running air support. He didn't want to think what might happen if that thing went down and Cacaxis was allowed to bring its full attention onto the two of them. That was perhaps the only thing that had let them survive unscathed as long as they had, that it was distracted.

In the studio, they had the best view of it all. Arnholt, Brendan, Pree Khan had all looked at each other as the great leather skinned bird had flown down and disabled both spirits. The power had faded moments later but still they could see. Hearing it had been difficult but they'd caught the gist. Arnholt had looked haunted by the appearance, but he'd shaken it off enough to unbutton his jacket. All three of them were armed. They hadn't expected anything but none of them had wanted to take chances. As the armed men and the doom dogs had appeared around the stadium, the feeling of terror had only grown. It was palpable even up in the observation box where they'd sat. Two of the armed men had tried breaking into the studio, Carlton Bond had screamed in fear until Pree Khan had shot them both in quick succession, neither of them registering what had happened until they were on the floor, bleeding out.

"We need a plan," Arnholt said. "We can't just hide here…"

He tailed off as the dozen kjarnblades roared into life, all around the stadium. Khan looked particularly interested at that sight, tearing her gaze away from the door and towards the overlook window. "What the hells?" she said, her voice laced with shock.

"Baxter," Arnholt said knowingly. "Cunning bastard."

Below them, it was chaos, Brendan had slipped a Unisco earpiece into his ear and could hear every transmission going around the area. His brow furrowed. "Derenko's got them mobilised. They'll be here soon. They're going to try and secure the exits, get as many people out as possible."

"The guys with the blasters aren't the problem," Khan said, continuing to watch the carnage below. The lower tiers of the stadium were dripping with blood, human and spirit, all running straight down towards the giant crater left behind by Cacaxis, a veritable lake flowing towards the hole. "If those doom dogs keep coming, they're going to get swamped sooner or later." One of the figures bearing a glowing kjarnblade moved through a crowd of them, cut a half dozen down in quick succession but already more were materialising out of nowhere.

"You think they're running a mass powered big area projector?" Arnholt asked, looking at her and Brendan.

"Makes sense," Brendan said. Such a device wasn't common, but some existed in military storage for ground engagements on a large scale, meaning individual combatants didn't need to use their own summoners in the heat of battle to summon spirits. "It'd also explain why the power went down. If we can take it out, it'll make things easier."

"You sure?" Khan asked dryly. "You two aren't the youngest anymore." She managed a smirk as she said it.

"We were both doing this when you were still in training," Brendan said dryly. "Any more comments like that, Agent Khan and these two old timers will put you on your ass."

"Come on!" Arnholt said as the three of them made for the door. "Mister Bond stay here. We have this. We need to get…"

Before he could finish, the door swept open and Harvey Rocastle stepped into the room, flanked by his thorned troll, a sickly grin on his face. He had a weapon in his one good hand, a long-barrelled pistol with a hint of ornamentation peering out the bit of the grip seen beneath his fist. "Look at this," he said. "The nerve centre of the entire operation. You get all that? Didn't she look fabulous on the screens. Everyone's going to be talking about this tomorrow."

For a moment, the three of them were stunned into silence, Arnholt was the fastest to react, went for his weapon and Rocastle shot him three times, would have been four had Khan not barged him out the way, taking one in the shoulder herself. Brendan's X7 spat laser fire at Rocastle, he turned neatly aside and dropped into a crouch, the barrel of his weapon parallel with Brendan's navel. "Byesies," he said cheerily. "See you in the next life, possums."

Something happened, something none of them quite saw but the next moment he was struggling for balance, nearly falling, and had to scamper back as Brendan's next round of shots hit the wall behind where he'd been crouched moments earlier. The troll sent a flurry of green needles towards Brendan who had to hurl himself out the way behind the couch. Rocastle's head briefly turned towards Arnholt and Khan, smirked wickedly as he saw the two of them entangled in an untidy heap, the smell of smoke and burned flesh prominent in the air.

"Don't worry," he said. "You're only going to miss the big finale. Your daughter won't though, she'll have a front row seat..." He turned his head, looked back out the door and blanched, turned to run. As the two of them fled, the troll fired more needles away from its arms, covering their exit. Wherever they were going, they had to be away quickly. Barely ten seconds later, Clara Wallerington rushed in, amethyst and white kjarnblade in hand, her hair tied back in an untidy ponytail and burns pockmarking her clothes.

"Oh shit," she said, seeing the scene in front of her. Bond had caught a shot in the throat, the wound smoking and he wasn't moving.

"I know you," Brendan growled, getting to his feet. He didn't lower his weapon.

"I'm friendly," Clara said as she deactivated her weapon. The blade retreated down into the hilt of the metal cylinder in her hands. "I'm with Master Baxter."

Khan let out a pained cough which turned into a splutter, tried to sit up and looked at her shoulder with distaste. "Bloody bastard," she said. "Why didn't you go after him?"

"I..." Clara didn't have an answer other than a sarcastic "You're welcome. Thanks for saving our lives. Oh, it was no problem, any time."

Arnholt laughed, a pained sound turning into a hacking couch, scarlet spraying the ground. It faded, he slipped backwards, his eyes going blank and pain-stricken features relaxing as he lapsed down into unconsciousness, his skin cold and clammy.

"Oh crap," Clara said. "What can I do to..."

She was cut off by Nick charging into the room, Clare turned to face him, weapon raised once again, Nick did the same. With the barrel of the weapon inches from her face, the blade of her weapon inches from his, he raised an eyebrow and gave her an uneasy grin.

"Friendly?!" Nick asked hopefully.

"He is," Brendan confirmed "Most of the time." Clara lowered her weapon, Nick did the same, looking past her at the stricken Arnholt.

"Shit!" he swore, already looking around for any sort of first-aid kit. There had to be one somewhere. "That's all we need..."

"Agent Roper!" Brendan said loudly. "We'll deal with the director."

"Who did this?!" Nick asked, still not giving up his search. He stuck his head back out the door. "Think I saw one..."

"Agent Roper!"

That caught his attention, Brendan at his most authoritative. He turned back, fought the urge to salute. "This was the work of Harvey Rocastle," Brendan said. "He fled rather than stand and fight. Agent Roper, I give you this order in simplest terms possible. Find him. Kill him, both him and Coppinger if you can. Do not let them get off this island. That is your only objective. Everything else is a distant second." He slid Arnholt's X7 from its holster and swept it across the floor towards him, an extra weapon just in case. Nick picked it up, slipped it into the back of his waistband and nodded.

"Understood." Ever since Rocastle had been mentioned, there'd been an air of cool implacability over him. "It will be done."

"One cannot survive without the other. The truth is, under duress, a spirit will always abandon all previous orders and move to protect its caller, if only for its own existence."
Little known spirit calling fact. Doctor David Fleck to students.

The ninth day of Summerfall.

In front of them, Noorland and Okocha had set up a schematic readout of the blueprints of the Carcaradis Stadium in full holographic display, the first stadium ever built on the island, always intended to hold both the opening bout and the final one. And now they needed to find the one design flaw inserted into it nobody had known about, and quickly.

"The thing with these projectors," Noorland said, not moving his eyes from the display, "is they're not small. You'd notice them if they wheeled them into the stadium, you'd need at least four to form a decent grid. Some sort of four-sided shape is usually best for a projection field. You could do it with three, but it'd be tricky. There'd always be safe zones over this size area, effectiveness would be compromised."

"So, are we assuming she had them built into the structure of the stadium?" Okocha asked. "I mean, the way she's gone about this; I think we have to assume she's planned this for a very long time. Everything leading up to this very moment."

Noorland studied the holographic image, pursed his lips. The stadium from above had been shaped like a diamond, two triangle shapes stacked base to base, eighty thousand seats surrounding a regular battlefield, complete with all the concessions and facilities ever needed by the masses. It was supposed to be cutting edge, he noted but now ironically being cut up on order of the woman who'd paid for it. Each of the four edges of the diamond bore a grand pillar rising to the sky, visible from every point of the island. He clicked on the display, magnified it to look at their peaks, the first vestiges of a theory forming, even as Okocha looked at him with a cocked eyebrow. "What? It makes sense tactically. Highest point of the stadium. Hard to get to. There's no stairway access. None. And those projection fields, the good ones anyway, they pump higher and deeper than they do wide, in case you want to launch from the air. It's military tech at heart, don't forget."

"So, if we can bring one of those pillars down…"

"Yep," Noorland said. "Bring one down, it should collapse the whole thing. A field of this power can't be maintained by three projectors alone. At the absolute worst, it'll collapse from a diamond into a triangle and there'll be a haven the other side of the stadium... Well, the guys with the guns'll be able to go there but one problem at a time. The dogs are the biggest problem currently."

"Okay, so how do we bring it down quickly?" Okocha asked. "You're the engineer, you tell me."

It had all been going so well, Anne thought as she emptied her X7 into the figure, watched him crumple and drop, several entry wounds visible across his body. She barely had time to push in a new power pack before two more of them rushed her, weapons held high and fingers on the triggers. She was dead, she knew it, reality just hadn't quite caught up with the truth yet...

You have the power!

The voice bellowed through her mind, she heard the clink of something metallic on the ground and almost instinctively she reached for it, and with one hells of a bounce surely, it sprang into her hands. It felt right, steel and rubber beneath her palm and she thumbed the activator switch. An azure and silver blade fountained into existence, the shots coming simultaneously at her. Moving to block them felt like a dream, as if someone else were in control of her body, a power she'd never known before guiding her movements. Two she beat down into the ground, the next she deflected into the face of the closest gunman, more came her way and she beat them aside before burying the blade into the second man's chest. He went down, as he fell, she became very aware of her surroundings for the first time, the death and destruction around her and beyond it all, the glowing weapon in her hand.

She looked up, Ruud Baxter threw her a salute from several rows above. "Keep it!" he shouted. "Might come in handy!" He spun around, four of them closing on him and he didn't have a weapon to defend himself from them. By the looks of it, one of them said as much to him and it brought nothing but a cold smile from him. He threw out his hands, thin needles of blue fire lancing from his fingertips, too many to count but they swept through the bodies of his enemies, leaving charred holes through flesh. One of them managed to get some shots off at him, Baxter's hand moved faster, face not changing as bolts crashed into the palm of his hand, he wasn't whimpering in pain, just smiling coldly. Not a hint of a reaction beyond that smile, the single scariest thing she'd ever seen.

Anne's eyes widened, if she hadn't seen, she wouldn't have believed. She'd always known Baxter had special powers. He'd been the one who'd taught her empathic abilities weren't a curse but rather a gift, only the start of something great. He'd done more for her than countless doctors and therapists in helping her get them under control. As far as she was concerned, he was nothing but the best of men, someone who absolutely could be relied on when it came down to it.

If he wanted her to have the weapon, she'd take him at his word. He tossed her one final salute and then turned out of view. Weapon still in hand, Anne glanced around, saw a group of people in trouble, doom dogs surrounding them, and she sighed. Time to go to work. She had the weapon, she almost had the knowledge. Time to put it to good use.

When it had all kicked off, Ritellia's first intention had been to run. Of course, it had, Alana Fuller noticed with disgust. He'd sown part of this, he wasn't the type who'd stick around to see it bear rotten fruit. By the same token, she didn't mind he'd run like the coward he was, just needed him to run to a certain place. She knew what needed to be done, the Mistress had told her as much. She had told Alana where Ritellia needed to be, how she had one final task for him before that usefulness ended.

In a way, she was sad, though in a lot more ways, she felt a sense of relief that had been missing from her life for so long now. She'd run with him, pushed him through a side door everyone thought a janitor's closet. To the best of her knowledge, only she and the Mistress knew what it really was. The people who'd built this specific passage of the stadium hadn't been left alive. It was just too dangerous. People talked, speculated. They couldn't be allowed to know what was here. It was a tough push, he was heavier than her, but she was taller, and he was off balance and they went through the door, she grabbed his hand.

"Come on," she said. "I know a safe place down here."

He didn't question it, the poor deluded fool as he followed her, first down the brief corridor and then down the steps into the bowels of the island. They were quite steep, yet he was determined to take them two at a time, apparently uncaring if he fell and broke his neck. A stab of anger flushed at her gut. That wouldn't do. She needed him to be alive. She had one part in this entire plan and she needed to get it right. It'd do even less than before to disappoint the Mistress now. Even more annoying was any sense of chivalry Ritellia might have previously shown, was now lost as he reached the bottom of the steps, lumbered forward into the darkness. She could hear his choked breaths, the sounds of his panicking. He'd not expected this, he'd thought he was untouchable and if anything, that made him move faster, determined to save his own skin, she be damned. It hurt but it wasn't unexpected. She'd always known what she was to him. An easy fuck. Someone to unburden to. Someone who could be discarded when the occasion came. And it was here. Unfortunately, that went both ways. She could hear him ahead, punching on the wall with his bare fists, breath ragged and panting.

Fool! He wasn't getting anywhere, not until she let him through. For all intents and purposes, this was a dead end. In truth, they just hadn't wanted anyone knowing the truth. Only she and the Mistress had access to get through, not even Domis had been granted the privilege. The rock wall moved as she approached, recognising her biological profile it had stored in the small but exceptionally complicated electronic brain left down here, protected against the damp and the dew. The Mistress hadn't wanted just anyone to stumble on it by mistake and Alana had felt honoured at the time. Now, she just got the feeling that she'd been guided to this point almost as surely as Ritellia had been down his.

There wasn't a sound of welcome, but she knew she'd been accepted, Ritellia was through the door even before it had slid all the way open and privately she was pleased by just how easy he was making it for her to lure him into this trap. The Mistress was waiting for them, here all along since everything had kicked off upstairs. This had been the whole point of it all. Everything had led up to this and finally it had reached fruition.

No matter how different the Mistress might be since she and that Wim Carson guy had returned from Burykia, it was the time. Alana could remember when she'd finally broached the subject and found the courage to finally ask why. Why? She'd asked, why did it have to be here on this unremarkable island in the middle of nowhere. She didn't believe the words given by the Mistress to the kingdoms, not when she now knew the truth, that there wasn't just one sole reason, although the shrine in front of them was perhaps closer to it than anything else. It lay illuminated in cheap lighting, the bodies of two Unisco agents laid close by. Guards, she guessed. Their hearts had been ripped clean out, not a clean kill but maybe they'd had the misfortune to have put up a fight against the Mistress.

The shrine of Kalqus. Once nearly opened a few weeks earlier with disastrous consequences. This could have been done elsewhere, there were more such shrines around the five kingdoms, but the Mistress had chosen this one for purpose. Claudia Coppinger turned to them, gave Ritellia a ghoulish smile that defeated even his sense of self preservation. "You!" he said, perhaps meaning it to sound defiant but it came out a whimper. Like a frightened child. "You won't get away with this."

"I have no intention of getting away with it, Ronald," she said softly. Her voice was different since she'd come back, it had a gravel to it now not present before, like she'd picked up an overtone somewhere, a voice beyond the voice. Alana hadn't asked, she wasn't entirely sure knowing the answer was something she truly wanted. And then there were the eyes, red-gold and horrific. She'd heard stories about an old statue of Gilgarus being completely decimated in Burykia, about the same time the Mistress was there, didn't want to know if it was more than coincidence. "Getting away with it implies that there's a sense of implicit guilt. I'm doing this for the best. Come, see."

She held out a hand and Ritellia turned, lumbering back the way he'd come. Alana stepped in his way, for a moment she thought he was going to barge her. He might have done had she not slipped the heavy weight from behind her, pointed the blaster at him. That stopped him short. "You're not going anywhere," she said scornfully. "Go listen to the Mistress. She told you to do something."

Confusion reigned on his piggy features just for a moment before being replaced by blind fury. "You... you bitch! You're a fucking whore!" She wanted to hit him with the blaster, might have done so had she not felt the eyes of the Mistress on her urging her not to.

"Language," the Mistress said idly. It came across as more for effect than any actual indignation. "Come to me, Ronald. Be a good boy for once in your life and do what you're supposed to." Each word gradually carried more menace as it left her mouth until it was little more than a growl. He didn't like it. But still he obeyed, largely because he saw he didn't have a choice, Alana imagined. Shame, he probably thought he was going to make it out alive. After everything he'd put her through, she wanted to shoot him in the legs because he'd tried to run. That itself would be a pointless exercise. There was no escaping what could come. He wouldn't have gotten out of the room. He was dragging his legs, face scarlet with anger and impotence but he obeyed.

"I'm... Well I'm not sorry," she said, placing a hand on his shoulder. Her eyes met his, Alana saw the tightening of muscle in her fingers suggesting she wanted to clench very hard. "I really am not. You've been running out of time ever since we first met. If you'd have known how much you'd borrowed, I'd imagine you would have spent it a little more wisely. Miss Fuller over there... Mine from the start. Every depraved little act, every sick fantasy, all under my directive." The look on Ritellia's face suggested had he not already known, he might have guessed. It was pure murder, the face that had bullied and cajoled ICCC executives, indeed anyone who'd tried to stand up to him really, for years but she stared back with pure indifference. He still made her skin crawl even in his moments of weakness.

"You bitch!"

"The blood of the man who would be king," Claudia said, looking up at the shrine. "Do you see it, Ronald? Do you know what this is?"

Ritellia turned, looked up at the statue of Kalqus and when he spoke, it was with a voice filled with scorn. "Is this why you brought me down here? To stare at relics?"

"No," the Mistress said softly. "I brought you down here to remove one unwanted relic from the world. It's all down to interpretation. Blut never could work this thing out, perhaps his passing was a blessing with hindsight. Alana…"

This was the moment, now it had arrived she was suddenly unsure, yet it still needed to be done. Stepping over to the Mistress' side, she handed her the blaster and took the ceremonial dagger from her, a beautiful piece of weaponry really, she found herself noticing the curve of the blade and the ivory polished handle as she moved to Ritellia. She'd waited for this moment, she steadied herself and dug it in deep, his eyes widening in surprise as she twisted it in his guts. Not content with a single stab, she thrust in again and again until his front was a mess of scarlet, blood gushing over her. Soon his legs gave out and as he dropped to his knees, she saw the pleading look in his eyes, the way his mouth opened ever so slightly with a beseeching look. It was to be the last sound he ever made, she slashed open his throat and stepped back, letting his body fall. It felt like blood covered every square inch of floor beneath the shrine, Ritellia's final breath coming out as one ragged bellow, his final movements little more than spasms before ultimately, he gave one final twitch and went still.

"Out of death comes life," Claudia said softly. "The price is paid, the bargain is struck, the king is dead, long live the queen." She clapped her hands together, the next words from her mouth Alana couldn't even come close to understanding. They sounded like a mixture of coughs, splutters and barks with the occasional howl thrown in. She could have sworn Ritellia's blood started to shine, just for a moment.

"This isn't going to work," Okocha said, looking at imagery from the team on site at the stadium. They'd relayed the tactical information about the pillars containing the spirit projectors, Aldiss and Leclerc had made efforts to try and get to one of them, either knocking it out or pulling it down. Their spirits had soared for the peak of the pillars, Aldiss' being a huge scarlet eagle, Leclerc hanging from the claws a huge bat, grabbed by the forearms. No sooner had they got within twenty feet of the projector, fresh doom dogs materialised below it, more than thirty streams of white hot fire shooting into the air, a web of destruction and death driving the two spirits back. "They can't get close enough. Defence matrix."

"Can't we get more people up there to deal with the dogs?" Nkolou asked. She'd made her way into the action centre, a blaster strapped to her hip, having woken for the crisis. "Seems like the best…"

"We're spread too thin," Noorland said. "If we had more people, we might be able to do it. Most of our people on the ground are tied up ensuring that civilians get out of there alive. We can't divert those resources."

"You take one of these towers out, you're making the problem smaller," Nkolou said. "It's standard warfare. Before you hit the enemy, you hit their resources, they can't hit you back as hard if they're already hurting."

"That doesn't work if you're the one being ambushed," Okocha said. "They really pulled a fast one on us."

"If I had a ship, I could blast it," Nkolou offered. "Direct hit from a HAX, they'd go up in smoke." The images showed Aldiss' eagle hit the ground and vanish, Aldiss rolled away, clearly struggling but he managed to get halfway to his feet before the first doom dog was on him, jumping on his back and tackling him to the rooftop.

"Fuck!" Okocha shouted, the image showing the spray of blood erupting as the dog bit down, they could hear Aldiss' screams. "You're right, I'll just pull a fucking HAX out of my damn pocket, shall I?"

"No need for that," Noorland said thoughtfully. "She might be onto something with what she said. We still have a hoverjet outside."

"It's not armed though," Okocha said, suddenly deadly calm again. "That thing couldn't win a fight with an oversized pigeon unless it got sucked into the engine." Noorland's response was to head for the exit. A few seconds later, Nkolou followed him and Okocha swore loudly. This day felt like it had been coming, one where all the bad shit on the island finally reached a breaking point and now the bill had become due.

In the confines of the spirit bout arena, it was considered proper conduct to be able to release a spirit anywhere within the boundaries of the battlefield on the condition its feet touched the ground when it appeared. Letting it materialise several feet above your opponent so it dropped on them was considered unsporting behaviour of the highest order and usually lead to disqualification.

Spirit battling outside the arena held no such rules, Wade noticed. Cacaxis went down, face hit the dirt hard, something stumpy and silver stood proudly on the back of its head. He narrowed his eyes, studied the four-armed figure. It couldn't be called humanoid. Only perhaps in the vaguest sense of the term. It was made of what looked like organic steel, a crude face scratched into the surface of the top part of its body, the effect strangely disturbing. Simultaneously it gave the impression of both blindness and an intense gaze, a contrast in experiences he'd never thought he'd see. Each of the four arms ended in thick metal claws, its legs shorter than each of the arms. It was amazing really that it could stand upright for any length of time. He'd seen the golem before, quite a while ago now. There'd been a few modifications made, but it was the same Iron-1 Ruud Baxter had fashioned for himself a very long time ago. The man himself stood high above them, peering down from the roof of the stadium. Wade could see him through the glasses, he raised a hand and waved. He knew Baxter could see him, at least until Cacaxis rose again, reared up like a ship in a storm, hurling Iron-1 into the stands, rounded on Wade and Theo with brutal anger. If the fight had gone out of it before, it was back now, roused with furious aggression.

Wade swallowed, reaching for another container crystal. This might yet still be tricky.

Nick ran, not entirely sure where he was going, all he could do was follow the general direction Rocastle had gone and hope for the best. It was all okay giving an instruction like Brendan had done, but sometimes you needed the means to be able to follow it through. That said, he was nothing if not resourceful. He'd hunt him down. Somewhere in this carnage, Rocastle was running. Finding him would always be the tricky part. He pulled up short, ducked a rifle butt swung at his face and tackled the attacker, smashing him into a wall. He yelled in pain, drew out a knife and swung at him, Nick twisted back, caught his wrist and broke it. That yell of pain became a screech, he flung out an elbow and sent his foe crashing to the ground, knocking his mask away. He knew that face, even if he didn't have time to dwell on it, he didn't know too many Varykian people, but he knew that one. He'd seen him twice in recent weeks, not just at the tournament but also on Coppinger's ship. One of Rocastle's special soldiers, Claudia had called them. Angels of Death? Something like that. Anything to be melodramatic apparently.

What drew his eye was the clip on Ulikku's belt, he reached down and snapped it off, looked at it with interest. He knew what it was only too well. When large scale spirit projectors were used in battle, the side employing them outfitted their own side with tags like these, ordinary-looking, unremarkable tags but containing a powerful pheromone inside which masked their presence to those spirits, marked them as friendly, meant the spirits sent rampant on the battlefield didn't accidentally attack them. He clipped it onto his own belt, put his finger to his ear and radioed the new information over, anything to turn the tide. It might buy people an extra few moments to deal with the hoards if they had an advantage.

Nick looked up, weapon rising at the same time as he heard approaching battle, an ice cat firing cold beams at two oncoming doom dogs. The caller... Jacobs... Nick could see he was trying to get away, failing miserably until Nick stepped in front of him and for a moment he saw their confusion in their eyes. Right up until the moment he put a flurry of shots between them. The bodies faded immediately.

"Shit!" Pete swore. "Where the fuck did you learn how to do that?"

"Never mind," Nick said. "You see Harvey Rocastle anywhere?" He didn't have time to be subtle. Pete's eyes widened in shock.

"As it happens..." he grunted. "We saw him, he came for us... Me, Matt, Sam... Mia! Where's Mia! He had a blaster!"

"Yeah, so do I," Nick replied grimly, hefting the weight of it in his hands. Mia Arnholt. It couldn't be, could it? He'd pulled that trick before, was he really doing it again? Rocastle had shot her father, was it even possible he was pushing his own agenda in all this? Coppinger couldn't know, surely. Or maybe it had been a hit on the director of Unisco and Rocastle had enjoyed a spectacular run of coincidence. "Where were you? Show me!"

Something in his voice must have told Pete he wasn't joking, not in the mood for playing about. He followed him, saw the Vazaran kid on the ground first, still breathing but shallow. He smelled like overcooked meat, smoke rising from the charred mess which had been his back not so long ago. Matt Arnholt looked in better shape, he had a welt the size of an egg above one eye, blood running down his face, but he'd live. "He... He took her," Matt said. He sounded numb, like he was in shock. "Grabbed her and ran. We fought but he tore through us like we weren't there."

This suddenly had the potential to turn ugly, Nick realised. Uglier than it already was. If they were taking hostages... He needed to get her back. She'd be where Rocastle was. He could kill two birds. Far too many had already died here to let her go. And there were plenty who loved her. He sighed. If this was how it had to be, so be it. He'd been unable to save Sharon. He wasn't going to let Mia Arnholt die as well, if he could help it. Her loved ones didn't deserve to feel sickness crawling through them the way he had in recent days.

"Don't worry," he said, wishing he was as confident as he sounded. "I'll take care of it. Get yourselves out of here! Now! Get to safety. Once you get out the stadium, you should be free of the doom dogs." He pointed to the tag. "You see any bodies, grab these tags and hold them yourselves. You SHOULD be okay with them but keep your wits about you."

"Errr... What about Scott?!" Matt asked. "He was here already. Found us before you did, he already went after them both."

Nick swore viciously. Little idiot! This was going to be hard enough to do without introducing a have-a-go hero into the mix. It should be left to the professionals. Last thing he needed was his quarry having two hostages in the mix. "Fine," he growled before turning for the exit. He was already running through the possibilities in his mind. Like as not, they wouldn't be going for the aeroport. Flying in would be reckless, the Vazaran military might not be the quickest to mobilise, but they surely had to be on their way, Okocha and Noorland had to have already gotten in touch. Which left the docks. A boat could sneak in and out of here, would probably have more chance of leaving undetected by the arriving rescue force.

Either way, they'd taken a risk, the way he was taking a risk heading for the docks. There was no guarantee they were going to make it out of here unscathed and yet they'd come anyway. There had to be something they were all missing. He saw the figure rush in front of him all too late, could only react with evasion rather than complete avoidance, he felt the shots burn through his side. Fire coursed up his body, he let out a yell and emptied the power pack of his rifle straight into the shooter's face, a rather petulant act but one that felt so good for a tiny moment.

Can't stop... Won't stop...

Running hurt like the hells but he wasn't about to give up, too much at stake for that.

"Want to tell me what the great plan is?" Nkolou asked, following Noorland out to the hoverjet. "You heard Will, this thing doesn't have any weapons. You can't shoot it down from here."

"I know," Noorland said. "I just want a..." He almost tripped over the words. "I just want a tactical appraisal of the situation, one gained first hand. You should know this, always trust your eyes over what the machines tell you."

"It's not going to tell you anything different," Nkolou said gently. "You know that."

"No, it's not going to answer my question," Noorland insisted, pulling the hatch door open. He was half inside when he felt Nkolou's hand on his arm, trying to stop him. He gulped. "Please, don't stop me"

"What question do you need answering?" she insisted. "Whatever it is, it's not worth it. You're hiding something."

"That's not true, Lieutenant Nkolou," Noorland replied. "Unisco doctrine. First thing they teach you in the academy. It's always worth it. No matter what it costs, no matter the price you need to pay, it is always worth it. Freedom isn't free, and lives are cheap in these five kingdoms. Somewhere, somehow it never quite adds up to how you want it to. Maths is a cruel bitch."

Her eyes widened. "So…"

"Don't make this harder than it has to be."

"Damnit, if you're going to fly in on some sort of suicide mission, it should be me!" she bellowed. "I'm a better pilot than you, I should be the one who dies in a cockpit. I'm more expendable than you."

Noorland shook his head. "No, you really aren't. You don't want to die. I've already made my peace with this. It's happening. If I can make it a little bit safer, give my life so that others can live, it's a good way to go."

"I won't let you…" Nkolou started to say before Noorland's fist flashed out, caught her a glancing blow across the side of the mouth and dropped her to the ground. She tried to spring up, he caught her kick and twisted her back down unceremoniously.

"You can't win," he said. "Just…" She tried again, he snapped out his hand in a chopping motion, caught her by the neck and squeezed, applying pressure to various spots until she dropped like a sack of potatoes, not permanently harmed but down for the moment. "Stay down!"

It wasn't even like she was unconscious, just momentarily unable to move any part of her body. He saw the anger in her eyes, tried not to look as he scooped her up and placed her out the way like she was a mere child. Alvin Noorland didn't look back as he made his way back to the cockpit of the hoverjet. This was the way it had to be.

He'd been right!

There!

Nick could see them all, a boat far below, fast bastard by the looks of it and there were some humanoid shapes nearby too distant to make them out entirely. He picked up his pace, every step fresh fire in his side and as much as he tried to ignore it, shut it out, each second it became harder. He took the hundred and three steps two at a time, trying not to think about what would happen if he missed a step or tripped. Halfway down, he looked up, saw the distinctive blue jacket Scott Taylor had worn during the bout worn by one of the figures.

Come on!

He forced himself to pick up the pace, working as hard as he physically could to get there, jumping the last three steps. Landing brought fresh new agony, he had to fight to stay on his feet and keep going. The docks were close now, he could see them both, Taylor and… Rocastle! Coppinger was nowhere to be seen for the moment but he could see Arnholt's daughter as well, being held by a seven-foot-tall troll who had a big fat arm around her neck. It looked ready to squeeze at any given moment, he got close enough and he could hear the conversation.

"Let her go!" Scott was pleading. "Or…"

The look on Rocastle's face bore full testament to sadism, ghoulish and gloating at the same time. "Or what, lamb chop? You come any closer and I'll see her snapped like a twig. She…"

Nick slowed to a walk, took the three steps to the dock very deliberately and strolled into view, Arnholt's X7 pointed at the fat man. "Or we could play this another way," he said, voice filled with authority. "Let her go, Harvey. You're under arrest for conspiracy to murder, conspiracy to treason, kidnap, resisting arrest, attempted murder at the very least of Prideaux Khan, Brendan King and Terrence Arnholt as well as the murder of Carlton Bond. If you go quietly now, they might not give you the chair. If you don't, I'll put you down like the mad dog you are!"

Other than the sob let out by the stricken-looking Mia when he named her father, the silence was deafening. Rocastle even looked to be chewing it over for a moment until his face broke into a grin. "Mad dog?" he said. "I like that. I like that a lot. Think I might get it in tattoo form. The question is, what are you going to do if I refuse? You shoot me, my cool Cacalti will kill that cunt right there, probably the boy…" Scott glowered at that. "And maybe even you. You're not fast enough to save them all." His face split open malevolently into a grin. "Just like you couldn't save your own woman!"

He nearly pulled the trigger right there and then, was mentally preparing for the sight of seeing his head snap back with a hole in the middle, a red third eye. Still Nick refrained. Just. Just. Would have been so easy. "She didn't die well, you know," Rocastle continued. "It was heart-breaking. Well if you care about that sort of stuff anyway. She cried your name. Wanted to know where you were. And you weren't there!" The last few words had a definite note of sing-song in them and Nick struggled to keep his finger off the trigger. He should pull it, he'd been given the order and yet he couldn't. Rocastle was right. He wasn't about to let more people die, even though he knew full well Rocastle deserved shooting in the back of the head and letting the ocean take care of the body.

He must have seen the twitch in his finger, the brazen amount of self-restraint because the fat fuck kept on laughing. "I don't care about that," he said stiffly.

"Sure, you do. You wouldn't be here otherwise," Rocastle giggled. "It's personal. Just like between me…" He jabbed a porky finger into his own chest, one of his good ones Nick noticed. Not the fake ones, he wondered what the story was behind that. One of them fake ones screwed into Mia's cheek, making her squirm. "And this bitch."

"Seriously what the hells did she do to you?!" Scott yelled. Nick grimaced. Shut the hells up, keep out of this. Don't antagonise him!

Rocastle only laughed. "Private, private. I'd have thought she'd have told you. Guess the budding relationship still has its secrets. You'll never ever get to know…"

Nick cast a glance over to the troll, realised those options sucked. It'd take a high-powered shot to get through its thick skull, more than a single X7 blast. Plus, their brains were naturally quite small, hard to guarantee a hit even if he could punch through with a lucky shot. He doubted it'd stand motionless and let him shoot it in the head without some sort of reaction. His side was starting to burn, his legs aching from the run. If he was going to do something, he needed to do it now. "So, who cut your hand up then?" he asked. "That looks like it hurt."

No response. Rocastle narrowed his eyes at him for a moment. "More than you can imagine."

"No. I really doubt that," Nick said, his voice quiet. Thanks to you, I'm no stranger to anguish and pain. Maybe he should just do it. Put him down and to hells with Arnholt's daughter. But then he could imagine the director's face if he lived through his own injuries, not a guarantee itself. He'd be devastated. There'd already been too much of that.

Although, there might be another way.

When a spirit's owner was killed in battle, the first thing an enraged spirit did was revenge itself upon all closest enemies. Having shared a consciousness with the deceased, it would be aware who that was. Cacalti would probably go through Mia, likely through Scott and even to Nick if he shot him. Nick had seen it before, he'd used it as a deterrent on more than one occasion. On the other hand, though…

He lowered his weapon and smiled sweetly. The pain in his side was forgotten, he felt the adrenaline flood his system. He was going to enjoy this. "Let me introduce you to the encore," he said. "You think you know pain? Not even close."

He moved, darted the short distance between them, saw the realisation in Rocastle's eyes and almost walked into the first punch. Nick ducked beneath it, tackled him with full force and caught an instinctive knee in the gut for his trouble. He might have been fat but there was some muscle there as well, like hitting a side of beef. Pushing him back, he threw a fist of his own, caught him on the jaw and Rocastle howled with pain as something cracked. With murder in his eyes, the fat man came back, spat out a tooth and went on the offensive, slow deliberate punches that held power but lacked precision.

Nick blocked the first two, spun and kicked him in his standing calf, buckling him to his knees. The momentum of his swing took him the rest of the way, suddenly down onto his belly and he had to roll out the way as Nick moved, trying to stamp on his spine. Suddenly the fat man was in motion, his legs sweeping Nick's out from underneath him. Nick hit the dock with a grunt, bounced his head off it. Vision swimming, he caught a kick on his injured side and bellowed in pain. Giggling manically at the result of his blow, Rocastle brought his leg back again, winding powerfully up as if he were about to kick a football downfield. This time Nick managed to roll and catch it both handed, twisting his ankle hard and simultaneously kicking into the standing leg. He heard vicious twin snaps of breaking bones and Rocastle went down screaming, wasn't getting back up. With his leg bent almost at a right angle, he tried to stand on one leg and failed miserably, Nick got to his feet and kicked out again, three, four, five times to the face, each of them a satisfying crunch and then rolled up into a standing position. He saw the pleading in the fat man's eyes amidst blood and bruises before he put his foot on his throat and started to apply pressure. It didn't take long for his face to change colour, Rocastle's breathing coming out harder and harder, his hands beating weakly against Nick's leg as he tried to get free and failed miserably.

Come on… Come on…

It was with a huge bellow the troll suddenly rose to its full height, tossed Mia aside and charged towards him, murder in its eyes. He'd had the desired effect.

Gotcha!

Nick barely had time to go for his summoner, didn't register the splash in the ocean as he jumped off Rocastle and barely evaded the charging troll. Empson appeared, flexed his wings and suddenly the two spirits were at it, penguin versus troll. He did notice Scott charge past him though, straight into the ocean and he stiffened.

Whoops!

Not what he'd had planned. Couldn't account for everything, but he'd partly succeeded. He'd gotten her away from this psycho at least. If she didn't drown, it was a job well done.

The salty water burned his eyes, threatened to stifle his lungs and made him want to retch but Scott tried to push it from his mind as he dove through the murky depths of the ocean. It couldn't be that deep here, surely. She couldn't have gone far...

There. Drifting. Not moving on her own, just sinking and moving further away from him. He cursed mentally, kicked his legs and went after her. He wasn't about to let her go. Not just yet. Not like this. He couldn't. He wouldn't. He needed to breathe, stupid, stupid, he hadn't thought this through properly and they might both drown for it. The harder he pushed, the faster he'd run out of air... That didn't deter him, he forced himself to go, reaching helplessly for her with his hand. Just... too... far away!

She twitched, whether a current had caught her, or she was coming around for sure, or the Divines loved him, Scott couldn't say. But as he felt her hand in his, he didn't question it, pulled her closer to him and wrapped his arm around her body. Her eyes weren't open, he kicked his legs and started the short climb back to the surface. With her dead weight... an unfortunate choice of term... it took twice the effort, his muscles aflame, the light spinning above his head, his lungs spasming out of control. When the first breath unconsciously escaped, he inhaled ocean water and began to splutter, almost lost his focus. Almost.

Just a little higher...

As he broke above the surface, he heard that shriek again, the same he'd heard at the stadium. Deep breath, he forced himself under again. He knew what it meant, and he didn't want either of them to be a target. Scott forced his mouth to Mia's, let some of his air into her Hopefully, it'd be enough.

Nick couldn't believe it, he snapped his blaster up and started to fire. Some of them landed but either the lizard-bird's skin was too thick to be affected or he'd misjudged and missed. One of the two. He couldn't let them get away. Not now. Empson had gone down from the shriek. Be interesting to know the properties behind that bit of power. And Claudia had swooped down on her mount, he'd gone for the weapon when he'd seen her creature scoop Rocastle by the legs up in its talons. In the distance, he could see aeroships incoming, just be a little faster and they could corner her here. It'd all be over.

He emptied the power pack, must have hit something but to no avail. Claudia only smiled sweetly at him, the sort of sweetness that turns sugar to bile in the stomach. At least one shot had been on target, he could see the rip in her jacket where it had landed, yet she didn't appear even slightly hurt by the blasts. "Oh, hard luck, Nicholas," she said. "I'd deal with you right now, but time does press. Even for me. You'll get your turn though. Don't despair." She waved playfully. "Farewell."

And they were gone, the spirit taking wing and accelerating off into the distance. By the time the aerofighters caught up, it'd be too late. Hells, even by the time he'd found Carcer's container crystal, they were already nearly out of sight.

Nick swore in anger, dropped to the deck, the fatigue finally threatening to catch up with him, before he saw the two heads break the surface and he moved again, went to throw them a hover ring. They'd been an upgrade on the old life ring, they held a highly-concentrated burst of superheated oxygen intended to create a brief hovering effect, enough to get them out the ocean.

As the two of them landed, Nick shut his eyes and grimaced. Judging by the state of Arnholt's daughter, it didn't look good. Scott crawled onto all fours, choking and retching but he'd be fine. He didn't hesitate, went to apply mouth-to-mouth resuscitation. She wasn't moving, her skin freezing cold. Four breaths, thirty chest pumps.

You're not fucking dying today, you little bitch! Come on, you best fight this!

Harder and harder Scott pumped, Nick only watched, not much more he could do for her. The technique was decent, most spirit callers did know rudimentary first aid techniques just in case the worst happened while they were out in the wild and he had a horrible feeling about the way this might end. Saltwater streamed down Scott's face, his own breath coming out ragged as he continued to work away, almost as if he hoped he could bring her back by sheer force of will alone. His hands continued to work away, against her chest, his face contorted in determination. For a moment, his eyes shone blue, Nick wasn't entirely sure he'd seen it and the younger caller let out a guttural bellow of something primal, as much frustration as anything else.

As she coughed up salt water and gasped for breath, Nick found himself thinking maybe today wouldn't be a total write-off after all. One small glimmer of hope out of a huge shit storm.

Everyone saw it, the hoverjet circling the stadium. Whether they paid any attention to it or not was up for debate, it circled three times, streams of fire coming to greet it every time it strayed too close to the pillars. The fourth time, it went in close and didn't pull out, the fires burning through the shields and the structure of the metal as it struck one of the pillars and exploded in a giant fireball, superheated gas and flame taking away most of the pillar with it. It wiped away the projector housed inside, immediately the doom dogs started to fizzle out and vanish as the other three projectors tried to pick up the slack, immediately pushed beyond their operating limits. Simultaneously, the debris falling into the stadium struck Cacaxis on the head, tonnes and tonnes of bricks, mortar and metal smashing down in great chunks, too many for the beast to ignore easily.

That might have turned out to be the breaking point for it apparently decided enough was enough. Trapped between tonnes of falling rubble, it started to shrink down again, digging down into the dirt, retreating, out of sight and gone back to where it had come from. Soon the only remnant left behind was the great gaping hole amidst a once pristine battlefield.

Around the stadium, those still inside stood silent for a moment, not entirely sure what had just happened. Those Coppinger gunmen who hadn't been killed made a run for it, many of them quickly killed in short order. In a matter of moments, the battle was as over as rapidly as it had begun, it didn't take long for comprehension to dawn and even amidst the sobering thoughts of what had just had happened, a few cheers broke out...

"Carcaradis Chaos Once Again…"
"Dozens of Dead in Stadium Massacre…"
"Ritellia Murdered in Ritual Sacrifice…"
"Unisco Promise Full Investigation…"
"Final Bout Declared Official Draw…"
"Coppinger Claims Island Attack Retaliation…"
"ICCC to Face Possible Suspension Due to Tournament Horrors…"
Media headlines following the Battle of Carcaradis.

The twelfth day of Summerfall.

Trying to avoid scratching at the bandage on his side, Nick stepped out into the afternoon sun, wearing his best black suit and did his utmost to fit in with the pervading aura of misery blanketing Carcaradis Island in the last days. It wasn't hard. The day of mourning for all those that had perished during the attack was well underway. The island had been silent, grave-like even, all previous days of joy felt so very far away.

They'd been burying the deceased throughout, everyone knew someone who'd fallen because of what Claudia Coppinger had done, he'd noticed the sense of disbelief permeating the place many times now. Maybe it hadn't affected him as much because he'd known about her before. He was noticing it in some of his co-workers though, some really struggling with the depths she was willing to stoop to. Madness was always difficult to comprehend at first, he'd found. Derenko hadn't been the same since what was now being dubbed the Battle of Carcaradis by the media, they did like their nicknames. The first shots fired in a war now holding a lot of speculation as to the causes and possible effects, with nobody having any sort of clear answer as to why. Political, social and religious commentators were suddenly finding themselves in high demand, speculating as to the ends, means and outcomes of what was now going to happen over the next few months, maybe even years.

Nick supposed it was true really, wherever there was to be war and strife, then there would be someone making a quick credit off the back of it. Word had it, every major arms company across the five kingdoms was predicting major profits for the next several years at the prospects for blood. He knew a guy who worked for BRO, he'd told him that they were already commissioning a new assault rifle for the hard times to come. Still, it wasn't time to think about that, not on a day like this. It felt like the rest of the world could wait until tomorrow. Today was a day to remember the past. He moved through the deserted streets, noted how different it was from the day they'd buried Sharon. Then, there had been people everywhere to pay their respects. Today, people had left the island as fast as possible, people were staying in their rooms in shock at what had happened, people wanted to be in their own little bubbles, suffer in their own solitary company. He couldn't blame them, but he didn't have that luxury.

Honestly, he was amazed that more Unisco agents hadn't been killed in the struggle, even if Arnholt and Leclerc were still in the hospital, the former not even having regained consciousness yet, Prideaux Khan had taken a flesh wound but had later been discharged after brief treatment. Fank Aldiss and Alvin Noorland were perhaps the two biggest losses, Tod Brumley had been treated for superficial burns, but they reckoned he'd recover the use of his arm in time. Beyond that, wounds had been not unlike his own, nothing that wouldn't heal with time.

Truth be told, he was still pissed at what had happened. He'd had Rocastle dead to rights, he'd blown it spectacularly. Someday soon, it was going to reflect badly on him. He somehow got the impression the director wouldn't be too pissed at him for making the choice he had, but maybe he should be. If he told Nick that he'd made the right decision, wouldn't that be him letting his personal judgement cloud the situation? Praise in circumstances like these felt hollow, pointless even. He didn't need it, didn't want it. Still he'd managed to defuse the situation okay. It had been a risk, getting that troll's survival instinct to kick in by choking its caller until it needed to intervene, but it had worked. By the time Empson had defeated the troll, Claudia Coppinger had showed up, defeated Empson and survived being shot. He knew he'd hit her at least once, knew that she'd shrugged it off. All in all, not the best things to report back to his superiors. Although, but for her intervention, he would have succeeded. The whole thing had been a mess from start to finish.

With Brendan King being nominally in charge of operations for the time being, it was an uncomfortable situation. He was loving his new circumstances; Nick could already see part of the Field Chief was hoping Arnholt couldn't continue with his duties. There were already whispers the Senate were still considering Unisco reforms to deal with the crisis. It looked likely he'd pull through; the train of thought he likely wouldn't be the same man. The injuries had been bad but considering what had happened to many others, he could be grateful to be alive.

He could see most of his fellow agents already in the cemetery as he entered, Brendan, Lysa, Brumley, Okocha, David Wilsin was finally out of the hospital, Wade and a tearful Derenko. He'd taken it hard, the loss of Aldiss. The two had been close for as long as Nick could remember, he'd never seen as close a friendship between two agents, always a dangerous situation given the volatile nature of the job. Good on them, he was sure it was good while it lasted. He'd never liked funerals and lately it felt like there'd been too many of them.

When Sharon had died... He remembered how that had gone, he'd thrown the punch at Ritellia, it felt like just yesterday. Ritellia's body had already gone, paid for by the ICCC to be shipped back to his home and buried there. A great homage for a great leader, they'd said. It might be the last time they were able to indulge themselves like this. He'd seen the headlines. Kate Kinsella had gone for them again, spreading her venom across the rest of them now that Ritellia was no longer a viable target. Even those softer targets like Adam Evans and Linda Alizaire, who she normally was marginally less unpleasant to, had taken the flak. In her writing, he got the impression in a strange sort of way, she was quite sad about the death of the man she'd criticised so frequently. Maybe No Fucks Given, the charming nickname bestowed upon her always making him smile, was only human after all.

They were doing Aldiss first, laying him to rest in one of the newly dug holes in the ground. He ran a quick count, winced at the sheer number still to be filled. Credit to the ICCC, they had stepped in to pay for it all. Probably trying to curry public favour while they still could, even if the gesture had much the same impact as offering to buy someone a new coffee maker after you've burned down their house. The zent looked tired, Nick supposed working non-stop the last few days would do that to you. But when he spoke, his voice was full of vigour and authority, above all else, comfort. Exactly what you wanted from a holy man. He spoke of how Fank Aldiss gave his life, so others may live. As was protocol when a Unisco agent died like this, the organisation had granted full disclosure of their status, the zent never mentioned it though. Too professional. Brendan King spoke a few words, talking about how it was a pleasure to have met him, to have known him, stopping just short of saying that they'd worked together. Wade stepped up and spoke briefly, said that he'd always have good memories of the times they'd battled each other. He'd been quite a popular city champion in Serran, had Aldiss. That many of his fans had tried to get out to pay their respects was testament to the man and the way he'd done things.

Then Derenko took to the podium, gripped the sides of it with gloved hands and despite looking shaky, when he spoke his voice was calm. "Yeah, I knew Fank," he said. "Bit of an understatement really. The man was probably my greatest friend in all the kingdoms. Someone who I could talk to, someone who got me when nobody else did. Someone who... Sometimes you feel like you're two parts of a whole. You know what? I loved him. He was one of a kind, someone special. You want to know what sort of man he was? He was the sort of man who knew how I felt, or at least I think he guessed but..."

He let out a big sigh, almost a sob. Nick felt a pang of regret touch his heart. He'd been there in Derenko's shoes. "He never felt the same way, but never let it come between us. When we were together, we were an army. And now that army has been routed. There'll never be a more beautiful soul to graze these five kingdoms. We've lost one of our best. Forever." He lowered his head, looked down at the coffin. "I'll miss you, buddy. I'll always think what could have been, what should and what might but there's no changing that now. Farewell and rest peacefully."

He stepped down from the podium and, in that moment, Nick had never seen a man who looked more broken from his loss.

Wade strode into the hospital, cloak billowing around him and the first impression he caught was the building was a lot quieter than it had been the last time he'd been here. Not when he'd been a patient but rather following the aftermath of the attack. Organised chaos might have been putting it lightly. Now, it was calmer. He knew there likely wouldn't be any sort of change in the director's condition, but with little else to do, he thought he'd come visit, something tugging at the back of his consciousness, telling him it'd be for the best. He checked in at reception, took the stairs up to the third floor. The atmosphere was electric made his hair stand up on the back of his neck. Something about it didn't feel right, no possible rhyme or reason for him to have that feeling. The source behind it didn't become clear until he stepped out onto the third floor, glanced to his right and saw Clara stood catching her breath, washing her hands in disinfectant. Her hair was a mess and her black ringed eyes were half closed with fatigue. At the same time, he could have sworn she looked about ten years older. Parts of her hair had faded, from blond almost to grey and he blanched a little at that. A faint patch of dried blood lay on her cheek.

"Cousin," he said, catching her unawares. He saw her jump, hid his smirk. "Sorry."

"Fuck," she said, glaring at him. "Can you not sneak up on me like that?"

"Shouldn't you have sensed me?" Wade asked. "Baxter always could. Guy's like a motion detector." He grinned as he said it, especially at the way she broke into a deep glare pointed at him.

"Master Baxter is a talented individual," she said. "He's had a lot more experience and training than what he has given us yet. Furthermore, he probably hadn't spent the last day and a half in this place trying to heal the wounded. I'm a Restorer, I'm not a bloody dispensary"

Wade raised an eyebrow. "That what you're doing?" He pointed to the corresponding point on his own cheek. "By the way, you missed a bit."

Clara cursed, rubbed at her face. "How long's that been there then? Someone else could have told me!"

"Probably upset about you crashing their workplace and using your fancy sorcery to do their jobs," Wade said. "I know I'd be annoyed if it happened to me in my workplace."

"You're a spirit caller," she said. "As well as that other thing… Master Baxter told me. Ha, you might not have a choice in that soon."

"What?!"

She grinned. "Sorry, not saying. Said as much as I know. Because you're my cousin and all that." Her grin faded. "But seriously, he volunteered us for this. Some of us have a knack for healing with the Kjarn and the hospital is seriously understaffed considering the circumstances. Nobody expected this. So, we're happy to help where we can. Besides he thought we could use the practice. Two bottles with one rock and all that."

"Yep, sounds like the Baxter I know," Wade said. "Practical if nothing else. Where is he anyway? Is he here?"

"He's with Terrence Arnholt," Clara said. "He came around earlier."

"What?!"

"Yeah, I think the two of them are in there discussing something right now. Looked important when I walked past earlier. They were plotting like mad."

"I'll catch you in a bit, Clara," Wade said, patting her on the arm. "Keep up the good work."

"Later, cousin. I'll get right back to it. Oh, and Wade…"

He craned his head back, curious as to what she might have to bring up.

"It's not fancy sorcery, you know!"

"I know."

"It's a gift. It's part of being one with something so much greater."

"Yeah, I've heard the mantra."

"You know, that power runs in our family, I've heard."

"Apparently." He shrugged. "What of it."

"Master Baxter says you have the gift too. It's how he helped you heal your eyes, he said."

"And he asked you to give me the pep talk? Not interested! I told him that before, I'll tell you that as well," Wade said quietly but firmly. He meant it as well. That discussion wasn't one he wanted to repeat. "My life's complicated enough as it is." Of course, it was a touch hypocritical. If it hadn't been for what Ruud Baxter had taught him, he might well still be having trouble seeing, he knew that. Just as he was aware how easy it had been to heal himself, it all making for troubling thoughts about his future.

He quickened his pace, left her behind as he crossed the short distance to Arnholt's room. Already he was surveying the surroundings, he knew what to look for. It was guarded, someone he didn't recognise stood outside the door to prevent intruders from entering accidentally. Made sense. Arnholt had already nearly been killed once, until he was back on his feet, it wouldn't do to give them a second easy shot at him. It didn't deter him one bit, the guy waved him through and he knocked on the door, waiting only for the permission to enter before going inside. Neither of them looked particularly good, Arnholt for obvious reasons, Baxter looked tired, but his eyes remained full of fire as he turned to greet him. "I knew you were coming," he said. "Wade."

"Ruud. Director. Good to see you up and well again."

Arnholt grinned weakly. "Yes well, don't advertise it just yet. There are some benefits to people not knowing that you've woken up. At least not for a few more hours yet." He coughed, made a face of discomfort, lay his head back down. "Although I wouldn't say completely better."

"I did the best I could under the circumstances," Ruud said. "Healing others never was my strong point."

"You've got other people doing it, I see," Wade remarked. Ruud stared at him with a raised eyebrow.

"What of it? They need the practice. No time like the present. It is the duty of the Vedo to give something back wherever they can. Speaking of which, Director…"

"Ah yes," Arnholt groaned. "Go on…"

"Well of course I'd love for us to come to some sort of arrangement," Ruud said. "A mutually beneficial one, of course. We have similar goals. You want to stop Coppinger; I want Wim Carson. Preferably alive but if needs be, I can negotiate to deceased. You won't be able to take him on your own. One of my people can." He paused to consider it for a moment. "Probably better than yours will. Less chance of one of mine dying."

"It's good that you showed up here like that," Wade remarked. "I dread to think how many people might have died if you hadn't."

"What did I say?" Ruud said. "Always giving something back. This time it might have been our lives."

"You all come through unscathed?" Wade wondered.

Ruud nodded. "More or less. Nothing a few hours healing won't cure. I trained them well. The only thing we lack is numbers. I have fourteen full Vedo, about half a dozen trainees. I had to leave two of them behind with the apprentices, otherwise I came full strength."

Just before he could ask why he needed to come full strength, Wade was cut off by Arnholt who cleared his throat noisily and painfully by the sounds of it. "I'm not entirely sure what sort of arrangement you think we could come to. I can't share Unisco resources with... Well technically you're a rogue organisation. We don't know anything about you, I certainly didn't know your group existed until the battle. I knew about you, Ruud, but... Well, that there are so many of you is a different matter. It's a shame as I'd love to have you by our side when it comes down to it."

"And you know it will come down to it," Ruud said. "This isn't going to be finished in a few weeks. It's going to be a long horrible bloody struggle. Claudia Coppinger means business. She's out for blood. You need all the help you can get. It's hard to come by these days, I hear. Not with what the Vazaran Suns did."

"Our organisation never bore a close partnership with them, though. Too many questionable acts committed in their name. I bore a professional relationship with Mazoud, I had a respect for what he's done in his life, but that aside, we never associated."

"My point is, she has allies. Powerful allies. And while my Vedo might not be on a par with that army, I think you'll find we can be of use to you in other ways. Infiltration. Espionage. Your training programs are presumably exceptional by now; they were pretty good when I went through them. My people are fast learners, I made sure of that. And besides, you're forgetting about the potential exchange of skills."

"Exchange of skills?" Arnholt asked. Wade found himself feeling more and more like a spare part. Also, he had a nasty feeling gestating in the pit of his stomach that he couldn't quite ignore, a horrible sensation that wanted to be heard.

"Well the required degree of sensitivity to the Kjarn needed to train as a full Vedo is present in more people than you might imagine, it just needs coaxing," Ruud said. "Given permission to test Unisco agents, I might find several suitable candidates. I train them, you have some on retainer then. Granted it's not a path I'd like them to take but at the same time, this isn't an ideal situation for anyone. It's happened before. You took Anne Sullivan on, she's potentially one of the strongest Kjarn users I've ever encountered in recent years."

"And you did it," Wade pointed out. "Combined the two."

"Hence why I'd rather not put anyone else through it," Ruud said. "I speak from experience, just as when I say people will do what they feel the need to. Can't change that."

"So, you become a part of Unisco for the duration of this conflict," Arnholt said. "You agree to render aid wherever it is needed..."

"No, I want to become an informal part," Ruud said. "Outside the regular command structure. I'll answer to you; I'll sign off on any missions you want to send my people on if I feel it's the right fit for them. These Vedo are a precious resource and I won't have you squander them on suicide missions. In exchange, we'll hunt down Wim Carson for you. Any resources, including people and equipment will provide for us will be greatly appreciated. Any assistance we can give you, we can."

"No," Arnholt said simply. Wade smirked at that. As much as he liked Baxter, there were too many horrible suspicions floating about his mind right now to just blindly accept anything he said as fact. "Not a chance."

"No?" Baxter asked politely. He hadn't even raised an eyebrow, Wade noticed. He always remembered playing Ruin with him. It was hard to forget. The lesson of the memory always remained thus, never gamble against someone who can read your emotions and at the same time give nothing away in exchange.

"You're asking for a lot."

"And think what you're getting in exchange," Ruud said pointedly. "This isn't the past. Back then, the Vedo were wasteful. They had all this power, they chose to sit on it. You saw what we could do. How much worse would it have been had we not been there in that stadium?"

"Still not explained why you had them all there," Wade muttered. At first, he'd thought they were here on the island to share their respects to Sharon Arventino. Seeing them all tooled up and ready for a fight in the stadium, he'd been developing suspicions of his own. If Ruud heard him, he chose not to reply. He couldn't have failed to miss the way Wade felt inside, though.

"At the very worst-case scenario, you would have been looking at a catastrophe instead of a disaster. You wouldn't be here yourself if not for the intervention of Agent Wallerington's cousin. She saved your life, I believe. In the past, that power was squandered. I'm bringing it out into the light. The times have changed, and we needed to change with them. Sometimes I think that's why the original order fell. But we are few and we lack resources to grow further. I've been financing them myself but I'm nearly out of credits. This alliance is mutually beneficial to both of us, you have to see that."

Arnholt, credit to him, Wade thought, avoided meeting Ruud's eyes. "You wouldn't be trying to put me under your influence, would you?" It came out lightly but at the same time doing little to hide the accusation in his voice.

"I wouldn't," Ruud said. "You can make this deal, or you can send me away. I want that to be your choice. Besides, that trick only works on those who don't know what they want. I think it's fair to say you are anything but. Terrence, believe me on this. I have only best interests at heart. I've spent these last years building the Vedo back up to anything even slightly resembling what came before. If I want control, it's only because I don't want to see that work fizzle out. It's not even anything against you..." He swallowed. "Believe me, I trust you. But you've just been shot. There was absolutely no reason to shoot you unless someone knew you were the director of Unisco. I trust you. I know you. You've earned that recognition. I have very little reason to trust whoever comes in after you. I'm covering myself. Better the enemy you know, for want of a better term."

"I'm flattered," Arnholt said. "But I still have to say no. If you and your people wish to join Unisco then you do it through the proper channels. Take the training and..."

"Then we have nothing further to discuss," Ruud said simply, cutting him off. "I'm sorry to have wasted your time. Maybe I'll go directly to the Senate instead. See if they'll give us the resources..."

"You won't," Arnholt said. "You'd have done that first, if it was a viable option. You're leery about your people coming under Unisco control. You'd hate it even more if they were under the bureaucratic thumb..." He paused for a moment. "And don't even try to deny that." Ruud said nothing, just stood stiffly with his arms at his sides. "Here's my counter offer. You and your people come into the Unisco fold and you'll be given any sort of resource you need, including any agents you want. I won't give you autonomy. I will give you a commanding role though under someone of my choice. You will be assigned missions and I expect you to fulfil them."

"Who's the commanding officer going to be?" Ruud asked.

"I have a few people in mind for the role. It's a new department I'm going to have to see created as soon as is possible."

"Don't forget as well, we have a library full of old books that might be able to help with this," Ruud offered. "This whole delusion of godhood mess that we seem to have found ourselves in with Coppinger."

"Do you really think she's become a Divine?" Wade asked. He couldn't help himself. "I mean it's a pretty bold statement to make."

"There was something not entirely right about her," Ruud said. "Even from a distance, I could sense her. It's like hearing warning bells chiming. You're aware, but sometimes you're not sure why until it's too late. I don't know." He rubbed his forehead. "But I do accept your deal by the way. I think it's in all our best interests if I do. We can't beat them apart. They've been preparing for this, the battle in the skies, the attack on the stadium. Together we might be able to do this."

"Then welcome back, Agent Baxter."

As they shook hands, Wade still couldn't shake that feeling rattling around in his head. He somehow couldn't entirely rid himself of the horrible thought that Baxter had known this whole mess at the stadium was going to happen. At the same time, he'd done nothing beforehand to pre-emptively deal with it other than ensure his own people were in a great position to look good during the aftermath. It was a horrible feeling to hold such suspicion about one of your closest friends, to wonder if they're capable of doing that. Being complicit in something so horrible. It's even worse when you knew in your heart every word was true. After all, Baxter had been trained by two worlds. The Vedo and Unisco. One had nearly died, the other was in a fight for its life. That he'd picked up some survival skills on the way and the savvy to use them, Wade shouldn't have been surprised. It didn't mean it didn't hurt any less though.

Betrayal always stung the most when it came from someone you trusted.

"I'm not going to be sad to leave here," Mia said. She sounded like she meant it as well, grim determination in her voice. At least her mood had picked up since she'd gotten the call her dad had woken up in hospital. They'd been to see him earlier. "Really. It's been nothing but bad luck for me."

Scott raised an eyebrow. "Nothing but?"

With a roll of her eyes she leaned up and kissed him. "Present company excluded. I've nearly died three times here. And my dad got shot as well! Can you blame me?! Never coming back after this. I don't believe in pushing fate further than I have to."

"Look at it this way," Scott said with a smile. "You could have died three times and you didn't. Does this make you officially a survivor?"

"We all survived this thing," she said. "You, me, Pete, Sam. When it all kicked off in that stadium... I was worried about you. You were right at ground zero. She could have killed you."

"She didn't though," Scott said. "Still here. Crazy bitch. Let's get as far away from her as possible next." He took in Mia's quizzical expression. "You know, assuming you want to come with me. I mean..."

"Love to," she said. "But where?"

"Well I'd love to show you my home city."

"Premesoir?"

"Delhoig in Premesoir. The iron city. Or so they call it anyway. I've never seen much attraction in calling it that. There's not much iron there anymore. Used to be a ton of steelworks there, now it all comes from Vazara, cheap." He scuffed his boot against the railings in disgust. "I remember growing up. It stank. I mean it, could smell it no matter where you were in the city. You... You've never smelled anything like it, believe me."

She squeezed his hand playfully. "And this is where you want to take me?"

"I've been away from home for too long," Scott said, looking out across towards the sun. This was the best part of the island, a small peak beyond the resort although not far enough into the unchartered parts of the island. Someone had made it into an observatory, a few long-range telescopes placed around the perimeter. They were alone but for each other. That didn't include Permear, the ghost hovering by one of the scopes, muttering angrily to himself. He'd not been the same since being knocked out in the fight. Scott assumed he'd get over it sooner or later.

"It doesn't have to be Delhoig," Scott said. "I'd follow you to the ends of the five kingdoms if need be. From here to Canterage." He winced, something coming back to him that felt so long ago. Like he'd been a different man back then. "Just... Not Burykia, okay? I did it recently. Wouldn't feel right going back there right now." Not with a different girlfriend. Two months didn't sound like it should have been a long time. Having lived through it, he realised it felt like an eternity.

"Serran?" she said. "There's some places I go there this time of the year. And it's beautiful. You ever been before?" Scott nodded his head.

"Not recently," he said. "Not for a long time. Think we lived there briefly when I was a kid before going to Premesoir." It wasn't as uncommon as it sounded. Plenty of people spent their lives never having set foot in all five of the kingdoms. He'd never been to Vazara before all this. "It would be nice to see it again. Home first though."

"Or we could go Serran first, since it's on the way. Travel across, head to Premesoir when we hit the other side."

She wasn't making it easy, he had to admit. Still he didn't care. Either way worked. Delhoig would still be there when he did get back. And he wasn't in a hurry. It wouldn't change drastically. "Sure, whatever works," he grinned. "You're the boss."

Her grin matched his at that comment. "That works for me," she said. "I like that, flyboy. Mia 'The Boss' Arnholt. Better than my middle name."

That piqued his interest. "What is your middle name?"

"Caroline. It was my mother's name."

"Oh. Nothing wrong with that." He didn't have much else to say. Couldn't think of anything, no benefit to further comment. And Mia Caroline Arnholt was a cute name, he thought.

"Not as good as 'The Boss' though, is it? Might adopt that for the dance stage. Try it out in Serran, I think. Maybe it'll take off."

"You could have your own merchandise," Scott laughed. "Your own brand. Isn't that like the dream for you people?"

She rolled her eyes. "You people?! What a tactlessly insensitive way to make your point." At least she gave him a grin while saying it. "But yeah, you're not wrong. There's some strange people in this game."

"Yours and mine," Scott said thoughtfully. "Hey, Mia."

"Yeah?"

"I seriously want to know. What really happened? Why does Harvey Rocastle hate you so much anyway?"

Mia let out a nervous laugh. "What, hatred to the point that he's tried to kidnap me twice and threatened me with death more than I can count? You'll laugh at this. Really you will."

"I'm pretty sure I won't. How come you never did anything about it before?"

"Well it was all just threats, he's always been petty and spiteful. And… And well, he thinks I stole some of his tricks on the stage."

"What?!" He genuinely couldn't help laughing, just as she'd said. "You're kidding!"

"Nope."

"But… That's…" Amusement turned to disbelief, it all sounded like some big joke now he heard her say the words. "Seriously?!"

"Yep."

"How petty can you get? Seriously?!"

"Apparently murderously so," Mia said wearily. "Shame really. Used to be friends. He'd had a hard life, there was always something cold in him. Never thought it'd end like this though."

"Where were you?"

Anne smiled weakly, it felt a strange emotion, alien to her lips right now. Every twitch of the muscles in her mouth felt like an eternity of discomfort. Maybe that was the way it should be. Her body ached, she was tired, and she just wanted to go to bed. Even above Ruud Baxter's offer, she didn't want to think about the future. Being around so much sorrow today, it had just been draining, even worse in a way than the horrors of the battle. She still bore the mental scars of that, she could hear the screams and smell the fire when she closed her eyes. She still bore Baxter's weapon on her belt. More than once in her room, she'd taken it out in front of the mirror and activated it, just to study the hissing blade, just to see how it looked in her hands. "Funeral," she said. "Friends died, you know."

"I'm sorry."

The strange thing was, he meant it as well. He'd always thought genuine apology was something beyond him. For that matter, he'd never been convinced he could do a convincing fake one. Apology wasn't something that ever really entered his psyche until recently.

"Yes well," she said. "Life goes on. Can't complain about stuff unfortunately. Being mad at life's like being mad at the Divines. It's not going to get you anywhere."

"Steady, I thought I was supposed to be the cynical one."

She managed a weak smile. "There's a margin of difference between cynicism and realism. Not a gulf but a glimpse."

"So, what will you do now then?" Theo asked. "Go back home, or...?" He let it hang, a curious brow raised.

"Can't say," she said. "I've been given a new... Yeah, I don't know."

"You're with Unisco, aren't you?" he said slowly. For a moment, she looked like she wanted to lie about it and then decided not to, nodding her head once gently.

"For a while," she said. "What gave it away?"

"The running around shooting people," Theo replied. "Was a pretty cool sight. You looked like a complete badass."

She shuddered. "Not a good thing to say, Theo. People died there. It was a bad day."

"The sentiment's true, even if the words are wrong," Theo grunted, his cheeks flushing at the reprimand. "I could have put it better. What I was trying to say is, you're amazing. A hero."

"I don't feel like a hero," she said, looking down at her feet. "You know what my new assignment is going to be? They're supposedly setting up a new department in the next few months, they want me to be a part of it. Don't know where I'll be based or how long it'll be for." She sighed sadly. "Shame because it does seem like a fantastic opportunity."

He swallowed deeply. "You should do it."

"Not like I have a choice," she said. "But I'm glad I have your approval," That last part came out a little sarcastically, he felt his cheeks flush again.

"Not what I meant," he said. "Anne, these days I've spent with you, they've been... Believe me, I've never used this word often before, they were fun. I learned a load from you. I wouldn't have gotten where I did without you." He reached out, took her hand. His stomach was leaping, he tried to ignore it. Wouldn't do to get the jitters. "I owe you so much. I'm not ever sure I can entirely repay you."

She smiled, stood up on her tiptoes and kissed him, her lips brushing against his, her arms around him. As best he could, he returned the gesture clumsily. He felt awkward but strangely, he wasn't worried about that too much. An unusual feeling for him.

"It's not about repayment," she said. "Consider it an investment in the future. You've been blessed with talent, tenacity, ferocity but no small measure of skill. Do you really want to be just a spirit caller for the rest of your days? Or do you want to actually do something to make a difference?" He didn't know what to say about that. "Think about it. There's always a need for talented spirit callers like you. It's just a case of where and when."

Harvey was waking, she could sense him coming around from the drugs they'd fed him, the stretch of his fogged mind grabbing for any sort of conscious thought. Touching the surface of his mind was like plunging face first into filthy water. She wondered if he could feel her touch, feel her fury. He needed to. To describe herself as furious with him was too gentle a term.

More than once she'd held back smothering him while he slumbered, it'd be far too quick and easy for him. What she had in mind was so much more useful. And painful for him, couldn't forget that. He'd screwed up badly, she'd given him orders and he hadn't carried through on them. More than that, he'd deviated from them. By any logic, it should have earned him a death sentence. She couldn't carry any sort of useless weakness.

But no. She'd chosen mercy after a fashion. If he continued to be of use, he'd live a little longer. If he didn't... She wouldn't lose any sleep over him leaving her new world. Not that she had slept recently. Fatigue had been something that escaped her. Strange. A moan escaped him as he tried to sit up, couldn't. He tugged at the restraints, she put a finger to his lips and shushed him gently.

"Quiet!" she said. "You've suffered traumas." It was true. He'd broken many bones through his fight with Roper, his left leg and kneecap shattered, several broken ribs and smashed teeth, his shoulder dislocated and wrist re-broken. His nose had almost been flattened by an elbow, Doctor Hota had commented on how he was lucky to be alive. The leg had had to come off, she'd made that decision and it had been carried out. If she said it had been totally benevolent for his health, it would have been a lie. It felt like a just punishment to make a point. The look of numb shock and terror on his face as he clutched at the stump was just delicious, she found herself drinking it in. For several long moments, he wailed and cried and begged, she thought he would stamp his foot if it wasn't beyond him now.

There was only so much of it she could take, she cleared her throat and glared at him, a silencing stare that shut him straight up. "Right," she said. "Consider this. We're already fitting you up for a prosthetic so quit your whining. You won't even notice. You've already got cybernetic fingers, what's a little more?"

"Because…" he started to whine before thinking better of it. Her eyes narrowed, she continued as if he hadn't spoken.

"You've screwed up a number of times," she said. "But you've had some successes in there as well so I'm willing to forgive you. Your obsession with that girl has proved to be your undoing once again."

"Not my fault she's surrounded by people tougher than me," Rocastle moaned. She grimaced. He couldn't really have just given that excuse to her, could he? It sounded pathetic, she fought the urge to strike him. Must have been the painkillers. "What can I do?"

She smiled coldly at him. "Get better. I have a few ideas. We're working on some stuff. And when we're looking for volunteers, I expect you to be the first in the queue. After all, it doesn't do for me to have doubts about where your loyalties lay." She grazed her fingers across his cheek, drawing lines of blood with her nails. "Sleep well Harvey, for the days will be long and hard ahead. But in this new world, a lord you shall be." If he had anything else to say, she didn't care, just turned to leave. Outside, Domis bowed to her. He didn't seem to be diminished by his recent traumas, like a mountain, he was just as she always remembered him. Giant. Terrible. Imposing. He'd shown up earlier in the day, none the worse for the wear without anything as much as a complaint. She could do with more like him.

"Goddess," he whispered. Even more than the term Mistress, that pleased her so much. "What can I do to enhance your cause?"

"It's starting," she said softly. "Soon the kingdoms will change forever, and I will have won. But for now, we all have work to do. The time of Coppinger is coming and the kingdoms are never going to be the same again. You and I, my son, we are going to bring it all down and then raise it anew from the ashes."

Ever since she'd started, since she'd taken to the skies in her fortress, or gone through the gateway, she felt at peace with herself. She was doing something, ensuring the visions she'd seen in her dreams wouldn't come to pass. No apocalypse of green, no end of the world, just a vision of her future. She'd been sleeping soundly since the war had begun, getting handfuls of hours wherever she could, peaceful if not lengthy. The dreams of death and destruction had faded, not completely but they troubled her less.

That alone told her she was on the right path. She'd set her first foot on it now and she wouldn't stop until she reached the end. Things were going to change in the kingdoms. She'd made a vow and she was going to stick to it.

The storm came out of nowhere, nobody saw it coming, not even the people at the Khazri Kel'an Institute of Weather, Vazara. What they did know was it appeared above the deepest, driest part of desert, covering almost the length of it, drenching it in an absolute downpour for six straight hours, no longer, no shorter. By the time they got people out to investigate, it had ceased. Although interviewed nomads had later told them there had been something quite not right about it, in their own superstitious way. They'd called it, in their own tongue, divine rain. A gift from the gods. The elder of the tribe had reached down, scooped up a hand of sodden sand and let it trickle through his fingers, along with the word 'alive' accompanying it.

The team had taken samples back to send off for study, curious as to what he'd meant. Less than a day later, the first shoots of greenery broke through the sands. At the same time, the deep gouges left in the desert by the Reims scar-mining technique saw water seeping through the base, more and more of it coming from somewhere unseen. Soon there were rivers all over the plains, the vegetation sprouting up first alongside them before the green spread out across the desert...

Never the End.

The story continues in Innocence Lost.

Coming very soon…

A Note from the Author.

Thank you for the time spent reading this book, taking the time to spend your days in this world I created. I hope that you enjoyed reading it just as much as I did when I wrote it. Just a quick note, if you did, please, please, please leave a review on Amazon for me. Even if it's just two words, it can make a lot of difference for an independent author like me.

Eternal thanks in advance. If you enjoyed this one, why not check out other books I've written available at Amazon.

If you wish to be notified about upcoming works, and even get a free short story from the Spirit Callers Saga starring Wade and Ruud some twenty-five years ago, sign up to my mailing list at http://eepurl.com/dDQEDn

Thanks again. Without readers, writers are nothing. You guys are incredible.

OJ.

Also, by the Author.

The Spirit Callers Saga.

Wild Card. – Out Now
Outlaw Complex. – Out Now
Revolution's Fire. – Out Now
Innocence Lost. – Out Now
Divine Born. – Out Now
Paradise Shattered. – Coming Soon

Tales of the Spirit Callers Saga.

Appropriate Force. – Out Now.
Kjarn Plague. – Coming 2018

The Novisarium.

God of Lions – Coming Soon
Blessed Bullets – Coming Soon
Spirit and Stone – Coming Soon

The Unstoppable Libby Tombs (A Novisarium Series).

Family Tradition – Coming Soon
Memory Lane – Coming Soon

About the Author.

Born in 1990 in Wakefield, OJ Lowe always knew that one day he'd want to become a writer. He tried lots of other things, including being a student, being unemployed, being a salesman and working in the fashion industry. None of them really replaced that urge in his heart, so a writer he became and after several false starts, The Great Game was published although it has recently been re-released as three smaller books, Wild Card, Outlaw Complex and Revolution's Fire, now officially the first three books in the Spirit Callers Saga, a planned epic of some sixteen books. He remains to be found typing away at a laptop in Yorkshire, moving closer every day to making childhood dreams a reality.

He can be found on Twitter at @OJLowe_Author.

Printed in Poland
by Amazon Fulfillment
Poland Sp. z o.o., Wrocław